ANCIENT DECEPTION

OF GOLD & BLOOD
BOOK NINE

Jenny Wheeler

Published by Happy Families Ltd

ISBN: 978-0-9951452-9-0 (Paperback)
ISBN: 978-0-9951452-7-6 (Kindle)
ISBN 978-0-9951452-8-3 (E-Book)

E Book Edition First published December, 2021
Paperback edition, 2022.

OF GOLD & BLOOD SERIES

The enemy of my enemy is my friend.
    —Ancient Sanskrit proverb

A man–or a woman–who desires revenge should dig two graves.
    —Confucius

Your name is like perfume poured out.
No wonder the young women love you!
    —Song of Songs, 1:3. (NIV)

Prologue

The nightmare came out of nowhere. Thrashing water, scarlet and stinking, filling his nose, his mouth. Salty water, choking him. He could taste it, that bloody smell of men gutting fish. Then the screams. Cutting into him, like a fisherman's knife in the stomach. His hands flew to cover his ears, to shut out the noise, but it went on and on. His eyes were wide open, stinging from the waves.

A hairy arm, as tough as a jungle vine, looped around his waist and scooped him out of the ocean. He flopped like a jellyfish, stomach down, onto the hardwood board.

Over the board's edge, he could see the dark shape hovering deep down. The screaming stopped, replaced by raspy noises, rumblings from a man's throat. Like the sound of crying.

Not Bully. Surely Bully wasn't crying? He closed his eyes tight against this new sound. He didn't want to open them.

When he did, the water was still gleaming red. And across Kanaloa's surfboard, a man lay, his leg a bloody stump.

Just like his father.

And he knew he would never feel safe again.

Chapter 1

The candlelight glowed. The silverware sparkled. Their hostess, "Countess" Elizabeth Westerhoven, sat at the head of the Epiphany dinner table, overlooked by the stately portrait of her husband, the late Charles Westerhoven, US envoy to France. In death, he displayed the same measured air of assurance as his widow showed in life.

She turned to Kaleo, seated on her left. "I apologize for Senator de Vile's absence tonight, Kaleo. It's a disappointment for you, I know." Her expression was gentle, but her dark brown eyes probed, searching his.

The second-term senator had offered his last-minute apologies, citing urgent government business. Elizabeth, a wealthy widow and benefactor to San Francisco's poor, decided it was too late to call the event off, so she'd gamely continued with the twelfth night after Christmas dinner at her Nob Hill mansion without the guest of honor.

"It's all right, Mrs. Westerhoven. No need to apologize."

The words left a bitter tang in his mouth. Hector de Vile, one of two California senators to Washington, was the father Kaleo Manolo didn't know he had until six months ago.

He'd long believed his father had died when he was a baby. Now he knew that was a lie, he'd developed a thirst that grew more debilitating every week. What it was like to have a father? He wanted to know, and he was sick of waiting.

Had this man left any stamp on his character and temperament, despite them never having met until six months ago? Did they laugh at the same things? Share a dislike for liver and cauliflower?

More important to him, was the senator willing to accept a role, however belatedly, in his life? Mentor him in business? And when he was ready, advise him on the choice of a wife?

His eyes traveled down the table, four chairs away, to where Sarah Wyndham sat, chewing her roast pork, her intelligent gaze flitting between her dining companions. Will Davenport, his immediate superior at Pike Consulting, sat at her right. On her left, Alex de Vile, Hector's adopted son and his new half-brother.

Sarah wasn't talking, responding instead with subtle non-verbal cues which left them in no doubt she was taking in every word. A slight hunch of a shoulder. "Who knows?" A brief smile. "You're right there." The crinkling of a brow. "Do you think so?"

When she was unguarded, the fleeting mobility of her expressions spoke volumes about her quicksilver nature. They'd struck an instant rapport when he'd first met her last July.

He was certain of it, though now, casting his mind back, he wondered if he'd imagined the whole thing. They'd talked with more ease than he'd ever known with another woman, and he hadn't lacked for blatant interest from numbers of young women over the years.

The problem was none of the women who'd chased him had raised a flicker of interest on his side. Sarah was different.

He turned his attention back to his hostess with a barely suppressed sigh, to find her alert, kind eyes resting on him. He'd been mistaken about Sarah.

Like a brief, false spring, her spontaneous pleasure at their chats had cooled into stiff politeness after the first couple of months.

When they met over their work at Pike Consulting these days, her penetrating hazel eyes roamed from the paperwork to an invisible spot fixed somewhere over his left shoulder. Rarely did she make eye contact.

It made it damned difficult working together in the busy import export office where she was a capable administrator and he an agent for raw material imports such as sugar from his family's Hawaiian estates.

"Sarah's a highly intelligent young woman, isn't she?"

Elizabeth Westerhoven's voice was quietly observant. She arched a sculpted brow, hinting at unspoken volumes. Kaleo's insides clenched. Was she suggesting that Sarah was out of his league?

Or was she making it plain she'd noticed he couldn't keep his eyes off the young woman's slender face, nor the exuberant blonde locks that sprang from the hairband at her brow when her mathematical calculations consumed her?

"She is," Kaleo readily agreed. "Brilliant." He stole a look to where she sat, laughing at some remark of Alex's, and returned his gaze to the Countess.

"She's got a deft touch in business, too. The company's taken flight with her managing things."

Elizabeth gave him a warm, approving smile. She reached out and covered his hand with hers, and gave it the lightest of reassuring squeezes. "Be patient, Kaleo. Your constancy will be rewarded. I'm confident of it."

She removed her hand and hesitated, as if considering whether to add to her remarks, then pulled back her elbows from the table in a negative.

She nodded to the attendant hovering by the sideboard on the nearby wall.

"Please serve the galette des rois, Mr. Bayreuther."

The portly gray-haired butler bowed and gestured to a pretty server to distribute the dessert.

"We might not have the pleasure of the senator's presence, but we can still eat king's cake for Epiphany," Elizabeth announced. "Frangipane tart traditionally marks the Three Kings' arrival in Bethlehem."

She gave Sarah a smile laced with motherly tenderness. "We've got a charm, a fève, hidden inside this sweet treat. Whoever finds it in their dish will be Queen for the night."

Kaleo suspected she'd already arranged for Sarah to be served the "charmed" dish.

***

An icy wind nipped at their cheeks as they huddled in the shelter of Elizabeth Westerhoven's porch, making their last farewells, reluctant to break away from the convivial warmth to venture home alone.

For Kaleo, that meant a bracing walk across town to the house he and his sister Leilani inherited from their unofficial godparents.

Cyrus and Misty May died tragically in a murder-suicide last year, leaving behind an attractive Queen Anne-style Folsom Street villa that had been the Hawaiian consul's office and the childless couple's home.

Lani was on a ship returning from Honolulu, so he had the place to himself. Mostly, he didn't mind. But tonight, the idea of going home to an empty house left him feeling hollow inside.

He wrapped his arms around his midriff and stamped his feet to keep warm. He intended to see Sarah to her coach and then step it out.

Light cast from a streetlamp picked up a fine sheen of black ice on the paved street; the thin, near invisible film formed on streets and sidewalks on frigid nights. It was a dangerous night for traveling anywhere, and he'd be wise to remember it.

Sarah was giving Will and then Alex a sisterly hug before making her way toward a hack that rumbled up. Kaleo fell into step beside her.

"Sarah! Let me escort you home. It's not a good night to be out alone."

She turned in surprise. "I'm not alone. Will's coming with me."

The slight, willowy figure of the office manager slipped in beside him.

"I've got it, Kaleo. You don't need to worry."

Kaleo halted, his heart pumping, fighting to keep his expression neutral.

"Oh sure, Will. So long as someone's taking care of it."

He gave his boss a cordial farewell tap on the shoulder and made to leave.

Sarah's voice reached out, sounding thin and reedy. "But thank you, Kaleo. I appreciate the offer." Her warm breath created plumes of mist.

He paused mid-step and dipped his head.

"I don't think O'Farrell Street is safe for you, Sarah, you know that. It's too close to the Tenderloin."

She smiled at him. "It'll be fine, Kaleo. I never took you for a worrier."

"It's common sense. I don't know why you insist on hiding in the shadows like you do."

The short vertical lines between Sarah's brows deepened.

"I'm fine." She sounded exasperated.

Will took her elbow. "I'll see her to her door, Kaleo. Don't worry."

"Sure thing." Kaleo stepped back to show he was disengaging. He hesitated, hovering on the curb in a no-man's-land as Will guided Sarah to the hack awaiting them.

He glimpsed back at the house. Alex was chatting quietly to Elizabeth in the entryway. The warm glow from within spilled out through the lead-light windows, creating dark silhouettes outside.

Elizabeth huddled into a fur cape over her dark red dress, the smoky quartz gray of her sable fur stole seeming to wrap her in welcoming warmth. Dancing red flares from the dining room fire lit their faces. They smiled at one another, and Elizabeth touched Alex's arm with her gloved hand in a gesture of affection.

Kaleo's insides swamped with frosty isolation. There would be no one to greet him, no welcoming fire in the hearth when he got home tonight.

He rotated on his heel, eyes tracking back to Will and Sarah's retreating figures.

They'd reached the hack. Will handed Sarah up into the cab ahead of him. She disappeared inside, gold-blonde hair momentarily glinting in the streetlight, before Will stepped in behind her.

That's when a dark figure came around the side of the vehicle, arm raised. The same beam that had caught Sarah's hair highlighted a burly silhouette, hat pulled low over his eyes, in a black coat with the collar turned up masking his face.

He wielded a lethal-looking bat. In seconds, he smashed it across Will's head and shoulders with skull-splitting force. His friend gave a short, strangulated cry as he fell onto the hard street.

Kaleo was already sprinting forward as the attacker bundled Sarah inside and the vehicle hurled away.

Chapter 2

Kaleo barely got level with the rear of the vehicle before it moved off from the curb. He made a desperate reach for the baggage rail that ran around the roof above the hack's rear window and grabbed, at the same time planting a heavy boot on the rear-guard rail.

As he hauled himself up, he was dimly aware of the sound of pounding feet as Alex—he hoped it was Alex—went to Will's aid. The wheels of the hack sliced through the ice film with a grating sound, very different from the normal rumble of rolling wheels.

His arms easily reached out over the low-slung cab roof, and he made child's play of hoisting himself up. He gave thanks for his strong thighs and sinewy shoulders, built up from hours thrashing in Maui dumpers. He lay splayed on top, taking a minute's rest, heart pumping with intense energy while his thoughts fluttered like panicked moths.

He noted Alex hadn't attempted to board the hack. He was on his own.

What's happening in there? Has he already killed her?

Almost in response, muffled curses sounded from inside, and the flimsy cab wall vibrated with a dull thud. Was that a body being thrown around? The hack swayed violently, unbalancing it on its wheels, and the driver yelled in protest.

"Oi! Watch it!"

Kaleo lay belly down, panting, his head mere inches away from the cabman's shoulder, his legs dangling over the back. He considered his options for a dozen heartbeats.

He tuned out everything but the accelerating thunder of the horse's hooves under the crack of the driver's whip. The screeching jolt as an outside wheel hit the curb. The slap of the untethered cab door as it smacked back and forth with the cab's every movement. All of it was background noise to his one thought; how to get Sarah out unharmed.

Why isn't she screaming? Is she already dead?

Still on his belly, he pivoted close to the edge, as if preparing to ride a wave, and like a circus gymnast, he readied himself to swing into the cabin through the open door, feet first.

With one hit, he'd knock Sarah's attacker senseless before he even knew he was there. But he had to ensure he didn't hit her by mistake.

He was counting on the advantage of surprise, and he didn't want to squander it.

Elbow jammed against the luggage rail to stabilize his flight, he prepared to launch into the opening, his tingling leather-booted feet braced for impact.

Legs down. Hold tight until you've swung far enough to see inside. Slam into him seconds after you let go.

In the last half-second before he catapulted in, he caught the glimmer of a long-nosed revolver. Sarah's attacker stood back on the cab entry, his feet braced to absorb the hack's movement, half throttling her from behind.

With one arm across her throat, he struggled to maintain his balance while bringing the gun up with the other hand.

"Don't." Sarah's strangled voice. Again. "Don't..." He choked her into an unintelligible garble.

Does she know him?

The thought hit him uninvited.

Why would you imagine that?

And then the cab lurched wildly again, the wheels hitting the curb as the driver fought for control in the black ice. A wind gust knifed across his back as another vehicle streaked by, the teamster roaring abuse as he passed.

Kaleo gauged he'd come within a hair's breadth of being squashed between the two vehicles.

He took a deep breath and thrust his body inside the cab. His feet slammed into the gunman's shoulder, slipping past Sarah with an inch to spare. The gun the man was clutching discharged with a roar.

The front window of the hack shattered, and the driver screamed. The hack pitched dangerously to one side, and then, just as abruptly, rocked onto the other.

Each dizzying lunge felt like it would be their last, but after seconds poised in mid-air, the hack miraculously righted itself and toppled back down onto four wheels. Sarah's attacker had momentarily loosened his hold on her, and she was scrabbling on the floor, trying to get out of reach.

The hack was barely large enough for two adults. With three of them jammed in, it was downright dangerous. Any move Kaleo made also threatened to crush Sarah. He wanted to bring her attacker down, but not by both of them falling on top of her. He noted with satisfaction the man's arm hung at an odd angle.

Good. I've probably dislocated something.

Kaleo leaned in and grabbed his dark coat by the back of his neck and whirled him to face him. He couldn't glimpse the man's face behind the upturned collar and jammed down hat. But the coat fabric was a heavy soft wool, finely cut, probably bespoke tailored.

He got a whiff of expensive cologne.

The collar fell back, revealing a smooth face with neatly trimmed sideburns, and dark, short hair fringing regular features. A plump, well-fed face, free of lines. A man who pampered himself. Not a hooligan, nor a street fighter.

Behind them, Sarah scrambled to her feet, panting and crying. Kaleo needed no further prompting. He hugged the expensive coat to him, his face inches from the man's snarling mouth. He pulled him close and fell backwards through the open carriage door, executing a twist like an underwater flip as they fell through the doorway.

By the time they hit the street, he was on top, his landing cushioned by the other man's body. They went down with a mighty crunch which momentarily knocked the breath out of them both, but Sarah's attacker was not giving up.

The shock of the landing lasted only moments before he clawed for Kaleo's face, aiming for his eyes.

The bastard's fighting dirty.

Kaleo rose to his knees and punched with all the venom, all the force and power in his being. Blood spurted from the first blow to his opponent's nose. His jaw audibly cracked with the second.

Then his head fell back, his eyes closed over, and he lay senseless, blood spilling over a fancy silk cravat that, until this minute, Kaleo hadn't noticed he was wearing.

Kaleo half sat, half knelt astride the attacker's limp form, trying to absorb what had happened.

Was he some toff Sarah knew from somewhere else? He'd had the distinct impression they knew one another from the garbled exchange he'd overheard.

He could have sworn she said a man's name. One that he couldn't make out. Had he tried to kidnap her? But why? It made little sense. She was a modest office worker, wasn't she?

Sarah. Was she all right?

He half rose and registered everything had suddenly gone quiet. The grinding of wheels on cobblestones had stopped. The only sound was whispers and footfalls from a knot of curious bystanders gathering on the sidewalk.

He turned, alarmed, expecting to see the hack overturned. Instead, it stood on its four wheels further up the street. Sarah was slowly coming toward them, supporting the driver, who was staggering against her, his shoulder a bloody mess.

Kaleo's mouth went dry. His heart jolted in his chest. All thought of the prone man at his feet forgotten, he started toward her.

"Sarah. Are you all right?" His voice, sharp and anxious, sounded loud in the icy night.

"I'm fine, thank you, Kaleo."

Her face glimmered, white and stricken in the light of the streetlamps.

"I can't believe all that just happened. Thank God you were there… And that you acted so quickly."

She halted and bent over double, as if in shock. As she let go of the cab driver, he tottered, and someone in the crowd lunged forward and caught him.

"Ah, I have to rest." The words came out on a long sigh. She sank to the ground, and Kaleo grabbed her by her elbows and held her up.

"You're in shock. Maybe injured as well." He led her to the curb. "Sit down." He surveyed the people who were gathering. "A doctor," he called, waving an arm. "Have we got a doctor here? The lady needs help."

A bespectacled gray-headed man carrying a doctor's bag emerged from the clustering crowd and made his way to Sarah's side, but she insisted she had suffered nothing more than a fright and pointed to the man bleeding on the street.

"He needs you more."

He kneeled and took the man's pulse. "This one will definitely need a night or two in hospital," he said. He pointed to a lad who hovered nearby. "Run down and tell the doc at the infirmary."

A police officer emerged from the crowd and approached Sarah. "Can you tell me what happened here, miss? This gentleman appears pretty banged up. What went on?"

He stared pointedly at Kaleo's bleeding knuckles. "I gather you know something about this, sir?"

Sarah stepped in. "He was protecting me. That man tried to abduct me. He would have got away too if it wasn't for Mr. Manolo here. He attacked one of our work colleagues in the street outside Mrs. Westerhoven's house on Nob Hill, as well."

The ginger-haired police officer raised his eyebrows, and the dark lines on his face seemed to lighten at the mention of the 'Countess.' The older ones all knew Elizabeth because of her charitable work for abused women.

This fellow had a beer belly that hung over his belt and Kaleo suspected was one of the crew who preferred to sit in bars taking money for not investigating crimes, rather than spending time out on the streets solving them.

The police officer swung to face Sarah. "So, who's this geezer? Do you know him? You're not a runaway wife, are you?"

Sarah's already stricken face drained of its last remaining color. "No… no, nothing like that." She bit her lip distractedly. "I don't know who he is. We were at dinner at Mrs. Westerhoven's and he jumped me when I left to go home."

The police officer turned to Kaleo. "And you, sir, you were at this 'do' at the Countess's too, were you?"

"That's right. Along with my boss, Will Davenport. He was seeing Miss Wyndham home when this fellow attacked him."

"Miss Wyndham, is it?" The police officer peered at Sarah through narrowed eyes, as if she'd done something wrong or stupid to provoke the attack.

She stiffened under his nakedly assessing stare.

"I'll need you both to come to the station and make full statements."

"But we know only what we've told you. He came out of nowhere and attacked us," Sarah protested.

"Might I observe that even a quick view of the victim suggests he wasn't intending to rob or ransom you? Look at his clothes. His fine boots. His nails. He's a right swell."

He peered at Sarah through thin, ginger eyelashes.

"You're sure you don't know him? This isn't your run-of-the-mill street fight, I can tell you that. I've been around long enough to know when something's fishy."

Sarah shook her head, eyes lowered.

He turned to Kaleo. "What about you, sir? What do you know? This young lady—she hasn't run away from home, by any chance?

"This geezer's too young to be her father. A brother, perhaps?" His mouth twisted into a mirthless smile. "What exactly is the nature of your relationship with Miss Wyndham, anyway?"

Kaleo's hackles rose. "My relationship? We're work colleagues, that's all. And I resent your insinuations. This lady has suffered a grievous assault that requires serious investigation."

"It's all right," Sarah mumbled. "Don't get upset, Kaleo. I'm sure it's all a terrible mistake."

The policeman scowled. "We'll find out when the injured party comes around then, won't we? *If* he comes around. If he doesn't, I'll bet he's the type to have expensive lawyers. Maybe there's a wife at home wanting to sue for alienation of affection."

"No. Oh no. Nothing like that. I've never seen him before. I told you." Sarah's eyes flickered in panic.

The threads of the police officer's nasty suspicions seemed to bind them there in a circle of light. Kaleo scanned his attention from the policeman's twisted face to Sarah's blank terror and knew the police officer's instincts were spot on.

Something wasn't right here. Sarah wasn't a guilty party, but she wasn't telling them everything either. He'd seen how it had happened. The guy had come from nowhere, attacked Will, and stormed the hack. He would hedge bets the hack driver was in his employ or was bribed to drive and not interfere.

His eyes moved from the police officer's sneer to Sarah's limp stance. She was staring at the ground, her shoulders slumped in defeat.

Buck up, he wanted to say. None of this is your fault. He stayed silent. And then the peculiar sense of threat defused at the urgent rumble of carriage wheels.

Elizabeth's Rockaway carriage pulled up alongside. Alex and Will were with her. They stayed seated while she alighted in a flurry of ruby red skirts, the smoky sable cape secured around her shoulders.

The police officer's accusatory attitude melted at her approach. He practically saluted as came toward him.

"Captain Adam Dearborn, Countess. Someone attacked one of your guests. Is that correct?"

She peered toward Kaleo and then Sarah. "You're unharmed, my dear? I was so worried."

Sarah gave her a weak smile. "Nothing a hot bath and a good night's sleep won't fix, Mrs. Westerhoven. What about Will?"

Elizabeth glanced back at her carriage. At a second glance, Kaleo saw blood trickled down the right side of Will's face.

"I'm taking him to the hospital to get checked right now. He's come around, but he needs his head bandaged." Elizabeth turned back to Dearborn.

"Forgive me, Captain. Yes, indeed. There was a ruckus when Sarah left to go home."

She gazed around her. The crowd whispered and pointed. The cab driver lay hunched over, bleeding on the curb. Two white-coated attendants loaded Sarah's attacker onto a stretcher.

She peered sideways at Sarah. "Is that the man who tried to abduct you?"

Sarah nodded. "Kaleo mounted a remarkable rescue."

Elizabeth Westerhoven's eyes widened with concern. "I can vouch for this young lady, Captain Dearborn. If you've got questions, come and see us in the morning. Meantime, I'm taking her home with me. She's not going back to her lodgings alone tonight. Not after this upset."

She gestured Sarah toward her waiting coach. "We're exceedingly grateful to you for your intervention, Kaleo. If you hadn't been there, goodness knows what would've happened."

Sarah wordlessly nodded and then followed Elizabeth.

Elizabeth turned back to Kaleo. "Can we drop you home?"

"No," he said. "You take care of Will."

"Rum business this one," Dearborn grumbled as Elizabeth drove away. "But there's no arguing with the Countess."

Kaleo watched as the coach turned the corner and was out of sight.

He didn't trust this suspicious cop. However, he had to agree with his conclusion. Sarah was lying about something. But what plausible motive could she have for doing so?

As he turned for home, he noticed he was limping, and decided he'd keep an eye out for a late-night hack if one came by. He'd have a badly bruised hip in the morning, but he was in much better shape than his anonymous opponent.

Anonymous to him, he corrected. He doubted very much he was unknown to Sarah. What was she running from?

Chapter 3

"I've never seen him before." Kaleo shook his head in disbelief as he hobbled home to the May house, his legs sore, his movement fueled by a rage that bubbled up from within. The further he walked, the more he hurt, and the more he hurt, the angrier he got.

She's lying.

There was no doubt in his mind. Sarah was a quiet woman. Some might even call her mousy, but tonight she'd shown unexpected steel.

He thought of the way she behaved around the Pike Consulting office. She was efficient in her work, gifted in her sharp calculations, but disinclined to draw attention to herself. Her fashion preferences leaned toward modestly cut pastel blouses and tidy but unremarkable business skirts.

She conducted herself with a restraint which underlined her preference for staying in the background, but he'd always sensed there was a lot more to her than met the eye.

He'd have been more inclined to believe her subterfuge if he hadn't seen the panicked flicker in her eyes as she disclaimed any knowledge of her attacker.

Sarah knows that man. So why isn't she willing to admit it?

No. That can't be… She's so straight up. She isn't a deceiver…

But what if Dearborn is on the right track? What if she is a runaway? And if she is, what is she running from?

As he passed by the Church of St. Joseph, and inhaled the fresh green scents of the City Gardens on Folsom and 12th, his heart twanged for Leilani, his twin sister.

A sudden longing filled him. He wished she was waiting for him at the May house, eager to hear about his unexpected scuffle, but she was on a steamship on her way home from Honolulu and wouldn't arrive for another few days.

Her cool head in situations like this one was a godsend, and he felt an ache behind his ribs as he remembered her sure instincts about almost everything. He corrected himself.

Everything except our father.

For all her talent for hammering out nutty problems, Lani had a blind spot about Hector de Vile. She'd wanted nothing to do with him. She was wrong on that score, and he hoped to prove it to her when she got back. But that would have to wait. Sarah was in trouble, and that was far more urgent.

He'd half fallen in love with the reclusive administrator before she'd put the chill on their blooming friendship. He told himself he'd read the signs all wrong, and he needed to back off.

But now he wondered.

Is she hiding something? Is she scared of someone getting too close because of some dark secret that shames or frightens her?

And if she is, what am I going to do about it?

***

Dawn flushed pink in the sky as Kaleo dropped into Cyrus's spacious bed with its carved oak headboard and luxurious goose down comforter. It had taken him much longer than usual to walk home.

The Spanish housekeeper had stoked the fire in the iron grate before she'd left for the night, and a consoling warmth wrapped around him as he stripped to his underwear and flopped between the fine cotton sheets.

Cyrus and Misty's lives had ended tragically, but they'd left behind them a gratifying sense of stability and security in the home they bequeathed the Manolo twins. He felt a rush of gratitude to them for their generosity and affection.

But even with that comfort, it had taken him a long time to drop into an uneasy sleep, and then he'd grabbed only short snatches of deep slumber interrupted by jolts of awareness, as if his mind was on high alert, unwilling to allow him peace because of an unseen but looming danger.

Several times he woke with a start, his heart pounding, his brain already ramped up, listening for unfamiliar sounds, for footsteps in the hall or knocks at the windows. The unease even infected his dreams when they came.

He was back in the ocean, belly down on a surfboard, his thin, boyish arms frantically paddling to get atop the next roller as it crested and carried him back to shore. Someone he trusted—a man—was close by him, but every time he turned to glimpse his companion, all he saw were drifts of hissing sea foam.

He was on watch duty, keeping himself and someone else safe. The lookout boy, Bully called him. He'd always teased him about that.

"We need your sharp eyes, kid. You can see further than any of us. We're relying on you."

Bully's voice had rumbling laughter buried deep within it. Kaleo knew he was playing with him. But he couldn't help feeling pleased, important somehow. He was *ohana*, part of the family, joined with his brothers as they—Bully and the others—all of them, were sons of the ocean.

Bully's ruddy broad face, his wide black beard sparkling with droplets of spray, was suddenly there, beside him, beaming.

Then he heard it. A piercing scream. The same scream that haunted his childhood nightmares. His surfboard flipped, as if nudged from underneath, and he was in cold water, gasping, swallowing the salty soup, his nasal passages stinging.

He would never reach air, would never breathe again. And then a brawny arm was around him, like a giant octopus tentacle, hauling him out; Bully was pulling him onto his thick *wiliwili* wood board—an expert's board. It was smooth on his thighs, and he could breathe again.

He gulped in great lungfuls of air, his body warming with a rush of gratitude as the oxygen brought him to his senses. But there it was again. He tasted it, smelt it. That awful odor of blood and guts. The aroma that hung around when the fishermen were gutting their catch. A noisome halo. And the water. The water all around him was red.

He remembered it then. His father. The shark got his father, and he hadn't been there to keep lookout.

I failed then, and I'm failing again now.

He pushed himself back up into a kneeling position, ready to paddle, and darted his eyes behind him, wanting to be sure that Bully, his second father, was there with him.

For an eternity he hung there, bewildered, waiting. The ocean faded. Bully wasn't there, but his arms still thrashed.

His face was wet, but there were no waves. His legs were damp and sweating, entangled in white sheets. He reared up off the soft mattress in terror. Saw the banked coals in the fireplace, the dying embers from last night, yet still the room felt too hot. He dashed the back of his hand across his cheek. He was crying.

He fell back into Cyrus's ample bed.

Sarah.

He'd failed all the others. He shuddered as he recalled Bully dying in his sister's arms last year, a stab wound in his chest, on the street outside the Occidental Hotel. That was when these childhood nightmares had started up again, he realized with a sudden jolt of understanding.

And now he had the chance to do it all over again, to prove he was a good lookout. That he could protect his *ohana.*

In Hawaiian, that word meant so much more than his diminished blood family. It meant wider kith and kin, those who bonded to you, not by blood, but by land, by sea, by spirit.

Whatever Sarah said, she needed a lookout now. Of that, he was certain. Something was badly wrong, and he couldn't stand by and pretend otherwise.

He hoisted himself onto his elbows and his eyes searched for the small mother-of-pearl clock Cyrus kept on the bedside table.

Eight o'clock.

He heard the muffled clatter of plates in the kitchen. Mrs. Leon was here, about to start breakfast. Everything was normal.

Except it wasn't. He had no choice. Sarah was special to him, whether or not she reciprocated his feelings. And he sensed that now, perhaps more than at any other time in her life, she needed someone to stand up for her. A lookout. This time, he wouldn't let anyone down.

Chapter 4

Will's faded parchment face brightened when Kaleo stepped into Elizabeth Westerhoven's Nob Hill parlor four hours later. The Pike Consulting manager was resting in a rocking chair, a newspaper open on the blanket tucked around his knees, his wire-framed spectacles slipping down his nose. Kaleo suspected he'd been dozing. In one quick, sure movement, Will removed the glasses and smiled.

"Good to see you, Kaleo. I gather you got a bit of a going over last night, too."

The remains of a light breakfast—a drained coffee mug, an egg cup holding an empty shell—sat beside some half-eaten toast on a rosewood side table at his elbow.

Kaleo laughed, holding up his grazed knuckles for Will to see. "You should've seen the other knave."

A dark-haired, middle-aged woman wearing a white smock interrupted them. "Mr. Davenport, the Countess asks if you'd like some coffee for your guest? And perhaps a refill for you?"

Will flashed her a quick smile. "Yes please, Mrs. Roderiquez. We'd be most grateful."

She nodded and left the room.

Kaleo gazed around him. A well-set fire flared in the hearth. On the mantelpiece, an earthenware pot of small yellow flowers filled the air with a jasmine-like scent. And before he could take his seat, Mrs. Roderiquez returned with the hot coffee on a tray and a fresh cup for him.

"Well, you're living it up, my friend, aren't you," Kaleo mock-chided after the housekeeper filled their cups and left. "I've traipsed all over the city to find you and satisfy myself you're still alive."

"Very much alive. But I've got one almighty headache. It's like someone's fired a gigantic cannon inside my skull and the reverberations are still coming."

He grimaced and gestured to the chair next to him. "I'm glad you found me. Once they'd checked me over and diagnosed nothing more serious than a concussion, Mrs. Westerhoven insisted on bringing me back here, rather than leaving me in a hard hospital bed.

"I'm a lot more comfortable than I would otherwise have been. Except for my headache, I'm fine. I got off lightly. It could've been a lot worse."

Kaleo nodded. "It certainly could. And you can't recall meeting the fellow who attacked you before?"

Will shook his head.

"I don't know who he was. And I haven't seen or heard anything from the sheriff or anyone else today. Oh, except Sarah. The Countess insisted she sleep here last night too, so I've glimpsed her." He shook the news sheet.

"She's upset our little contretemps made the newspaper. You know how she is about not wanting to make a fuss. Obviously, the only newsworthy thing about it was the Countess's name being dragged into it. Otherwise, it would have been one of the multitude of random skirmishes that occur in this city every week."

"How is Sarah?" At the mention of her name, his stomach churned uneasily.

Will shrugged. "She seems okay."

He'd been standing next to Will, but he now sank into an armchair closer to the fire.

"A 'random skirmish'? Is that what you think it was? It didn't appear random to me."

Will frowned. "Why would it be anything else? What are you suggesting?"

Kaleo shrugged. "'Random skirmishes' don't normally involve well-tailored fellows wearing expensive leather boots. Not unless they're in their cups. I don't know. This fellow doesn't fit the picture of a brawler."

Will's cheeks sagged along the jawbone, and dark shadows ringed his eyes. Everything about his posture appeared weary and drained, and he suddenly appeared much older.

"I guess I didn't have time to notice his tailor," he said listlessly. "He clobbered me before I even lit eyes on him." He turned his coffee cup round in his hand reflectively.

Kaleo moved to stand in front of the fireplace, staring into the flames, letting their warmth strengthen him, his back to the door.

"I don't know, Will, I really don't. It seemed planned to me. I think they knew who—or what—they were after. And I suspect Sarah knows too."

"I know what?"

He whirled to the sound of her pert voice.

Without him realizing, Sarah was standing quietly inside the parlor doorway.

"Sarah! How are you?" His words were breathy.

She walked around to the back of Will's chair, limping on her right side.

Will stood as she entered. Kaleo stepped forward and gestured for her to take the seat he had been occupying.

"You're limping. Please! Sit down."

She shook her head and remained standing.

"Would you like some coffee?" asked Will. "The pot's still hot."

"No, I'm fine, Will. Don't worry."

"Did you sleep okay?" Kaleo asked.

Her shoulders hunched with a distracted, tired air. He saw the fine fatigue lines around her eyes, and the bruising at the base of her throat.

"I've been better, but I'll recover." She gave him a thin smile.

"How about you? I didn't say a proper thank you last night. I don't know how it would have ended if you hadn't been there." Her worried hazel eyes searched his face.

"I'm very glad I was there," Kaleo said hotly. "That fellow meant serious business."

Sarah peered at Will, then settled on Kaleo, her eyes flickering with uncertainty, as if unsure of what to say next.

Kaleo filled the awkward silence. "We're no further ahead in understanding what's going on, are we Will?"

The office manager gave a vigorous answering nod. Too quickly, by Kaleo's lights.

Is Will in on this too?

"And Will was saying you've had no more information from Dearborn?"

She shrugged her shoulders. "Nothing." They stood in a pregnant hush. Kaleo tasted a foreign sourness on his tongue.

Lying doesn't come naturally to them, he thought. I suppose that's a good thing.

A loud hammering on the front door shattered the silence. Although the parlor was located several rooms down the hall from the entryway, whoever was there made it clear he or she expected immediate access.

They heard someone answer the door. Raised voices echoed in the hall as a man demanded entry and a staff member insisted the lady of the house be called. There was a scurrying of feet, and then the Countess's serene presence imposed its own authority.

"Captain Dearborn, do come in. We're all very interested in hearing what you have to say."

A gabble of male voices answered in response—more than one visitor it appeared. The door to the parlor opened, and the room was suddenly full of too many people.

Dearborn stood, cap in hand, beside a scowling man in a fine wool suit and polished black boots. With the Countess behind them, they surveyed the room, eyes narrowed, mouths tight, as if expecting more trouble.

"Well, well. I'm glad you're here, Manolo. Just the man we're seeking." Dearborn turned with a dismissive hand wave to the man by his side. Kaleo gauged him to be in his early thirties, with a pencil-thin mustache that magnified the natural sneer of his upper lip.

"My name is Heatherington. Ralph Heatherington. I'm representing my client, the man you attacked last night. And I'm insisting Captain Dearborn arrest you immediately for unprovoked assault and battery.

"My client is a wealthy and respected businessman and he will not put up with being randomly attacked."

He stared expectantly at Dearborn as the rest of the room subsided into shocked silence.

Will's jaw had dropped open. Sarah bent over and clutched at her middle, as if she was about to faint.

"Sarah! Are you all right?" Will's blanket fell to the floor as he reached toward her.

"Fine. I'll be fine. It's a little warm in here, that's all."

She dropped unsteadily into a nearby chair.

Dearborn spoke up, his voice steely and certain. "Now Mr.

Heatherington, sir. I told you. I won't be arresting Mr. Manolo or anyone else until after our investigations are complete. And at this time, sir, they are ongoing."

Heatherington was a tall, lean man with a powerful jaw, a beaky nose, and a shock of dark hair above piercing black eyes. He carried the air of someone used to being obeyed.

He drew himself up to his full height and glared, first at Dearborn, then at Will and Kaleo.

"There's far too much brawling and misfeasance in this town, and the leading merchants have had enough," he thundered. "If you won't take action, they will."

He fixed his eyes on Will. "You rely on the goodwill of our local businessmen for your livelihood, Mr. Davenport. I can tell you that benevolent attitudes are likely to be in short supply if you protect this rabble-rouser in your organization."

Behind his gold frames, Will's eyes took on a flinty sharpness.

"Mr. Heatherington, I was present last night. I know who attacked who. The supposed victim is lucky he's not facing the gallows, if you ask me. If he'd broken my skull, that could well have been the outcome."

Heatherington puffed out his chest. "How dare you besmirch my client's name with such lies, sir?" His cheeks puffed out in pompous outrage.

Throughout this exchange, Elizabeth Westerhoven stood poised at the back of the room. Now she stepped between the newcomers and her guests, as if providing a bulwark of peace and common sense.

Her gray silk dress trimmed in red lace seemed to underline the natural authority she radiated. She raised her hands from her sides, palms open, in a conciliatory gesture.

"Gentlemen, I was watching from my porch, as was Mr. Alex de Vile, Senator de Vile's son, who is not present here today. We were eyewitnesses to what occurred last night. And I can assure you, a male person attacked Mr. Davenport with no provocation outside my home.

"He then bundled Miss Wyndham into the waiting hack and drove off. It was only because of the valiant efforts of Mr. Manolo that she is here with us today. Goodness knows where she'd be if he hadn't come to the rescue."

The Countess's dark brown eyes fixed on Ralph Heatherington's flushed face.

"Thus far, Mr. Heatherington, the name of this person, this attacker, is unknown to us. If you claim your client is this person, pray tell us, what's his name? We're all curious to know it."

Heatherington's eyes flickered toward Sarah, who was staring at her hands in her lap, as if this was the last place on earth she wished to be.

"I… I'm not at liberty to say. Perhaps there's been some case of mistaken identity, Mrs. Westerhoven. Far be it from me to challenge the accuracy of your account."

Sarah's head jerked up, and for the first time since Heatherington had entered the room, she turned in his direction. Her narrowed hazel-green eyes were beseeching and alert.

She knows, Kaleo thought. She damn well knows who he is. And she's sheltering him.

A long silence followed the departure of Dearborn and the swanky lawyer from the Westerhoven parlor.

Then Will spoke in a measured, quiet voice. "Goodness only knows what's going on here, Kaleo. But I want you to know you're an essential part of our team.

"Don't let that fellow's threats scare you. If he thinks he's going to bring out the big guns, well, we've got a cannon or two of our own."

He took off his glasses and pinched the bridge of his nose. The indent of the metal frames left a pink mark, which he massaged between thumb and forefinger as he considered the situation.

"For starters, your newly discovered father, the senator, will object to their strong-arm tactics. He doesn't like anyone encroaching on his territory."

Kaleo felt an ache of dread at the back of his throat. The last thing he wanted was Hector de Vile thinking he needed rescuing. Oblivious to his discomfort, Will grinned at him and then turned a concerned frown toward Sarah.

"Are you okay, Sarah? You appear rather upset, I have to say."

She peered anxiously, first at Will and then Kaleo. Her face was deathly white, her mouth pinched.

"I'm upset that rescuing me could leave you in such an unpleasant position—both of you," she said.

"Maybe I'm the one who should leave." She stared from one to the other, her green-flecked eyes suspiciously bright.

"Sarah," cried Elizabeth Westerhoven. "I won't hear such talk. It will all blow over in a few days." She bustled forward and placed a consoling hand on Sarah's shoulders.

Kaleo slouched against the mantelpiece, enjoying the radiated warmth from the fire, the picture of a relaxed detachment he was far from feeling. Inside, he was a boiling cauldron.

Sarah had come close to peril last night. Rape, abduction, death? Who knew what the man's intentions were? But one thing was certain. They were for her harm, not her good. And she knew him. She knew who he was, and she probably also knew why he'd taken such rash actions. And yet she was protecting him. Why?

He peered into her closed face. Perhaps she was terrified of the repercussions… Has she done something she doesn't want disclosed? Is she frightened of what they might do to her next time? And what will they do next time?

Because suddenly Kaleo knew there would be a next time. And he'd have to be prepared for it when it came.

Chapter 5

"How in hell's name did Otis land us in this mess?"

Samuel Hollows stood behind the big leather director's chair at the Uncle Sam Silver Company office in Virginia City, his mouth so full of bitter saliva he turned and spat into the smouldering fireplace in disgust.

He cricked his thick bull's neck to ease the jagged pain that had stabbed him below the ear all night, ever since he'd heard the news of the San Francisco debacle, but no amount of craning it this way and that eased it. He thumped the desk with his meat plate hands in frustration.

The mining office occupied the ground floor of the three-storied house on South D Street—an elegant French Empire building imposing enough to be called a "mansion" by the locals, though regarded as merely superior accommodation in New York or Boston.

It sat like a white-tiered wedding cake, narrowing on each level as it rose, backed by the mountain behind. Like many such houses in the town, it was officially the mining office on the ground floor, with private accommodation for the mine owner or manager on the upper levels.

The man staring back at Sam from the strange milky green orbs recoiled, but in distaste, not fear, at his explosion. Clifford Jensen hated drama. The opaque eyes, which some initially took as sightless, bored into him.

"Easy does it, Sam." Jensen's voice was ice cool. "One of your offspring has already gone off half-cocked. You can't afford to follow up with something equally stupid."

Sam rolled the big chair out from the desk and flopped his ample backside down on cushions that released a satisfying squelch of rushing air.

"It can't get too much worse. The kid's in hospital. The police are involved. And Rebecca knows we're onto her. The only good thing is no one's dead." Sam leaned back and his fingers drummed an angry tattoo on the desktop. "He couldn't have whipped up a worse mess if he'd tried."

"Calm down." Jensen's voice echoed in the room, with its ornately corniced fourteen-foot ceiling, like a mine wagon rolling along a deep underground track, rumbling and threatening.

Sam flushed at his own silent admission that "the kid"—his son— was thirty-six years old, the same age as Jensen himself, something the Jensen had restrained himself from mentioning.

Leaning on the chair on the opposite side of the desk, Jensen met Sam eye-to-eye, his stance communicating total command of himself and his surroundings. He'd pushed the sleeves of his fine cotton shirt up to the elbows, exposing powerful hairy forearms, at odds with the elegant fingers that braced either side of the chair.

One foot rested, deceptively casual, on a chair strut a few inches from floor level. Samuel Hollows had known Clifford Jensen long enough to know he was never casual about anything. And especially not this morning, when they'd learned of Sam's eldest son's fiasco.

The iceberg eyes didn't waver.

"You got yourself into this and it's your job to get yourself—and me—out of it."

They'd been colleagues in business for more than a decade, and uneasy rivals long before that, but Sam adjusted himself awkwardly in his chair because there was no "us" in his partner's statement.

Jensen had agreed only grudgingly to the idea of sending Otis out to bring Rebecca back home, and now he was letting him know he would not share responsibility for the disastrous outcome.

Jensen's deep voice had an edge. "All I know is we need her back here, and now. It's ridiculous that you allowed the filly to trot off like she did."

"All right, all right. You've made your point." Sam knew he sounded scratchy and defensive. "I didn't exactly 'allow' it."

Jensen: "Need I remind you of our agreement?"

Hollows shook his head. "No need."

Jensen twirled the chair he'd been leaning on around to face him and finally sat down. He was a good-looking fellow, with finely chiseled features and a purposeful mouth. But his eyes were ice cold, and an intense austerity was the closest he came to displaying passion. His humor always held a sardonic edge.

"You agreed to give me your daughter in marriage in return for me backing your ruinous forays into silver," he said. "No wife, no money. It's as simple as that."

He paused, and Sam leaned forward in anticipation. "Oh, and I should have added, no sheriffs. I hadn't thought it necessary to state, but now I see it is. No cops."

His mouth twitched in a contemptuous curl. "And if there's any suggestion at all that Rebecca is going to be talking to that police captain, then I trust you'll stop her. I don't care how."

He stood abruptly. "If you don't stop her, then I will. I'm watching, Sam. I mean it."

Sam jumped up from his desk, unwilling to let Jensen leave on that note.

"Cliff, you're the only one who can sort this out. You know that. Get down there right now and see to it."

His voice held a plaintive note he despised in himself. "Damn fool of a girl. What's she playing at? Sarah Wyndham indeed. What's wrong with being Rebecca Hollows?"

Jensen glared. "I'm glad you understand who's really in charge here, Sam. At last, you're getting it. I own your business, and I'm going to have your daughter too. From now on, understand this. You're nothing without me."

He walked to the door and then turned back to face him. "Nothing personal, you understand, Sam. It's business. That's all."

***

Clifford Jensen did not exit the Uncle Sam Silver building when he left the company's ground-floor office. He ascended to the second floor, moving like a sleek cat up the wide staircase, barely disturbing the air in the silent house.

With Otis away, there would likely only be Sam's wife Charlotte, and stepdaughter Petra here. Sam's second son Rufus was away at a fancy engineering school on the East Coast. Charlotte would be in her private suite, and Clifford was certain he knew where he'd find Petra.

Rather than enter the main living area, he slipped out through an arched doorway onto an open Victorian walkway that ran all the way around the second storey, making an airy terrace that gave spacious views out over the town and up to the mountains

He briefly hesitated to let his eyes adjust to the dazzling morning light, then moved with deceptively languid strides around to the south side where he knew he'd find Petra.

He passed full-length windows set into the white-painted timber wall at regular intervals, each one topped by decorative carved brackets and ornate window hoods, all in homage to the French Second Empire and Napoleon III's desire for affluence and character.

At the back the walkway broadened to accommodate a wrought-iron glass-walled tunnel house, the windows steamed up by an ingenious heating system fed up from the mines underground.

Petra's paradise and her obsession. A secret jungle filled with rare plants and brightly colored songbirds. All designed and implemented by Bekka.

Amazing what that woman can come up with.

As the tunnel house door closed noiselessly behind him, a clean, sharp citrus scent assailed his senses. Small white flowers with golden centers smothered a tree in a marble urn in the entry. A Tahitian lime or Spanish clementine? Who knew? He wasn't interested enough to ask.

In the middle, the tunnel broadened out into a separate structure with a pagoda roof over a three-chambered aviary, its fine mesh walls embellished with curving spirals like fern fronds, mimicking the grape tendrils that twined across the roof. The pièce de résistance.

I guessed right.

He made out the slender figure of a young woman standing inside the aviary, the door slightly ajar behind her, her magnificent mane of burnished red hair tumbling down the back of an unadorned white gown.

He slowed and reminded himself to adopt a solemn mien. He knew what was in store.

Normally, the air would be full of the sound of songbirds—native mockingbirds, canaries, linnets and bullfinches. But this morning there was no music; only sound the sound of a woman's sobs.

"Petra?"

He tapped lightly on the half-open door to attract her attention. She whirled around, eyes wide in panic. When she recognized his dark shape against the morning glare, her shoulders slumped forward again.

"Oh, Clifford. It's you." A wariness replaced her panic.

"Who would do this?" she whispered, extending a shaking arm in front of her. "How could they?"

Bloodstained sawdust lined the floor of the cage. Small, delicately boned bodies lay at the girl's feet, some still quivering. A blizzard of blue, green, and yellow feathers floated in the surrounding air.

"Oh, my goodness. What's happened?" Clifford asked.

Her tear-stained face pointed to a lower corner of the sturdy wire-walled enclosure. At floor level, a hole ripped open the durable netting. "Someone let the cat in." She swung around wildly. "I'm scared it's still in here somewhere. A big ginger tom."

A not-quite-dead bird fluttered in the sawdust and, as if on cue, a long-haired tabby leapt and pounced on the dying linnet. Petra screamed and covered her eyes with both hands.

"No! No! I won't look! No…" Her cry turned into a long, moaning wail.

Clifford observed, unmoved. Two sisters, similar in appearance but so different in character. Rebecca would never stand in the middle of a disaster wailing about the loss. She might grieve in private, but she always met hardship full-on.

She engaged that pragmatic temperament, the steel-trap mind and the iron will, and in a flash, she'd have a new strategy. That's why she was so valuable to Uncle Sam's Silver, and why Clifford needed her as his wife.

He gazed over at her dishrag sister and stepped fully into the enclosure. He scooped up the cat in one focused movement, his long, strong fingers holding it tight on either side of its rib cage.

"Come away from here, Petra. There's nothing more you can do."

He led her out of the apiary and down the terrace with its waist-high picket fence railing, releasing the cat back into the garden as he went.

Then he shepherded the sobbing girl upstairs to the bar set up in one corner of the dayroom. It was cold after the warmth of the conservatory, but the fire the staff had re-lit from last night took the chill off the air. Shutters muted the light from the long windows.

"I'll organize for Mrs. Murphy to get some coffee in here," he said. "You sit down."

She perched on a barstool like a shadowy phantom, hardly aware of her surroundings.

His neck prickled with irritation. "Bad stuff happens," he said as he went to the door to call Mrs. Murphy. "Get used to it."

She gave him a sleepy, blank-eyed stare that went on and on. And then she erupted into laughter, a crazy, high-pitched convulsion edged with hysteria.

"Ever the sympathetic guardian," she gulped. "I wouldn't have expected anything different. Rebecca always said you were a cold sod."

"Rebecca knows nothing," he said. "But that's why I'm here. We've found Bekka. We're bringing her home. In fact, I'm leaving to get her later today."

The hysteria stopped as abruptly as it had begun. Petra's pale face turned so white the freckles on her cheeks and nose stood out like the spots on a baby fawn.

"Rebecca? She's alive? You know where she is?"

"Yes. We do." He decided against the coffee. He stepped behind the bar and poured two glasses of water from a jug that sat there. "But there are complications."

Chapter 6

They've found Bekka.

Petra closed her eyes and gulped down the cold water as she absorbed Clifford Jensen's amazing news.

My sister's alive. I'll see her again.

Exhilaration surged from the soles of her feet to the top of her head. She jumped off her stool. Clapped her hands over her head. Her body was on fire with joy.

And then she remembered what discovery meant for Rebecca, and the joy fled, replaced by trembling over her whole body. She never wanted to remember that last night when Bekka was at home. But nor did she want to forget.

Bekka had run away for good reasons. Forcing her to return would put her in chains. And she'd never accept the fate her father and Clifford had planned for her.

Petra slid back onto the stool she'd leapt up from minutes ago and blinked up at Clifford through long lashes.

"Where is she? And when is she coming home?"

She saw by the momentary flicker of doubt that passed across his soapy, green eyes that Clifford didn't know the answer to at least one of those two questions. She hoped it was the first.

He cleared his throat. "She's in San Francisco. Never mind where. We've found her. That's all that matters."

She searched for the minute telltale signs she and her sister had learned to read in his stony face. The fragile lines that ran out from the corner of his eyes when he was uncertain of winning.

A tightening at the corner of his mouth when he was being questioned on a topic he didn't welcome. The slight frown of annoyance that appeared in the dip between his eyebrows when he was losing an argument.

And the unconscious flicking of his long fingers in his belt, as if he wished he could pull out a gun and force everyone to do his bidding.

He stared back at her, saying nothing.

"So, when is she coming home?"

The fleeting dip between his brows, the one you'd miss if you weren't watching for it, immediately rewarded her attention.

He doesn't know. Maybe there's still a chance…

"Soon enough. We've a few details to sort out."

He stepped up to her, far too close to be comfortable, and before she realized his intentions, his powerful arms turned her, stool and all, to face him. He placed his hands on her shoulders and leaned in so close she could smell the lemony mint on his breath.

"Thing is, Petra, we need your help to bring her back. Sisterly affection and all that." He threw the phrase away like old trash.

Sisterly affection. Like he knew anything about affection. Anything at all.

She thought of the agonized months when Bekka pleaded with her father to change his mind about the marriage. Tried to bargain with him to avoid it. She'd stay in the company even though she loathed the work. She'd do anything except marry Clifford Jensen. And her father had been obdurate.

Petra tried to pull back, but Jensen increased the downward pressure on her shoulders. His face was a frozen mask of dislike. Leaning in even closer, specks of spittle hit her cheeks when he spoke next.

"I know how much your sister loves you. I'm sure she wouldn't want anything unpleasant to happen to you."

He was a hissing snake in her ear.

"She'd hate to see something even nastier than today's unfortunate event with the birds," he said, stroking one elegant hand down her cheek in a charade of tenderness.

She wrenched her head away from his touch. Chills ran up her arms. "You! You killed my birds."

She reared back, pushing away from him. The stool clattered to the floor, and she fell with it, grovelling on the wooden floorboards in her full skirts to escape. She scrambled to her feet, took cover on the other side of the bar and glared at him, disbelieving.

"How could you? They were pretty, innocent creatures. They've got nothing to do with all this."

Hot tears surged behind her eyes, and she squeezed hard to shut them and him out. When she opened them again, Jensen had picked up the toppled stool. He slouched against it, his long legs stretched out as if he didn't have a care in the world.

"You're despicable," she gasped. Her voice was raw and harsh.

"Oh, Petra. Pretty little Petra. What a pathetic little creature you are. So unlike your warring soldier of a sister." His voice curled in scorn. "You really don't have a clue, do you?"

"A clue? About what? I can't make my sister marry you. Why don't you go find someone else?"

"Because your sister is a moneymaker. Unlike every other woman, who spends it." Almost as an afterthought, he added, "Besides. She needs to be taught a lesson."

She ran her hands through her hair, tugging at the roots as she did, trying to use the dull pain she inflicted as a focus point for understanding his meaning.

"What are you talking about?" she cried, her voice anguished and desperate.

"Your father relies on her to do the calculations for his business. You wouldn't eat as well as you do without Rebecca's brilliant mind. It's not only the lightning speed with which she calculates numbers.

"She's got an instinct for business. If she doesn't come back soon, your father will be bankrupt by the end of the year. And that will mean, my pretty little maid, your plate will be empty too.

"There'll be no hopeful suitors lining up to marry a rich mine owner's daughter. You'll be wiping tavern tables for a crust of bread. I'm surprised you haven't figured it out yet."

She ignored the scorn in his voice and said, "What can I do about it? I'm not clever like her."

"You, Petra, are going to persuade your sister to come home. Because if you don't, something much more unpleasant than losing a few useless birds will befall you and this house. That, I can promise."

Chapter 7

Kaleo wended his way home from the docks where he'd successfully convinced Jag Bennett, one of their fellow Hawaiian sugar exporters, to send his sugar to Diamond Sugar—the processing plant the Manolo family now held shares in, thanks to Senator de Vile's deal with Leilani and its main stakeholder.

He'd won an important contract, meaning more business for their family company and—he hoped—accolades from his new father.

He glowed with the warmth of achievement, turning over in his mind what he was going to do about another dinner alone, when he noticed a familiar figure hunched forward ahead of him on the street.

Alex de Vile was leaning into the notorious Market Street afternoon wind, one hand simultaneously holding his hat in place and shielding his face from the dust that whipped up around him. His other hand clutched his coat to his chest, as if holding in the warmth.

Kaleo quickened his pace and dodged around slower-moving shoppers to draw alongside.

"Alex! I thought it was you."

Alex de Vile stopped in his tracks and turned, his face open and welcoming at the sound of his voice.

"Kaleo Manolo. Fancy bumping into you." He clapped a friendly hand on his shoulder.

"The rescuer of maidens in danger, and my very own half-brother. Elizabeth and I couldn't believe what we witnessed last night. You've got to tell me all about it."

He gestured up the street. "My studio's only half a block away. Come back with me and have a coffee. We deserve to get to know each other a bit more, anyway."

Kaleo felt his mouth quirk up at the corners in response. "Why not? Every time we've met so far, there's been so much else going on."

They fell into step, edging away from the fish, lumber and marine oil smells of the wharf end of Market Street to the up-and-coming smart new residential section.

The top end of Market Street sprouted new buildings everywhere, with the sand dunes that blocked access removed in the last few years. The broad thoroughfare was already a dividing line between upper-class homes in the north and gritty working-class dwellings to the south.

"It'll get lively out here tonight," Alex observed as they crossed a busy intersection.

Taverns on opposite corners were already filling with boisterous workmen, leaning out of the windows offering jocular insults to passersby, beer mugs in hand.

"After all, it's Friday night. Along with Saturday, it's the only night a lot of these fellows can let their hair down. They find any excuse for a party or a parade practically every other week."

Kaleo grinned. "Can't blame them for wanting to add a bit of joy to their lives."

Alex paused on the pavement and took in the front door of a pretty single-storey Victorian villa painted in pale yellow with mint sills and eaves. "Here we are. La Casa de Vile." He deferred to Kaleo and shrugged.

"I'm a total fraud, of course. My father was a Spanish photographer, but he died long before I ever knew of his existence. I barely speak a word of his language."

He turned and made his way up half a dozen steps to the front door, Kaleo on his heels. As they stepped inside, a welcoming smell of beef stew wafted down the hallway. "Something smells good," said Kaleo.

"Mrs. O'Donovan must already have my dinner under way," Alex replied. "You must stay and eat with me. I hate dining alone."

He gestured to a comfortable sitting room. "Take a chair in there while I let her know we're here and that she's got an extra mouth to feed. She'll be delighted. She's used to feeding eight at home."

He disappeared down the hall, and Kaleo sank into a deep brown leather armchair. A restful gray silk lined the walls, hung with a series of old daguerreotypes, family studies of a young mother and three small children—an older girl of about five years and toddler twins.

Kaleo walked over to inspect. The young woman was captivating, but that wasn't what hooked his attention. There was a wistful depth in her face, a face that held secrets behind the wide eyes haloed by wild blonde curls.

She's so young, but she already knows deep sorrow.

Kaleo turned at Alex's footsteps.

"Ah. You've found my mother." Alex stepped beside him. "Can you believe it? I befriended a photographer in Nevada City, rescued these prints from a fire, and it turned out they were historic photos of the family I didn't even know I had."

He pointed to one toddler. "That's me with my twin sister, Isabella. You know? She's married to Sebastian Russell now?"

His finger wandered to the older girl. "And Graysie, Nathan Russell's wife? She's my half-sister."

He paused and his dark eyes bored into Kaleo with an intensity that belied his light-hearted words. "Graysie and I have the same mother, but different fathers. You couldn't make it up if you tried, could you?"

Kaleo nodded. "You're right. It seems odd, suddenly being connected to all these new people, even if its remotely."

Alex smiled. "You'll get used to it. They're pretty decent people."

He took the top off one of the two elegant decanters that sat on a side table.

"Now, let me be a welcoming host. What will you have to drink? Whiskey okay?"

"Please," said Kaleo.

He poured two drinks, and they chinked glasses.

"This calls for a celebration." Alex beamed. "I know we're not blood brothers. I'm adopted. You're of Hector's blood. But I've known him as my father my whole life. And you've only just found him, so I'm confident we've got plenty to talk about. I can give you some hints, for starters."

"Hints?" asked Kaleo, feeling like the class dunce. "What hints?"

"You know… the 'How to keep Hector happy' sort of hints. Which I confess I summarily fail to do most of the time. I know what he wants from me. But be blowed if I can deliver on it most of the time."

He slumped into the chair opposite Kaleo and gestured for him to take the chair opposite. "Relax. Mrs. O'Donovan says we've got an hour before dinner. We've got plenty of time."

"So, what is it that the senator expects? And why can't you give it to him?"

"I sound like the most ungrateful son alive, don't I?" Alex gestured around him.

"What does he give me? A comfortable home. Good education.

Plenty of good food. A good life. He might have a reputation as a ruthless competitor in business, but I can't fault him. He's given me everything, and he's been patient with it."

He stretched out his long legs and swirled his drink in his glass, watching as the amber liquid moved.

"I guess it's really that with all that, I'm my father's son. My actual father, I mean. Blood will out."

"Who exactly was your father?" Kaleo felt awkward asking, but he'd never given it much thought until now.

Alex took a quick sip and put down his glass. "His name was Rafael Castellanos. And the moment I saw my photographer friend Charles Durant developing a daguerreotype, Hector's business lost me."

He gave a deep, windy sigh and gazed at Kaleo with earnest eyes.

"I didn't even know much about my father. Still don't. But photography? It was like falling in love. Seeing that image appear from nothingness? Pure magic."

He sighed. "I don't want to be a magnate, running a business empire. I want to be the best photographer in California. On the whole West Coast. Or further."

"The world." He laughed in self mockery.

"And you knew that in an instant, with no doubts?" Kaleo's chest twinged with envy. If only he could be so certain about his future.

Alex leaned forward to emphasize the point.

"I'm not cut out to run the de Vile empire, and the guilt burns every time I see myself letting the senator down."

He cast an arm toward the back of the house. "I've converted two rooms into a darkroom here and this is where I could happily spend all my days, working on my art. It's become more and more obvious to us both. Me and my father. Business is not my game."

He got up to refill their glasses. He paused in his pouring and flicked his eyes across to Kaleo. "So, what about you, oh half-brother of mine? Are you going to fulfill our father's vaunting ambition?"

Once again he introduced an element of jest, putting down his own grand designs.

Fulfill my father's ambitions?

Kaleo suppressed the urge to squirm in his chair, like a mouse spotted by a red-tailed hawk. Alex's expression betrayed nothing other than friendly candor, but the words carried an ironic edge.

Behind them, Kaleo sensed a tidal wave of unhappiness and frustration. Perhaps even suspicion. Was the new boy, the recent discovery, going to supplant him?

A heaviness lodged in the pit of his stomach.

First Sarah. Then Will. Now Alex?

Who could he really trust in this town? Each one had their own secret agenda. And until last night, he'd taken their friendship at face value, blissfully unaware of what they were keeping hidden.

Talk about the hick boy from the sugar plantation, only good for surfing. He might be a prince of the curling waves, but that carried no prestige outside of Hawaii.

He steeled himself, remembered the warm glow he'd enjoyed only a couple of hours ago, after his deal with Jag.

He accepted the refreshed glass from Alex and flashed him an artless smile. He's not the only one who can play this game.

"A bit too early to say, don't you think, Alex? I've barely got here."

Alex responded with an apologetic shrug. "Didn't mean to put you on the spot, old man. Truly."

***

They relaxed over Mrs. O'Donovan's hearty beef dumplings, followed by apple pie and cream. They were lounging in the sitting room, having an after-dinner port in front of a roaring fire, when

Kaleo finally felt comfortable enough in Alex's company to ask him for his version of last night's events.

Standing on the porch with Elizabeth, Alex might have seen something Kaleo missed.

"I still don't know who the toff was who tried to abduct Sarah last night," Kaleo said into the companionable silence. "The police know who he is, but they're not telling because the cur wants anonymity."

They'd moved on to after dinner brandy, and Kaleo took a sip and savored the burn as it went down.

"Frankly, I think Sarah knows him too, but she's not telling. It's all too weird if you ask me. I even wonder if Will's in on it. Maybe I'm the only one who doesn't know who he is."

His voice trailed off, and Alex's eyes sharpened over his crystal tumbler.

"Well, I certainly can help you there, Kaleo. It will make up for my social incompetence earlier." He laughed.

"The fellow who tried to kidnap Sarah last night? Father's got impeccable sources in the San Francisco police department. He's Otis Hollows. From a Virginia City mining family. They're into silver mines in a big way, as far as I understand it.

"What the connection to Sarah is, I don't know. But they've got a lot of clout with the local constabulary, here and in Nevada. Hell will probably freeze over before they lay any charges, especially if Sarah won't cooperate."

A surging heat filled Kaleo's veins. "Otis Hollows? He's the one behind it?" He swiped his hand across his forehead. Suddenly, the room felt hot and airless.

Alex shook his head. "Not Otis, no. It will be his father, Sam Hollows. Otis will have simply been obeying instructions. Sam's the owner of some big silver mines in Virginia City, the Golden Bowl among them.

"It's been a share market star for the last couple of years. Its share price went through the roof a while back, but it's been dropping over the last six months.

"There's been a lot of grumbling from shareholders. Suggestions they've deliberately falsified test results to get punters excited."

Alex tapped his glass. "I'm afraid mine owners in this state are notorious for fiddling the share prices. Playing tricks like keeping miners shut in underground for a week to make investors think they've made a big new ore discovery. That kind of thing.

"Hollows has got a name for playing dirty. His henchman's a guy called Jensen. There was some rumor he was marrying one of Hollows' daughters, but nothing ever came of it."

He held up a decanter. "One for the road?"

Kaleo held out his glass and Alex topped it up and continued.

"Hector's made some sharp business deals over the years, but even he keeps the Hollows outfit at arm's length. He says he can't have his reputation sullied, especially now he's a politician."

Kaleo stared into the fire and rolled the smooth liquor around his mouth.

"I can't see why they'd want to abduct Sarah. She's an office administrator who prefers to keep a low profile. It's all head down and get on with the job with her. What interest could Sam Hollows have in a woman like that?"

Alex shrugged. "Beats me. Maybe she's got some hidden talent we don't know about. Or maybe she knows something they don't want others to know. Something to do with their mines? Where did she work before she came to you?"

"Do you know, I've never thought to ask. I'd assumed it was somewhere very similar to us."

Alex twirled his empty glass in his hand as Kaleo talked. He put it down and brought the back of his hand up to his mouth to mask a yawn.

"If you think it's relevant, then maybe you should ask."

Chapter 8

"Drop it, Kaleo. I don't want to discuss the topic any further."

Sarah's throat closed around her strangled words.

She stood in the Countess's parlor, her hazel-green eyes suspiciously bright, her slim form erect and defiant, fists clenched at her sides, a warrior princess standing in the breach.

But her complexion was chalky white, and Kaleo suspected she was clenching her fists so that no one would see her hands were trembling. In his eyes, she'd never been more beautiful.

"Sarah! I'm only trying to help." He hated it sounded like an impotent plea. This exchange was not working out at all as he'd expected.

He peered at Will, who'd moved to stand protectively at Sarah's back. His pale-faced boss was shaking his head in a wordless warning: Step back. Let it go.

It's all right for him. I bet he's in on her little secret.

Kaleo swallowed against the sudden bitter taste in his mouth.

He'd gone straight to Elizabeth Westerhoven's Nob Hill mansion the morning after his dinner with Alex, intent on finding out more about Sarah's attacker.

He'd ask her where she'd worked before Pike's if he got the right opportunity. He was hoping to protect her from further harm. But she'd been adamant she didn't need protection from this guy Otis or anyone else.

"It's a private matter. I can't say any more than that."

"But Sarah! How do you know they won't try again?"

For a moment her lip trembled, as if she was losing her nerve, and then she stiffened her shoulders. "I'm… We're…" She couldn't continue. The words seemed to freeze in her throat.

Will stepped closer and placed a consoling hand on her shoulder. "The Countess is arranging security," he said. "Sarah's moving in Elizabeth in the meantime.

"She can't live in that apartment downtown alone any longer, that's clear. She may have to work from home for a few weeks until things settle."

Kaleo felt as if someone had stuck a knife in his ribs. They were all in on this. Whatever "this" was. He was the only one left out. And he probably cared more than any of them.

"I don't understand. Some rich dude attacks you and we're supposed to fold up our tents and go home? Not even seek protection from the police? How can they intimidate you so? They don't scare me."

"Well, they should." Sarah's eyes flashed, and her face flushed in sudden anger. "Keep out of it, Kaleo. I'm begging you. You don't know what you're getting yourself into."

"Then tell me. Who are they? And why are they out to get you?"

She shook her head. "Please go. We have nothing more to discuss. And really, it's none of your business."

The pain in his chest twisted his insides.

None of your business.

He stared at her, humiliation firing up his cheeks as he stood his ground.

She clenched her jaw tight, but her lips were trembling as she fought back tears.

He picked up his hat to leave. "Don't bother showing me out. I know my way to the door."

***

The day she'd been fearing ever since she ran away from home had arrived. And the terrible thing was, it wasn't her despicable half-brother's actions that hurt the most. No. The worst thing of all was the devastation on Kaleo's face when she told him her situation was none of his business.

He wants so much to help me.

The immediate sense of intimacy they'd shared when they'd met five months ago had done much to heal the wounds scorched into her soul by that pig, Clifford Jensen.

But she'd known, right from the start, that she could never tell him her secret. Their intimacy was false. She was a fake. Her name wasn't even Sarah.

That's why she'd had to pull away from him, although it pierced her heart, and she'd confused Kaleo beyond measure.

Why, she imagined him wondering, had she gone so cold on their friendship, when everything seemed to be developing so beautifully?

And what could she tell him? That if her father and his torturers ever found her, they'd force her to return home, or they'd annihilate her little sister? Would anyone who stood between her and her tormenting family be in danger?

She couldn't let Petra suffer, and she certainly didn't want Kaleo to get caught between her ruthless stepfather and his plans for her.

She threw herself down on her soft eiderdown and, for the first time since Otis attacked her two nights ago, she cried.

***

Kaleo had little recall of his walk back to the May house on Folsom Street. The well-heeled burghers of the upper-class neighborhoods he strode through were enjoying Saturday family time, with three generations seated around a scarred dining table, the grooves and bumps of many years of joy and tears sealed in furniture wax.

He blundered through the quiet streets, desperate for solitude to go over it all in his head one more time, Sarah's words ringing in his ears.

It's none of your business… None of your business…

A knot of irritation lodged at the bottom of his rib cage, like a dose of unshakeable indigestion.

What? Would she prefer it if he left her to her fate? Did she see him as an interfering busybody? And if Alex was right, what kind of family did she belong to, anyway?

His cheeks were hot with shame and indignation. Had he so badly misjudged the situation, and her? And what was Will doing? Was there something going on between him and Sarah he'd been blissfully unaware of?

The wafting odor of roast beef and gravy two or three doors down from his home distracted him. He paused and sniffed, suddenly recalling he hadn't eaten today. He'd been too keen to catch up with Sarah.

Uninvited, another smell hit the back of his throat, the salty scent of the sea. He was instantly back in his dream, kneeling on his board, on the lookout for his family, his *ohana*.

Sarah was *ohana*, but she didn't want him as her lookout. Somehow, without knowing why or how, he'd failed again.

He only registered he was at his own front gate when he saw the Hawaiian flag Cyrus always flew as a sign of his office as consul, dangling limp in the late morning air.

When he'd taken over the house after Cyrus and Misty's deaths, he'd clung to the idea of retaining the flagpole, a sentimental reminder of their old friends, and of where he and Lani came from, of their sugar planter legacy.

He pulled up at the front gate to savor the reality that this was his house, his and Lani's, when he saw he wasn't alone.

Two men stood, dark-suited backs to him, one with an enormous fist raised about to hammer on the front door. He registered their presence with a spike of dread. Sarah's warning rang in his head.

Stay out of it, Kaleo. You don't know what you're getting yourself into.

Seems like I'm about to find out.

He treaded silently up the stairs, ignoring the spiking of his heartbeat.

When he reached the top step, he paused. Dearborn, apparently sensing his presence, he swung around, face reddening into a scowl at the sight of him.

"Manolo. I need to see you."

"Why is that?" Kaleo raised the brow permanently scarred by a surfboard's cutting edge and gazed at him steadily.

He was easily three inches taller than either of the men who stood before him. Like a threatened dog, Dearborn pulled his lips up into a snarl and tried to stare him down.

Kaleo held his ground, aware that the sun had broken through the morning cloud. His temples were damp with sweat, and his shirt stuck to his back. On the street, a boy of ten or eleven wobbled along on a bicycle with a squeaky wheel.

Kaleo turned back to Dearborn. The policeman was still glowering, but he stepped away from the doorway to allow Kaleo passage.

"I want to ask more you more questions about the attack the other night. I'm still not satisfied."

Kaleo stepped past them and let them in with a quick flick of the front door key. Dearborn's offsider was a young copper with protruding teeth and bushy blond sideburns. Dearborn didn't introduce him.

Kaleo led them into the sitting room and gestured to the sofa, but remained standing with his hands clasped behind his back.

"I've told you everything I know. It was a blind attack all over in a few minutes. That's it." He rocked on the balls of his feet, as if to emphasize his words.

Dearborn's brow furrowed in irritation. "All the same, we've got problems. The man you beat up is part of the Cabal."

"Cabal?" Kaleo raised his brow again, determined not to play into Dearborn's hands. He waited.

"A powerful lot in Virginia City. They own pretty much all the silver up there. They're too big to ignore. And they play by their own rules."

Kaleo stood his ground, arms folded across his chest.

"Old man Hollows has this fancy lawyer. He's out for his pint of blood."

"So?" Kaleo said.

The policeman seated next to Dearborn shifted uncomfortably on the sofa. His voice when he spoke was unusually high and squeaky.

"No one bests Hollows and gets away with it, Manolo. You'd better understand it."

"Hollows? Who is he again?"

If I'm the dumb Hawaiian outsider here, I may as well play the part.

Dearborn's lip curled. His piggy eyes narrowed and disappeared into puffy flesh.

"He's one of the most powerful men in Virginia City, that's all. He's pushing for you to be arrested. And money talks. Mr. Manolo, I'm formally advising you.

"You're a person of interest in our inquiry. And I'm warning you, don't leave town without seeking the police commissioner's permission first."

Kaleo shook his head. "What are you talking about? I went to the aid of a defenseless woman. If anyone should face charges, it's her attacker."

Dearborn stood, hands in his pockets, and sauntered toward the fireplace. "You don't get it, do you, Manolo? He's untouchable."

Kaleo had heard talk in the pubs of corruption in the police force, but he'd thought things were improving.

Dearborn sat back down again. He jostled his offsider in the ribs, and the tubby, dirty-blond-haired fellow pulled out a small notebook and drew a stubby pencil from behind his ear.

"How well do you know the victim, Manolo?"

"Sarah? She's a colleague. That's all. I usually only see her at work. Thursday night's dinner was an exception."

"She's not your sweetheart or anything?"

Kaleo's heart lurched. "Sweetheart?" He ground the word out. "Nothing like it."

"That's good. Because I'd suggest keeping your distance from now on."

Kaleo stared. "I'm missing something here, Captain. What's going on?"

"Miss Wyndham—if that's her real name, which I doubt—is trouble, Manolo. I'm warning you. Keep away from her."

Kaleo took a step back, positioned his butt up against the hard edge of a side table and leaned back.

"And who told you this, Captain? Your commissioner? The patsy lawyer?"

Dearborn's face shone. His breath wheezed in his throat. "I'm warning you, Manolo. She's not exactly backing up your story. If you're not careful, she'll hang you out to dry."

Kaleo's stomach twisted. He fought to maintain a bland expression under the vicious cramping.

"Then there's something else going on here. She's badly frightened, or something. What happened on Thursday night isn't complicated. Someone jumped her. I fought him off. End of story."

"Sadly for you, that's not what she says."

His hands were sweaty, as if he had something to be guilty about. "I don't understand. What does she say, then?"

Dearborn shook his head. "I'm not at liberty to divulge that. I'm telling you. Back off. You don't want to tangle with the Cabal. I'm warning you, and you should thank me for it."

Chapter 9

Elizabeth Westerhoven used both carrot and stick to persuade the pimple-faced young policeman on guard outside Otis's Occidental Hotel room to let them in. Senior men like Adam Dearborn were in awe of the 'Countess.' They knew her from San Francisco's streets because she'd given charitable support to downtrodden, deserted, and abused women in the poorest districts for years.

But after one too many narrow scrapes with bully boys and pimps, she'd pulled back from that involvement in recent times and the younger officers were not as familiar with her reputation.

With a combination of her beguiling charm, and veiled hints of dissatisfaction if Captain Dearborn heard he'd refused her request, the young copper opened the door to Otis Hollows' suite and called out ahead, "The Countess and your sister to see you, sir. You're allowed ten minutes, but then I'm afraid I'll have to ask them to leave."

Dearborn had confided they'd discharged Hollows from the hospital to the hotel, but were keeping a guard on his door to ensure he was available for questioning.

"We're not through with this case yet," he'd said.

As the young officer ushered them in, the Countess turned and said sotto voce, "The gentleman may be in an unpredictable mood, Constable. I trust we can count on you for protection, if that should be the case."

The young man stared at Sarah's soft blonde hair, and flushed a bright pink that highlighted his pimpled cheeks. "Of course, madam."

The air in the large room was heavy with blue cigar smoke. A stuffy dryness hit the back of their throats with their first breaths. The second-floor room's dark wood paneling and soft red velvet furnishings made a perfect retreat for injured male pride.

And Sarah's stepbrother Otis Hollows—nearly a decade older than her—reinforced the sense of a rich man licking his wounds by lolling back against a mountain of pillows on top of a four-poster, clad in a dark maroon jacquard dressing gown.

On the bedside table sat a silver tray bearing a brandy decanter, and a lit cigar burning down in an ashtray. His hand jerked as he caught sight of them. The brandy sploshed over the lip of the glass and soaked the front of his dressing gown.

"What the devil are you doing here? The cheek of it! Get out!"

He was a big man, broad shouldered, with tree trunk thighs and a ruddy complexion flushed brighter than normal from the hot room and the alcohol.

Swollen fingers, like fat cigars, peeped from the end of his bandage swathed hand. Sarah's breath caught in her throat, and she suppressed a cough.

The Countess slipped a consoling arm around the back of her waist. "A wounded bull," she whispered. "Take no notice."

He glared at them through puffed up eyes, the right more noticeably swollen than the left, Sarah observed. His face was a palette of purple and blue bruising, complemented by an angry rusty graze down his right cheek. A sense of bitter-edged triumph rose from deep within her.

He probably got those injuries when Kaleo tossed him out of the coach. Good job.

"Mr. Hollows," said the Countess, drawing herself up in her most regal fashion a few yards short of the end of the bed. "We need to talk."

Her voice could have cut glass as she fixed glacial eyes on him. "This shameful business has got to stop."

Otis's bloated mouth turned down at the corners. "Trust you to stick your nose into other people's business. You've got nothing to do with it."

"Ah, but that's where you're wrong. I have everything to do with it. And I won't stand for your disgraceful mistreatment of Sarah."

"Sarah," he said, scorn dripping from a rasping voice. "Since when was she Sarah?"

Sarah stepped closer, right by the bedside, and fixed him with a steady eye. "Since I took back my own life," she said, her voice strong and low. "I'm not coming back."

"Pa and Cliff will see about that," said Otis. "You've got no idea how furious the old man is."

Sarah shook her head. "No. He's got to understand. There have been..." She hesitated and her eyes flicked to Elizabeth. "Developments. There have been developments in my life. I can manage thing for myself. And I want Petra with me. She doesn't deserve to be left in hell."

Otis jerked his bandaged hand and accidentally doused the front of her dress with the last dregs of the brandy. She licked a few burning drops from her fingers.

"You're mad if you think he'll agree to that, Rebecca. In fact, you've guaranteed she's in for trouble. You, of all people, should know better than that."

Sarah's face flushed bright red and Elizabeth slipped closer to her side.

Otis made a show of taking the decanter in his left hand and awkwardly refilling his glass. He took a slow sip before lifting scornful eyes to her.

"'Developments.'" He rolled the word on his tongue. "What the hell is that supposed to mean?"

Cold shivers ran up Sarah's arms. She'd never heard a word imbued with so much hatred. She didn't respond.

"If you think you're going to swan off into the sunset with that lover boy who beat me up, you can think again. He's got a target on his back now. Nobody humiliates a Hollows like that and gets away with it."

He took a morose slurp from the glass. "I don't know why Pa doesn't get rid of the lot of ya. Cut ya all off for good, but unfortunately, he says he needs you back."

Sarah stiffened. Elizabeth, sensing her distress, slipped her arm around her shoulders.

"Sadly, he's promised you to Clifford, and he can't afford to go back on his word, not when he owes him as much as he does. So, you can forget about 'developments.' And about lover boy as well."

Her hands and fingers felt numb, but she had to respond.

"Lover boy?" she barked. "You've got it all wrong. The man who saved me—the man who banged you up, and you deserved it—is one of Bully's employees. Nothing more. He was there on Thursday night, and he doesn't like to see women manhandled, that's all. Nothing more to it than that."

Otis gave a jeering roar. "Pull the other one, sister. It's got bells on." He grinned.

"As soon as I'm out of this deuced jail, I'm reporting back to Pa. I'm going to enjoy doing that. You won't have time to worry about Petra, you'll be too busy worrying about yourself. You and lover boy? Start looking behind your back, sister. Your lives won't be worth living."

Chapter 10

When Will walked into Pike Consulting's second-floor office in the Occidental Hotel on Monday, Sarah was already at her desk, her face pale but determined.

"You're early. Are you all right? Fully recovered from your ordeal?"

She gazed up from the paper she was reading and gave him a wisp of a smile. "As well as can be expected."

He stood beside her, uncertain of how to continue, glancing at the work in front of her. She was deep into the sugar processing contract that Kaleo had been working on—getting one of the key Hawaiian producers to come over to Diamond Sugar's facility at the end of the Bay.

Will tensed up as his eyes flicked over the document.

Another Hector de Vile complication. Since the senator had discovered the Manolo twins were his children six months ago, he'd benefited their business interests, giving them a substantial holding in Diamond Sugar and taking a close interest in their personal affairs.

It was good for Pike Consulting. As the intermediary agent, every new client was a good client. But it left a sour taste in his mouth that they had de Vile to thank for it.

"Working on Kaleo's new sugar contract? We're really seeing

good things coming from our Manolo connection. Kaleo's doing a great job," he said.

Sarah's hazel-green eyes flickered. "He is, but we must thank Hector, too. If only we all had fathers like him."

The nausea in Will's stomach grew. "I wouldn't know. Mine died years ago."

That, at least, is true.

"I wish mine had too." The venom in Sarah's voice caught him unawares.

"I'm sorry. I didn't know. You never mentioned…"

Sarah switched her attention to the papers on her desk, signaling she was getting on with it.

"No reason to," she muttered, staring down. She peered up, her eyes magnified behind her reading glasses. "Isn't Kaleo in this morning?"

"I think he's got another meeting down at the wharves. Probably be in later."

She nodded, as if satisfied with his response. "And what have you got on today?"

Will itched with irritation. Was he answering to her now? They'd joined Bully Pike's business within months of one another, not long before his violent death, him as an assistant agent, her as the office administrator.

Bully had no obvious successor, and they were still waiting for probate on his will to be settled to know what was going to happen to the company. Maybe someone like Hector de Vile, who already owned a quarter share and was a good friend of Bully's, would buy it.

The familiar sense of loathing crawled over him at the prospect. He had to do something about that man before it was too late.

When Sarah had first joined them she'd been a mousey, retiring little chit of a thing, hiding behind her glasses, happy to fade into the background and work at her filing and her numbers. She was very good at the calculations an office like theirs relied on.

The mark-up they could put on incoming exports, gauging the maximum charge for processing, working out shipping fees for exports. All that stuff. Like a walking calculator, she did it all in her head. But she hated to have attention drawn to her brilliance.

She reminded him of those pale blue moths which camouflaged themselves in sage bushes. You wouldn't give them a second look, but when you did, you noticed their exquisite delicate markings.

Will peered at her again. She was wearing a deceptively austere outfit—a white blouse of the finest fabric with a rounded collar, tucked into a double-layered skirt in contrasting pastel plaids, slate gray sitting over a misty marine blue.

Lately, she'd been like a moth coming out of its cocoon. She'd turned her brilliant organizing capacity to the wider management of the office. And truth be told, he suspected she was nudging him aside.

He tamped down his prickly pride. Only a few more weeks—a month at the most—and they'd know the contents of Bully's will, surely?

"I've doing the contracts for our wheat exports to Britain. I'm happy to let you see them before I send them out, if you want."

Will hadn't realized until a few months ago that California grew and shipped significant amounts of wheat and barley to Europe every year.

"Thanks, Will. That would be good."

There was a brisk tap at the outer door and a familiar, elegant head appeared around the office door.

"Good morning," said Elizabeth Westerhoven. "I thought I'd pop by and see how everyone is doing. I've got some pain relief if anyone needs it. You all took a bit of a battering last week."

Will was grateful for the deliberately light tone the older woman adopted.

Sarah rose from her chair, laughing. "I only left your house an hour ago, Elizabeth. Not a lot has changed since then."

The Countess put down a box she carried under one arm on Sarah's desk, and they exchanged an affectionate hug. Sarah scanned the box. "What's this?"

"A special messenger delivered it not long after you left this morning. It's addressed to you." Her dark brown eyes flashed a warning. "I thought it best not to wait till tonight for you to see it."

Sarah peered at the package, and her already wan face drained of its last color. Will sensed her breath quickening.

The box covered the area of a small side table. It was wrapped in brown paper and securely tied up with rough twine and red sealing wax. The scripted address was in black ink, handwritten with an angled calligraphy pen.

Miss Rebecca Hollows, 18 Pine Street, Nob Hill.

Sarah peeked up at Will. Her pupils had shrunk to black dots. "There must be some mistake," she said, but her voice lacked conviction.

"Open it, Sarah," said Elizabeth quietly. "No point in putting it off."

As Sarah stood rigid in front of the box, Will leaned around her, opened her office drawer, and drew out a pair of scissors.

"Here," he said. "Or do you want me to do it?"

She eyeballed him, as if he'd interrupted her when she was escaping far away. Then her hand darted out to take the scissors. "No, it's all right. I'll do it."

Within a half a minute, she'd broken the sealing wax and peeled the paper back. Then she broke through the seal on the box itself.

Will could see edges of fine blue tissue paper inside. Packaging for a precious item a suitor might send to show his love—a silk scarf or a fine nightgown. And then the smell assailed them; the odor of rotting flesh, mustiness, and decay. What on earth was in there?

Sarah's right hand flew to her mouth. She stifled a sharp cry, then gazed at the Countess for a moment, terror in her eyes. After fractional further hesitation, she leaned forward and opened the box.

Will's eyes widened in horror behind his steamed up glasses

Nestled in the blue tissue lay a dozen small mutilated bodies, a cloud of tiny, brightly colored birds, their wings torn off, heads decapitated, tiny clawed feet pointing skywards in rigor mortis. Stinking songbirds, packaged for delivery. A rusty red liquid stained the paper.

As Will peered in disbelief, he saw movement, and in a rush realized what the most disgusting smell of all was. The earthy, mushroom smell of maggots, writhing amongst the pretty creatures' desolated remains, hungry for final obliteration.

Sarah's hand darted forward and retrieved an envelope that was tucked to one side of the disgusting display. She tore it open with trembling fingers. Inside, the violet-scented paper momentarily displaced the foul stink of the birds. Petra's notepaper. She opened the letter and read:

My Dearest Bekka,

I'm so excited to hear from your beloved fiancé, Cliff, that you'll soon be coming home to those who love you. Mother, me of course, and Cliff (especially Cliff) and Father. Oh, and Otis too.

Sarah squeezed her eyes tight. Within one sentence, she recognized Petra's note as a parody, written under duress. Her stomach tightened with dread. How much were she and her mother suffering already? She read on:

What wonderful news of your imminent arrival, dear Beks. You've been away so long, and Mother and I can hardly go another day without you. Though I hasten to assure you, we're in good health and being looked after wonderfully here. Dr. Morpho is attending Mother daily. You can imagine, I'm sure.

Dr. Morpho. Their shorthand for the quack their father had 'taking care' of Lottie. They knew he was dishing out far too much laudanum for "women's troubles." Her eyes skimmed the page, and she smiled grimly to herself. Petra was a lot smarter than she gave herself credit for.

We're not the only ones missing you. Your friend Jenny S. at Gold Hill has been asking after you. She is missing you and plans to send you a message as soon as she has an address.

Jenny S. Shorthand for the Gold Hill telegraph clerk, Johnny Skeates, who was a good friend. She missed the business gossip they often shared.

Remember Prince Prospero, and Mother's stories about him? Well, the Prince is up to his old tricks. He's still "happy and dauntless and sagacious," just like in the old days of Mother's story, even though his kingdom is depopulated.

You recall? He invited a thousand friends to join him, and they had everything they needed. Remember? Buffoons and songbirds and Beauty and wine. And no one wanted to leave the kingdom?

We so loved that story? And then at the fabulous masquerade a stranger asked to venture out, even though it meant facing the Red Death? We both know it so well. We used to recite it with Mother in our secret place.

"Who insults us with his blasphemous mockery?" Prince Prospero demanded. "Seize her and unmask her, that we may know whom we have to hang at sunrise from the battlements."

I've forgotten how this story ends, my brave and clever sister, but I'm sure you'll remember. You can tell me when you come home.

We love you so, and we long to be with you. See you soon.
Remember Beauty had a capital B and Prince Prospero sends
his love.

Prince Prospero. From Edgar Allan Poe's story *The Masque of the Red Death*. A clever allegory for their own story. They used to giggle about their nickname for Clifford. He was Prince Prospero because he ordered their father around like he was the boss of everything.

Petra was covertly telling her to stay away, while Clifford was forcing her to encourage her to come home.

This was his own weird version of carrot and stick, including this letter with the dead birds. In the story, the Prince's Kingdom fell under the thrall of the Red Death, and Darkness and Decay had dominion over all. Their lives were turning out exactly how Poe had described it.

So appropriate.

Sarah screwed the letter into a tight ball and dropped it into the wastepaper basket. She sank to her chair, put her head in her hands, and wept.

Chapter 11

Kaleo had shaken off the cloud of threat that hung over him for the rest of the Sunday after Dearborn's visit, but more shark dreams disturbed his sleep.

He'd risen early and given himself a good dousing in cold water in the copper bath to wake up. He daydreamed of home, of paddling out toward the low horizon at dawn, breathing air not yet warmed by the day, scented with the acerbic saline snap of the ocean he loved.

He was out the door and down to the wharves to check out any overnight arrivals as dawn broke on this side of the Pacific. He told himself it was every bit as uplifting to be out in a fresh San Francisco morning with the breeze to himself, before the crowds hit the streets, and he was right.

He'd soon fallen in with a newly arrived ship's captain with news of Honolulu that they'd chewed over together, breakfasting on warm cornbread and Folger's coffee at one of the port market stalls.

As he strode up Market Street to Pike Consulting, his spirits rose. There was a "do or die" spirit about the Bay that he loved. It reminded him of that moment when, poised on his board, he decided whether to shoot for this wave or wait for the next.

Once committed, there was no going back, and that's the way a lot of the people he met here in San Francisco approached life. With a brash vigor, a boldness and sagacity hardly matched anywhere else.

He bounded up the stairs two at a time. Thursday night's events were all but forgotten. Dearborn's warnings were a faint echo. He was ready to take on the world. As he entered the public reception area, he saw Will, Sarah, and Elizabeth were there ahead of him.

The first two? Hardly surprising, as they were both punctual timekeepers. But Elizabeth? He wasn't sure why she'd be here. Even more unusual than her presence was the musty, unpleasant odor rising from a box on Sarah's desk.

Sarah was leaning over it. And what? Was she crying? Surely not? A wave of giddiness threatened to overwhelm him.

Will hovered close by, wringing his hands, shifting his weight from one foot to the other as if he couldn't decide what to do or where to go next. Elizabeth's body was rigid, her face drained and stony.

Kaleo hesitated in the entryway. He took off his hat. Regained his balance.

"Is something wrong?"

Sarah met his eye but did not answer. She touched her throat with a shaky hand.

Will's eyes flashed him a message which said, "Not now." He ignored it and moved toward the desk.

"What's that smell?"

Uninvited, he leaned over and peered into the box, which lay open on the desk. The gorge rose in his throat, his senses invaded by the rotten smell of death.

Maggots writhed on the exposed flesh of small feathery bodies, blue and emerald and gray with red-tipped wings—every color of the rainbow seemed to spill out of the box, along with the horrendous smell of rotting meat.

He halted and stared in disbelief. "Sarah! What is this?"

She closed the box with rapid, anxious movements and stared up at him, still not speaking.

Her lower lip trembled; her eyelids fluttered like hummingbird wings. A long, drawn-out silence played out between them.

"Sarah. Tell me. What's going on here?"

She collapsed back into her chair, and Will placed solicitous hands on her shoulders. The placatory move riled Kaleo more than he cared to admit.

What is this? Have they got something going on I don't know about?

Sarah avoided meeting his eyes.

"Have you called the police?" He addressed the question to Will. Will shook his head. His chest heaved. "No. No, we haven't."

We haven't. Ah, he was involved somehow.

"We? Are you involved too?"

Will jerked his hands away from Sarah's shoulders. "Me? No. No, not at all. I was offering Sarah support."

Sarah ran her fingers along the edge of the box, her eyes squeezed shut. "This is his way of threatening me," she gasped. "They're my sister's birds. They're the only thing that keeps her going."

Her voice cracked, and she wiped a hand over her eyes. "Now see what he's done. It's so cruel."

She broke down and sobbed into a white handkerchief while they stood around her, staring and helpless. Through her gasps she coughed out, "It's meant to frighten me. Make me do what he wants. Or else…"

"He? Who's he?"

Elizabeth spoke into the silence. "I think Sarah is referring to Clifford Jensen."

Kaleo remembered Alex mentioning the name last night but played dumb. "And he is…?" He patiently awaited an answer from one of the women. When Sarah didn't respond, Elizabeth did.

"He's Sam Hollow's business partner."

Kaleo stretched out his hands and picked up the box. It weighed nothing in his gnarly hands, the knuckles still banged up from Thursday's fight.

"I'm taking this down and locking it up in the warehouse where it'll be safe until the police come. And then I'm coming back up here with coffee and you're going to tell me what's going on."

Elizabeth Westerhoven shook her head. "She's not up to talking, Kaleo." She placed a consoling hand on Sarah's back. "Sarah, dear. Maybe you'd better come home. You need some breathing space."

Sarah dabbed her eyes and abruptly stood up. "No, Elizabeth. We'll talk later. Right now, I've got work to do and I'm not letting this stop me."

Mrs. Westerhoven hesitated, her face mirroring concern. Then she gathered her skirts in one hand and faced the door. "Very well, dear girl. I wouldn't have expected anything else from you. But we will talk later. There's still a lot we need to decide."

Kaleo held the box at arm's length to lessen the smell. "I'm taking this to the storeroom. It's evidence that should go to the police."

He and Elizabeth walked out together. Outside the office door, Elizabeth paused. "Go easy on her, Kaleo. She's carrying a tremendous weight on her shoulders."

He shook his head in frustration. "And she doesn't have to carry it all alone."

Elizabeth stared at him for a minute, and then left.

***

Sarah crossed the room and opened the windows wide. A sweet cinnamon and sugar aroma flooded the room, supplanting the other horror. Dan the Doughnut Man was hard at work at his street stall immediately below.

A whiff of horse dung, a cacophony of wagon wheels, and the rising volume of pedestrian chatter all infiltrated the room, seeming to insist life was proceeding as usual. Except here.

Will watched as Sarah turned away from the window, her eyes glazed over, as if in a daze. She muttered something to herself. Will caught the words.

"Normal. A normal day. Unbelievable."

Then she lifted her eyes to him.

"I can't tell Kaleo. He's determined to help. And it will get him killed."

Will leaned against the wall closest to her desk, arms folded, his face thoughtful.

"You can tell me. I'm as much in the dark as he is, but I promise I'll avoid getting killed."

He slid his back down the wall, sank onto his haunches on the soft Oriental carpet, and patted for Sarah to join him. "You can start by explaining who Rebecca Hollows is."

Sarah gave a sharp intake of breath, and her already pale face drained to deathly white. He hunched his shoulders forward in an apology.

"I saw the name on the box."

She moved with quiet grace and joined him on the floor, her long legs spread before her, her back hard against the wall as if she feared she couldn't hold herself up without it. She stared at the floor for half a minute, chewing her lower lip. Then her eyes flashed up at him.

"You noticed," she whispered. She took another breath. "Please. Don't tell anyone. It's my secret."

Will gave her an assessing glance that wasn't unfriendly. "I guessed that much."

Another silence.

"Come on, Sarah. Who is she? Rebecca, I mean. Or perhaps more to the point, who are you? We've worked together long enough, worked happily, I thought, for me to deserve some answers.

"Especially when it seems we all might be in jeopardy because of it."

She reached out her hand and placed it on top of his in a sisterly gesture. "You're right, I suppose. It's hard to know where to start."

Will shot her a sympathetic grin.

"I think someone famous had the idea. Something about 'Begin at the beginning and go on till you come to the end, then stop'?"

Sarah gave a breathy laugh. "The King. You know *Alice in Wonderland*? How so?"

"Oh, I have nieces who love bedtime stories…"

"Really? You've never mentioned."

"You're not the only one who has secrets," he said, the retort sounding sharper than he'd intended. He paused. "Sorry. Didn't mean it to come out like that. Poor form."

She shook her head. "It's okay. We're all a bit rattled after Thursday."

She cleared her throat nervously. "Rebecca Hollows. That's me. And why I've been using another name, calling myself Sarah? Well, it's an endless story. Too long to tell now. Life as Rebecca became unbearable. So I ran away."

"Oh? And your father is Sam Hollows?"

"That's right."

"And the birds? What about them? Apart from being an especially vile trick. Surely someone didn't think that was a joke?"

"No joke, no. Intended to intimidate."

They sat in a tense silence.

Then Will ventured, "And this Clifford that Elizabeth mentioned? How about him?"

"He's the main one I have to get away from."

More silence. Will sighed.

"Well, I can't say I understand, because I don't. But what happens next? Do you run again, or what?"

"No. No more running. I'm here to stay. I have to work out how to do it."

Will shifted closer and tentatively clasped the back of her hand. "I hope you're not trying to do this alone? Who do you have to back you up?"

She didn't move her hand.

"Elizabeth is a gale force hurricane. She's all the help I need. Her and Dolphie, her nephew. He's a great man in a tight spot."

"You're a woman of surprises, Sarah. You still want me to call you that, right?"

Sarah nodded.

"Until that Epiphany dinner, I wasn't even aware you knew Elizabeth."

She shrugged. "There wasn't any reason to mention it. I mean. We're not big on confiding secrets, are we?

"I know very little about you, come to think of it." She regarded him with a curious glint. "Those nieces, for example. You've never mentioned them before."

And never will again.

He raised his shoulders to his ears. "As you say. No reason to. We've got plenty on our plates without getting personal."

Once again, her eyes roved his carefully neutral face.

"I'm worried about Kaleo. He's such a hero. Goodness knows what would have happened if he hadn't been there the other night. But he can't keep coming to my rescue. He'll get himself hurt, if not killed.

"That's partly what those poor little birds are all about. Promise me you won't tell him anything."

Will laughed easily. "My lips are sealed. It'll be our secret. But Kaleo won't like it."

Chapter 12

Kaleo dropped the box off in the warehouse and side-tracked to organize coffee at the Occidental's café on a floor below their office, then bounded up the stairs ahead of the cheerful waiter, eager to get back.

He soft-footed through Pike Consulting's main door and a low plea stopped him in his tracks. A woman's voice, soft and confessional.

"Promise me you won't tell him anything."

Sarah's voice. But who was she talking about? He hesitated, waiting for the coffee bearer to catch him up, reluctant to break in on what was obviously a private conversation. Will laughed. He sounded relaxed, not like a man who'd witnessed a sinister delivery minutes before.

"My lips are sealed. It'll be our secret. But Kaleo won't like it." Will's voice.

He froze.

Kaleo.

They're talking about me.

His throat tightened. The waiter was at his back. He stepped aside and gestured for the man to precede him in, taking the seconds to compose himself. The last thing he wanted was for them to suspect he'd overheard them.

His face heated at the same time as his core temperature plummeted. He ran his hand down one cheek, as if his flat palm could absorb his high color and camouflage his distress.

As he followed the waiter in, he momentarily stalled. He'd heard their voices, but where were they? The office appeared empty.

Then he spotted them, huddled on the Oriental rug. Hip to hip, shoulder to shoulder, at floor level, holding hands. What a cozy scene. His breath came rougher, faster. He gave them another minute to register they were no longer alone.

The waiter paused in front of the desk, unsure of where to deposit the tray.

Kaleo interceded. "Leave the tray there on the desk, thanks, Ricardo. We'll manage the rest."

His voice had such an edge of false bonhomie he expected them to react, but if they noticed he was cracking false, they didn't show it.

Sarah jumped up and shook out her skirts. Was that guilt that crossed her face?

"Oh, Kaleo. So good of you. Coffee's exactly what I need. It smells divine."

His eyes scanned her slim form. Her arms dangled awkwardly at her side, and her eyes were downcast. Her body language contradicted the positive words.

Will got up more slowly, like a zoo animal who'd had an afternoon snooze in the tropical sun.

The thought slashed through him. Had there been any indications? *Are Sarah and Will a "thing"? Attracted? Romantically attached?*

He flexed his shoulders, suddenly overcome with cramping pain.

What do people call it, anyway? The thing that stirred him up inside whenever he saw Sarah? Like he wanted to keep her safe from every bad thing?

He was like a surfer marooned on a mirror-slick ocean without a wave in sight. If he'd been on his board, he'd be daydreaming, waiting for things to change. Either that or paddle in. As it was, he stood paralyzed, inside and out. Stranded at sea with the sharks.

How blind am I? Is this why Sarah went cold on me a few months back?

He leaned on the back of the chair, feigning nonchalance, as Will and Sarah took their coffees. Sarah sat down at her desk. Will slouched against the side wall to her left.

Kaleo remained standing in front of them both, neck and torso prickling till he wanted to toss off his jacket and rip open the top buttons of his fresh white linen shirt.

But casting his jacket aside would suggest he was settling in for a long chat, and after what he'd heard, this was the last place he wanted to be.

"Your parcel's downstairs in the warehouse storeroom." He addressed Sarah in a sober, level voice. "The police will need it as evidence, so I've put it somewhere safe."

"Evidence?" Sarah's tone was high and querulous. She swallowed hard. "I mean, why?"

Kaleo arched his scarred brow in disbelief. "Because they'll want to see it. They can't rely on your say-so."

"But... I don't see why it needs to be a police matter at all. Someone's playing a nasty trick. That's all."

He held onto his gut as if someone had punched him. "A nasty trick? Is that all you think this is?"

She leaned forward and rested her elbows on the desk's edge. They both could fake detachment. "Well, um. What do you think it is?"

"I think it's stepping up the threat on whatever started on Thursday night. Like when a shark first takes a bite of your board and then circles back for the kill. Just like that." A shiver ran up his spine.

Sarah's face softened. "Oh, Kaleo, I think you're overreacting."

She gestured for him to sit in the chair on the opposite side of her desk and reached for her coffee. She took a sip.

"This is so good. Thanks so much."

He remained standing, though he picked up a coffee. "A nasty trick, then? Not a circling shark?"

Sipping her coffee, she narrowed her eyes, as if trying to decide if he was making fun of her or not.

"I'm serious," he said.

"So am I. It's a misguided attempt to browbeat me. And it's destined to fail."

"Oh really? How can you be so sure? These people appear out of nowhere. They seem to have limitless resources. How are you going to match that? I know you're a capable woman, but you're an office manager with limited resources..."

Sarah drew in a sharp breath. "Elizabeth is helping me. She has people she can call on to help. Even your father, Senator de Vile, if necessary."

She shot him a quick, doubtful smile. "But we won't be going to those lengths at the start. First, we're going to hire better security." She leaned back in the chair and folded her arms in front of her.

What's coming next?

He jumped in before she could say whatever it was she had on her mind.

"Who are they, Sarah? You obviously know more than you're letting on." He glared in Will's direction. "Or that you're willing to tell me."

Her fingers tightened into a white-knuckled knot. Intense emotion flashed across her face, like lightning on a spring day. What was it? Fear? Fury? Longing? It was gone in a split second, too fast for him to read her.

She continued as if he hadn't spoken. The small room echoed with the false brightness of her upper register.

"Kaleo, I know you're a gallant man. Valor personified. You proved it the other night. But I'm begging you. Please. You've done enough. It's a mess and you could get killed."

Her voice cracked. The slim column of her throat pumped.

He planted himself squarely in front of her. "Which one is it, Sarah? Nothing but a 'nasty little trick'? Or serious stuff?"

She pursed her lips. "Listen, I'm arranging security for us all. You, me, and Will."

She peered at Will, who was silently watching, his coffee nursed in both hands. His face was blank, as if he hadn't registered she was speaking of danger. Of potential death.

"As long as we're careful, it will be all right."

Kaleo felt as if a transparent bubble enclosed them, the three of them together, in this silent room. For a long minute, he stared at her.

"Security? A good idea for you, for sure, but don't worry about me. I don't need it."

Her face pinched in exasperation. "Don't go all horns and rattlesnakes on me."

"All what?" Despite his stunned annoyance, Kaleo laughed.

"An old cowboy saying. Don't get yourself all lathered up. You look like you want to pitch a rattlesnake on your horns."

At that, he did laugh. "I've got to give it to you, Sarah. You're incorrigible. But as for arranging security for me? Forget it. I can take care of myself."

She shook her head. "Humor me, Kaleo. If anything awful happened to you, I'd never forgive myself."

Her eyes lingered. They drew him into their shimmering warmth. And then, as suddenly as she'd made the connection, she dropped her gaze to her desk.

I'm never going to figure you out. Hot and cold. I never know where I am with you.

Will hadn't spoken since he'd arrived with the coffee. Maybe he would get more information out of him.

"Well, Will? What do you make of it? Do you know any more than me about what's going on?"

Will flushed pink. His eyes flicked to Sarah's face and then darted away, as if guilty he'd caught him out.

"I'm as much in the dark as you are, Kaleo. I guess we'll have to trust the boss."

The words sounded truly earnest. At least the guy could fib better than Sarah.

In it together. Both liars. And I thought they were my friends.

Kaleo knew his eyes glittered with anger as he turned first to Sarah, then Will.

"Trust. A simple matter of trust, is it?"

He balled and opened his fists, arms stiff at his sides, wanting to raise them and hit something, or someone. The wastepaper basket sat at his feet, overflowing with brown wrapping paper.

From that damned parcel this morning, he guessed. He shoved at it irritably with his heavy leather boot, and the wicker basket rolled over, its contents spilling across the carpet as it rolled to a stop.

"I guess I'm wasting my time here."

Sarah's face had paled to a chalky white.

"A gallant? That's it? That's what I am to you?" He stared at her, boiling inside. Better to vent his frustration than allow the pain of rejection to gnaw at him.

"One thing you should know about us 'gallants,' Sarah. Simple fellows like us hate thugs who attack women. But even more than thugs, we despise liars."

He skimmed his eyes to Will, and then back to Sarah.

"Keep your security for yourself, boss. I don't need it." And in three long strides, he was gone.

***

As the door slammed behind Kaleo, Sarah buried her face in her hands, but no sound escaped her lips. Her chest was so tight and painful she could barely breathe, let alone summon up the energy to cry.

The vile box of birds had devastated her, but she still had the fight, the raw indignation, to keep going.

That scene with Kaleo had wasted her, left her like one of those dead birds herself, wings torn from her body, abandoned at the bottom of her cage, with no hope of escape.

He'd obviously overheard her and Will talking. He knew they'd lied to him, that she'd lied to him. And there was nothing she could do to make it right. No excuse, no explanation.

Given a repeat, she would do exactly the same thing all over again. Because telling him the full story of her mortification was more than she could bear. And once he knew her past, he would never see her with those same bright, searching eyes again.

She lifted her head at the sound of Will's footsteps. He put his hands to either side of the coffee tray and stared across the desk, his eyes gentle and inquiring.

"That was awful bad luck, on top of everything else," he said. "Is there anything I can do to make it better?"

She shook her head, suppressing the bitter laughter that was bubbling up from inside at the absurdity of the offer. There was nothing anyone could do. And it was all her own fault.

These last few months she had been walking a knife edge, trying to hold on to a thin wafer of faith that everything would work out in the end.

That she could take Kaleo into her confidence, to explain to him why she'd resorted to an audacious ruse to escape. But after this morning, she'd shattered any hope of a future together.

He despised her, and with good reason. She knew integrity came first with him; before power, before money, before popularity. Kaleo was a prince of fortitude, quietly commanding, discreet, and purposeful. She'd met no one like him.

And she'd never so wanted with all her heart to bask in his favor. But now, not only was that never going to happen, but he was in grave danger because of her.

She pushed herself up from the desk. "I'm really sorry, Will, but I need to go out for a couple of hours. Make a few arrangements. You understand?"

He gave her an ironic grin.

"Not really, Sarah. I'm still rather short on facts." He shrugged lightly and picked up the tray.

"However, I accept that's how it is for now, and I appreciate you have an emergency on your hands, so go for it. I'll expect you when I see you."

A few minutes later, she was out on the street and the hotel's floor manager was calling for a hack.

The only thing she could do now was to focus on protecting the people she loved.

First, she had to rescue Petra before Clifford did to her what he'd done to Rebecca.

And second, whether or not Kaleo liked it, she had to keep him safe.

Otis had the idea he was her "lover boy." And if Clifford believed Otis, he'd do anything he could to get at her through Kaleo.

Chapter 13

Screwed-up paper and other debris littered the floor. The air was dusty, and his breath wheezy as Will gazed at the office floor with unseeing eyes and asked himself, What's next? He'd landed at Pike Consulting eight months ago and talked his way into a job with Bully Pike based on his years of experience in exporting and importing in New York.

He'd carried a recommendation from a merchant Bully knew and trusted, and within weeks he'd been up and running.

Bully appreciated having young legs and a sharp new mind in the business, and Will had dreamed of one day buying a share. Bully was a bachelor with no children, and he'd taken a fatherly interest in Will's growing familiarity with the California trade.

"One day soon you'll make an excellent factor man, son," he'd said one afternoon as they sat around discussing business at the end of the working day. "You've got all the makings—a quick mind, an affable personality, and the ability to get on with people."

His father would have been so proud to see it, he'd fleetingly thought to himself. And, as always, reminded of his father, a chill gripped his entrails. He'd endured a life hampered by ill fortune. A premature death. And it was all Hector de Vile's fault.

He took a deep breath. He was going to get that bastard, and at Pike Consulting he'd perfectly positioned himself to keep close tabs on de Vile's comings and goings and plot his revenge.

De Vile was a lifelong friend of Bully's, a frequent visitor and a minority shareholder who took a close interest in what Bully was doing. So, it had been an awful shock—a disaster for them all—when a jealous husband murdered Bully six months back, although the business had survived remarkably well without him.

Office admin was in Sarah's capable hands, and they'd taken on Kaleo to work as the junior alongside Will. De Vile had taken a closer interest—and pushed business their way—partly because he'd discovered after a lifetime of ignorance, he was Kaleo's father.

Will prickled with irritation. Being beholden to de Vile for anything set his teeth on edge.

Bide your time, sonny. You'll get your chance.

That's what Bully would say, though he didn't know Will's connection to de Vile, nor his blinding hatred for him.

The rolling thump of heavy wooden barrels being unloaded into the kitchens below interrupted his reverie. The hotel was receiving its regular delivery of the booze—the wine, cider and beer—which kept the Occidental's thirsty patrons well-watered. He stared at the crumpled brown wrapping and smiled grimly.

Kaleo, falling over himself to know what was going on so he could protect Sarah, didn't know how close his boot had come to revealing her identity.

The silly lovesick fool.

He leaned over and picked through the rubbish, returning everything except the paper from the box—a few ripped envelopes, fragments of string and sealing wax—to the bin. He smoothed out the paper on the desk in front of him, and considered the address, immaculately scripted in black ink with a broad-nib calligraphy pen.

Miss Rebecca Hollows.

Sam Hollows' daughter. That's who Sarah was. Where could he find out more about the family?

An idea formed in his mind. If Sarah wouldn't come clean, he'd have to do his own research. He couldn't afford to have the business ripped out from under him because of some woman's problems, even if he respected Sarah's clever brain.

The stakes were too high. His first obligation was to protect himself and his family's future. And if he had to sacrifice a friendship to do it, then he would.

He placed the carefully folded wrapping paper in his briefcase and hurried downstairs. A strategy was half forming in his mind. Visit Dearborn and offer a bargain.

Give him the information about the box of birds in return for more information about the case. Clearly Sarah was Sam Hollows' daughter Rebecca.

But did Dearborn know that? And why was she hiding out under a false name? What was happening to the fellow who'd attacked them? Otis Hollows. Obviously related. As one victim, he had a right to know.

And then the strangest thing happened. Coming toward him along one of the Occidental's narrow back corridors—the one leading to the warehouse—came none other than Captain Adam Dearborn.

And at almost the same moment, he realized the policeman was pausing outside a room where a young police constable stood guard.

Snap! He'd heard rumors of the cops keeping men of the "higher classes" who were "wanted for questioning" in comfortable premises outside the jail.

Will took a leap of faith and posited that the man who'd nearly brained him the other night was in this hotel room, close to the warehouses. He raised his hat as he passed Dearborn in the corridor, exchanged pleasantries, and then continued on.

He'd likely be able to do a far better deal with the scum who'd attacked him than the cop who had him in custody. He'd wait a while. And then go in for the kill.

***

"She said what?" Clifford stared at Otis Hollows, mouth open in disbelief, his eyes shooting daggers.

"She says she's not coming back. There are 'new developments' and she's managing her own life now." Otis shot him a satisfied smirk and took another long swallow of brandy.

Clifford wondered yet again how the woman he planned to wed—he would wed her, there was no "maybe" about it—Bekka of-the-brilliant-mind, could be the sister of the smug pea-brain lounging around like Lord Muck in a shiny patterned banyan top hanging over street trousers.

And then he reminded himself once again, they shared no common blood. Sam and Charlotte were both widowed with two children when they married, so Rebecca and Petra were Sam's step daughters.

Otis was the spoiled younger son of a rich man—correct that, a once rich man—and he hadn't yet cottoned on to the unwelcome reality that there was no Hollows empire left for him to inherit. None that he was going to get his hands on anyway. It was all going to go to him. Clifford Jensen.

So, Mama, put that in your pipe and smoke it.

The towering figure of his Jezebel mother loomed up in his memory, the fingers of her left hand digging into his shoulder to stop him from running away. She stood tall and gaunt, like a clothed skeleton, her leather-soled slipper raised in her strong right arm, about to bring it down with walloping force across his backside.

A snapshot of my childhood.

She'd never believed he'd make anything of himself, and she'd tried to beat that into him. But he was proving her wrong. The only reason he wished her alive today was to rub her nose in his success.

Within a couple of weeks, he would have control of the Hollows silver fortune and control the brains behind the business—as his wife. It had been a long time coming.

But it was all dependent on a few last key moves; getting Rebecca back to Virginia City where she belonged and forcing Sam Hollows to stand by their deal. Once he had the sole command of the key to the safe, Otis and his brother Rufus would be out the door.

Otis's round face with pouched chipmunk cheeks and small beady eyes darted around the room, as if he was expecting to be surprised by something unpleasant. The bruising from the beating he had received showed through his waxy complexion, a paler shade of purple than his robe.

Clifford punched down his rising irritation at Hollows' puffed-up complacency as Otis, oblivious to his mood, opened his mouth to continue.

"Oh, and she plans to get Petra to come and join her."

For the second time in less than five minutes, Otis had left Clifford momentarily speechless. He swallowed hard, fighting to control his anger. His mouth was dry, his throat prickly. It was as if he'd got a mouthful of sawdust. He coughed to clear his throat.

"And you know all this? How?"

"She came by and told me herself." Another pleased-with-himself smirk.

"She did what?"

"Yeah. With that witch of a Countess." Otis was revelling in being the man on the scene. "That old woman's sticking her nose in everywhere."

Clifford chomped down on his back teeth as Otis watched. For the first time since he had come into this infernal room, the man sprawled on the bed wasn't twitching all over the place. He'd got Clifford's full attention and was loving it. Clifford's heightened pulse thumped at his temples.

The dumb sot.

He, Clifford Jensen, had left Virginia City against his will and come to San Francisco to clean up the mess Otis had made of what should have been a simple task. It had taken their spies and lookout men months to locate Rebecca, while the business went into near terminal decline.

Without her fiendishly ingenious calculations on silver share prices, her fast re-positioning against other shares when needed, they'd seen nowhere near the same success in their efforts to play the market as they enjoyed when she was heading the Brains Trust.

Truth be told, without her quick mind they were left holding stock they didn't want, leading to big losses.

And they'd attracted unwelcome attention because of the Golden Bowl's sinking value, though Lord knows they were doing their best to prop it up. Fact was, they relied on Rebecca's brilliance to calculate and strategize. Without her, their too-clever strategies floundered.

When she'd escaped without warning, she'd been smart at covering her tracks. But now they knew where she was, her return should be straightforward.

The law was on their side. An unmarried woman had to obey her father, or her fiancé. Or both. Nobody liked the idea of single women swanning about the state without family protection.

Dearborn had taken a dim view when Clifford called on the police captain an hour before and outlined the situation. Told him how she'd flown into some tizz understood only by women and absconded from her father's safekeeping.

He'd related how Sam Hollows' worried efforts to trace his eldest daughter had run into brick walls until this week.

Once he knew where she was, he'd sent her stepbrother to bring her home. It was as simple as that. Perhaps Otis had overreacted, but the whole thing was an unfortunate misunderstanding.

Rebecca wasn't being kidnapped, she was being returned to a loving father and fiancé.

Dearborn had told him that police inquiries were complete, and they were no longer holding Otis in custody. He was free to go, so when he arrived in Otis's hotel room, he expected he'd be falling over himself to get home.

Far from it. Instead, he'd found him cuddled up with the brandy decanter, talking about bringing some women in.

After all, he'd told Clifford, he'd got the thin end of the wedge. Getting beaten up when they'd told him picking up his stepsister was going to be as easy as stealing candy from a baby.

He became aware Otis had said something. "I didn't hear you. What did you say?"

"I said, I told Rebecca her lover boy wouldn't save her a second time."

"Lover boy? Who are you talking about?"

"That bruiser who beat me up. He's sweet on Rebecca, and she's not running away from him. Far from it."

"What would you know about it?" His lungs squeezed so tight in his chest he could barely breathe.

"I tell you. She's on with him. You'd better move fast if you want to lay claim to her."

He paused, savoring another sip. A calculated gleam in his eye had replaced the hangdog attitude.

"Oh, my apologies. I forgot. You've already staked your claim, haven't you, Clifford? That's why she ran away before. Maybe she prefers lover boy's gentle touch to your barbarianism."

"Shut up, Otis. You know nothing about it. I'm only here in San Francisco because you blew it."

Otis's thick eyebrows came together in a frown. "Not my fault, Clifford. No one told me I'd be dealing with two guys, one of them the blinking size of Hercules. I was lucky to get out alive."

Jensen scoffed. "You're lucky you're not in irons. Anyone else would have been. Now shut up and tell me what Rebecca said. How did she react to the parcel she received today?"

"Parcel? She said nothing about a parcel. What did you send her?"

A warm curl of satisfaction lodged in his ribs as he recalled the disgusting potage he'd shoveled into the box for delivery to Elizabeth Westerhoven's house. He could still smell the decay in his nostrils.

Serves her right for leading me on a merry dance.

"Nothing. Never mind."

Whether or not she'd reacted to Otis, as sure as bread always falls buttered side down, he bet it devastated her seeing Petra's dead birds. She'd be beside herself about the note.

Petra sounded so pleased to have her home. He didn't get all the girly stuff about fairy stories and princes, but that didn't matter. The point was her sister was asking her to come home.

The only thing she would hate more than what he'd done to her the night she'd run away was to see Petra get the same treatment.

He grinned to himself. Helping himself to a second Hollows virgin wouldn't be a bad thing. Rebecca had an iron will for standing up to him and her father, but she'd always been a protective Mama Bear around her sister.

But before he dealt with the Hollows sisters—both of them—he was going to settle the score with the plug-ugly who'd taken out Otis.

Lover boy?

He wouldn't be much of a lover boy with a bullet in his chest.

Otis might not be right about many things, but he was sure right on that one.

Lover boy wouldn't be around to save her a second time.

Chapter 14

Will tapped diffidently on the door of Room 102, and it opened with a flourish within seconds, as if the occupants inside were expecting someone, though it plainly wasn't him.

The man who stood in front of him was tall and dark, his strong Roman nose and chiseled cheekbones strangely at odds with the boxer's shoulders and hairy forearms. His dark brows pinched in an irritated frown, as if to say, Who the devil are you?

This was not the same man who'd attacked him the other night. That was clear at one glance. His second glance got no further than a pair of cloudy pale green eyes, which gave the impression of seeing right through him while not actually looking at him.

Will had to steel himself to avoid making eye contact as he thrust out his hand with forced aplomb. "Will Davenport at your service. Captain Dearborn mentioned you were here, so I thought I'd drop by and see if I could be of help."

The man who'd answered the door stepped back and stared at his proffered hand, but did not grasp it. Behind him in the room, someone uttered a guttural howl. "In the name of Beelzebub. What's he doing here?"

The fellow at the door turned back into the room. "You know

him?" he asked with a perfunctory shrug, as if it mattered not a whit to him whether he did.

"Know him? He's the dude who was seeing Rebecca home the other night. I took him down before that other brawler came and punched me out."

The man's voice was rough and indignant. Will poised awkwardly on the balls of his feet, ready to run if they came at him.

Not this time. The man beside him stepped aside and made a gesturing motion with his arm, though his face remained closed and distrustful.

"You'd better come in, Mr. Davenport." The well-modulated voice carried the rounded tones of higher education. Will wondered if he was another Hollows family lawyer sent to oversee the rabble-rouser's release.

The opaque eyes flicked over him, and Will was aware of his clothes—his casual sandstone corduroy jacket over a rumpled plaid shirt didn't hold up against the stranger's crisp white shirt and slick bespoke jacket. In one sweeping glance, this guy had dismissed him as of little consequence.

He preceded the lawyer—if that's what he was—into the room, coming to a stop at the foot of a four-poster bed where the man who'd attacked him lounged with a brandy glass in hand.

"I gather you've already met Otis," the man said without a hint of irony. "I'm Clifford Jensen. Sam Hollows' primary business partner and Rebecca's fiancé." He kept his hands tightly at his side.

"Fiancé?" Will, normally placid and unshockable, couldn't suppress the surprise in his voice. "I see."

Sarah really does a good turn in deception, he thought. She's taken us all in with her sob story. He adjusted his expression to one of nonchalance.

"I'm here to find out what's going on, because we didn't know about Sarah's real identity either. It's not good for business, being caught out like this. Our clients like to think we're straight as a die.

"Any funny business makes them jittery, and coming so close after Bully's death… It's all very unfortunate." He flashed an enquiry at Jensen, then at the man in the bed.

"Dearborn tells me he's letting you go. I wanted to come by and say 'No hard feelings.' These things happen."

He turned to Jensen. "But I would like to hear exactly what's going on. We'll have to square it all off with our clients, as I'm sure you understand. And de Vile will want to know, too."

"De Vile?" Jensen's distrustful face darkened to thunder. "What's he got to do with anything?" Will detected ice in Jensen's tone and cursed himself for the name dropping. He'd been trying to make up for the casual jacket, the fashion faux pas. Damnation.

"Senator de Vile? He was a very close associate of Bully Pike's, as you probably know. He's taken an even closer interest in the firm since Bully's death because of the association we have with the Manolo twins.

"We handle all their sugar imports and de Vile takes a paternal interest in all the comings and goings." Jensen clamped down on his jaw. Will could see the tiny muscle working in his cheek.

"Is there a problem?"

A kaleidoscope of opportunities was opening up at the back of his mind.

If Hollows hates de Vile too, he'll make a perfect ally for me. Couldn't be better. His heart was pounding. Jensen, too, was apparently re-considering.

"I think you need to sit down, Mr. Davenport, and share some of the brandy Otis is hogging there. Tell us all about it."

Will peered at the man in the bed. "Otis? I'm not sure we've been introduced."

The other man barked a mirthless laugh. "Not introduced? I like it. Mr. Davenport, this is Otis Hollows. Rebecca's brother."

Yeah. Like I guessed. As if things aren't messy enough already.

Will took a deep breath and stood his ground.

"Oh. I see." He scanned the room, suddenly awkward.

"I'm thrilled to talk, Mr. Jensen, but it can't be all one-sided. I need to know what the heck's going on with our office administrator. Sarah or Rebecca or whoever she is.

"The woman we thought was Sarah. And funnily enough, she doesn't seem keen to tell us much about herself."

"You've had a lucky escape, Davenport. That woman is hell on wheels. You're fortunate we'll be taking her off your hands."

Hell on wheels? Were they talking about the same quiet, methodical, wouldn't-hurt-a fly Sarah? And why had this Jensen fellow reacted like the senator's name was poison?

Will moved tentatively to the chair Jensen gestured to and accepted a glass of brandy, but before he had even taken one sip, there was another knock at the door, this one loud and impossible to ignore.

"Come in," called Jensen, turning toward the entry.

A disheveled underling tumbled into the room. The man had eyebrows that met in the middle and he was panting, as if he'd run some distance.

He didn't wait to be invited to speak. "Mr. Clifford. Mr. Clifford, sir. She's gone. She's not there anymore."

Jensen banged his brandy glass down so hard the amber liquid slopped over the tabletop. "She's what?"

"She's gone. When we made our two o'clock check, the place seemed awful quiet. Dusty went around the back and found two hulking scrappers guarding the place. Armed to the teeth, they were, and they ordered us off the property."

Jensen's urbanity slipped, and Will's prospect of a convivial brandy evaporated.

A furious energy propelled Jensen across the room to the door, where he grabbed the messenger by the front of his shirt. He was a big man, but Jensen lifted him onto tiptoes in one galvanized swipe.

"What do you mean, 'She's gone'? Your job was to make sure that didn't happen."

His rage strangled his words, which he spat out through clenched teeth.

The messenger responded with a garbled protest that was indecipherable because Jensen's fist was at his throat.

Jensen dropped the man like a hot coal, and he folded in half into a coughing spasm. Everyone stood in silent shock, waiting for the man to regain his composure. After some more deep breaths, he stood up and glared at Jensen.

"The Countess. She's brought in security, Mr. Jensen, sir. We did what you said. We stayed out of sight. But she must've guessed we were watching the place."

"So, how do you know she's not there?"

"Dusty got hold of the housemaid. She was on her way home, and he stopped her for a little chat. Says the Countess and her young guest have left town and they won't be back until after St. Pat's day, and maybe not even then. The staff have all got two months' paid leave."

***

Clifford knew it was useless going to Nob Hill, but he couldn't help himself. He had to see the evidence with his own eyes.

He fumed as the hack thundered uphill toward Pine Street

Sheldon, the guard, shrank into the farthest corner of the cab, his face white and set. Otis and that odd fellow, Will Davenport, bounced around on the seat facing him.

He didn't know what to make of Davenport, who seemed a queer fish, but he couldn't think about that now. He had to satisfy himself that his men were correct—that Elizabeth Westerhoven had helped Rebecca give them the slip.

As soon as the hack drew up outside the ornamented St. Anne's mansion with its turret and tiled gables, Clifford knew he'd lost the second round in the battle.

Despite the obvious presence of the men patrolling the grounds, the house had a closed-up air. Shutters covered the windows, and no smoke rose from the chimneys.

At the sight of the hack on the curb, the property minders made a display of planting themselves at the front door, arms folded across their chests, glaring. No "Do Not Disturb" sign required. There was no point in alighting.

He stuck his head out of the hack door and called to the driver, "Auction Lunch Saloon on Washington Market."

The Auction was owned by a couple of Irish miners-turned investors, William O'Brien and James Flood, and was a booming "bit house"—so-called because the bar sold two drinks for a quarter and, like many San Francisco watering holes, provided a free savory lunch for their patrons.

The city's stock exchange stood a short distance away in Montgomery Street, and tips and insider information flowed with the drinks, as touts, brokers and speculators buzzed at the bar like bees in a hive. The Auction was like a second home to Clifford. And you never knew. Maybe he'd pick up some whiff of where Rebecca had absconded to this time.

As the cab rattled down the hill to the grill, Clifford burned inside with a fever like he'd never experienced before. The most urgent thing to do—more pressing than life itself—was to find Rebecca again.

But this time, he wouldn't be letting her out of his sight. He'd manacle her to himself if he needed to make sure he returned her to the Hollows home in Virginia City and got her to the altar.

Nothing would stop him this time. He swore it to himself. Not Petra. Not this so-called lover boy. No one would stand in his way. They could all be sacrificed if that was how it played out. He had to win.

*****

Clifford sat at the Auction Lunch Saloon bar and swallowed down on the raw sting of cheap brandy. It seemed an appropriate punishment for the folly of losing Rebecca twice. The hostelry was serving free oyster, chicken, and gumbo soup, and the full-bodied aroma as it arrived reminded him he hadn't had breakfast.

Like birds on a fence, they sat in line—Clifford, Otis, Sheldon and Davenport. Clifford sat next to Will Davenport.

"Sorry. Where were we before we were so rudely interrupted by the news of Rebecca's escape?" He flicked Davenport a wry grin.

Bumping their way down the hill to the Grill, Clifford had come to one glaring conclusion. Will Davenport, the colorless clerk who'd seemed insignificant in the scheme of things, a mere flunkey, had suddenly become very important to his task of finding Rebecca again.

This instant. Before Elizabeth Westerhoven had time to spirit her away, perhaps even out of the state. Or the country.

Davenport probably had more knowledge of where she'd be likely to go than anyone he knew. And, most important, Davenport knew where Clifford could find that 'lover boy.' He sensed he could be a very important chip in the Rebecca retrieval game.

His priority was now finding that bruiser and making sure he was in no position to rescue Rebecca again. If it turned out he meant something to Rebecca, he could also be a useful bargaining point.

"Where were we?" Davenport was peering at him over the top of his pen pusher's glasses, waiting to claim his full attention. "I believe you were about to tell me why this woman was running around with a fake identity. What's going on?"

Clifford gritted his teeth in annoyance. He might be an anaemic factor man, but he knew how to seize the initiative.

"Not quite," he ground out. "First, I want all the information you might have on where she might've gone and who with. That other fellow in your office, the one who hit Otis, for example. Where can I find him?"

Davenport's face kept its bland, clouded expression. Either he was very good at concealing his feelings, or he didn't care a whit about either Rebecca or her offsider.

"Oh, you mean Kaleo? Kaleo Manolo?"

"Yes, him. I seem to recall you mentioned something about a link between him and Hector de Vile? What's the story there?" Davenport shrugged, as if it was of little import.

"Kaleo and his twin sister Leilani are Hector de Vile's children from his first wife, but he's only recently found out about them. Apparently, there was some family drama, and he was told they'd died.

"He only discovered the full story recently, and he's taken an enormous interest in them since. Assisting them in business and so forth. Why? Don't you and de Vile get on?"

The inquiry sounded as disinterested as the rest of Davenport's rendering, but the glint behind the thick glass of Davenport's spectacles told Clifford the answer was far more important to him than he was letting on.

"Fascinating. I hadn't heard about the sudden expansion of de Vile's family." He took a considered sip. "As for de Vile, let's say there's been a longstanding rivalry between Hector and our Hollows' interests. Competition over silver mines, silver stocks."

He fixed the office manager with a stare.

"Hector played as fast and loose as the next man until he went to Washington. Now he's turned all 'holier than thou' with this nonsense about cleaning up the share market. He's become quite a thorn in the Comstock boss's sides."

"Ah, I see." Davenport nodded as if he sympathized with their predicament.

Clifford took this as a promising sign. "So, this Manolo character. Is he in de Vile's pocket?"

"Not exactly. No. They're still circling. Getting to know one another. But de Vile's hot on him and the sister. He wouldn't want to see their interests compromised, if you know what I mean. Interests or well-being."

"And where can I find him? This Manolo fellow? For a friendly chat, you understand?"

"Oh, that's easy," said Will. "He's at the old Hawaiian Consul's house."

Chapter 15

Clifford left the Auction Lunch Saloon comforted by a belly full of oyster, chicken, and gumbo soup and furious with determination to stop Otis's 'lover boy' in his tracks. Whether there was any truth in Otis's rumor or not, he was going to make sure no one—but no one—could move in on Rebecca.

She was his. He'd already stamped his mark on her. Whether she accepted that, he didn't care… And thanks to Will Davenport, he knew exactly where he needed to go to find his quarry.

However, Davenport had been less forthcoming with details of his rival's personality—apart from saying he was some kind of Hawaiian royalty and had a twin sister. If the Washington Senator really was this islander's father, he'd have to tread softly.

I don't want to leave any trail if things get rough.

Otis was still pretty banged up, so he would leave the bulk of the work to Sheldon. Otis would be backup.

The senator wasn't a man you'd choose as an opponent—they'd already discovered that to their cost. De Vile was relentless, and anyone harming his potential heir would pay.

He smiled grimly as the hack made its way out to the old Hawaiian consulate near Mansion Row, where Davenport said the toad lived. If Sheldon bungled things, the blame wouldn't come back to haunt him.

He wondered idly if this varlet had his father's looks. De Vile was a handsome devil, even though he must be close to fifty. Maybe even older.

He stopped the driver a few houses down the street from the old consulate and briefed Otis and Sheldon on what they were to do. Stay hidden until the gutter-prowler came out. Move on him then.

He marched up to the front door with determined purpose. He was on legitimate business. One businessman calling on another to discuss matters of joint interest. That's all this was about.

The stiletto blade he carried strapped to his leg? The revolver in his shoulder holster? For insurance. Any man determined to leave his mark on the world needed to plan. Of one thing, he was certain. This time, Rebecca and her Romeo weren't getting the best of him.

***

Kaleo had served himself from the platter of fried chicken and taro that Mrs. Leon had left ready for him. She knew he was homesick for his sister and food from home. He'd told her so when she had asked what he missed most and she'd had done her best to plug the gap.

He was carrying his laden plate from the kitchen to the dining room for another solo meal when the doorbell rang. He put his food down on the dining-room table, wandered back down the hall, and opened the door. A powerfully built man with oddly opaque iceberg-green eyes stood on the doormat.

"Mr. Manolo?"

"Who's asking?"

The man stepped forward and thrust out his hand. "Clifford Jensen. Chief executive of Pan Pacific Exporting. We ship raw materials out of San Francisco.

"We're interested in talking business with Pike Consulting. I know it's unusual to call like this, at home, unannounced, but I'm due to leave town later today and it's my only opportunity. Can you spare a minute?"

Clifford Jensen? I can't believe the arrogance of the churl. To come here like this? Unbelievable.

Kaleo was grimly aware he wasn't carrying any weapon. He'd considered it unnecessary in his own home.

He scanned the new arrival from his expensive calfskin boots to the crown of his casual but stylish barbered head. He wore a black jacket and high-notch collar vest over fawn trousers.

At his throat, a slim silk flat bow cravat edged the sharply pointed collar in black to complete the picture. All crafted, Kaleo surmised, to appear smart and menacing at the same time. He couldn't figure out how he did it.

"How did you know where to find me?" He kept his voice light, only mildly interested.

"I bumped into Will Davenport at lunch, and he said you were the man to talk to."

Kaleo hesitated, the fragrance of his fried chicken beckoning. "I guess…" he said. "I was about to have lunch, but I can spare a few minutes. Come in."

He led Jensen into the sitting room Cyrus had used as the consulate office, all the while debating whether he was stupid to let him in the house.

What if he pulls a gun and shoots me in the back?

As they entered the sitting room, he paused and deftly stepped aside so the stranger was now in front. Jensen was tall, but Kaleo still had the advantage of a couple of inches.

He studied Jensen's hands. They were unusually slender for a man of his size, with elegant long fingers, and pale soft skin. Not the hands of a brawler.

"Forgive me for being unusually cautious, Mr. Jensen, but would you raise your hands?"

Jensen gave a barely perceptible start. He wasn't expecting the request, but he obliged with no objection.

Kaleo quickly frisked him, back and sides. Running his hands down the voguish waistcoat with jacquard panels, he hit an angular object. A gun.

He stared into Jensen's face. "You've come here armed? For a casual business meeting?"

Jensen's cheeks flushed, and the iceberg eyes seemed to cloud even further. He gave a dismissive huff of a laugh. "A precaution, you understand. Can't be too careful these days. Your pal Will told me what happened to him the other night."

Kaleo reached inside Clifford's jacket. "Shoulder holster too. Not a last-minute addition then. Do you usually carry metal, Mr. Jensen?"

Jensen shrugged. Underneath the first flush of embarrassment, Kaleo detected a darkening tint of anger. "Virginia City is still a pretty wild town, and I'm sure you'd agree, you can't be too careful."

Kaleo kept hold of the gun and gestured with it to the sofa. "We're not in Virginia City, though, are we, Mr. Jensen? Have a seat. I'm sorry our housekeeper is on a day off, so there aren't any refreshments."

He kept his voice perfunctory and remained standing. His height advantage increased as Jensen sat. Kaleo hoped his tone made it clear he had no intention of offering this man anything except the way to the front door.

"Virginia City, you say. What's your line of business, again?"

"Silver mines, railways, share trading on silver, real estate—"

Kaleo stopped him with a hand gesture. "And why would any of that interest Pike Consulting, Mr. Jensen? We're an import-export agency, as I imagine Will would have explained."

"Ah, yes, but we're forming important new partnerships with British firms interested in lumber, in salmon, a whole range of possible natural exports. I'd have thought you couldn't afford to ignore an enormous opportunity."

Kaleo leaned back against the table and folded his arms across his chest. The man's strange eyes stared insolently back at him, their veiled nature making it impossible to read him, but the hairs on the back of Kaleo's neck stood on high alert. He knew from the moment Jensen walked in that he was casing his home.

"You speak of 'we,' Mr. Jensen? Who exactly is the 'we' you are referring to?"

"Oh, no worries there. My business partner's very well known in Virginia City. He's a former mayor and a real philanthropist."

"And his name is?"

"Sam Hollows."

Sam Hollows…

As he suspected. No surprise there, either.

"Sam Hollows, eh? Fancy that."

"Why do you say that?" The man's voice rose in querulous uncertainty.

"Because Sam Hollows is not a man Pike Consulting wishes to do business with."

Jensen pressed his lips together, assessing. "That's not what Will Davenport said."

"Mr. Davenport may not be in the best position to make an informed decision. I am."

Jensen rose to his feet, his arms stiff at his sides. "You are? Some bumped-up coconut kingdom aristo no one's heard of?"

Kaleo laughed. "Coconut kingdom? Bumped-up aristo? I confess I've never been called that before. I love it." He slouched against the edge of the table, casually gesturing with the hand which held Jensen's revolver.

Jensen glared, mouth in a sardonic twist. He sat stock still, but he was flexing his fingers in a tense rhythm. Kaleo could see he wasn't used to being needled.

"And you, Mr. Jensen. What gives you the liberty to pull rank? Born with a silver spoon in your mouth, were you?"

Kaleo felt a pulse of triumph as the fingers curled into closed fists.

"My origins have got nothing to do with you."

"Really? I'm trying to figure out why a man like you—a Virginia City aristo, if you don't mind me saying—would abduct a harmless office clerk like Miss Wyndham. I'd have thought if I'm beneath your notice, she'd be even more so."

Jensen ran his hands down the lapels of the expensive black coat, as if seeking reassurance he was still boss here. "I don't know what you are talking about."

"Come. Mr. Jensen. You know very well."

Jensen fixed him with a challenging stare. "I'm finished here. I'll see myself out. It's been a waste of my time to come here. Your loss. Not mine." He hesitated.

He's unsure if I'm going to shoot him or not.

Kaleo's body buzzed with fresh energy.

He checked the gun. It was loaded. He emptied the bullets out into his hand. Pocketed them, and pointed the barrel toward the door.

"After you."

They tramped down the hall in silence. As they halted at the front door, he offered the gun to Jensen, who made a show of opening his jacket and placing it back in his shoulder holster. Kaleo opened the door, and Jensen tipped his hat. He tossed off a departing shot as he stepped over the threshold.

"Be seeing you."

"I hope not," Kaleo muttered under his breath.

Lured by his chicken lunch, he started back up the hall. Too late, he registered a heavy footfall behind him. And the bite of cold steel at his left temple.

Chapter 16

A glimpse out of the corner of his eye told Kaleo all he needed to know. The man holding the gun to his head was the same hedge-creeper who'd attacked him the other night—or, more accurately, who'd attacked Sarah. He must have been loitering outside when he had let Jensen out.

Otis Hollows, the guy Alex said was responsible. Brother of the dude who'd just left, he wagered. The de Vile intelligence would be right. Same bullish jaw, same heavy black eyebrows, and the finely tailored coat—the same coat, in fact, that he'd worn that night. Fine black wool, with a generous collar the wearer could turn up against the wind.

Kaleo had failed to make sure he'd latched the door securely, and this charley had slipped in while he was thinking about his lunch.

He stared down the hallway. The house was growing on him, and he wondered if he'd ever wake up in the big soft bed in the sunshine-yellow bedroom again.

"Don't move," Otis snarled. "You're not getting away from me a second time."

Kaleo did what he was told. He stood, arms hanging loosely at his sides, and cursed himself for not being more careful. If only he had taken Sarah seriously when she'd warned him.

The muzzle, which had first felt cold when placed at his temple, grew warm, seeming to draw heat from his roaring blood. The barrel point trembled.

Kaleo wondered if indecision paralyzed the gunman. He waited, his mind blank, for the bullet to come. His stomach was a jittery chasm.

So, this was what it was like to face death. He thought of Lani, who he hadn't seen in months. She was coming home to get married in a few days. He didn't want to miss that.

Then the surrounding energy shifted dramatically. The hand holding the gun convulsed, digging the barrel into his brow, lacerating the bony ridge. Immediately after that, the pressure eased.

The gun was still present, but no longer biting into his skin. Warm blood dripped down his cheek. He continued to stare straight ahead, as unmoving as an Easter Island monolith. And then, the sound of an unfamiliar male voice came, low, slow and menacing.

"Put the gun down. Now. And slowly…" Every word enunciated with authority and the hint of an accent. Kaleo tried to place it. European? French like Aristide? No. More like the German sugar magnate, Claus Spreckels.

He held his frozen stance for a few more seconds as the barrel wobbled and then pulled away altogether. He steeled himself to continue staring straight ahead. Was this some kind of trick?

"You can relax now, buddy. That grafter won't be bothering you again. Not right away, anyway. And no. I will not kill him. Or you."

Kaleo warily turned to face the speaker. He stood shoulder to shoulder with a lean tiger of a man clad in tight-fitting black fencing garb. His hair was a dappled gold, and when he parted his lips in a satisfied smile, his dazzling white teeth showed as slightly pointed through dusky red lips.

He held guns in both hands, one firm against Otis's neck, the other casually pointing at the floor. Kaleo presumed one was his, and the other he'd taken from the man who'd held him up.

His rescuer man-handled Otis back to the entry, pulled the door wide open and shouted, "Jensen! Take this useless bit of blubber with you and get out of here. The lot of you. Go back to where you belong. I won't give you another chance."

He thrust him out over the doorstep. Otis half stumbled, half ran for the gate at an ungainly gait that highlighted the dancer-like grace of the man who'd routed him.

"I'm counting… You've got till ten to leave… One, two, three, four…"

A shame-faced sidekick struggled free from the undergrowth of a straggling guava tree near the front gate, pulling twigs from his hair and beard as he fled. Kaleo saw it was the hack driver from the other night, his bandaged arm hanging at his side.

The man in black bid him farewell with the flexed gun. "Get out of here, Sheldon. If I see you anywhere near Manolo or the girl again, it's curtains. Understand?"

The driver ducked as he ran, as if expecting a bullet, closely following behind Otis.

"And you too, Jensen. I know you're hiding out there, watching others doing your dirty work as usual. Your time's up."

Two quick blasts rang out from the street, and one of the front windows exploded in a fountain of shattered glass.

With narrowed eyes that made his tensile body appear even more feline, the man in Kaleo's doorway answered with three quick shots. There was a roar from the hedge that partly obscured the front gate.

"You devil."

Gesturing Kaleo to stay back, the tiger man surveyed the street with narrowed eyes, searching from street to house with the intensity of a lighthouse beam. Kaleo imagined he saw things others could not.

After a long silence, he gave a satisfied nod and backed through the open front door, closing it decisively behind him.

"They won't be back for a while."

He grinned, and Kaleo half expected this man who had saved his life, and whose name he still didn't know, to lick the lips that sheltered the vulpine teeth, as if finishing a meal.

Instead, he slapped Kaleo on the shoulder and made as if to start down the hall.

"Jensen will have to see a doctor about that hand. The tame goose. If he hadn't had fired at us first, I'd have let him go."

"How did you know where he was?"

"I've been watching the house. I expected him to show up sometime."

"You were watching the house?" Kaleo shook his head in wonder. "I didn't see or hear anything until that gun was against my head."

Now the excitement was over, he had a roaring headache coming on.

Sarah. She tried to warn you. But you wouldn't listen.

He ran his fingers through his hair distractedly.

"Who are you? And who sent you?"

"Adolphus Maximilian Westerhoven at your service." The new arrival gave a playful half bow. "People I trust call me Dolphie."

His tanned face showed he spent a lot of time in the sun. Kaleo would bet he was a fine horseman as well as—from his garb and grace of movement—a skilled fencer. And yes. A man he could trust.

"Westerhoven? Does that mean you're related to the Countess, Dolphie?"

Adolphus hitched a quizzical eyebrow. "Only by marriage and gratitude. I probably wouldn't be alive if it weren't for Elizabeth and her late husband. The family name comes from Charles. I'm a distant cousin."

Kaleo stared back at him. Glass fragments peppered Dolphie's left shoulder. He nodded toward the jacket. "Take care there. You've still got some glass on you." Kaleo gestured down the hall, and Dolphie followed him into the kitchen.

The stranger helped himself to a glass of water from the tray on the bench and wiped his hand across his mouth in satisfaction.

"You're going to have to get a carpenter in to board up that front window before we leave."

Kaleo had been about to put the coffee on to brew. He wheeled on the newcomer. "What did you mean 'before we leave?' Where are 'we' going? And what the heck happened out there?"

Dolphie hesitated, as if having preternaturally detected they were about to be interrupted. A loud knocking echoed down the hall.

"Kaleo! Open up! It's your sister, home to see you at last."

Kaleo stared at Dolphie in disbelief.

"Have you got eyes in the back of your head? A dog's hearing? You pick up signs we ordinary mortals miss." And then he bolted down the hall to welcome his twin home.

Chapter 17

I'll make her pay for this. Clifford cradled his bleeding hand against his chest and gritted his teeth at the hack's every judder. The bullet had grazed the top of his flexed hand, as he was about to fire again on the ass who'd got to him first. He clenched his teeth as another wave of pain wracked him.

The knuckle of his index finger was a mess, but the last thing he wanted to do was moan in front of Otis. He considered his pulped hand once more. It'd be a long time before he'd be chucking any doxy under the chin, but that didn't matter. What he had planned for Rebecca and her sister didn't require sweet lovin'.

Otis lay half sprawled on the bench seat opposite, his face an expression of mingled wonder and sneaking delight.

"How in the blazes did he do that? He must be the cussed devil hisself."

The words fueled a red fury that made Clifford's pain that much harder to bear. He'd have pulled the trigger on Otis right there if he could. "Shut up, you oaf. If you'd done your bit, I wouldn't be in this state."

Otis took on the well-worn role of the wounded sidekick. "What do you mean? How was I to know the cur was hiding there?"

Clifford put out his hand to brace himself against the side wall as the hack took a sharp turn. He cried out despite himself. Otis was in full flood. "You can't blame me. He was like a demon out of nowhere."

A demon, maybe. But out of nowhere? He didn't think so. Paid for out of the purse of Westerhoven, or de Vile or… who knew? Who knew what Rebecca was up to now, who she'd got on her side?

For a few seconds he was back to the night he'd shown her who was boss, inflated with the glorious heat of it. He'd forced her to submit then, and she would again. She would pay. In the end, she would pay. And if he couldn't get his hands on her right now, he'd get his revenge on her damned sister.

They pulled up outside the emergency department on Stockton Street. Sheldon, who'd had the sense to remain silent, helped him down, bracing his left side. As he drifted off in a laudanum haze, his pain eased by the drug relief the doctors had given him, the answer to the question he'd asked himself in the hack came to him.

Where is Rebecca now?

He bet that Will Davenport character knew a lot more than he was letting on. He might even have tipped off the gunman who'd showed up at the Hawaiian's house.

Yes. Davenport. As soon as he felt better. First thing tomorrow. First stop Davenport. Second stop Virginia City to show them all who was boss.

***

He pressed Otis into action before the day was out.

"Take this and get him. And if you mess it up, I'll have your head on a platter. Understand?"

Clifford passed the Colt revolver to Otis with his left hand and glared. "Be back here with Davenport within the hour. We've got no time to waste. The longer we dilly dally, the more chance she has to get away."

Otis's mouth set in a mulish line. "What if he's not there?"

A red mist passed in front of Clifford's eyes. "He will be there, you useless oaf. It's a normal working day, and he's the only one left."

Clifford had a sudden, unwelcome thought: What if that coconut aristo went into the office today and told Davenport about their encounter?

"Get out there," he growled. "And don't come back here without him."

While Otis did his errands, Clifford sat on his hospital bed nursing his bandaged hand, going over the day's events.

He'd underestimated that Manolo fellow. He assumed he had no connections. That cove who had turned up and disarmed Otis—well, he wouldn't worry too much about him. But if de Vile's money was behind it…

If Davenport was right about the Hawaiian being de Vile's son, he should have worked out a better strategy. He wouldn't make any more mistakes. He lay back in his chair, closed his eyes, and got thinking.

Will Davenport had some grudge against de Vile. That was clear in the way he'd talked about him the first time they met. He hated the guy. What was that all about?

He barked for Sheldon. "Get me some paper, man, and take something down for me. With my hand like this," he raised his bandaged maw, "I can't write. I want to send a telegram."

Sheldon bustled around to oblige.

After a false start, they completed the task.

"Now take it down to the exchange. I want it sent immediately. Then come straight back here."

Sheldon was gone less than ten minutes when Otis walked in,

accompanied by a relaxed Will Davenport.

"Heavens, Clifford. I only heard now that you're injured. That's mighty bad luck. How are you?" Clifford flicked his eyebrow in inquiry for a millisecond, and Will opened his mouth to continue.

Otis jumped in before he could speak. "Will was planning to see us today anyway," he said. "I'm glad I caught him."

He glared significantly at the older man. "Sure thing," said Clifford. "We've still got plenty of talking to do. I'm interested for a start in why you appear to dislike Hector de Vile. What's with that?"

The normally mild-mannered manager bristled. "Dislike? Who said anything about dislike?"

Clifford regarded him and cleared his throat. "Let's say I got the impression he was a foul smell in your nostrils. Is that not the case?"

Will Davenport deflated like a slow-leaking balloon. He pouted. "He did my family wrong. I'm not going into details, but I'm not letting him get away with it. And seeing as he isn't your favorite pal either, I thought we might take him down together."

Clifford grimaced. "Well, hell, that's a mighty ambitious goal for a mild-mannered mouse. He's a powerful man. How do you propose to do that?"

Davenport shrugged. "I've got some ideas. But I'd like to hear yours."

Chapter 18

Leilani and Kaleo's reunion was ecstatic, but all too brief. They barely had time to fall on one another's necks, laughing and crying, before Dolphie was at their backs, urging them to move right along.

"You'll have plenty of time to catch up in the coach we're taking north," he said. "We don't have a minute to lose."

"North?" said Kaleo. "But that's not what I'm doing. I'm finding Sarah and keeping her safe."

Dolphie leveled him with a granite gaze. "And how are you going to do that? Jensen knows where you live and as far as I'm aware, you don't know where Sarah is."

He spread out his arms to embrace the rooms. "We're leaving a twenty-four-hour guard on this place. If we don't, they'll torch it by morning. These boys don't play games."

"But…" Kaleo couldn't think of one sensible thing to counter Dolphie's reasoning. He fell silent, momentarily stumped.

Dolphie turned and gathered in Leilani and her fiancé, Aristide.

"I'm taking you all to a safe house. Our version of it, anyway. That's why I got my men to collect your sister from the docks."

"You what?" Kaleo raised his scarred eyebrow in a question.

She shrugged. "He's right, Kaleo. As soon as we stepped off the boat, he had someone there explaining you were in trouble and we needed to skip town."

"He did?" Kaleo felt as if the situation was slipping further and further from his control or understanding.

Who are the good guys here? And who the bad?

He sighed. He sure didn't know any more.

He allowed his eyes to settle on Lani, cataloguing how she'd changed during her months in Honolulu.

Six weeks ago, Aristide Laurent had gone to the Paradise Islands to protect Lani's interests. He could see by the glow on her face that she'd appreciated his efforts.

Kaleo raised his hand and slapped the French winemaker on the shoulder. "Forgive me, Aristide. I've barely said hello." They shook hands and drew closer for the traditional French hug, a brief brushing of cheekbones to the right and the left.

He drew back, still holding Aristide's forearms.

"You're both looking very good. The sea air obviously suits you."

Leilani laughed, a delighted musical sound that lifted his spirits after his heavy morning.

"The sea air? Yes, it was bracing. But even better than the sea air was unmasking Max Moeller and seeing the way our sister has come into her power. Malia's a different woman, Kaleo. You won't recognize her. There'll be a wedding coming soon, too, if Titus gets his way. Mark my words."

"Looks like that makes it two," Kaleo said. He flicked a glance at Aristide, who was watching his sister with adoring eyes.

Dolphie stepped between them.

"There'll be plenty of time for the lovely dovey talk in the coach, people. Grab what you need for a stay of a week and let's get out of here."

Kaleo resisted the tap on his elbow. "Maybe I haven't made myself clear, Dolphie. I'm not leaving town without Sarah. I promised myself I'd protect her, and I plan to still do that, even if doesn't want me to."

He stepped clear of Dolphie's restraining hand.

"It isn't right to leave her to the mercy of a creep like Clifford Jensen." He gazed at Lani.

"I've been pretty useless so far. This fellow here saved me from a fate worse than death. But I can't give up on Sarah."

"No one's asking you to give it up, Kaleo. Be assured." Dolphie smashed a broad-brimmed black hat down on his head—one Kaleo couldn't recall seeing till this minute—and started down the hall to the front door.

"I'm leaving Sam Potter in charge here. He's handy. He'll guard the place and arrange for the front window to be fixed. Now get moving. We leave in five minutes. And don't worry. We're not leaving Sarah behind. She's already far, far away."

He stopped mid-stride and swung back dramatically to stare at Kaleo.

"And if you're so concerned about protecting her, you'll be a lot more useful where we're going than you would be here." He started toward the door.

"Five minutes. That's it. We need to beat it before Jensen even realizes we've gone."

Chapter 19

Elongated tree shadows lengthened across the road as the carriage barrelled down an oak-lined driveway to a large Spanish-style adobe house set in rolling vineyards. Kaleo had never been here, but it became clear during the half-day journey that they were going to Sir John Russell's Vino d'Oro wine estate, where Aristide lived and managed both the vines and the wine produced from them.

Aristide trailed one arm out of the carriage door and lifted his eyes appreciatively to the transparent late-afternoon light.

"Mmm... smell that air. Nothing like northern wine country. That faint hint of salty sea spray and grape must from the fermenting barrels. I know I'm home when I smell it."

His lean face glowed from his weeks in the Hawaiian sun. He took Leilani's arm and beamed at her. "I can't wait to show you around."

Kaleo dug Dolphie in the ribs. "Is this where Sarah's staying?"

Dolphie, seated beside him, opposite the lovebirds, jostled him back. "No, she isn't at the Russells, and I think it's best at this stage we leave it at that, apart from saying Sarah is safe. The fewer people who know where she is, the better."

Kaleo stiffened. He was close to a day's journey from town and was still no closer to satisfying himself that Sarah was safe? His chest tightened.

Dolphie put a restraining hand on his thigh. "Take it easy, Kaleo. No need to get uptight. But you'll have to take my word for it for the time being. Sarah is fine."

The carriage slowed and turned into a spacious central courtyard that opened onto stables, generous cellars, and the homestead. The odor of horse manure and equine sweat drifted in through the coach window.

Barely waiting until the carriage had drawn to a stop, Aristide threw the door open and jumped out. He danced in a gay jig across the tamped earth pathway toward the cellar door. He circled back as the coach stopped, and Leilani tentatively slid forward to disembark.

Aristide offered her his hand as the front door of the house opened and a tall dark-haired woman hurried to greet them, a broad smile lighting up her handsome face.

Aristide handed Leilani down and turned in anticipation, as his sister Madeleine embraced him with obvious affection.

"Mon frère," she cried. "Welcome home!" She ruffled his hair affectionately, then clasped his sleeves and stood at arm's length to examine his face.

"Hawaii agrees with you! You're rested and so tanned!" Aristide laughed and disengaged his right arm encircling Leilani's waist.

"Not so much Hawaii, as the island's most beautiful daughter. Leilani Manolo, meet my sister, Madeleine."

Aristide grinned at Kaleo, who'd joined his sister's side. "And her dashing twin brother, Kaleo. Kaleo, meet my sister… We'll be family soon, I know, so it's time we got acquainted."

With a hint of shy reserve, Madeleine turned from Leilani to Kaleo and gave him the traditional French greeting, a light kiss on each cheek. She made a playful bobbing curtesy in a flaming orange dress before each of them in turn.

"We're so thrilled to have you here. Between our house and Sir John's we've plenty of room for you all, so come inside, do. John and Pania are back in Grass Valley at present, so you've the house to yourselves. Caleb's boys will unload your trunks and bring them in."

Aristide stepped aside and gave Leilani an apologetic grin. "I'll leave you and Madeleine to get acquainted while I see what Caleb's been up to."

He started for the cellar, and Kaleo saw a broad-shouldered cowboy had emerged from the dark interior and was standing in the arched doorway, grinning.

"Laurent! Glad to see the sharks didn't get you!" Madeleine's husband, Caleb greeted Aristide.

Briefly, Kaleo's eyes followed their backs as they entered the cellar, and then he sensed Dolphie standing beside him. A new constraint had replaced the gayness of the initial greetings, and his eyes followed Dolphie's gaze to the front path.

An older man, with a neatly trimmed gray beard and straight, erect carriage, emerged from the house and was striding toward them, serious intent in every step.

Dolphie stepped forward, his hand outstretched in a formal greeting.

"I'm Adolphus Westerhoven, Senator. Retained by Countess Elizabeth. And if you're here, I'm confident she's been in touch with you, too."

Senator de Vile's eyes flickered from Dolphie to Kaleo.

"You've got yourself mixed up with this business, I see." He gave his son a warm hug, and Kaleo felt instant reassurance.

Hector spun his attention to Dolphie, grasping Westerhoven's hand and shaking it vigorously.

"Westerhoven ay? Elizabeth told me she's called you in. What is it? Count Westerhoven?"

Dolphie's face showed he didn't like being reminded.

"Not till pater quits this mortal coil."

De Vile stood for a minute in silence, as if digesting the significance of Dolphie's presence, and then cleared his throat.

"Your assumption is dead right. Elizabeth is anxious about the safety of her sister and niece now that Sarah's bested the Hollows mob twice. Sam doesn't take kindly to being a loser."

Hector considered Leilani, who stood beside her brother.

"Excuse my poor manners, my *ohana*. My family."

He leaned forward to kiss Leilani on the cheek. "Leilani—so glad we pried you out of Maximilian's clutches and got you home."

There was a pregnant pause, and when Leilani didn't speak, De Vile turned and regarded the house. "Kaleo. I want to hear all about the contretemps you've had with the Hollows' men. I gather you've acquitted yourself remarkably well. But I'm afraid the pleasantries will have to wait."

He took the lead up the path to the front door, glancing behind to speak as he walked. "Elizabeth will arrive any minute. She wanted my advice about how to proceed.

"We've got to settle on a strategy for rescuing Petra and Lottie."

Kaleo reached out and placed a hand on his father's arm. De Vile halted.

"Petra and Lottie? Who are these people, Father? Um. Sorry. Senator? And why don't we seem to be concerned about Sarah? Isn't she in danger too?"

De Vile's handsome face cracked into a brief smile. "Father? It's fine to call me that, son. After all, it's the truth. As for Sarah? You're right to be concerned about her long-term safety.

"We'll have to find some solution for that. But at present it's her mother and sister in most urgent need of protection."

Kaleo stared into de Vile's dark eyes and saw in them a concern he'd never witnessed before. "Her mother and sister? Hang on a minute, I'm catching up here. Are you saying Sarah's related to Elizabeth Westerhoven?"

"Indeed, I am, son. Sarah's mother Charlotte is Elizabeth's sister."

Kaleo clapped his hands together.

"Ahh. That explains a lot. The Epiphany dinner, for example… Elizabeth seemed to take a close interest in Sarah's coming and goings, and I wondered why."

De Vile nodded. "Elizabeth and Charles were away in Europe for most of the time Charlotte and Noah were married. Elizabeth has really only got close to Sarah since Charles's death, when she came back West to live.

"She and Charlotte have spent more time together in recent years, and I think Elizabeth has loved the opportunity to get to know her nieces."

Chapter 20

Sarah is the Countess's niece? Kaleo trailed behind his father into the Russell homestead, his head spinning with the latest revelation. *The more I find out about this woman, the more I discover I don't know her at all.*

He thought back to the enchanted short period when they'd shared what he had thought was a special friendship. When they'd laughed and bantered and were at ease in one another's company. He'd enjoyed being with Sarah more than any woman he'd ever known—except for his sisters, of course.

She was so easy to be around, with none of the posing and preening he'd found in so many of the females who threw themselves at his feet. She was natural and unassuming, a straightforward young woman of modest means who needed her office job to survive.

Or so I thought.

He now knew she was a total fraud. Her name wasn't Sarah, and her stepfather was one of the Comstock Lode's wealthiest men. Why she was doing a modest office administrator's job under a false name, he didn't know.

He blushed at the assumptions he'd made unwittingly. No wonder she'd frozen him out. He'd been such a fool to take her at face value.

He'd even imagined they might form a more lasting relationship. She was probably laughing at him behind his back all the while.

He threw his overnight bag into the corner. The room Madeleine had shown him into had a capacious bed covered with a quilt appliqued purple and green grapes along the top edge.

It was so appropriate. Through the arched windows, he could see vines in regimented rows rising up the slope to the horizon. On a bedside table stood a water flask and a glass. He plopped down on the bed and poured himself a drink, suddenly aware his throat was scratchy. He was parched and desperately tired.

He didn't need to be concerned about this woman, Sarah or Rebecca or whatever her name was, anymore. She had the power of a Washington senator and the Countess of San Francisco to call on.

The last thing she needed was a hanger-on whose chief claim to fame was that he was an excellent surfer—a skill useless in San Francisco, where no one had even heard of surfing until Mark Twain wrote about it.

He drained the glass and fell back on the pillows, closed his eyes and within minutes was asleep.

***

He was about to catch a massive wave when a jaw-like grip fastened on his shoulder. Sinewy tendrils reached in and dug under his collarbone, sending excruciating pain up his neck and into the top of his head.

Kaleo reared up, instantly awake, heart pounding. He fell back onto the mattress with a great sigh, opened his eyes and saw Dolphie leaning over him.

"Dolphie. What the devil," he muttered, his thinking obscured by a sea fog in his head. Where was he? "I'm breast stroking awake," he breathed.

"Well, stroke faster," said Dolphie, his voice loud and cheerful. "The senator wants to start our meeting."

"Meeting? What meeting?"

"Weren't you listening earlier? The meeting with Elizabeth."

"I heard him—but why am I needed? I don't know any of these people. They've got all the resources of San Fran at their disposal. They don't need a Hawaiian drifter."

"You're already involved, blockhead. First, you beat up Otis. Then you colluded in shooting Jensen."

"I colluded? Since when?"

"Since you were there to witness his humiliation. That's unforgivable in Jensen's book. If we don't settle this now, he'll be your enemy for life."

Dolphie grabbed his right hand and hauled him upright. "Besides, aren't you one of the good guys?" His pointy white teeth flashed from inside red lips. "Come on. Hector's waiting."

***

Still groggy from his quick nap, Kaleo dutifully followed Dolphie into a comfortable sitting room furnished with welcoming sofas in Spanish red and gold. They sat at right angles to a stone-walled fireplace filled with blazing logs. Between the sofas sat an ottoman, covered in the same red and gold fabric, and set with a tray carrying a coffee pot, cups, and a decanter.

Coffee with a dash of brandy. What a great idea! The room smelled of pine and brandy mingled with wood smoke, and it hit Kaleo that next to the salty tang of the ocean, smoke from a good fire was one of the homeliest smells he knew.

His short sleep had clarified nothing. His confusion about what was going on was as dense as ever. Maybe the reinforced black coffee would bring the world back into focus.

He relaxed into an armchair plumped with extra cushions that sat to one side of the fire. He would treat this as a spectacle. Hector stood with Dolphie, both men with their hands behind their backs, near the doorway, as if waiting for someone. He would watch his father play Big Boss and be entertained by Count Dolphie's antics.

Two, three more sips, and the flames from the fire grew hot on his face. If he wasn't careful, he would drop off again and miss it all. He rallied himself, set his cup aside.

He glanced to where Hector and Dolphie stood. His father was shifting his weight from one foot to another, passing an occasional remark to Dolphie in a low voice that didn't carry clearly to where Kaleo was sitting. They tempted Kaleo to cross the room to join them. If something didn't happen soon, he would fall back to sleep.

Aristide and Leilani slipped in with quick greetings to the men on the door, but before he had time to say hello, everything became clear.

He heard the tap of female shoes on the parquet hallway, and Elizabeth Westerhoven appeared in the doorway, as regal as ever in a midnight blue dress with a blue and yellow ruffle at the throat.

At her side was Sarah, relaxed and laughing, as if she'd she's spent the last few hours doing whatever young ladies did on a pleasant Northern California afternoon. He couldn't imagine it was needlepoint.

She wore a pretty flowered dress with velvet collar and cuffs, appearing like a herald of early spring. Her gold hair with red highlights tumbled out of the pins designed to keep it in place. Her lips were fuller and pinker than he remembered.

His body flooded with a warm wave of releasing tension, as if seeing her in this safe place, secure and happy, swept away his fears. And then almost immediately intense irritation overtook this new ease as he recalled again her lies and distancing.

Hector greeted both women warmly, kissing Elizabeth on both cheeks and making a gallant bow in Sarah's direction. "Miss Wyndham. I understand that's how you prefer to be addressed?"

Sarah cast him a quick smile. "Sarah will be fine, Senator. But yes."

Hector gestured to the sofa, the chairs. "Do sit down. I understand you already know Kaleo and Dolphie."

Sarah raised her eyes to meet his, and her cheeks flushed a light pink. "Of course. I'll always be grateful to Kaleo for saving me the other night."

When Kaleo said nothing, she turned away and hurried to sit beside Elizabeth.

"Right. Let's start, shall we? We've no time to waste."

Kaleo noticed Elizabeth Westerhoven held a daguerreotype in her hand. She pointed at the image.

"These are the women we need to free. Sam's wife, my sister, Mrs. Charlotte Hollows, and her daughter—Sarah's sister—Petra."

She was obviously making the presentation for his sake, Kaleo guessed, because Dolphie already knew them all. He'd done surveillance on the Hollows' establishment at the Countess's behest.

He leaned across and took the frame from her hand.

Charlotte Hollows was a fair-haired, middle-aged woman with the full figure of her years. It was hard to tell in the picture whether her hair was prematurely white or naturally blonde, but even in this studio portrait, her eyebrows creased in a permanent frown.

She had deep anxiety lines around her down-turned mouth. The daughter at her side was slight and pretty, with bouncy darker curls framing a pixie face.

She appeared much younger than Sarah, although he'd been told only two years separated them. She had dreamy eyes, as if she'd rather escape into her thoughts than face the real world. Alongside her organized, pragmatic sister, she was like a child.

His eyes met Sarah's. "Will she be willing to come with us if we can locate her? Don't take offense, but she appears a dreamer."

Sarah gave a brief smile. "She is a romancer, but don't worry. If she has a chance to escape, she won't hesitate. She knows what's likely to happen if she doesn't."

"And what's that?"

Sarah's face flushed a deeper red, and she flicked her eyes away to Elizabeth. When she returned her gaze in his direction, she couldn't meet his eyes.

"Clifford Jensen uses any tactic at his disposal to force his will. Humiliation, bullying, assault. He'll use her to get at me." Her voice was so quiet it was almost a whisper. "Goodness knows what he's capable of, but I don't want to wait to find out."

***

Leilani caught up with Kaleo on the Vino d'Oro verandah, where he'd retreated from the suffocating warmth of the drawing room fire. He was gazing out over the bare vines that climbed up the rise to the horizon, pruned-back stems shrouded in the fast-falling dusk.

He guessed what had upset her apple cart. He'd had the temerity to call Hector "Father" in there. She'd thrown him a visual dagger of disbelief even as he'd done it.

She stood alongside him, and he smelt her familiar fragrance—a mix of lemony soap and her warm floral perfume. She nudged him with her elbow, examining his face with an intensity which irritated him.

"Father?" She crossed her arms in front of her chest and gave him a spiky smile. "Since when do you call Hector Father?" She was launching an interrogation.

His eyes searched the early evening calm of the vines for the peace that eluded him. His chest tightened and his throat closed up, making it difficult to speak.

He resorted to the silent treatment, dismissing her query with a flick of his eyes, and returned his gaze to the sky. Night had blanketed to the horizon in the last few minutes. He was observing a sleeping landscape. Somehow, that helped him find his voice.

"What's it with you, Lani? He is our father, isn't he? And you, more than anyone, have good reason to show him some gratitude."

"Wow. What's put you in such a snitch?"

He swung around, leaning his back against the veranda rail, glaring directly into her annoyingly amused face.

"Nothing. I think it's time you dropped your stupid antagonism toward Hector and gave him credit for the way he's supporting us. First in rescuing you from that mess you got yourself into in Honolulu, and now, with sorting out this snake's pit for Sarah."

Lani frowned. "What is it with you and her, anyway? When I left last year, I thought you were all sweetness and light. Now I'm back and you're all prickly. Didn't things go the way you'd hoped?"

"I wasn't hoping for anything, Lani. And it's none of your business, anyway."

"Well, that's a plain lie for starters, Kaleo. You're clearly upset. I'm your sister, for goodness' sake. You can talk to me."

"I'm upset because I don't like seeing women mistreated. That's it. Nothing more. Forgive me if that's hard to understand."

Leilani stepped back from him, her brows raised in surprise, her eyes still searching his face. "Kaleo. Please. I can tell you're upset. I didn't mean to step on your toes. Really. But you're not your normal self. Tell me. What's wrong?"

He shook his head. "Nothing. Nothing's wrong, Lani." He shrugged.

"Well, nothing that a ridiculously complicated and risky rescue mission won't fix, anyway."

She reached out and touched his arm. "Kaleo. This doesn't need to be your fight. I mean, we've never even met these people. What are their names? Charlotte and Petra? Leave it to the professionals like Dolphie, why don't you?"

"I can't Lani. I don't want to let Hector down. And I owe it to Sarah."

Chapter 21

Leilani had left him to seek out Aristide, and Kaleo had stepped onto the lawn, intent on taking a before-dinner stroll to settle his nerves, when Sarah emerged onto the veranda. She called out to him. "Are you going for a walk?"

He ignored her and took another step toward the driveway.

"Can I join you?" she persisted.

Without waiting for his agreement, he heard her trip lightly down the steps and run across the grass to his side. She grasped his wrist and peered up with questioning eyes. He stopped moving, and she dropped her hold on him.

"I wanted to catch you." She sounded breathy, even a little nervous. "I wanted to apologize for getting you caught up in all of this."

She hesitated, as if waiting for some comment, some reinforcement from him he that he was ready to listen, to let go of the rancor that had risen between them.

He remained silent. She took a deep breath. "I wanted none of this… You don't need to…"

He pulled his shoulders back irritably and made as if to step along the path. She bustled alongside him, keeping up like a partner in a quadrille.

"Kaleo, please…" Her voice was pleading.

He stopped suddenly and rounded on her. "Sarah, first, I stepped in and took on that guy. It was my choice. And then you fenced me out. You wouldn't tell me a thing. You confide in Will, the traitor of all time, but not in me."

He swung around and began walking again at a furious pace, glancing over at her as she ran to keep up with him.

"You failed to mention your mother and sister are in dire danger. I had to learn that from the senator. As for involving me, it's a bit late to be apologizing about that now.

"You know that the maniac who considers himself your fiancé came around to my house? No doubt Will gave him the address. Goodness knows where I'd be now if it wasn't for Dolphie.

"But I suppose you organized that too, didn't you?"

He stopped mid-stride. "Come to think of it, Clifford Jensen. Do you consider him your fiancé? Because I can tell you, nothing you say or do would surprise me now. It's all lies as far as I can tell."

He resumed his march under the bare-branched oaks toward the front gate.

She was getting breathless, keeping up. "I deserve that. I know I do. And I can never make it up. As for Jensen? He's pure poison to me. I'd rather eat arsenic than marry him.

"And Will? I don't think Will would betray you. Or me. There must be some misunderstanding."

"No misunderstanding, Sarah. He's in Clifford Jensen's pocket."

"Oh, no. He can't be."

"Why not? If you're so sure you have some 'understanding,' then why isn't he here lining up to rescue your mother? If he loves you so much." A surge of fierce energy, fueled by rage, supplanted the fatigue he'd felt earlier.

Sarah paled and bit her lip. "It's not like that, Kaleo."

"Oh? Then what is it like?"

"You understand now that Elizabeth is my aunt? My mother is her sister? And Sam Hollows is only my stepfather. Not my actual father. He died when I was young.

"My stepfather and Clifford, they're ruthless, Kaleo. They won't kill Mum and Petra. They'll torment them instead."

She clenched her fists at her sides as she scurried to keep up with his long strides.

"Let me rephrase that. They might kill them, in the end. But first, they'll torment them. I know that's what they'll do because that's what they tried to do to me."

She grabbed him by the wrist. "Please. Stop going so fast. I can't keep up, and I want to explain."

Kaleo allowed his steps to slow. Ahead of them, a little off the drive, lay a massive oak trunk, brought down, he suspected, in a winter storm.

He gestured to it. "Over there. Let's sit for a bit and you can do all the explaining you like. I'm not sure I'll believe any of it."

She gave him a sickly grin and held her rib cage with one hand. "Thanks," she muttered. "I was running out of puff."

They settled on the damp wood. Sarah was wearing a red wool jacket over her flowery white dress, and it was long enough so she could sit on it and stop the old log staining her frock.

Kaleo noted, despite himself, that the jacket fell in a loose arc that moved as she did. A red bow tied at her throat perfectly enhanced her cream complexion and gold-red hair.

Sarah cleared her throat. "There's nothing going on between Will and me." Her eyes flickered and her cheeks reddened. "I'm simply grateful to him for tolerating me at Pike's. Until the last few days, he knew nothing about anything. Bully gave me the job, and he didn't object."

"Bully gave you the job?"

She hesitated. "As a favor to Elizabeth. They were close. You know she's his executor?"

He nodded. "Of course, now I think of it."

"When I escaped from my family, I went straight to Elizabeth. She found me the house in the Tenderloin. We knew they'd watch her place, so I couldn't stay there. She knows lots of people downtown from the years when she helped all those women left on their own to fend for themselves.

"It was somewhere Clifford wouldn't search for me."

She sighed. "I still don't know how he found me. Elizabeth also persuaded Bully to take me on. I had to keep a very low profile, become a real mouse, so no one would notice, but that wasn't hard. I've always been the quiet type."

He thought of the sparkling young woman she'd been at the start. "You weren't particularly quiet when we first met. In fact, you had a lot to say for yourself, if I recall."

Her cheeks flushed carmine. "Kaleo, that was unusual. You brought something out in me. Honestly." Her hazel eyes flashed. "But it couldn't last. I was living a lie. I shouldn't have let it happen. How could I let it go on?"

"You could have brought me in on the secret. Months ago."

"And put you at risk, too? I couldn't do that."

"It's happened anyway now. Without the trust there would have been before."

She shook her head sorrowfully. "I know. But if you knew the full story, you wouldn't like me, anyway."

"Why do you say that?"

"Because it's true."

"Why not tell me and let me be the judge?"

She put her hand up, palm flat, towards him.

"You're wrong about Will. He's got nothing to gain from siding with Clifford. He loves being the manager at Pike's and he's still got ideas about buying the business once we know about Bully's will. I don't think he'll do anything to endanger that."

Kaleo shifted uncomfortably on the log. "For a clever woman, you've sure got your blind spots." A flicker of movement up the drive caught his eye.

A large hound with a shaggy blue-gray coat was bounding toward them with all the fervor of an animal glad to be off the leash. Trailing behind, he could see Lani and Aristide's sister Madeleine.

Madeleine called: "Nero. Come here."

The dog did a free loping circle around the log, as if to satisfy himself their presence was friendly, and took off back toward the women.

"We've got visitors," said Kaleo.

Sarah stood up as the women approached.

"Kaleo," Leilani called out as she drew near. "Hector wants you back at the house."

He stood too and stretched his frame. The temperature had dropped with the sun, and his body had stiffened with it.

"What's up?"

"He's apparently heard from his spies that Clifford has left town, likely heading for Virginia City. He says there's no time to lose. Oh, and Clifford's got Will Davenport with him. Or so the senator's been told."

Kaleo lobbed Sarah a triumphant stare. "See," he said. "I told you."

Chapter 22

"I want to go with you. I have to go. I know more about that household than anyone else here." They'd assembled, again at de Vile's behest, in the Vino d'Oro library, having shared a quick but hearty supper of thick vegetable soup and chunky farmhouse loaf Madeleine had magicked from the kitchen with the cook's help.

Sarah knew she was barking like an overexcited lapdog, and she hated herself for it.

Keep calm. You won't win them over by sounding hysterical.

They were all there. The senator and Elizabeth, Dolphie, Kaleo, Leilani, Aristide and Madeleine and her husband Caleb. And her. Rebecca Hollows, alias Sarah Wyndham. The cause of it all.

"My mother and sister are in dire danger because of me. If I hadn't run away, this wouldn't be happening. I have to go with you."

She gazed around her, pleading in her voice and eyes. "I can tell you things about that place no one else can. I know all their secrets."

De Vile shook his head. He was still debonair for an old man, his salt and pepper hair neatly trimmed close to his temples, giving him the aspect of one of those antique Roman busts she'd seen in her schoolbooks. And he exuded the same air of imperial authority she imagined Julius Caesar carried. His hooded dark eyes flicked with searching intelligence.

"My first impulse is to say absolutely not. It's no place for a woman." He steepled his fingers under his chin and stroked his trim beard. "But my next thought is that you're no ordinary woman, Miss Wyndham."

"Please call me Sarah," she said. "And I'll take that as a compliment."

De Vile had opened the meeting a few minutes earlier by relating the new information he had received in a telegram before supper.

Will Davenport definitely appeared to be in cahoots with Jensen and the Hollows Cabal. De Vile suspected they had their eye on taking over Pike Consulting, and were using Davenport as their stalking horse.

"I don't know yet which came first," de Vile said, turning to Sarah. "Whether they placed him there to report on Bully, or on you. Or whether he was there for other reasons and they've tied up with him since.

"But it's possible he's the one who recognized you somehow and reported your presence back to Hollows."

He waved a copy of the message he'd received in the air.

"The evidence we've gathered here shows everything he's told us about himself is a lie. His name isn't Will Davenport, and he hasn't worked with any of the New York agents that he's claimed.

"Not under that name, anyway. He clearly knows a lot about the export business, but something's fishy. His story doesn't add up."

His eyes softened as they fixed on Elizabeth. "I think they're targeting Bully's business, Elizabeth. I presume Bully getting murdered was a lucky break as far as they were concerned, because they obviously had nothing to do with Bully's death. We know that was a crime of passion much closer to home."

He surveyed the circle. "I'm a minority shareholder in Bully's business. Bully and I go back to my early days in Hawaii."

He angled a wry smile at Kaleo and Leilani. "There's no way I'm going to stand aside and let crooks like them get control. I've got too much affection for Bully's legacy to allow that."

He gave a nod in Kaleo's direction. "Besides, I know someone who can take over on my behalf."

Sarah caught Kaleo's eye. His shoulders gave a helpless little flex, as if to say, I told you, he's a traitor. Believe me now?

She flicked her eyes downwards, unwilling to meet his gaze.

From things she'd overheard in her father's house, she knew nothing escaped de Vile's eagle gaze. But there were still some secrets even he didn't know.

Kaleo spoke up. "Do we know anything about this man, Father? The one who calls himself Will Davenport, I mean. Apart from the fact that he's not who he says he is?"

"Not yet," said de Vile. "But we will. Make no mistake. We will."

De Vile's attention turned back to Sarah. "Sarah, one thing I don't understand. You're taking the blame for this mess. You say you put your mother in peril by running away.

"What was so dreadful that you needed to do that? And why haven't they retaliated before this?"

There was a long, excruciating silence.

How was she to answer that? Her stomach clenched, and her lungs felt as if they'd had all the air squeezed out of them.

Her wrists burned with the memory of the ties that held her, the crushing humiliation of her helplessness as Clifford bore down on her, spreadeagled on a snooker table, while her stepfather stayed in the room next door and pretended he didn't know what was happening.

Never in a million years could she speak of that despicable, foul act. The event that, like no other, made her untouchable. Why Kaleo would never want her.

She coughed out the only answer she could.

"He used me. My stepfather, I mean. He used me to put together the figures for his thieving schemes. When it started, I was young.

"I didn't realize he was using the numbers to swindle ordinary people—bank tellers and waitresses and widows—until much later. But the final straw was when he sold me to Clifford Jensen."

Tears welled up behind her eyes, and she steeled herself to hold them back.

A stunned silence fell like a thick blanket.

"Sold you? What are you talking about?" De Vile sounded disbelieving.

"He intended to force me into a marriage with Clifford Jensen. He'd done a deal. Clifford would forgive the enormous debt my father owed him if he got me as his bride. I was a golden goose, to be trussed up and delivered in a sack."

She felt a surge of fresh confidence as she scanned the group. Kaleo's face was alert, drinking in every word.

Leilani's eyes were wide with shock. De Vile, his face unreadable, had moved to stand close to Elizabeth Westerhoven, one hand resting on the back of her chair. Elizabeth gazed straight back at her with warm admiration. Nothing she was about to say was a surprise to her aunt.

"Sure, Sam's made money out of cheating others. But he's also had disastrous losses with mines that didn't come to anything.

"Clifford saw a way to benefit from that, by extending endless credit and then pulling the noose tight. He demanded my hand as payment."

She smiled ruefully at Elizabeth. "It's not as if he cares a jot about me. He wants me for my ability to make calculations, and I suppose I wounded his pride because I made it clear I'd rather die than be in the same room as him. My only choice was to escape."

The room hushed. De Vile flicked a silent inquiry to Elizabeth, who gave an infinitesimal negative shake of her head that said, Ask no more.

De Vile nodded in the silent conversation.

"I see. I had no intention of prying. My apologies."

The quiet in the room hung on like a fog. And then Sarah asked in a timid voice, "About tomorrow. Are you agreed? I can go with you?"

Once more, de Vile's dark eyes snapped to Elizabeth, as if seeking female direction. This time, her brief nod was affirmative.

"It seems so," de Vile said. "You've made your case."

***

Long after the rest of the house was in darkness, Sarah hugged her knees to her stiff, frozen body to warm herself. The Russell house, with its thick adobe walls and burning fires in most rooms, was like a firebox. But the surrounding coziness didn't penetrate to her marrow.

Even the full-length flannel nightgown she snuggled into failed to ward off the icy fear which had overtaken her when she'd left the camaraderie of the library and went to bed alone.

She was going back to the house in Virginia City, which represented everything foul and frightening in her life. And the reason for her return was to ensure her mother and sister didn't suffer the revenge she knew Clifford Jensen was intent on wreaking on them, to pay her back from escaping him twice.

First, she'd had the gall to run away. Then she'd rebuffed being recaptured.

She rolled restlessly under the thick eiderdown, willing her mind to stop whirring from one image to the next.

Her mother's distraught gray face. Jensen with sweet-natured

Petra at his mercy. If it came to it, she would walk in there and offer herself as a trade for her sister's freedom. Her breath froze, and her arms went numb at the thought.

Only if there's no other option. Only if I'm desperate enough to die.

She lay in the safety of d'Oro's thick walls and willed her body to escape into sleep.

They would leave early tomorrow morning. Leilani and Aristide and Madeleine and Caleb would all be staying here. They had work to do.

For the rest, it would take them two days, first in two carriages to Oakland and then by train to Sacramento. A night there, and then a second and third train over the Sierra Nevada mountains the next day. The track for the last link, the Virginia City train, had been completed in the last year.

She needed rest. Badly. But when she closed her eyes, all she could see was the soft light that glowed in Kaleo's lean masculine face, the scarred brow lending him a piratical air, as he devoured every word of her account of Jensen's abuse. What she'd shared had left a deep impression on him.

She relaxed onto her back, her legs sprawled comfortably down the bed, remembering all over again her delight in those early days with Kaleo. The weeks when they had joked and laughed, as spontaneous as young kittens at play, the blessed period before she had understood this was a friendship that could go nowhere.

Clifford Jensen was always going to haunt her, and she couldn't drag someone like Kaleo into that future. She tossed restlessly to her right side, then her left, quenching the memory of the affinity she had felt.

There had been something between them, and she was pretty sure he felt it as well.

She'd never thought of the long-term consequences when she'd fled Virginia City six months ago. She hadn't had time to do anything except grab a few possessions and run, battered and bleeding, Clifford Jensen's sickening smell leaking from every pore.

If she hadn't taken her chance and fled then, when he'd least expected it, she'd be an abused wife, forced into despised submission night after night.

She'd imagined she could escape him. That if she ran to Elizabeth and found a safe hiding place, she could outwit him. She counted on him giving up and finding someone else to victimize.

She realized now she should have gone far away, to New York or even London, while she had the chance, but it was too late for regrets.

She couldn't ask Kaleo to share a life on the run, forever looking over his shoulder, severed from everyone he loved. To ask him to sacrifice his bond with his twin sister? It was unthinkable.

And anyway, he'd made his disappointment plain. He hated nothing more than dishonesty, and she'd forged a distrust she'd never overcome.

The numbness in her arms and upper body crept back.

For a few moments, she allowed herself to daydream about what it would be like if everything was different. If they had continued to share their lives and stories and become ever closer…

But Clifford Jensen had spoiled things for that kind of life.

The best she could do now was to save her mother from the pain of losing two daughters instead of one. She had one last chance to make her life count for something, and she wouldn't lose it daydreaming about true love.

Chapter 23

Kaleo had to be on his sharpest mettle for the coming fight. He knew that. But his body didn't want to submit to his demands. He slept fitfully, and he'd barely closed his eyes when he woke again with the first birds calling from the bare trees. He sat up, scratched himself, and scrambled into the clothes he'd worn the night before.

Slapping his face with rough handfuls of cold water from the bedside basin, he slipped outside, his breathing shallow, hoping the cutting dawn air would wake him.

His foot had barely crunched onto the crushed pebbles of the rose walk when he heard light footsteps behind him. He stopped and turned.

Elizabeth Westerhoven stood on the pathway off the deck, the full skirt of her deep green gown glowing iridescent in the pearly morning light.

"Countess." He stood and waited for her to approach. "Whatever brings you out so early?"

Her dress was in the new walking style, of a shorter length for freedom of movement, and she wore round-toed black boots polished to a high sheen. The corners of her mouth tilted in a smile which acknowledged his gentle courtesy.

"I could ask you the same thing, Kaleo Arnold Liholiho Manolo."

His shoulders stiffened in shock. "How do you know my full birth name?"

"I knew your mother," she said.

He took a step back and faltered. "Every time I turn around here, I get another surprise. I'm not sure I like it."

She stepped forward. Her voice was gentle as she took his elbow in a motherly gesture.

"Let's walk together. Slowly. It's too cold to sit, I know that. But I've got something important to tell you, and I can't be rushing to keep up and talk at the same time."

She smiled, confident she would get her way. "Let's set a pace we're both comfortable with to both talk and keep warm."

He hesitated and allowed her to steer him back in the direction he'd been taking when she'd interrupted him.

He shook his head. "The things that go on in California. I'll never get over being confounded." They stepped out for a few minutes in silence, as Elizabeth took her time to begin. She cleared her throat and her eyes gazed down the aisle of bare oaks as she spoke.

"You know Bully loved you and you sister very much, don't you, Kaleo? He took it hard when his business forced him to move here and leave you behind in Honolulu."

He thrust his hands into his pockets to escape the chilly air and flicked his gaze sideways. Her eyes had a distant glaze, as if remembering a much younger Bully, from years long passed.

He nodded wordlessly and said, "No one ever replaced him for me. As a kid on the verge of manhood… Well, it would've been good to have someone like him around."

His eyes roamed the treetops, where black clouds of birds roosted and then rose in waves, as if saluting the rising sun. "Perhaps that's why I've been more open to Hector than Lani is. I've always wanted a father to talk to."

Elizabeth nodded sympathetically. "And then, so soon after you got back together again, he died. He had so much he could have imparted."

The hard stone of grief that rose in his throat whenever he allowed himself to see Bully, bleeding on the ground with Leilani crouched over him, choked him again.

"I wish…" His voice was a croak. He cleared his throat and glimpsed Elizabeth watching him with soft eyes. "I wish it could have all been different," he murmured. "We lost not only Bully, but Cyrus and Misty, too. All of our elders—our *kupuna*—lost together."

He paused, his hand clutched in front of him. "It's great that Hector is here, but we hardly know him. He's no replacement for Bully."

She nodded in understanding. "Hector wants that to change. The thing he wants more than anything is to get to know you both better." Kaleo stepped on. It was too cold to stand around even for half a minute.

"What about Hector's family? Do you know anything about them? Apart from Alex, I mean. It seems strange he's never married, never had other children. And what about his father? We haven't had the chance to talk about any of this yet."

Elizabeth gave a faint smile. "Hector has always been a dark horse. He cut his family connections long ago, and not happily. He never talked about it, even when we were younger."

They reached the end of the vineyard driveway, and in silent agreement, circled to walk back to the house. The day had crept to full brightness. Already a faint warmth penetrated the night chill, striking his shoulders with stealthy zeal. Vino d'Oro's adobe walls shone with an apricot glow through the trees.

"This is all part of why I wanted to see you privately this morning," said Elizabeth. "Before we go to Virginia City, I mean. I felt it was important to give you extra information."

Curiosity surged inside him. "Oh? Like what?"

She halted and drew a tissue-wrapped object from the side pocket of her voluminous skirt.

"Like this. Bully left it for you in his will."

She passed it to him, their fingers brushing as he took it from her. He hefted its weight in his hand. It was light, and it carried its own peculiar energy.

He heard the whisper of ocean, the gentle sigh and surge of the waves, and he knew what the soft paper enclosed. He cradled it in his hand, a sacred totem.

"Bully's pendant. His ancestral necklace. The *lei niho palaoa*," he whispered in awe.

The ancestral whalebone hook, originally hung from human hair, passed down through countless generations to Bully, a rare heirloom given to noble-born boys when they came of age. Bully wore it at his throat until his killer ripped it from him at his death.

"How did you know?"

"It sings to me."

"A perfect confirmation," said Elizabeth. "He was certain you were the one to have it."

She stepped out again, her stride smooth and supple. "As you well know, I am Bully's executor. There have been unforeseen delays in clearing his estate, but I wanted you to have this before we leave with Dolphie and Hector this morning.

"It's a dangerous undertaking, this mission you're on, and I'm hoping it will offer you some protection."

"We? Are you coming too?" Kaleo couldn't keep the shock from his voice.

"Hector's got an important meeting there I'd always planned to attend with him. And now I'm concerned about my sister and niece, there's even more reason to come. But I'll be keeping out of your way, I assure you."

They were nearing the house, and the need to ask Elizabeth things he had never asked before overcame him. He was like a soldier going off to war. Would he ever get another chance?

He reached out and gently caught Elizabeth's arm in mid-stride.

"Countess." His voice was soft, apologetic. "Please. What's the true nature of Sarah's plight? Really? I suspect I've haven't heard the full story."

She lifted her compassionate brown eyes to his and gazed at him for a long minute, as if assessing what she could say.

Then she sighed. "Kaleo Manolo. There are many things I'm not at liberty to talk about. It's not my story to tell. I'm sorry. But one thing I can say. Sarah's family is in real danger. And Bully would want you to be helping them.

"Sarah is Bully's niece. Sarah's mother was married to his brother Noah before she wed Sam Hollows. That's why he gave Sarah a job."

Bully? Sarah's uncle? When are the surprises going to stop?

"If anyone would want Noah's wife and children protected, it would be Bully. And I reckon he'd want you to have the whalebone with you when you do it."

Her face opened up in a self-deprecating grin. "For protection. See, some of the old Hawaiian, buried deep in here." She tapped her chest.

He gave a slight shake of his head. Opened his mouth, but no words came.

She smiled again, this time with warm sympathy. "I know. It's a lot to take in. But one day you'll understand."

A call floated through the warming air. "Kaleo. Where are you?"

Lani.

"And that's our signal. We need to get back," Elizabeth said. "You'll learn all that you need to know at the right time and in the right place."

Chapter 24

"Bully's heirloom looks good on you, Kaleo. I'm glad Elizabeth gave it to you when she did." Kaleo locked eyes with his father across the distance of the carriage. The motion of the train had slowed as they neared Sacramento. They were only half an hour away from their destination. Dolphie had disappeared to the dining car.

"Did you know he'd left it to me? And that Elizabeth was going to give it to me yesterday?" His chest hollowed at the thought of the two elders discussing him behind his back. The emptiness eased as de Vile's alert eyes flared in surprise. He hadn't known.

"No, no. Not at all. Elizabeth is the model of discretion." He gave Kaleo a cheeky grin. "It's been irritating sometimes. Like trying to open a clam, getting her to talk when she doesn't want to."

Kaleo raised his hand to his throat, where the whalebone pendant nestled against the dip in his collarbone. Already it felt destined to fit there. Like he was born to wear it. He imagined it gave off a silent hum, discernible only to his inner spirit.

Nothing audible, but a sense of presence there. If he woke up without it, he'd be instantly aware of the loss.

"It belongs with me, that's all. It's inevitable. Like an incomplete circle that's been joined. That's the best way I can describe it."

This was the first time since they had left Vino d'Oro that he'd talked privately with Hector. He'd spent the hours reading newspapers that left your fingers grimy with newsprint ink, or playing interminable games of euchre with Dolphie, broken by intermittent dozing.

And all the time, fragments of Elizabeth's confidences rang in his head. The little that she'd said raised so many more questions. He realized with a thump of his heart that this might be the only opportunity he'd have to ask de Vile about them.

"Elizabeth told me yesterday that Sarah was Bully's niece. Did you know that?"

"Not until last week. I have a vague memory of Bully's brother Noah marrying Charlotte, but I never connected Sarah to it.

"I never saw Noah's children. He died when Sarah was young, and anyway, I lost touch with them. Elizabeth and Charles were away in Europe, and I only ever saw them at the Westerhovens."

De Vile gazed out of the carriage window, and Kaleo followed his line of sight. Away to the east loomed the snow-capped Sierra Nevada mountains, majestic and mysterious.

Closer to the railway line, the train crossed a swampy area covered in tall rushes. A dull plain stretched before them, dotted with occasional mid-sized trees, hung with clusters of dark creeper.

De Vile turned back to him. "Apart from the addition of the train, it's much the same as when I first came here in the late forties."

His voice was flat, sad. He shifted in his seat and pulled his shoulders back. "But where were we? Oh, yes. Noah. Elizabeth and I have really only renewed our acquaintance in the last twelve months. We lost touch for years."

De Vile's face lit up with what, for him, was an unusual tenderness. It struck Kaleo that his father was still an energetic, virile man. Maybe he entertained thoughts of marrying one day. He banished the idea as fast as it came.

"Do you recall much about what Sarah's father was like?"

"I guess all I remember is that he differed from Bully. He was a quiet chap. Not the forceful sort of fellow Bully was. But I think he did well enough.

"He set Charlotte up. They had the house in Virginia City and some funds. When he died, she was a promising catch for someone like Sam Hollows, a man with vertiginous ambitions and no money to realize them."

Kaleo glimpsed the likely dynamics of such a marriage.

"What about your family, Father? Are your parents still alive?"

De Vile's jaw tightened, and a nerve flickered under his left eye. The senator raised his hand to his face and stroked the spot. "No. They died years ago."

"And you've no brothers and sisters? Nieces and nephews?"

"No nieces and nephews–at least not that I know of." Hector scowled.

"I had a brother, but we lost touch. I'm afraid it's not a cheerful story." He gave a weary sigh and rubbed his eye again. "And I suppose you want to hear it."

"Well, yes, Father, I would. It's quite a novelty to have a new family. Even if they're not around anymore."

***

Father. De Vile rubbed the irritating tic that twitched under his right eye and observed the young man who sat across from him with an air of calm authority that marked him as a born leader. His son. And unlike Alex, his own blood.

His and Abigail's, the only wife he'd ever had. Apiakali Kamamalu Arnold—a high-born Hawaiian—was his wife for exactly four months before her incensed missionary father Archie Arnold intervened and had the marriage annulled.

The familiar spear of pain lodged in his ribs at the memory. Abigail had died in a measles epidemic when the twins were babies, and Archie's messenger, Elizabeth Westerhoven, had led him to believe—he had believed until six months ago—that they had died with her.

It wasn't an unusual fate—hundreds of native Hawaiians had died in the fall of 1848 after visiting sailors infected the 'Paradise' islands with the deadly disease. But before that happened, Archie—Abigail's adopted father in the Hawaiian *hānai* tradition—had already dissolved their native Hawaiian wedding rite and married her off in church to someone approved by the king.

The young man who sat across from him mirrored his mother's elegant profile, the sharply wrought cheekbones, the piercing black eyes. But his personality was quite different.

Where Abigail was a tempest of wilfulness, the man before him wore a gravity appropriate for someone far older.

His dark eyes were tranquil, and though they occasionally sparked with mischief, they carried a steady integrity that unsettled de Vile. He wore his raven hair tied back in a ponytail that nestled between broad shoulders.

Anyone else would come across as an artless jerkwater. On Kaleo, with his hawkish profile and one scarred eyebrow, his unorthodox hairstyle softened a nonchalant, devil-may-care masculinity that warned he'd be a dangerous man to cross.

How do I tell him about the desperation of that time without him hating me?

De Vile cleared his throat and deliberately brought his wandering hand down from his face to settle in his lap. "Those were hard times, Kaleo. It's hard for me to recall now how bad things were."

Kaleo shifted his weight imperceptibly. "Anything you can remember. I'd like to hear it. Did you know Matthew Manolo? I never knew him or my mother."

Manolo was the man Archie Arnold replaced him with—and he'd died in a shark attack within a year of Abigail's death.

De Vile gave a wry chuckle. "That makes two of us. I only saw the man on a couple of occasions—your mother's funeral being one of them." The knife dug into his ribs again, reminding him of his mortality.

"When I went to sea, I'd already broken with my family. My father brought us to America from Europe in the 1830s. Things weren't good in our homeland. Prospects were much better in America—a lot of our people were emigrating because of the economic conditions and political unrest."

Kaleo's dark eyes fixed on him, drinking in every word. De Vile diverted his gaze to his wrinkled hands.

When did I get old? I'm older now than my father ever got to be.

"It saddens me to admit I never got on with my father. He seemed to favor my younger brother. We clashed. No other way to describe it.

"I was in a rush to conquer the world, and he was a much more cautious spirit." He gave a deep sigh, and the pain in his chest eased.

"I can understand today why he'd be skeptical of my big talk. But it felt like he had it in for me. He made demands. Dictated that I marry and present him with a son and heir before I turned thirty or he'd disinherit me.

"He'd had three children by the time he was twenty-five, but only two of us survived. My brother was like him. Circumspect, always worried about the family name, his reputation."

Kaleo watched his father's changing expression. The grooves that ran in vertical lines on either side of his mouth deepened. Confiding his personal story was painful.

"Coming to America was the riskiest thing either of them ever did. My father wanted to bypass me, give my brother a hundred percent of the family business. And I suppose that was understandable.

"Even though I was the eldest, I never settled in the firm. I worked for him for a few months, but I left home when I was sixteen."

Hector's eyes closed momentarily, and Kaleo saw the flash of pain in them as he opened them again.

"I suppose throwing me out was my father's way of forcing me to 'settle down.' He wanted something very different for me than going to sea, captaining a whaler, rubbing shoulders with the Gold Rush forty-niners…"

"You did all that?"

"Running passengers and cargo to California? That's where I made my first fortune, yes."

"And your father didn't approve?"

"He only knew one way, and it was his way. He wasn't interested. My brother stayed faithfully at his side, working in the family importing business, believing one day it would all be his."

De Vile steepled his fingers in front of his chin. "They were both angry when I turned up with Alex and his mother and demanded my share. They weren't expecting me to do it." He watched as Kaleo's dark eyes narrowed in confusion.

"Alex's mother? But I thought Alex said she died when he was a baby?"

De Vile waved away the comment, as if it was of no consequence. "His adopted mother."

Kaleo's brow remained creased in a frown. "Adopted mother? And your father was okay with that?"

But Hector was back in that unlikely reunion.

Something had triggered like a lightning bolt in his brain. He could smell blood, sense its syrupy stickiness. He clenched his fists to stop himself from putting his hands over his ears to block out Thirza's screams.

His eyes flickered to Kaleo, who was staring at him.

"Are you all right, Father? You look like you've seen a ghost."

Arms rigid at his sides, de Vile growled in the back of his throat. "I don't believe in ghosts."

"So, you got your share, even though you weren't married?"

"What did it matter? I played him at his own game and won, didn't I? I forced him to give me what was mine." There was a long, painful silence, and then Kaleo asked, "And your brother? Is he still alive?"

"I don't know." He wasn't about to explain that after their father's death, his brother fell to pieces. There was nothing left of de Vile and Son now. But if he played his next hand right, Pike Consulting might become the new de Vile and Son, and he'd have scored a royal flush.

Chapter 25

Hector de Vile gazed at the tanned young man across the railway carriage from him, but he wasn't really seeing the deep brown eyes, the sculpted mouth that usually carried a hint of a smile, the scarred eyebrow that gave an air of danger.

The strangely comforting smell of coal smoke, the gentle sway of the carriage, the soporific clacking of iron on iron, all faded, and Hector de Vile was Kaleo's age—perhaps a year or two older, standing in the claustrophobic overheated library in the Fifth Avenue house on the last day he'd seen his father alive.

They had been apart for over ten years after his father had cut him off with the cold precision of a surgeon amputating a diseased limb. Rather than simply disown him, he'd set inheritance conditions impossible for him to satisfy. He'd been confident Hector could never claim his birthright.

But Hector had beaten him at his own game. He'd turned up unannounced from California with a wife and son.

"Father, may I present my wife, Madame Bertha de Vile, and our son, Alex de Vile."

Bertha held Alex protectively on her hip. The boy gurgled joyfully and waved his chubby little hand at his grandfather, as if delighted to meet him.

His father's pale gray eyes—the color of icebergs, Hector had always thought as a boy—stared at him with an unbelieving, deathly glaze. The last thing he'd expected was to have his eldest son arrive with a wife and son in tow to collect his inheritance.

He took a step toward his father's stern figure. "As you may remember—or you may not—I turn thirty at the end of the year. I've all the documents here to satisfy your requirements."

He drew his heels together with a satirical click. "I claim my birthright."

Hector opened his eyes and rested his gaze on Kaleo's rapt face.

"It was the last thing your grandfather expected, and he wasn't pleased."

His son's dark eyes flickered in momentary surprise. "Why was it a surprise? Surely, he'd have seen you're a force to be reckoned with? You usually get what you want?"

Laughter bubbled up from inside, and Hector coughed to disguise his enjoyment of his son's dry wit. "That was part of the problem. He didn't enjoy having a son with big ideas. He wanted someone who'd stay home and follow his directions like an obedient little paper pusher.

"That would never be me. Anyway, I've not always got what I wanted. Take your mother, for example."

Hector fleetingly thought of his pathetic bid to bully Graysie Castellanos into marriage. And of Elizabeth Westerhoven, who he hadn't got around to asking yet. Somber-faced Kaleo knew nothing of them.

"I can see how Archie, interfering with your marriage to Abigail, messed things up for you. Did he think you were using her to get at your father?"

Hector ran his tongue over his teeth. "I can't prove Archie knew about my father's will, but I've got strong suspicions. He had good connections. He was into business in a big way before he found God."

There was an awkward silence.

"And were you?" Kaleo's jaw set at a determined angle.

"Was I what?"

"Using her as a pawn to get even with your father?"

De Vile glared at him for half a minute and then shrugged.

"Not at the beginning. That woman was a whirlwind who swept me away. But after she got pregnant? I admit it. Then it occurred to me it would be an immense advantage to marry her."

His eyes roved over his son's stern face. "Your mother was a beautiful, spirited woman, Kaleo. But she wasn't cut out for life as a steady, docile wife."

Their carriage door banged open and a railway inspector peered in. "Tickets please."

The spell that caught them in a locked, intimate bubble vaporized. They were back to being like any other father and son, sitting knee to knee on the Sacramento train, talking about the ancient past. Kaleo flexed his shoulders, as if easing the tension.

De Vile cracked his knuckles, left hand over right. Stared outside again. "I don't come out of this looking good, do I? But I'm not guilty of the things they've accused me of."

Chapter 26

Sarah sank onto a stool at the small lounge table where Dolphie and Kaleo were enjoying an after-dinner nightcap in Sacramento's Orleans Hotel on Second Street. The glamorous seventy-five-room multi-purpose salon hotel was the senator's second home in the state capital.

"Mind if I join you?" Her soft, melodic voice set up a familiar heightened awareness whenever she was around Kaleo.

"Sure thing, Princess," Dolphie said with light familiarity. "What can I get you to drink? Hot chocolate?"

"You know me so well," she said with a grin.

They had an early start tomorrow, boarding the connecting train from Sacramento to Carson and then changing to the new Truckee-Virginia railway for the last leg, but despite the fatigue of the journey, none of them were ready for an early night.

"You two know each other?" Kaleo strove for nonchalance, but he was fooling no one.

Dolphie shrugged. "I'm Elizabeth's ward, her protector, her flunky." He grinned. "Honestly, I owe Charles and her my life. Not literally. But in every way that counts. Her wish is my command.

"And over the last year or so, her wishes have extended to concern about her sister's well-being in the Hollows household."

"Ah, I get it now." Kaleo gave them a quick smile. "That's why, when you came to my house, you knew their names. Jensen and so forth. I wondered about that. You've dealt with them before?"

Sarah leveled her sparkling hazel eyes to meet Kaleo's cool gaze. "He's dealt with them before. I'd be dead if it wasn't for Dolphie."

Some days, her eyes showed green flecks. Today he saw dark charcoal specks in with the green. His heart stuttered.

"Hot chocolate would be wonderful, Dolphie," she said. "Thank you."

Dolphie rose with his fencer's grace and signaled to the barman as he crossed the room to place his order.

An awkward silence stretched between them.

So, what the heck am I supposed to say now? I seem to always be behind the play here.

"You'd be dead without Dolphie? Care to explain?" He scrambled for what seemed the least touchy subject.

She smiled like a sphinx. "Of course not. Too long and boring."

She leaned in more closely. He braced himself to stay focused.

"Kaleo, I know I've said this before, but I can't help it. I'm saying it again. I don't want you to get hurt on my behalf. Please. Get out while you can. You don't have to do this."

Her voice was a plaintive whisper. A rush of hot annoyance replaced his awkwardness.

"Sarah, it might surprise you to find I'm not here for you. You've made yourself perfectly clear, so don't worry. I'm not a dumb ox."

The words came out with a bitter edge he barely recognized as his own. He rushed on. "I owe it to Dolphie. He saved my life too, don't forget. And to Bully. Even Elizabeth agrees Bully would approve of me being here.

"And I'm here for my father. My newfound father." He picked

up his glass, tossed back the dregs, and thrust back from his stool with a screech.

"Despite what you choose to believe, Will's up to no good. He doesn't give a damn about you, no matter what you think." He reflectively stroked Bully's pendant at his throat. It was warm and smooth, reassuring him he belonged somewhere.

"The senator's got it right. He's out to seize control of the consulting business—Bully's business. So, I'm protecting my family interests. He won't win, whatever he and Clifford have cooked up."

He grabbed his jacket from the back of his chair and slung it over his shoulder. "Now excuse me. I'll leave you and your friend Dolphie to catch up."

He stalked off, a wretched loneliness tugging at the hollow places inside.

Chapter 27

How had she got everything so wrong? Sarah slowly undressed for bed in the suite she shared with Elizabeth. Her aunt was accompanying them because Hector was due to make an important political speech in Virginia City in a few days' time, and she had agreed to stand at his side for moral support.

Keeping the punters happy was what de Vile called it. Something to do with mining interests and the building of the Sutro Tunnel. She could hear her aunt's steady breathing through the wall. Good, at least one of them was getting rest tonight.

Sarah doubted she'd sleep a wink. Tonight's sharp exchange with Kaleo was like the final nail in the coffin. And a fever of anxiety at the task ahead threatened to overwhelm her.

What if they didn't get there in time? What would Clifford do to Petra? Had Will turned traitor on them, as Kaleo suggested?

Hector's information that he was traveling with Jensen didn't automatically mean he was conspiring with him, did it? They might have taken him for a ride. He wasn't a warrior like Dolphie and Kaleo. He was a pale-faced pen pusher. Perhaps he was waiting for his chance to escape.

But Kaleo? He was a different man altogether. Every time her eyes skittered over his tawny, hawkish profile and dark glittering eyes her breath hitched. Her head could tell her heart there could be nothing between them, but her soul refused to accept it.

A gaping hole of despair opened up inside.

She was going to free her mother and sister. Free them all from the clutches of the despicable Hollows empire. But what then? She would live out her life without Kaleo to laugh with, to tease, to love?

It hardly seemed worth going on if that was how it had to be.

She pulled back the deep bedcovers, wriggled down into the soft mattress and turned out the bedside lamp.

The only thing worse than living without him was the possibility of Kaleo dying protecting her interests. Because it didn't matter what he said, she didn't believe she meant nothing to him. Or that he was here solely for his father and Bully and Dolphie.

She linked her hands behind her head and stared overhead. They'd garlanded the ceiling with a pilaster fringe of smiling cherubs, their rounded tummies and chubby arms reminding her of the children she would never have. A sturdy little boy with Kaleo's serene sparkle. A dancing girl with Leilani's natural grace.

Her throat filled with a hard lump as she balled her fists in the soft bed.

How have I made such a mess of things? And how am I ever going to fix it?

Chapter 28

Kaleo stalked from the Orleans cocktail bar, furious with everyone, including himself. Would this woman never stop pestering him? And when would he stop caring?

What I choose to do is none of her damn business!

Had he truly known anything about her when he'd imagined their special closeness? Every time he turned around, there was some new revelation he hadn't accounted for. How he hated being always pushed to the fringes of her life. It was humiliating when he'd hoped for so much more—another reminder of how foolish he'd been.

A rush of homesickness overcame him, for Waikiki, for the fresh salty air, the hissing surge and ebb of the waves on the sandy beaches. He was hungry for somewhere people knew and loved him.

That was it. He needed air. He swung out of the hotel's impressive columned facade and turned toward the Embarcadero, drawn to the sound of water slapping against chunky wooden piles. It was a poor substitute for his beloved ocean, but it would do.

Hands in his pockets, a wide-brimmed hat shielding his face, he strolled toward the schooner masts and the rising bulk of steamer funnels—now cold and smokeless—tied up in the downtown basin.

An unpleasant odor blew off the water—a combination of offal and dung and filth. The city's fathers had acknowledged the serious contamination of Sacramento's water, but had not yet found a solution for purifying it.

Kaleo pulled his scarf over his nose and mouth, blocking out the stink, and prayed Honolulu would never get into the same predicament.

A black cat that stalked a gangway to an old salmon boat meowed as if saying "hello." A street back from the docks, he heard muted music and men's cries—some downtown gambling joint, he surmised, probably open for all kinds of illegal activity. As for the rest, the street appeared deserted except for a lumpy form in a doorway—a drunk sleeping off his excess, most likely.

Kaleo's hand slipped to the small revolver he carried in his coat pocket. No point in getting rolled before he'd even got to Virginia City. The evening paper he'd seen in the hotel lobby was full of stories of "garroters" ready to attack and rob passersby armed with nothing more than a knife.

According to the report, an innkeeper embarking on a San Francisco holiday, his pockets stuffed with his night's takings, was assaulted and robbed of two hundred dollars in this very area the night before last.

Hector had taken part in building this city—and others like it in the region—for the last twenty years. He'd seen it grow from a tent town that flooded every winter to the state capital, with its cupola-topped building in the finest Greco-Roman style.

The growth included "international quality" hotels like the one their party was staying in tonight, and the development of a bustling transport hub—with cross-country trains and inter-city steamers departing every day, carrying people and produce across the prospering state.

What if Hector's marriage to his mother had lasted? What if

they'd come back here, and she'd occupied a role like Elizabeth Westerhoven did—as benefactress and consort?

From what he'd heard of his mother's nature, he doubted that would ever have worked out And here his father was, twenty years later, still a bachelor, hungry for a family and someone to inherit his legacy.

He'd prospered beyond his dreams—a US Senator, a magnate with multiple interests in mines, railways and property, but still with an ache for more.

The sound of running feet brought him to an abrupt stop. He listened. A man's cry. He swung toward the source of the noise in time to see a slight man in a heavy overcoat bracing against a coming blow, one arm above his head.

A man twice his size swung at him with a baseball bat. Light from a sidewalk gas lamp caught the bat's blinding white arc, and an exposed ghostly face. A face Kaleo knew.

With a yell, he sprang forward, revolver out of his pocket before he had given it conscious thought. He grasped the barrel end and, wielding it like a cosh, struck down on the attacker's arm.

The blow sunk with spongy impact, reverberating through the big man's frame. He crumpled, going down with a howl, arms protectively raised over his head, scuttling crabwise on his buttocks to escape further blows.

Kaleo knew by instinct, by a sixth sense, he didn't need to worry about any further retaliation from that quarter.

He focused his attention on the victim. The man had dodged sideways to escape his attacker's blow. He stumbled on the jetty edge, dangerously close to toppling into the icy poisonous water.

Kaleo shot out an arm and grabbed the lapels of the man's coat, catching him at the point of falling. He hauled him back, wedging his toes under the warm bulk of the fellow lying at his feet to maintain his own balance. The man's overcoat bunched in Kaleo's right fist.

Terrified, pale eyes stared back at him from behind wire-rimmed spectacles. He let go of the overcoat and stepped back from the prone man at his feet.

"I thought so!" He let out an angry laugh, pointing at the man at his feet, who was snuffling and moaning. Slowly coming around.

"And if this rogue dies, I suppose you'll turn me in?" He glared at Will Davenport, who was sucking in deep gulps of air, too choked to speak.

Will brought one hand to his throat. Drew one more raging draft of air and steadied himself. "Kaleo… By Beelzebub, thank you. I was a goner."

Kaleo stowed the revolver back in his pocket. "That you were." Will stepped around the downed man and thrust out his hand.

Kaleo stared back, hands firmly in his pockets.

"Why are you here, Will?" His voice was cold, clipped.

Will waited out a long silence.

Kaleo lost patience. "It's not as if you're Jensen's prisoner. You're his willing aider and abettor." He stared at his workmate's frozen face, then searched around him in a theatrically exaggerated pose.

"So where is he? Has he got you under house arrest? Is there a gun at your back? I can't see it." Will licked his lips. A bruise on one side of his face was already leaving a purple stripe down his cheekbone.

"You're a traitor, Will. A sell-out to Bully, to Sarah, to everyone who gave you a chance." Will took a big breath, as if suddenly fired into life.

"And you're a fool if you think you'll get any thanks for loyalty, Kaleo. An absolute dolt. All muscle and no brain." His lip—already swelling and mottled red—curled up on one side of his face.

"You think de Vile is going to thank you for being his good little boy? He's a murderer and a cheat. When he's done, he'll knock you down and walk away.

"And Sarah? She's already taken, you idiot. She's damaged goods. As good as already married to Clifford Jensen, one of the most powerful men in this part of the state. You think you can stand up against him and his backers?"

Swaying unsteadily on his feet, still the worse for his near miss, he jerked away.

"If you've got any brains—any brains at all—you'll get out now, before de Vile and Sarah eat you for breakfast. And if they don't do it, Clifford Jensen certainly will."

Chapter 29

Snow began falling in the early afternoon, an hour before Sarah approached the front door of the decorative French Empire house on Virginia City's South D Street.

She presented a vulnerable figure, standing under the colonnaded porch, waiting for her tentative knock to be answered. From their hiding place across the street, Kaleo and Dolphie watched the door open, and heard the joyful note of surprise in the voice that answered.

"Miz Rebecca. Welcome home!" One of the faithful retainers in the Hollows household, Kaleo surmised, glad to see the prodigal daughter return. Probably unaware of the reason she'd disappeared.

Kaleo felt the rock-hard tension in his rib cage, the terror that would not end until she was safely out of there again.

Sarah was returning of her own free will. She'd insisted it was the best way to make an initial approach, to discover as best she could what was going on behind the palatial three-story dwelling with its series of double-bayed windows either side of the front door and a widow's walk on the top, edged in curlicued wrought iron.

It went against the grain with him to let her take the risk, but Dolphie and de Vile had gone along with the feint, saying that if Hollows or Jensen attempted to restrain her again, they'd be ready to take action.

She was supposedly on a courtesy call to make peace with her stepfather, and then leave again, having taken tea.

They'd given her a maximum of an hour to complete this reconnaissance before they intervened. If all was going well, they'd agreed she'd leave a sign—a teddy bear mounted in the window of the upstairs bedroom facing the street—to indicate no one was in immediate danger.

She'd been inside for thirty minutes, and there was no sign yet of a teddy bear. The snow fell more heavily with every minute, dampening down the street noise, creating a peculiar cotton wool softness that was foreign to Kaleo's experience.

So this is how it feels.

He stamped his feet to keep the blood moving in his toes.

As if reading his thoughts, Dolphie sidled over.

He grinned as he too stamped his feet. "You're in luck. It only snows for six days at the most in Virginia City in January. This is obviously one of them, and it's settling in for the night."

Kaleo blew on his gloved hands. "What do you reckon's going on in there?"

Dolphie shrugged. "Hard to say. It depends if Jensen's there or not. She might have more chance of pleading her case if he's not there. If he is, he'll need to save face by acting the big man."

A trickle of doubt ran down Kaleo's spine. "I still don't like it."

"Sarah's a resourceful lass. And she knows she's got backup."

D Street was in a section of town where the richest mine owners and merchants had homes. Men like James Mackay, whose garden they were loitering in, thanks to Hector's contacts.

Mackay was away in San Francisco, but the woman who ran the house happily agreed to them keeping watch from the mining baron's front yard. Piper's Opera House, where the senator was giving his speech, was down the way.

De Vile. Thoughts of his father was never far from his mind.

Melting snow dripped off the brim of his leather hat and penetrated through the woolen scarf wrapped around Kaleo's neck. He shivered. Was it the cold or Will Davenport's words that prompted the chill?

"He's a murderer and a cheat."

He'd worked with Will for six months, and he'd never have believed he'd so readily desert them—him, Sarah, and Pike's—unless he had good reason.

He recalled Will's twisted face, the certainty and determination in his voice as he spat out his hatred. There was personal vehemence there. Something had made Will hate the senator with frightening passion.

What connection could an ordinary office clerk like Will Davenport have with one of the state's—the country's—most powerful politicians and magnates? Alex had mentioned no problems. De Vile himself had acknowledged no dealings between them.

The treacherous uncertainty that assailed him ever since he'd discovered everyone around him was lying returned. The knife-in-the-ribs stab of not knowing who to trust. Like being in turbulent seas in a tiny boat.

He was leaning against a tree—a deciduous oak, so it provided little shelter, but it was better than nothing—when he heard Dolphie growl quietly in his right ear.

He jumped.

"I didn't even hear you—" He stopped mid-sentence as Dolphie pointed to the window, the one where they had organized for the teddy bear sign.

A white-faced figure stood in unobstructed view, holding up a sheet of paper with scrawled bright red letters.

HELP.

It was Petra.

As they darted back out of view behind the painted brick wall which surrounded the house, someone hauled her away from the window. Seconds after she had delivered her SOS, she was gone.

***

Even as Sarah stood at the front door, her inner turmoil tempted her to turn and run. The only thing holding her back was the terror that hollowed out her stomach and left her so weak she feared if she bolted for the street, her legs would give way from under her.

She reminded herself for the umpteenth time since she'd conceived this mad scheme, that Sam and Clifford wouldn't kill her. She was worth too much to them alive.

This was the most straightforward way to go about finding out if her mother and Petra were unharmed, she told herself. If this didn't work, she had the senator and Elizabeth and Dolphie. They would work something out. Dolphie… And Kaleo…

The thought of the steely eyed Hawaiian filled her with renewed confidence so that when the front door creaked open, her legs held her upright and she stepped forward into the housekeeper Nessa Murphy's broad, welcoming hug.

"Miz Rebecca…"

Nessa circled her with arms made sturdy from beating rugs and working bread dough. Sarah's legs strengthened in her embrace. She jammed her nose up against Nessa's warm, damp neck and smelt strawberry jam.

Jam and other homey smells—of Nessa's fresh-baked bread, her mother's cologne and the yeasty wet fur odor of her stepfather's mastiffs, Dancer and Blitzen.

As if on cue, the dogs surged into the entry hall and sniffed around her skirts until Nessa reluctantly released her and Sarah put her hand down to let first Dancer and then Blitzen sniff her fingers appreciatively.

If it wasn't for that horrible scene with Clifford, and Sam's callous disregard for both her safety and the integrity of their business… Sarah paused, stroking Blitzen's neck.

This could still be my home. If that nightmare hadn't happened.

"Welcome home, darlin'." Nessa's thick Irish accent brought her back to the task in front of her.

"Are my mother, or my father at home, Nessa?" Her voice sounded nervous and squeaky. She cleared her throat. "Petra too, of course."

"Surely, my girl. I'll get George to find them."

George Patrick Murphy, her husband, was the household's right-hand man for practical household maintenance.

"But first ye must come into the kitchen and take a little soup to warm your gills. It's going to carry on snowing today if I'm not right and certain. My arthritis has been playing up something dreadful."

Despite the complaint, and a slight limp as she led Sarah down the hallway, Nessa's face was pink with pleasure as she headed for the kitchen. The dogs padded languidly after them.

They hadn't reached the door into Nessa's cozy domain before a rattle of heels on the stairs signaled someone coming. Petra threw herself into Sarah's arms.

"Princess! What are you doing here?"

The nickname—a joking reference to Sarah's ability to carry a kingdom on her shoulders like the Old Testament wife of Abraham—had never been one Sarah liked.

She wrinkled up her nose in distaste. "Here to see you, of course, Pet."

A flicker of irritation momentarily blurred her sister's ecstatic face.

"Ha! And you don't like being called Pet either, do you?"

They fell into each other's arms again, laughing.

Petra tugged her arm, pulling her into the kitchen, closing the door behind them.

"No, I mean really." Her voice was a low whisper, her eyes stormy and serious. "You can't stay. You know that. Didn't you read my telegram?"

"Of course, sweetheart. I'm not stupid. But we have to put an end to this nonsense. I'll not hide for the rest of my life. And you shouldn't be in danger either. We need to sort things out."

It was happening again. She always sounded and acted more certain, more determined, when there were others around her who needed reassurance.

The weakness that had nearly overwhelmed her on the threshold had vanished, replaced with fierce determination. She'd make this work. She had to.

Nessa seated them both at the plain oak table and poured each of them a mug of chicken gruel. The first mouthful confirmed she was back home. The next steeled her resolve, as hot, fragrant goodness slipped down her throat.

Chicken and saltiness, a hint of carrots, onions and celery. Goodness knew where the cook found these vegetables in Virginia City in the middle of winter, but she magically did.

They sipped in silence for a minute, and then Sarah asked in a low voice, "How are things? You haven't been…"

She hesitated. "Clifford hasn't…" She peeped around furtively, but Nessa was out in the pantry at the end of the roomy kitchen, humming a low tune to herself, well out of earshot.

Petra blushed and shook her head. "He's been awful. He's threatened dreadful consequences. But so far, Dad has kept him under control. I make sure I'm never alone with him."

She hesitated. "That and I always have the dogs with me. They sleep next to my bed at night."

Sarah nodded in approval. "Excellent idea. And Mother?"

"She's stressed out of her mind about you and what's going to happen. Elizabeth has tried to reassure her with her 'secret messages,' but she's taking it hard."

They knew Elizabeth regularly sent notes to Lottie through the housekeeper, with a shared understanding they were not for Sam's eyes.

Petra snuck her an anxious sideways glance. "She's still taking her 'medicine' from Dr. Morphine. Half the time, I honestly don't know if she knows what's going on around her."

"Dr. Morphine," alias Ebenezer Jacobs. Sarah doubted the man was a qualified physician, but he was someone Sam Hollows insisted knew about "female troubles."

Sarah suspected he was dosing her mother with opiates of some sort. Laudanum, most likely. Her stomach churned.

What if she's out for the count right at the time we need her to leave?

"She doesn't have to be stressed any further. It's a good thing Clifford found me. Now we can get it all out in the open."

Her voice rang with a confidence she couldn't find inside. She clutched her soup mug to hide the tremor in her fingers and swallowed the hot draft down on her rising fear.

The kitchen door opened and George Murphy preceded her stepfather into the room. He stepped aside for the master of the house.

Sam's bullish face sat between hunched shoulders. His cheeks were a fiery red, his dark eyes bright with anger.

"Peter, Mary, James and John! What are you doing girl, coming back here as if nothing's the matter, after all the trouble you've caused?"

Sarah rose from her chair, the panic reflex irrepressible. The chair legs screeched against the wooden floor and the frame toppled backwards with a clatter.

Petra shot out a restraining hand on her forearm, as if expecting her to bolt.

"Nice to see you again, too, Father," Sarah responded in a pert tone.

Dammit if she was going to let him see he intimidated her.

"And I'm not the one who has caused the trouble. If you hadn't hatched that mad plot to kidnap me, then Otis and Clifford wouldn't have got hurt. What sort of jape was that anyway, for goodness' sakes? We're not living in the Wild West."

Samuel Hollows glared, fists clenched at his sides. The lines under his eyes had deepened in the last six months, the double chin grown heavier. He'd aged ten years in the time she'd been away.

"I see your attitude hasn't improved." He surveyed the kitchen, his eyes settling on George, and then Nessa. "This isn't the place to discuss this. Come to my study."

It was an order, not a request. "Now," he barked. His bloodshot eyes flicked to Petra. "And you can stay here. What I've got to say is for Sarah's ears only."

Chapter 30

The minute Sarah stepped into her stepfather's Persian-rugged study, the back of her throat closed up, hit with the blue haze of pungent cigar smoke that hung from the ceiling to eye level like a Sacramento swamp fog.

She bent over and rattled her rib cage with violent coughing, then slowly drew upright again. The room was as she remembered it, a classic gentleman's study with leather armchairs, expensive oriental floor rugs, and shelves of books, the novels and classics which were her mother's delight. Sam Hollows wasn't interested in anything but money.

"What's he doing here?"

Sarah glared at the source of the suffocating cloud. He lay sprawled in a wide-armed chair set to one side of the big leather-topped desk Sam Hollows lumbered clumsily to fit in behind.

Otis Hollows adopted his usual couldn't-care-less pose, his injured arm in a sling across his chest. He held a cigar awkwardly in the fat fingers of his left fist. He did not sit up. His lip curled in an arrogant half sneer, half smile.

"It's my home too, Princess. Or have you been away so long you've forgotten? I needed somewhere to recuperate from a most unfortunate attack."

He gestured around the book-lined room with his bandaged arm in an ironic salute. "But you already know all about that."

She sent him a scorching, scornful stare. "So. The puppy dog has limped home with his tail between his legs," she said.

She rounded on Sam Hollows, who was settling his big backside into the fat leather chair behind the desk and reaching for a cigar.

"I don't want him here. What we have to discuss is private business. If Petra's not allowed in, then neither's he." Sam fiddled with the matches. He didn't look up.

"Otis is part of the team. Petra isn't. "He purposefully struck a match, lit the Havana and sucked a big draw, peering over the cloud that billowed from his pouty mouth, eyes challenging her.

"You could show some sympathy for the pain you've caused him, daughter. He is your stepbrother."

"He's the thug who unsuccessfully tried to kidnap me. That's who he is."

Her face lit with a furious heat that she conveyed in her voice. "If we're going to come to any arrangement, Father, then you'll have to learn not to rely on thugs like Otis to do your dirty work."

Sam's eyes glowered over the burning cigar, fired by an inner rage as hot as the red tip.

"Remember your place, girl, and watch your mouth."

"I'm here to make a deal, Father. That's got to mean something. But I'm not doing it with anyone but you."

"You're not in any position to make deals." Her stepfather's voice dripped with ridicule.

"You're in my house. Surrounded by my men. And you'll do what I say."

Sarah stepped forward and placed her hands palms down on the front of the desk Sam occupied like a throne. She leaned forward so she could drill into him at eye level. Her jaw clenched. She knew from the tightness inside that her eyes were diamond bright and relentless.

"I'd have thought you might have learned your lesson last time around, Father. You won't get your way with me by force, or threats of mistreating Mother and Petra. Or by setting my rabid stepbrothers onto me. If you want me to cooperate, we have to talk turkey. You and me."

She glared at Otis, who'd pulled himself up in his chair, erect enough to take a slug from the crystal glass that had replaced the cigar in his left hand.

She leaned even further in, so she and Sam Hollows were almost nose to nose.

"Naked force won't get what you want. You could kill me, but what good would that do you? You still won't get the numbers."

She set her jaw and willed herself to show no signs of doubt or fear. But inside, her stomach churned. She'd never been an actress, but today she had to pull off the biggest performance of her life.

Her father leaned back, seeming to move out of range of her intense challenge, his eyes betraying a flicker of surprise before he withdrew into his usual mask of contempt.

He opened his blubbery lips to speak, but a clatter of feet and shouting interrupted him. Women's voices, protesting, and a male voice overriding them.

The study door burst open and Petra and her mother stumbled in, being hustled and pushed from behind by a man.

Clifford Jensen.

Sarah turned, leaving one arm on the desk to brace herself as she took in his powerful dark figure.

The abject fear of that last night she had spent in this house threatened to engulf her. Her knees sagged. She fought to breathe.

Air sucked out of her chest as if by some involuntary ghostly force.

Sheer terror momentarily blinded her. The arm supporting her on the solid desktop was all that kept her upright.

She steeled herself again and fixed her eyes on the doorway. Her mother stood in front of Petra, holding her chest as if she too was having trouble breathing.

Lottie Hollows had once carried herself with the same regal elegance as her sister, the Countess, but she'd always been of a softer constitution than the resilient Elizabeth.

Her mother's fine, sandy gray-flecked hair hung in disheveled waves over her face. Like her stepfather, her mother had aged ten years in the months that Sarah had been gone.

But it was her eyes that frightened Sarah the most. They were vacant black hollows in a haggard face, registering nothing. She wondered if she even recognized her.

"Rebecca…" Charlotte Hollows staggered toward her, arms outstretched. "Oh, Rebecca. You're home. You came home. And you shouldn't have."

In two steps, Sarah covered the space between them and wrapped her mother in her arms.

She recognizes me.

Hugging Lottie was like embracing a wraith. The bones across her back stuck out through the silk of her dress, fragile and thin. Her mother wept on her neck, great shuddering sobs, her tears soaking Sarah's bare skin.

She spoke in heaving gasps. "It's not safe. Not safe for my darling." She pulled back and gently ran her thumbs down Sarah's wet cheeks.

"I wanted one of us to get free." She gazed wildly around her, seeking her younger daughter.

"It's too late for us. But I so wanted you to stay free. And now it's too late for all of us."

Sarah stroked her mother's cheek, comforting her. "There, there,

Mother," she whispered, quiet enough so neither Clifford nor her father could hear.

"It will all be fine. I'm here now. It will all be fine." She dissolved into inarticulate shushing noises, the sound mothers make when getting a new baby off to sleep.

Slowly, her mother's wild anguish died away, to be replaced by a confused, slightly vacant light in her blue eyes.

Laudanum. Petra was right about the doctor.

She'd heard from Elizabeth how the soiled doves she'd worked with in San Francisco's Tenderloin district often resorted to laudanum to ease their pain.

She remembered Petra's hint in the kitchen about the doctor prescribing her mother medicines. They'd been controlling her with laudanum, and the poor dear hardly knew where she was.

Sarah eyed Petra, standing inside the door, her right arm restrained from behind by Clifford Jensen's iron-fisted left hand.

The right one, she saw with satisfaction, was bandaged. The sisters exchanged knowing looks.

"Well, well," Clifford said in a jeering overtone. "Who do we have here? Come in from out of the cold, have you, Princess? Did life get too hard on the outside?"

Coming off second best to Dolphie's fast draw had not muted his arrogance any.

The fear that had almost overwhelmed her at his entry evaporated, replaced by a fierce indignation at the man's swaggering insolence.

What had Clifford Jensen ever done to earn the right to lord it over others?

"Let her go." Her voice was icy and commanding.

"Make me."

"If you think you're ever going to get me working the numbers again, let her go."

"I'm not only going to get you working the numbers, Princess, but so much more…" He devoured her with his eyes, a starving man contemplating his next meal.

And then, in a moment, he let go of Petra, drew a gun from his jacket pocket, and placed it at the base of Petra's neck, restraining her on the other side with his bandaged hand.

"You'll do exactly as I say or she gets it," he snarled, the jeering replaced by hard-edged contempt.

Before Sarah had time to react, her mother screamed and lunged at Clifford's gun-wielding arm.

Petra tilted sideways. The gun exploded.

Blood and plaster rained down on everything.

Chapter 31

Nessa Murphy beamed like the headlamps on the Central Pacific locomotive when she opened the door and saw Adolphus standing on the threshold. She threw open her broad arms in a delight.

"Dolphie! You've been away far too long. Mrs. Hollows will be so pleased to see you."

Dolphie ducked her embrace and gave her a quick peck on the cheek. "Lovely to see you too, Mrs. M, but we're here on urgent family business." He took a few quick steps into the front hallway and paused. "This is Kaleo. Where's Sarah?" Nessa gestured to the study.

The sound of screams interrupted any further explanation. Then they heard gunshots, two in rapid succession. Nessa threw her hands up to her face and wailed into them.

Dolphie glanced over his shoulder. "Remember our agreement. You keep Petra safe. I'll take Sarah and Lottie."

Kaleo nodded, and they raced down the hall, Dolphie in the lead.

They halted at the closed door, backing themselves against the wall, and pausing briefly to listen.

Sounds of chaos came from inside. A woman screaming. The light patter of falling masonry—probably plaster from the walls or ceiling, damaged by the gunshots. And Sarah's voice rising alongside the other woman's.

"Are you all right? Mother? Are you all right?"

Okay, so the woman screaming was Charlotte.

Dolphie placed one hand on the doorknob. The other held his Remington, cocked and loaded. He fixed Kaleo with a determined stare and silently mouthed. "One, two, three…" He turned the handle and burst in with Kaleo on his heels.

Clifford Jensen stood with his back to them, his gun raised in his left hand, but in the chaos he didn't hear the door open.

Before he knew what had hit him, Dolphie swung his gun around and cracked the butt down on the back of Jensen's skull. The big enforcer crashed to the floor like a heavy sack of potatoes.

An older woman who surely must be Sarah's mother—they had the same blonde coloring and tall, lean form—was standing in the middle of the room bleeding. Her hand pressed against her side was already red and sticky. She was screaming at Sarah to "leave. Leave now.'

Sarah stood unmoving at her side, her arms linked around her mother's waist, seemingly about to drag her clear. Blood stained Sarah's skirts—whether her own or her mother's, Kaleo had no way of knowing.

Petra was crouched on the floor, out of the reach of Jensen, her hands over her eyes, head tucked down protectively, like a bird on a night roost. He took three steps into the room, took her arm in a firm grip, and hauled her to her feet.

She stiffened and gave a terrified cry. "It's all right, Petra. I'm here with Dolphie to get you to safety."

She stared up at him with disbelieving eyes. "I'm your rescuer. The knight in shining armor."

She stood stock still, in shock. He grabbed her hands. "We've got to go."

Petra took a deep breath, flung a last crazed glance around the room and ran with him, light steps at his heels, out of the room, down the hall and out the front door.

As they reached the street, Kaleo thought he heard someone yell Will Davenport's name, but he didn't stop. He kept running, his hand linked to Petra's, so he never lost contact with the young woman they'd entrusted to his care.

It felt so wrong to be running away from Sarah, from Sarah's mother. The pain in his chest increased the further from the house he ran, and he didn't think that had anything to do with his fitness or lack of it.

He prayed as he fled Dolphie would do his bit too, and bring Sarah and Charlotte out alive.

Chapter 32

Clifford had shot her mother! Lottie had risked her life for them. Their gentle mother, who never so much as raised her voice. Nausea hit Sarah in the back of the throat. She suppressed a gagging reflex as she fumbled in her skirts for the pocket Derringer she'd carried since the night of Jensen's attack.

She took three quick steps to her mother's side. Docile, ladylike Lottie was clutching her bloodied side and screaming abuse at her husband, a hollow-eyed druggie no longer. Sarah wondered for a second if the first guise had been camouflage.

"Sam Hollows, may you rot in hell for what you've done to this family!" She bent over in pain and straightened again. "Rot in hell," she gasped out.

Sarah reached her mother's side, her gun pointed a mere foot from Clifford's chest, when the study door behind him swung silently open.

Her eyes flew to Clifford's face, but he seemed to be oblivious. He'd fixed his eyes on her and her little pistol, daring her to pull the trigger.

Men derided pocket-book pistols as "women's weapons" because of their short range, but this close to a beating heart they could still do deadly damage, and God knew she had due cause for revenge.

But he didn't realize. The cavalry had arrived. She sensed, rather than saw, the blow which felled him.

I'm not shooting you this time, buddy. But one day, you rapist bastard.

She turned back to her mother, who was keening her name.

"Bekka… Go. Go now while you've got the chance."

"Not without you, Mother."

Her eyes darted around her in desperation. To Otis, who sat in the chair he'd been in all day, a silent audience. To her father, who leaned back in his chair, his hand under the desk.

"Mother needs a doctor!" She screamed out the words, even as she registered her father was calling for reinforcements. The desk. He had an emergency button under the desk for desperate situations such as a robbery.

Her head was in such a whirl she barely registered what happened next.

Kaleo grabbed Petra's hand and pulled her toward the door.

Jensen went down under a blow from Dolphie.

Then Dolphie was at her side.

"You're coming with me," he hissed in her ear. "There's no time for anything else."

"No…" she wailed. "I can't leave Mother."

Even as she spoke, her mother collapsed, an unconscious heap at her feet.

Dolphie grabbed her by the shoulders. "The Murphys will take care of Lottie," he hissed. He propelled her through the door into the quiet hall. "We need to disappear." He hesitated on the balls of his feet, darting his eyes right and left.

"Father's already pushed the emergency button," she rasped urgently. "I saw him do it a minute ago."

Dolphie acknowledged her with a quick nod and turned left up the stairs. "They're coming from down there," he said, nodding toward the kitchen on the right and the servant's alcove off the front porch. "Your mother's room. Maybe we can hide there."

They flew up the stairs and into her mother's spacious quarters, a bedroom and private sitting room fitted out with a small pianoforte and a book-lined alcove.

She barely registered the pretty four-poster bed with its floral comforter and plumped up cushions, the comfortable seated area where her mother loved to relax and play the piano. She knew exactly what she needed to do.

It had been their secret. A hiding place her mother had created in the original house when their father was alive. Charlotte had always been anxious about their safety, especially if Noah was away on one of his frequent business trips and she and the two girls were home alone.

When her mother married Sam, and his two raucous sons joined the family, they'd held on to the secret. Just for the three girls.

"They'd spoil it," Sarah agreed.

"They stink," said Petra, giggling.

When her mother and Sam started having their frightful rows and Sam slammed out of the house and stayed out all night, the three of them would slip into their safe space and Charlotte would tell stories about courageous woman warriors to keep their spirits up.

Sarah closed the bedroom door behind Dolphie and paused in front of the three-panelled bookshelf. She slipped her hand behind the monster volume of Grimm's Fairy Tales that always sat in first place on the sixth shelf up from the floor.

She felt for the lever the hollowed book concealed, and within seconds, the middle section of the bookcase turned and let them through into the space behind.

"Wow," said Dolphie. "That's pretty neat."

She quickly re-adjusted Grimm's Tales to conceal the handle and pulled the shelves into place behind them.

Dolphie put his finger to his lips as they both sank down the wall to the floor, strung out by the drama of the last few minutes.

Sarah gazed around her, caught in a time warp. The four-poster bed covered with a familiar faded flower print eiderdown stood in the middle of the room. A heavy oak bookcase, shelves near-empty and filmed in dust, ran along one wall, opposite the windows with a view of the garden.

The air smelt shut up and stale. "Probably no one's been in here for years," whispered Sarah. Dolphie put his finger to his lips. "Don't say a thing," he mouthed silently.

They'd been there for what seemed like mere seconds when they heard thundering boots coming upstairs, and then doors banging open and shut up and down the hall.

Sarah registered a familiar voice amongst the rabble of comment that penetrated through to them.

Will Davenport's distinctive nasal New York twang. He seemed in charge of the search, which continued, up and down, in and out, the comments growing louder and more frustrated as they failed to find their quarry.

"They're here somewhere. You can bet on it."

"They've got no food or water. Nowhere to relieve themselves. They'll have to come out, eventually." And finally. Direct appeals.

"Come on, Sarah. Don't be silly. No one's going to harm you."

She grinned at Dolphie and whispered, "Sure. I believe you."

He shook his head. "Amazing, isn't it? They must think you're stupid."

A fixed canvas blind covered the second-floor bay window that faced out from the back of the house, letting in enough light for them to watch as the afternoon faded to evening and then nightfall.

"He's right," Sarah muttered as a silvery moonlight trickled in around the edges of the blind.

"We've got no food or water. But he's wrong about one thing. We have somewhere to pee." She pointed to a ceramic bedpan that sat in one corner.

"Oh well," said Dolphie. "We've got everything we need then. Don't we?" He squeezed her hand and gave her a sickly grin. "Here's hoping Kaleo brings relief as soon as he can."

Chapter 33

De Vile leaned back in his chair and sucked on a cigar. Kaleo and Petra had charged into de Vile's Old Washoe Club rooms on South C Street as he and Elizabeth were sitting down to coffee.

Elizabeth was delighted to see Petra, but her eyes widened in shock when Kaleo explained that Charlotte, Dolphie and Sarah were still—as far as Kaleo knew—stuck in the Hollows' house.

"Charlotte was bleeding. She needs immediate medical attention," he told them. Elizabeth wrapped her arms around Petra, who was wide-eyed and trembling.

"Mother was incredibly brave," Petra said in a tremulous voice. "She walked right up to Clifford and challenged him. I've seen nothing like it."

De Vile ordered more food and drinks from the kitchen downstairs and then gestured to Kaleo to sit in a chair beside him. Elizabeth gathered up Petra and led her to a window seat they could share.

"Let's start at the beginning and you can both tell us what you saw. Slowly. You never know, Dolphie might be back here before you've finished the story. If he isn't, we can decide what to do next once we've heard the facts."

Elizabeth appealed to Hector. "Surely Sam wouldn't leave Lottie without medical attention. He'll have organized something immediately, I'm sure."

Petra stumbled through her version of what happened before Kaleo arrived on the scene, stuttering and anxious. But she had a clear recollection of the events and a shrewd appreciation of the power play at stake.

"Clifford wasn't there at the beginning," she said. "Father said he wanted no one but Rebecca present. He wouldn't let me in, and I didn't realize Otis was already there.

"When I heard Father shouting at Rebecca, I thought I'd better put out the sign that she'd whispered about in the kitchen. She said to do so if she got into trouble."

"And you did that very well," said de Vile with a quick glance in Elizabeth's direction.

She nodded agreement. "You certainly did. Without you, Kaleo and Dolphie wouldn't have known Bekka needed help."

Now, with the tale told, Kaleo studied his father, lounging over coffee, and noted the faint tinge of yellow on the neatly trimmed gray hairs at the corner of his mustache.

What was it with men and their stinking smokes, Kaleo thought irritably. Sam Hollows' study was fogged up so badly you could hardly see across the room. And now they had to endure the same nuisance here.

Impatient to escape the haze, he crossed the room to open the window a few inches. He didn't want to be sitting around talking; he wanted to get out of there and find Sarah.

De Vile grinned and stubbed out the offending tobacco. "You don't like cigar smoke?"

Elizabeth broke in. "I don't know about Kaleo, but I certainly prefer not to have to put up with it this early in the day. Best left for the late-night port when I'm not present."

Petra leaned against Elizabeth's shoulder, silent and withdrawn after her torrent of words earlier. Elizabeth stroked Petra's brilliant auburn hair. Watching the soothing strokes calmed Kaleo.

It seemed like hours since he'd escaped the Hollows' home with Petra in tow, but in fact, it must be only thirty minutes since they'd burst into the senator's suite.

"Did you see Will Davenport?" de Vile asked Kaleo.

"He was there, yes. Not in Sam's study with the others, and we didn't see him, but I heard someone calling his name as we were leaving. He was there somewhere. Being called in to help, no doubt. Why? It doesn't surprise you, does it?"

He recalled the previous night's encounter. Sacramento already felt like a year ago.

"He's a murderer and a cheat."

"Do you know Davenport, Father?"

"Know him?" said de Vile testily. "Of course I know him. He's been working for Bully for months, so I've met him here and there. That's all."

"No, I meant other than that," Kaleo said. "Because he seems to think he knows you."

"What do you mean by that, lad? Did he say something?" De Vile's eyes sparked with interest.

Kaleo shrugged. "Oh, it's nothing. I wouldn't take a turncoat like him too seriously."

"Let me be the judge of that. What did he say?"

Kaleo felt the muscles across his abdomen tighten. He suddenly felt reluctant to say any more, but de Vile was glaring at him with gimlet eyes.

"Last night. When I rescued him—a lot of thanks I got for it— he called you a murderer. And a cheat. Said I'd regret trusting you."

He stared straight into de Vile's surprised face. "Have you any idea why he'd say such a thing?" Kaleo asked.

De Vile shook his head and laughed, as if delighted by the charge.

"None. But if I worried about every slander spoken against my name, I'd never sleep at night. He's worrying a badger in his hole until he comes out to fight."

Kaleo frowned. "Pardon? I don't understand."

"He's picking a fight. For what purpose? Only time will tell."

"Hector's made a lot of enemies during his years in public life," said Elizabeth soothingly. She patted Petra's head.

The girl's eyes were ringed in dark shadows. Her teeth worried her bottom lip.

"Let's get back to the urgent business, shall we?" said Elizabeth. "Sarah and Lottie? What are we doing about them? Dolphie shows no signs of returning."

De Vile gave a heavy sigh. "You're right, as usual, Elizabeth. Seems to me we're in a damned tough spot because we don't know where any of them are.

"Sarah, Dolphie, or Charlotte. We can't go charging in there claiming they've detained them."

"We can't stand aside and do nothing either," said Elizabeth with an exasperated tone. "From what Kaleo says, Lottie needs medical attention. The least we can do is call and ask after her welfare. Ask them which doctor or hospital they've taken her to."

Elizabeth paused, then continued, as if struck by a fresh thought. "We could take Sheriff Roger along with us. He could say he was checking on reports of a disturbance. He's satisfying himself that everyone in the house is safe. Hollows surely couldn't object."

"Let's get going then," said Kaleo, straightening up from where been sitting next to his father.

De Vile raised his bushy brows derisively. "Get going? You're not going anywhere, lad. I want you to stay here and protect Petra. You did an excellent job of getting her out of there. Now we need you to make sure she stays alive."

"But Sarah…"

"Dolphie will take fine care of her wherever they are. You turning up there would only aggravate things. Particularly if Davenport is still kicking up dust."

Elizabeth's face softened in sympathy. "He's right, Kaleo. You're best to stay here and keep Petra's spirits up. Hector and the sheriff can do the rest. They won't dare attack them."

Kaleo took in Petra, whose eyes sparkled with unshed tears.

Elizabeth rose and gently detached herself.

"Kaleo won't let anything happen to you, sweetheart," she said in a low, melodic voice.

"You stay here and try to rest while Hector and I find out what's happening with your mother."

***

A loud hammering came at the door of Hector de Vile's rooms. Kaleo's eyes flicked from the card game laid out in front of Petra to the door. No one outside the family knew they were here.

Hector and Elizabeth had left ten minutes ago, and he had been trying to teach Petra how to play euchre, although the poor kid was too distracted to concentrate.

The banging came again.

Kaleo froze. No mistake, it seemed. Unless Sarah was sending a message.

"Kaleo, I've got to see you."

Will Davenport's voice.

Petra's eyes flickered to his, seeking reassurance. They were marine in this light, more blue than green. The thought of home flashed for a moment until he remembered home was never like this.

He ushered her into the bedroom, putting a finger to his lips and shutting the door soundlessly behind her. Then he swept up the cards and shoved them behind a sofa cushion, out of sight.

With Petra clear and the cards no longer visible, he moved to the door on silent feet, gun drawn.

"What is it, Will?"

Silence, a sense of hesitation, and then Will spoke. "I've got to see you, Kaleo. Sarah's in danger."

"Really? Tell me something I don't already know."

"No, you don't understand. Her project. The secret project. She's gone missing and something's come up she needs to know about."

Project? What secret project?

Kaleo faltered. If there was one thing he knew about Sarah, it was that she was a woman of secrets.

"I know nothing about secret projects, Will, and I'm confident you've got a much better idea of where she is than I do.

"Go back to your friends in D Street, before I call the club security and tell them you're making a nuisance of yourself. You, and whoever else you've got there with you."

"No, Kaleo. You've got it all wrong. I'm here alone, and I'm not your enemy."

"You're working with Clifford Jensen, who is Sarah's enemy. Did you know he was coming to abduct her, Will? Did you tip them off and then play at heroics that first night, all for show? You already knew what he was up to, didn't you?"

A long silence.

"No. No, I didn't." Will's voice sounded genuinely stressed. There was a shuffling sound against the door, like a body leaning into it. "Have you ever heard the saying 'The enemy of my enemy is my friend,' Kaleo?"

Kaleo shivered. This was all too weird. "I haven't, Will. Now you'd better leave. I've got no interest in talking to you."

"You're making a big mistake. I'm not your enemy. I'm not Sarah's enemy either."

"Then why are you in cahoots with Sam Hollows and his cronies? They're certainly no friends of Sarah's, even if Hollows is her stepfather."

"Because of that saying. The enemy of my enemy is my friend. And Hector de Vile is my enemy."

Kaleo turned away in disgust. "You're talking in riddles, Davenport. Go away. I'm not interested."

"I know he's your father, Kaleo. I know you're in the first flush of infatuation at discovering a big important man like the senator is your father. You think it's going to be so wonderful to find the family you've always wanted?"

Kaleo heard a rustling noise, a sound of fabric against wood, and the door shuddered slightly. It sounded like Will had put his back to the door and slid down it. He could sense him sitting on the carpet on the other side.

What was it with this fellow? Was he mad?

"I can tell you what it's like to have Hector de Vile in your family. It's a nightmare. He's worse than Sam Hollows, worse than Clifford Jensen. At least they don't murder people."

Kaleo wrenched the door open. Will half fell into the entry. He was alone.

"I don't know what the heck you're going on about, but I don't want you making a spectacle of yourself out here. It reflects badly on us."

He waved Will inside with the gun barrel.

"You've got ten minutes to tell me what you're on about, and then you need to get the hell out of here."

Chapter 34

The suite smelled of de Vile. The scent of an old rich man and his wealth. Of the creams his fortnightly manicurist applied to keep his nails in perfect condition; and the resiny cologne, imported by a French emporium in San Francisco and supplied to only their most exclusive clients.

It oozed from him—the Rogue Baron odor of leather and mine damp and the best Spanish port. And the sweat of the poor.

Will fought the urge to pinch his nose to stop the memories that came with that aroma. His grandfather's house smelt of it, too. He'd noticed a faint whiff of it when the Big Man visited Bully, but nothing as overpowering as here in the suite de Vile regularly occupied on his political tours.

"This place smells of him. De Vile, I mean."

Kaleo shrugged. "It's a rich man's hangout. Nothing different from a hundred other hotel rooms like it."

Oh, but it is. When it's the smell of the man who killed my father and my grandfather, it's very different.

Kaleo gestured toward the sofa with his revolver. "Sit down and tell me what the heck's going on, Will. And stop talking crazy."

He pulled a pocket watch from the inside pocket of his jacket and checked the time. "Start talking. You've got ten minutes."

Will leaned forward, elbows on his thighs, hands clasped under his chin, in a confessional pose. "How can I make you believe I mean no harm to Sarah? My sole interest in all this is Hector de Vile."

Kaleo shook his head in irritation. "See, that's the part I don't get, Will. You had a good job with Bully—and Hector has a small share in Pike Consulting.

"If he's such an ogre, wouldn't he make sure you didn't get a job with the company? How come you have it in for Hector?"

"Will Davenport isn't my real name. He doesn't know who I am. Believe me, if he did, I'd never have got a job there."

Kaleo gave a bitter laugh. "Now, why doesn't that surprise me? First Sarah, now you. What is it with you people in California? Are you not satisfied with the name you're born with?"

He laid the gun across his knees. "Or is that another little thing you and Sarah have in common?

"You're both there under false pretences. Did you have little parties after we'd gone home at night, where you laughed at how dumb we all were to not guess you were incognito?"

Kaleo is hurting something terrible at being left out of the story.

Will was on a high cliff edge with wild dogs at his back and no choice but to jump.

"It wasn't like that." A bone-wearying fatigue seeped through him, and he was suddenly grateful to be sitting down. "I had to use another name. De Vile was hardly going to welcome me in if he knew who I was."

He hesitated. Kaleo was losing interest. He was gazing into mid space, flicking his fingers impatiently, as if limbering them up to be quicker on the draw.

Kaleo came back to himself and darted a testy squint in Will's direction. "It's all sounding too much of a shaggy dog story to me,

Davenport. Get to the point, will you? Ten minutes, I said."

Will took a deep, anxious breath. "I suppose the fact that he killed my grandfather and stole my father's inheritance might have something to do with it."

"He what?" Kaleo collapsed against the back of the chair he'd perched on and ran his free hand across the top of his head. He smoothed his hair held in a ponytail as if to calm himself.

"He killed my grandfather. And he stole my father's inheritance."

Kaleo raised his brows in disbelief. "Start with the part where he killed your grandfather. How's that supposed to have happened?"

"He got thrown out of the de Vile family when he was a teenager. His father was Rolf de Vile, and he owned De Vile and Sons. They were one of the biggest import-export houses in New York twenty years ago."

Kaleo leveled him with a skeptical gaze. "And today?"

"Today we don't exist, thanks to Hector."

"I can't see how it's Hector's fault when he was on the other side of America all that time. But that's where you got your training in the business?"

"There was a shadow of an agency left—enough for me to get a bit of experience."

Kaleo still appeared unwilling to believe him. He peered at the watch again and then tucked it back in the pocket of his soft suede jacket.

"And how is de Vile supposed to have killed your grandfather?"

"They had a big argument when he came home to demand his share of the business. He stabbed my grandfather. Grandmother didn't want any scandal, so they kept it quiet. The family doctor signed it off as a heart attack. But my mother told me the true story of what happened. Hector did it."

Kaleo seemed to weigh his words, maybe finally taking him seriously.

"Why didn't your father carry on with the business? It sounds like he was the 'favored son' in all this."

"You don't understand. My father was counting on inheriting everything. De Vile spoiled all that. When he killed my grandfather, it destroyed my father too. He broke down. He died of grief."

Kaleo got up suddenly and paced the rug in front of the fireplace. Back and forth. Hands behind his back, but the gun still held in one of them.

"You must have been a kid when all this happened, Davenport. You didn't actually see any of it, did you?"

Will's heart pumped harder. "No, I didn't, but my mother did. She's told me the entire story. Many times. I tell you, you don't know who you're dealing with. De Vile is a killer."

Kaleo came to a decisive stop. "I'm not interested in ancient family vendettas and who's right and who's wrong. I'm interested in the now and in making sure Sarah's safe. And that Charlotte gets the medical attention she needs. What's the story about that?"

"Mrs. Hollows? They called a doctor. I didn't stay around to see what happened next. Sarah? As I keep telling you, I don't mean her any harm. I don't know where she is. I thought you would."

Will's eyes narrowed with pleading. "As I've been trying to explain. I've got to find her. There's something I need to tell her."

Kaleo let out a long, disbelieving breath. "Secret projects. Family vendettas. You've got a colorful imagination, I'll give you that. I'm not sure why you're wasting my time with this stuff. I don't believe a word of it. Now get out."

Chapter 35

The door to Sam Hollows' study stood wide open. Hollows sat at his desk holding a steel nib pen, the inkwell at his elbow, horned-rimmed glasses slipping off his nose. In the far corner next to the windows, Otis hunched over a chessboard, setting out the pieces for a new game. Clifford watched.

George Murphy led them in, clearing his throat to announce visitors. All three men stared with narrowed eyes, and Elizabeth had the odd sensation that the room itself was holding its breath at their arrival.

Hollows rose and pushed back his chair with a muffled scrape of legs on the carpet. Clifford gave the senator a knowing smile, intended as much for his own private amusement as a greeting.

Elizabeth sniffed the room. A heavy fog of cigar smoke obscured a view of the ceiling and upper shelves. She detected the faintest whiff of spilled whiskey, but she could see no evidence of a shoot-out on her first cursory glance around.

No blood on the Persian rug, no overturned chairs or damaged upholstery. Any remnants of the fight Petra and Kaleo had described in vivid detail—the skirmish which wounded Charlotte—had disappeared.

She fixed Sam with her sternest gaze and with no preliminaries demanded, "Where is she, Sam?"

Hollows gazed over his glasses with a distant air, as if she'd interrupted him in detailed calculations which were taking up all his brainpower. Working out the monthly losses on the Uncle Sam mining stocks, Elizabeth thought sourly.

She surveyed the ceiling and saw one detail Hollows and his henchmen couldn't conceal. The elegant plaster molding that encircled one of the room's three chandeliers was bullet-scarred. Several of the once sparkling lights dangled from the fitting, doused and dead.

"Where's who, Elizabeth?" Hollows bore a bemused expression, the picture of a wealthy magnate interrupted going over his books on a quiet afternoon.

"I'm not sure who you're talking about. Marching in here, making demands."

"I'm asking after your wife, as you well know. I have an eyewitness report that someone wounded her in here earlier today."

Elizabeth's eyes moved to where Otis and Clifford sat. They had stopped their game and eyed her and Hector with thinly disguised dislike.

Sam brought his hands up to a prayer position in front of his mouth. "An eyewitness report, you say? Well, I never. Who have you been talking to?"

Hector stepped forward, blocking Elizabeth's unhindered view of the man standing behind the big leather desk.

"Come on, Sam. Let's not play games. Naturally, Elizabeth's concerned when she hears Lottie's hurt. She wants to be reassured she's receiving good medical attention and being made comfortable. We trust it's nothing serious."

Sam Hollows made a conciliatory gesture with his hand. "Sit

down, Hector." His smile didn't reach his eyes. "You too, Elizabeth. I admit. There was an unfortunate incident, but no lasting harm done."

He cast a significant glance toward Clifford and Otis before turning back to them. "That bothersome fellow you're apparently calling your son… It's all his fault."

De Vile objected, but Sam waved him off.

"Have some tea and then you can satisfy yourselves that Lottie is receiving the best of care. An unfortunate incident, but one of those things."

Elizabeth remained standing, her hands inserted into the muff she'd brought for the carriage ride. Despite the fire smoldering at Hollows' back, the room was chilly.

"We don't have time for tea, Sam. We want to see Charlotte. And Sarah. She's still here too, is she not?"

"Sarah?" Hollows' eyes were icy.

"Oh, you mean my daughter, Rebecca? I'd rather like to know where she is myself. She left with the Hawaiian, I believe." He opened his palms up in a gesture of giving. "If I knew her whereabouts, I'd be the first to tell you," he replied, his eyes wide with innocence.

"And Lottie?"

Sam shifted uncomfortably, and then renewed confidence filled his sails.

"She saw the doctor earlier today, and he recommended full bedrest and absolutely no visitors. His specific instructions. I'm sorry, Elizabeth, much as I'd like to, I can't let you see her. You'll have to take my word for it. She's enjoying total rest and some of Mrs. Murphy's excellent chicken soup."

De Vile broke in. "We can come back with the sheriff if you insist, Sam. He's out on another job at present, or we would have brought him with us this time."

Sam hesitated for a long minute, then shrugged. "They don't believe me." He was addressing Clifford Jensen. He shook his head at de Vile.

"Such an unnecessary fuss, Hector. Clifford, take the lady upstairs to see my wife. Meantime, Hector, what's all this nonsense about 'changing the laws to protect investors'? Aren't the investors perfectly well protected as it is?"

As Elizabeth followed Clifford's footsteps up the wide carpeted staircase to the first-floor suite, she pondered the many afternoons she had spent drinking tea here with Charlotte.

Sam and Charlotte's marriage had always been one of convenience for both of them. Charlotte, a widow with two young daughters, of good family and moderate estate, in need of a husband to provide security—physical if not emotional, for herself and her girls.

Sam, a widower, and a rising business success, who needed a wife to run his home and discipline two unruly sons who were a few years older than Charlotte's girls.

It should have been a union that worked. Charlotte was an elegant, measured woman who knew how to manage servants and establish their social credentials as a successful young couple on the rise.

Except Sam had the same impatient blood he'd passed on to his sons, greedy for instant wealth, careless about legal niceties, always ready to play fast and loose if he could see personal benefit. And Charlotte was not cut out to manage rambunctious boys.

As the dissatisfaction set in, Sam belittled Charlotte's good breeding, and humiliated her with a parade of cheap floozies who hung off his neck at the gambling halls and booze parlors which were his favored haunts.

He allowed his sons to ride roughshod over Charlotte's wishes at home, and gradually the marriage had descended into one of dignified disillusionment on Charlotte's side, and a demeaning disregard from her loud-mouthed husband.

Elizabeth followed Clifford into Sarah's private sitting room with its small piano, comfortably paired with yellow and mist-green sofas and a book-lined wall. Charlotte's spacious bedroom was next door, double-hung windows letting in shafts of sunshine and a view of the tree-lined street at the back of the house.

Lean out some distance from the windows, Elizabeth knew, and you'd glimpse part of Petra's beloved aviary on the floor below. Except not today.

She'd followed behind Clifford in silence, their footsteps soundless on the thick carpet. The sitting room was empty, a faint fragrance of Earl Grey tea lingering from the tortoiseshell tray loaded with a rose-painted china teacup that sat on the occasional table separating the two lounge suites.

Clifford stopped abruptly as they reached the bedroom. Remembering she was on his heels, he briskly stepped aside to let her into the room first. It took only a second for her to understand the reason for his display of good manners. The bed was empty, the pulled-back linen the only hint of anyone recently in bed.

"She must be in her bathroom," said Clifford. "Though she shouldn't be out of bed at all."

The occasional table beside the bed held another tray—this one large and silver, on which sat a bowl of clear chicken broth. The smell of rosemary and thyme, celery and onion lingered over the uneaten dregs, golden melted butter congealed around a spoon sitting in the cooling dish.

Elizabeth stepped around Clifford and put her hand on the soft bottom sheet. The mattress dipped in a gentle impression of a recent body. Her hand smoothed over the fine cotton depression, picking up a lingering sense of body warmth. As she turned away, she saw a faint smear of pink. Blood, she was sure.

"Someone's been here recently," said Elizabeth.

She scanned the room. Everything seemed in its usual place. A cluster of silver-framed daguerreotypes on the wide dressing table. Sam and Charlotte on their wedding day, Charlotte in a slender cream satin and a halo of flowers across her forehead, Sam broad shouldered and immaculate.

Alongside them, portraits of Rebecca and Petra, along with Charlotte's silver-backed hairbrush and hand mirror. On the table on the opposite side of the bed, a copy of Jane Eyre bookmarked a third of the way through.

Nothing appeared out of the ordinary. She stepped across to the corner where a water closet and basin sat in a private cubicle. She tapped on the door, and when there was no answer, she tentatively opened it. Also empty.

She searched Clifford's face. Was this an elaborate setup, and Charlotte had never actually been here? Sam Hollows loved to be the man in control, and she knew he enjoyed boorish practical jokes. Was this one of his unfunny japes?

"So where is she?" Elizabeth asked. "I'm far from reassured by what I see. Or more accurately, don't see."

Clifford backed away to the door, shaking his head. "She was here. The doctor saw her here. In that very bed."

"I could believe you. But where is she now?"

Clifford turned and exited the room. A second or two later, he heard him bellowing from the top of the stairs. "Mrs. Murphy? Mrs. Murphy! Come here this instant."

A long delay. Then the urgent sound of feet thundering up the stairs. Not only Mrs. Murphy, by the sound of it, but a small army.

"Yes, sir?" said a breathless Nessa Murphy; her husband George was hard on her shoulder. "Is something wrong, Mr. Clifford?"

Jenny, Lottie's personal maid, trailed behind the Murphys, her face pale and anxious.

Clifford led them through the sitting room to where Elizabeth stood. "So where is she?" He glared around the small band. "Why isn't Mrs. Hollows in her bed, as the doctor ordered?"

The trio gaped. George Murphy, at the back of the group, flicked a nervous glance behind, back into the sitting room.

As he caught Elizabeth's eye, he blinked.

Elizabeth closed her eyes, momentarily at a loss for words.

I believe George knows where she is.

She watched Clifford Jensen as he ranted on, his voice raspy and perplexed. She was confident the empty bed genuinely dumbfounded him.

It came to her in a flash of intuition that Sam Hollows would be furious. This wasn't one of his practical jokes, and Sam never liked to have the initiative stolen.

She searched the surrounding faces. Nessa and Jenny were red faced and astonished. George? She caught his eye again, too briefly to read his expression.

Clifford Jensen. She'd caught his rising pitch when he'd spoken. Clifford Jensen was frightened. And she didn't think it was only because of Charlotte's disappearance.

Chapter 36

Kaleo paced restlessly up and down the front walk of the Old Washoe Club, impatiently awaiting the senator's arrival back from the Hollows' house. Not only was he desperate for news of Sarah, but he also awaited with mixed excitement and dread the bombshell he was about to drop about Will's true identity.

"He's your nephew. Did you have any idea?"

He rehearsed it in his head as he trod a worn track up and down the street, illuminated as it was by gas-powered lamps which burned day and night.

He tried to imagine what de Vile's reaction would be. Did he have any inkling this was the case? He was famed for his spider web of informants that kept him primed of anything momentous, and Kaleo shivered at the thought of breaking this piece of news. He would be the one telling the senator something he didn't know—and his heart was in his mouth at his likely reaction.

He was leaning against one of the marble doorframes, idly surveying the passing crowd, when Hector and Elizabeth emerged from their carriage at the curb's edge. He hurried forward, ready to assist, eager to hear their news, but as soon as he drew alongside, he picked up their dark mood.

Hector's grim expression and Elizabeth's quiet, worried air told him that things hadn't gone well. They were not ready to embark on any conversation, at least until they got into the privacy of Hector's suite. Maybe not even then.

"Order some coffee and then follow us upstairs, will you, Kaleo? Tell Waterman I want the usual."

Hector took Elizabeth's elbow in a protective gesture and nodded toward the maître d' who stood in his black tie and tails near the front desk. "Waterman will see to it. Put it on my account."

"Certainly, Father. Be with you shortly."

When Kaleo entered the room a few minutes later, Elizabeth and Hector were semi sprawled on velour sofas, plainly wearied by their encounter.

"That bad, was it?" He took an armchair next to Hector. "You need a stiff brandy instead of coffee."

De Vile gave him a weak smile. "Perhaps 'as well as' rather than 'instead.'"

Elizabeth matched his wan smile. "Has Petra been all right? Where is she?"

Kaleo nodded. "She's slept all afternoon. The strain of being in that house is taking its toll."

Elizabeth nodded. "I can quite believe it. Even more so now than before."

Kaleo felt his heart turn over. "Why? What's going on there?"

There was a knock at the door and a manager and a younger house boy arrived with trays loaded with a silver coffeepot and cups and cocktail snacks from the bar. The portly manager bowed. "Fritto misto, Senator, sent with Mrs. Benson's best wishes."

Kaleo sprang to the door and ushered them in.

"One of their specialities," said de Vile with a smile. "Tiny logs of batter filled with a surprise—a piece of artichoke heart, or chicken liver or brains, or some other tidbit."

He turned to the server. "Thank Mrs Benson for us. We've all had a demanding afternoon and it's most appreciated."

They fell silent as the staff placed the refreshments down and offered to pour the coffee.

"Don't worry, we can manage," said Elizabeth. "Thank you for the prompt service."

They waited for the door to close, and then Kaleo couldn't restrain himself any longer.

"Is Sarah safe? Is her mother all right?"

Elizabeth shook her head slowly, her lips turned downward. "I'm afraid we don't know the answer to either of those questions."

"What do you mean?" Kaleo's innards twisted like octopus tentacles.

"We didn't see them. Sam Hollows claimed he didn't know where Sarah was. And when we went to see Charlotte, who was supposedly resting under the doctor's instructions, she'd vanished."

She turned to de Vile. "As I've already told you, I believe Clifford was as astonished as I was that she wasn't there. I don't think he was putting on an act."

Kaleo jerked to his feet. "Then what…" He gazed at his father. "What are we going to do? We can't leave it like that, surely? Call in the sheriff. Have the house searched. We have to do something."

De Vile picked up the steaming coffee cup Elizabeth poured, studied the savories for a few considered seconds, and plucked one up from the plate.

"Hold your horses, boy. Elizabeth and I have already decided the situation might be a lot more complicated than we'd thought. We need to think our next step through carefully."

Elizabeth gestured to a freshly poured cup. "Here you are, Kaleo. Help yourself to cream and sugar."

"What's so complicated? They were in that house and now they've gone. Hollows, Jensen—someone must know where they are."

Elizabeth tilted her head to the side, like a wise sparrow considering its next meal. "I believe someone does, Kaleo. And we'll tell you all about it over dinner. What have you been up to all afternoon, apart from pacing the floor and worrying about everyone else?"

It was at that moment Kaleo recalled it. The earth-shattering news he had for his father.

He planted himself in front of de Vile. "You won't believe this, Father." Kaleo's throat was hot and tight, and his words came out pinched and slightly strangled.

De Vile's eyes lifted, picking up on the charged excitement in Kaleo's voice. His father fixed him with coal-black eyes that seemed to read a man's innermost thoughts.

"Believe what?"

"Will Davenport was here this afternoon."

De Vile's brow furrowed. "Hell's bells," he said. "What did he want?"

"Your head, it seems. He claims he's your nephew."

A flare lit de Vile's eyes, a sapphire arrow of shock that registered and then quenched. Like a flaming torch doused in a barrel of cold water.

"My nephew? Good God. Whatever will he be claiming next?"

Chapter 37

A skinny man with ginger mutton-chop sideburns was waving a finger in Will's face and chiding him.

"Come on, Davenport! Keep up!"

O'Grady. Liam O'Grady. That's the fellow's name.

O'Grady was a printer for Virginia City's much-admired newspaper, the Territorial Enterprise, published nightly on a steam-powered press which was the pride and joy of the entire town. Proving, beyond any doubt, that Virginia City could match any new-fangled inventions found in much bigger cities.

That's what they'd told him, anyway. And from what Will recalled in the jumble in his head caused by too much alcohol—he never drank, for goodness' sake, and they'd plied him with hard liquor all night—Virginia City's engineers didn't just match the rest of the world.

Rather, they led the world in the ingenuity they brought to dragging billions of dollars' worth of silver out of the gluggy blue mud on which the insubstantial township sat, rows of single-storey weatherboards splayed across the hillsides in the shadow of Mount Davidson.

By nothing but the grace of God, he remained upright and steady, despite the fuggy cloud in his head. He slid the mug of foaming dark Guinness back to his new friend.

"I'll be fine, O'Grady. I've had enough. I haven't been in training like you fellows."

O'Grady nodded understandingly and happily lowered his ginger whiskers to the rim of the returned handle, picking up a smudge of white foam on his mustache as he did. He wiped his face with the back of his hand. Relaxed. Unconcerned.

"Sure thing. Ye be a mighty fine fellow anyhow. Any friend of Sam's is a friend of the Territorial."

"Oh? Is that so?"

Will cast a sidelong glance back down the table. A few chairs distant, Sam and Clifford engaged in an intense discussion with the man he'd been told was the Territorial's owner, Joe Goodman.

He was in one of the swankiest premises in the city—Barnum's Restaurant, frequented nightly, as he'd been told, by the mining magnates who owned the biggest producing silver mines—and regretted he was not in a fit state to take advantage of it.

He could hardly keep track of the places they'd cycled through as Sam and his offsider picked up on the latest gossip from various acquaintances. The hairiest of them had been a place called The Howling Wilderness—scarier than any bear-infested, snow-covered pine forest, as far as Will could tell.

It felt like a lifetime ago that he'd willingly complied with Sam's insistence that he must introduce him to C Street—the town's major thoroughfare—by celebrating with a typical night out on the town. It was said that every second door on C Street opened into a saloon, and Will Davenport could certainly believe it.

They'd shot a man dead in the "entertainment hall" out the back of the Howling Wilderness last week. Or so he was told. The city coroner couldn't attend to the body immediately and the man had lain where he had fallen, dead as a dodo, half under the billiard table, half out, while players stepped around him intent on their game. They'd explained the earliest the coroner could get there was well into the next day.

This place is unbelievable.

Amidst the hurly-burly of Barnum's—with the hooraying and the friendly jibes of fast mates, the Hollows crew was still conducting business, and he objected to being left out.

Did they really not know where Sarah had gone, or were they lying to him when they disclaimed any knowledge of her whereabouts?

He quaffed from a big water jug on the table in front of him and watched the unfolding scene, wondering how to break into the select little group.

Territorial editor Joe Goodman was a local legend, considered by all and sundry—well, everyone except bank boss William Sharon— to be the first citizen of the Comstock, a friend of the slain President Lincoln who'd read a poetic tribute he'd written at Lincoln's memorial service. That was a few years ago now, but they related the story to Will within the first few hours of drinking.

How many hours ago is that now?

The Howling Wilderness had a cheap pine bar and a modest range of black bottles lined up on a flimsy shelf behind. Barnum's, by comparison, was spacious, with a walnut bar backed by massive mirrors and glittering rows of decanters.

The "room out the back" was no brawling gambler's den, but a cozy retreat where the owners advertised their distinguished clientele could "have a quiet little game of chess or euchre with a friend."

He'd drunk one too many of the deadly Sazerac's, a lethal cocktail brought to the town from New Orleans, the place where it originated, by Julia Bulette, Virginia City's first and most beautiful courtesan.

Bulette had died a miserable death a couple of years back, strangled by a jealous lover, but the blend of cognac, absinthe bitters, and sugar with the kick of a mule lived on.

He caught Clifford's eye and the mine owner beckoned him over.

"Will," Clifford shouted down the table, yelling above the roar of general conversation. "Come and meet our good friend Joe Goodman."

Will needed no second invitation. The luck of the Irish must have rubbed off on him tonight, because miraculously his head cleared on cue with Clifford's invitation. He wouldn't wait for a second.

The dark eyes that fixed on him like a hawk on prey sparkled with intelligence. The slim, tall figure of Joe Goodman as he rose to take his hand left Will momentarily dazzled. He had a sudden sense that this man understood power and how to use it.

The owner-editor's dark hair lay smoothed back from the hint of a widow's peak above a wide forehead. Dark brows and a matching neatly trimmed mustache sat above a finely chiseled chin.

The newspaperman carried himself with sure confidence. With a slight smile, he took Will's measure, like a cat observing a bird. Will cast a nervous eye over his shoulder, suddenly aware he was in the presence of a man of iron will and purpose.

There were almost no women present, but he was certain when they were, Joseph Goodman was at the center of their attention.

"Will Davenport, is it? And what brings you to the Comstock, Mr. Davenport? Not dreams of instant wealth, I hope?" Goodman's deep-set eyes twinkled with kindly mockery.

"Unless you've got someone like William here on your side." Joe turned and gestured to the man sitting next to him at the long table, with eyes as deep set and intelligent as his own. "Or should I say Dan." Piercing eyes flicked his way with a polite nod. "Dan de Quille."

De Quille, The Territorial's most famed journalist and the man who "discovered" Mark Twain, was better known by his pen name than the name he'd been born with, William Wright.

Joe Goodman paused long enough to swallow another draught of beer. "You've heard of him, I'm sure. He's known throughout the land, our mining editor. The Territorial wouldn't be half the paper it is, without his profound knowledge of the Lode in its every detail. He's the best-informed man on diggings anywhere in California and Nevada."

The man in question turned back to his glass and the conversation he had been engaged in.

"You're staying with Sam? Been to the Lode before?"

Will shook his head. "My family's from New York. Importers and exporters. I've come West to see what's happening in San Francisco. See if it's worth opening a branch here. I've been working for Bully Pike for nearly a year now."

He broke off and rubbed the back of his neck self-consciously. "I *was* working for him," he corrected. "Before he was murdered. I'm still there, helping. Not sure what will happen next."

Goodman's penetrating eyes bored into him.

Will felt the need to explain. "We haven't heard about Bully's will yet, so it's too soon to say. But I get the impression Clifford and Sam might be interested in buying Pike Consulting if it's for sale." He shrugged. "Who knows?"

Goodman continued to eye him keenly. "If it is for sale, wouldn't the senator be interested? So far as I know, he already has a minority share." The newspaper man drew on his pint and swallowed. "Can't see him agreeing to go into partnership with Sam, though. They've never got on."

Will felt a chill inside. "De Vile? That man has lived a charmed existence. Why he hasn't been found out before now, I'm sure I don't know."

Joe lifted a quizzical eyebrow. "Found out for what? The robber barons might have been ruthless to get where they've got, but de Vile's not by any measure the worst of them. What makes you think he is?"

Will snorted. "I doubt any of them are guilty of murder."

Goodman's dark brows met in the middle. "Are you alleging Senator Hector de Vile is guilty of murder? You'd need pretty hard evidence before it would be worth your while making that sort of accusation too loudly around here. His stocks are very much on the rise in Silver City since he took up the part of small investors."

He grasped Will's arm and guided him to a quiet corner of the bar. "Why do you sound so sure of yourself on this? If it's wild talk…"

"It's not." Will faltered, suddenly unsure of how to proceed. The booze had made him run off at the mouth, and now he didn't know where to go from here.

Goodman stared at him, implacable. "Well then. What's your evidence?"

My mother told me?

Will stared back for several long seconds as he felt the heat rising through him, turning his ears red. He dropped his eyes to the floor, unable to meet Goodman's challenging stare. "Let's say I have inside knowledge."

Goodman shook his head. "You'll have to do better than that, sonny boy."

He leaned back on the bar and surveyed the room. A monarch surveying his domain. No wonder they called him the foremost citizen of the Comstock.

"You see that man there, by the door? He's just arrived—" He drew out his pocket watch. "Quarter past ten. Funny, he usually comes here later than that." He nodded his head toward the door.

The man who'd entered had a drooping handlebar mustache that shadowed a dour, down-turned mouth. Everything about him shouted his disdain for the common crowd.

The receding hairline, the narrowed eyes, the stiffly erect posture, and the immaculately tailored suit. A man who didn't expect to be liked and returned the favor.

"William Sharon. The most hated man on the Lode. Now there's someone who's destroying hundreds of lives, and doesn't care a whit. He enjoys it."

Sharon. A name whispered everywhere in California. Through the Nevada agency of William Ralston's Bank of California, he'd siphoned up control of a dozen silver mines, bankrupting their owners and establishing a monopoly which benefited no one except himself and big money interests.

"He's angling to get Hector's job," Goodman said with quiet venom. "It'll be over my dead body."

***

Sharon. William Sharon. Will leaned into the corner at the end of the bar, glad to have slipped from notice, digesting the impact of the editor's words.

Recognition flooded through him, warming his cheeks. He squeezed his eyes shut against the sudden recall. The Territorial was conducting a vitriolic campaign against Sharon's bid for a Senate seat.

Joe Goodman's editorials excoriated Sharon for "merciless rapacity" and "fastening yourself on the vitals of the state like a hyena." There was no way he was going to get Goodman to go after Hector de Vile when he already had Sharon in his sights.

He scanned the bar. Goodman was only a few feet away, but he might as well have been in a different universe, hauled into the epicenter of another whirlpool of speculation and excitement, surrounded by high rollers and hopefuls fishing for Virginia City's latest hot tips and gossip.

Where the most promising new strike was. What stocks were on the way up, or the way down. The latest mine in danger of flooding. The ore seam that was about to run out—or throw new veins in whatever direction. They hung at Goodman's shoulder for the latest tip.

Will tapped his fingers on the shining walnut surface of the bar, his heart rate beating a faster than normal tom-tom, as he considered his options.

He'd come to California with one purpose. To repay his treacherous uncle for destroying his family. In his mind's eye he saw his mother's face, arrested in a stony fury she was released from only in death. His father, a wraith-like echo of the man he'd once been. Dead at thirty-eight. All because of de Vile.

He rehearsed in his mind the story he had been told by his mother many times. He was a little boy, only four or five, but the calamitous night when his grandfather died remained with him like a childhood nightmare.

He'd never forget being woken by a terrifying dream. His screams had brought his nurse rushing to calm him, but he wouldn't be comforted. He'd broken free from his nurse's grasp and run to his mother.

She and his father were in the drawing room. His father was bending over a man lying still on the patterned carpet. A man with long white hair and a white beard.

His mother was screaming. He knew it was still nighttime because the fluffy red curtains he loved to stroke hung closed across the windows. He grabbed his father's trousered leg. "Papa! Papa!"

Strong arms reached down and scooped him up, held him on a shoulder, facing away from the old man on the floor.

"Will! William…" His father patted his back consolingly. "What are you doing here, son?" He held him for a long time, patting his back while he sobbed.

After a while, his mother stopped screaming. Then the only sound was his mother's sniffles and his father puffing like their old dog Geronimo. And then his father carried him back to his nurse. Placed him in her arms. He'd stroked his face until it stopped being as hot as a burning fire.

"Everything's going to be all right, son. Now you let Nurse Ryan put you back to bed. Everything's going to be all right."

But it never was all right again.

Chapter 38

"Will! There you are. We're ready to move on. One more call and we'll be heading home." Clifford Jensen stood beside him, an inquisitive gleam in his eye. "Are you all right? You look like you've had a bad dream."

Will bolted to his feet like shot out of a gun. "I'm fine. Where to next?"

"The Sawdust Saloon. Bill Sharon has moved on there. He often hangs out there until he knows the Territorial gang has cleared out of here." He shrugged. "You know the story. Like oil and water."

"Ah yes, the famous feud. I heard a bit about it." He picked up his hat and jacket that hung on the seat back behind him. "You'll have to give me the good sauce."

***

"Sam, old chap. The man I want to see." Sharon lifted his whiskey-bearing arm in a wide welcoming arc, without spilling a drop on his impeccably tailored suit.

"Sit down. Sit down," he instructed. He surveyed the nearby drinkers before asking, "You got a drink?"

Clifford responded with no further instruction from Sam. Will followed him as he headed for the bar.

"So, tell me about William Sharon." Will stood beside Clifford while he waited to catch the barman's eye.

"Sharon? He's the one man in town you don't want to get offside with." Clifford sucked in his breath through his teeth, making a whistling sound. "You'll live to regret it if you do. Take my word for it."

Will took in his surroundings while they waited to order. The Sawdust Saloon was right next door to Barnum's, entry by an anonymous mahogany door you could easily miss if you weren't in the know, but he saw in one second that geographic location was the only thing the two venues had in common.

While Barnum's had been brightly lit and heaving with the boasts and salacious laughter of the town's movers and shakers, the Sawdust was hushed and intense, so dimly lit Will could barely make out the man whose influence Sam was seeking to cultivate.

If he squinted through the murk, he could make Sharon's immaculate silhouette at the hub of an all-consuming dark energy, as if every ounce of oxygen in the room was concentrated on the tight circle that surrounded the Bank of California god in his spindle-backed wooden-armed chair.

Despite its plebeian name, he saw instantly this was no one-bit bar populated by porters and mule drivers. Clifford tipped his head in Sharon's direction.

"He's here holding court most nights of the week," he said. "Eats it up. He might be the most hated man in the Lode, but in here they treasure his every word."

He and Clifford headed back a few minutes later with the drinks, and Will watched in awe as Sam Hollows tackled the forbidden topic. Sharon's recent defeat in his bid for the Senate. Sharon shrugged off the commiserations. Sam nodded sympathetically.

"Joe was completely out of line. Like a rabid dog." Sharon took a long, thoughtful draft and licked his lips.

"I'll win next time, if I have to buy the damn paper to do it." He stared at Sam long and hard, as if considering something else entirely. "That's not what I wanted to talk about, though, Sam."

The full-to-overflowing whiskey tumbler Clifford had brought him dangled carelessly between his thumb and index finger, as if the man who controlled millions in bank deposits couldn't care less if his liquor spilled onto the sawdust-covered floor as long as not a drop marred his suit.

He took his time, putting the glass down, and pulling out, tapping, and lighting a cigar before he continued.

"I wanted to ask you. What the heck's going on with the Golden Bowl? You're the man with all the answers. The shares are seesawing all over the place. Last month, they were at nine hundred dollars. Now they're down to one-fifty and still sinking. And yet you're still claiming you've got a bonanza in the works.

"Does someone know something I don't about what's going on down there? Have you had some bad assays that no one's told me about?"

Will felt, rather than saw, Clifford stiffen beside him.

Sam's fingers froze to his glass, and his cheeks noticeably paled at the banker's inquiry. Then he braced his shoulders and his response, when it came, was a tad too robust. "One fifty, you say? Must admit Bill, Cliff and I have been out of town. We haven't been paying much attention.

"But there's definitely no cause for panic. We've got a firm hand on the Bowl. There are no poor results. Quite the opposite, in fact."

He drew in a deep breath and exhaled it out in a booming, dramatic laugh. "No one else is going to be dipping their dirty mitts in there. We've been around too long to let that bonanza slip through our fingers."

Sharon took a long slurp and savored it as he swallowed. He gave Sam a bitter, calculated grin. "That's what I'd hoped to hear, Sam. 'Cause there's no way I'm going to stand behind you if you lose control of the Bowl. You know that."

He lowered his voice to a harsh whisper, so Will could barely hear what he said next.

"You've loaded all the rest of your loans against that as collateral. You remember that." He stared at Sam with black, strangely cold eyes.

For a man who had been proclaiming his "hail fellow well met" confidence only minutes before, he sure was unfriendly now, Will thought.

Sharon threw a quick, shifty glance around him and drew Sam and Clifford into an even tighter circle. Will shuffled forward and leaned in.

"I've been hearing disconcerting whispers of shares changing hands. Of some San Francisco widow who holds a previously secret little packet of the double bangers. If the wrong fellows got their hands on that little haul, you boys could well be in trouble."

Sam darted an anxious glare in Clifford's direction, and then his face crumpled in astonished mirth.

"Bill… what do you take me for?" The words fell in a disbelieving arc, trailing off into uncertainty.

"We've been around… Cliff and I have been here too long to fall for a ruse like that. There's nothing to worry about. Take my word for it."

Sharon slapped him on the shoulder, holding his glass carefully clear of spillage. "Glad to hear it, old boy. You don't know how glad."

Will took a quick step back. No point in being obtrusive. He nursed his iced water and watched the drama unfolding before him, like a moth drawn to a flame.

As Sharon's words sounded around the tight, suddenly quiet circle, he thought back to a day in Pike's cheerful consulting office, the week before they'd all left. And how the usually warm camaraderie of the daily office had evaporated when he'd got too nosey.

He'd ventured into Sarah's office to check on an order he was expecting. She hadn't been at her desk, and he'd leaned over and shuffled through the papers lying on top to see if he could find it.

His eye fastened on a sheet buried down in the pile, covered in Sarah's feminine black handwriting. Her loops and swirls were like no one else's. He leaned over to make out the note she had apparently written herself.

Cassandra Florence Whitecliffe: Widow. 18 Vallejo Street, Russian Hill

Golden Bowl. 1000 shares on her husband's death.

Dolphie—underlined.

The words were ringed with frivolous circles, as if Sarah had played the information over in her mind, ruminating on what to do with it.

Will paused, puzzled by what he was seeing. Why was Sarah interested in Golden Bowl shares?

She was a humble office receptionist. The Golden Bowl was topping out the share prices. Last time he'd checked, they were at $1200. No way could Sarah afford to buy into that hot property.

He felt his brow knit together. He reached and pulled the sheet closer. Maybe he'd read it wrong.

The air shifted almost imperceptibly around him and his eyes stabbed up to the doorway where Sarah stood, hands on hips, her mouth set in a tight line.

"What do you think you're doing?" She was practically barking.

He jumped back, dropping the paper, as if it had suddenly caught fire.

"Um… sorry… um… nothing. I was searching for the purchase order for the Kansas wheat. It hasn't come through yet." His voice sounded wheedling and breathless. "That's all… for the Kansas order."

Sarah stalked over to the desk and shuffled through the top few sheets, whisking one out with unerring confidence. "Here's the purchase order. The rest of it doesn't concern you."

Furious red spots dotted her normally pale cheekbones. Her eyes blazed.

Will was backing out, bewildered by her attitude. He'd never seen her so angry. "Sure. Sure. I'm sorry. I didn't mean to pry."

"Good. There's nothing to pry into."

The memory dissolved. He was back standing next to Cliff Jensen, who was staring from Sharon to Sam Hollows, their eyes locked in silent outrage.

A widow. With Golden Bowl shares. Dolphie.

And suddenly he knew how he was going to destroy de Vile. Now he couldn't rely on Joe Goodman to do it for him.

Chapter 39

Each footstep they took squeaked in the fresh snow as they labored up the slight incline to the Hollows' house, Clifford in the lead, his gait more halting than usual because of the sling he wore to protect his bandaged hand.

Behind him, Sam stomped in slow, powerful strides, his breath rasping, his face florid from their night of heavy drinking. A lifetime of overindulgence had given him the capacity to conceal how drunk he was, but it showed when he needed to exert himself physically, and Will guessed tonight was one of those nights.

Will came up in the rear, wriggling his frozen toes inside his San Francisco street shoes to stop his feet from turning into solid blocks of ice. It was only a short walk back, but he feared frostbite if they didn't get to Sam Hollows' white picket fence soon.

Moccasins were hardly fit for the challenge of Virginia City's heavy snowfalls, and Will hadn't had time to buy more sturdy boots.

But even with his inadequate footwear, he gauged he was in the best shape of the three of them. His head had cleared in the hours since he had swapped the deadly Sazerac cocktails for iced water.

Clifford paused before starting up the front steps, stroking his sling as if easing some discomfort. As he went to take a step, his foot slid on the snow-covered step and he pitched forward, protecting his arm as he fell.

He cursed through clenched teeth as he pushed himself upright with his left arm, brushing the snow off his injured arm as he did.

"Those bastard night watchmen are meant to be keeping this clear," he snarled to Sam. "What have they been doing all night?

"You'd better go and see." Sam scowled. "I need a bedtime brandy."

"For Pete's sake, Sam, there are more important things than grog." He paused on the top step and listened. "And why aren't the dogs barking? We're making enough of a racket."

Will saw then that while the house was open to the street, a second picket fence ran from the front wall of the house out to the fence on either side, enclosing the garden around the house. On the right-hand side stood a small watch house—about the size of mare's stall, with a single shining window lit from inside.

"Come with me to check, Will?" Clifford turned to Sam. "We'll see you inside in a minute."

They ploughed into the uncleared garden, where the snow was much deeper than it had been in town. Will suppressed a groan as freezing wetness leaked in around his ankles and soaked his trousers up to his knees.

This was turning into a right pain, he thought, as Clifford thrust the watch house door open and stared inside. Will peered around him. The warmth that hit them in the face was in stark contrast to the outside temperatures.

Not so surprising then that the two watchmen were asleep, one slumped in a chair in front of a small coke-fired heater and the other with his head in his hands on a table.

Almost simultaneously with Clifford's roar, they ricocheted to their feet.

"Sir," they cried in unison.

"Asleep on the job?" Clifford let rip with a rich flow of profanities. "And where are the dogs?"

One man, a burly fellow who was almost as wide as he was tall, rubbed one eye with his fist. He cleared his throat. "The dogs, sir? They should be out, prowling about like usual."

Clifford whirled around and stared out into the flat, white space. "Do you see any dogs? Hear any dogs? For Beelzebub's sake, man. What's going on here?"

Chapter 40

Sarah peeked through a two-inch chink between the blind edge and the window ledge, open wide enough for the thick jute rope that snaked through the gap, the other end tied around a heavy oak bookcase on the far side of the room.

Minutes before, around midnight, Dolphie had delicately slid the double-hung window up, inch by inch, as silently as was humanly possible to avoid notice from anyone in the yard, until it was open wide enough for Dolphie to ease through, his body stretched to horizontal.

He was lean, taut, his body as tough as the rapiers he wielded. And across his body, roped to his chest, lay Charlotte.

Once clear of the window, he swung to the vertical and slid into a "fireman's chair" he'd set up earlier that day, a skill perfected in years of mountain climbing in the European Alps. Sarah once again marveled at the man's remarkable range of unusual talents.

After they exited, she pulled down the window again with equal care. The tiny open sliver where the rope wound through remained her one promise of freedom. Through it, she listened desperately for the telltale sounds of success or failure.

If all went according to plan, Dolphie would deposit Charlotte safely on the other side of the Hollows' garden fence where Kaleo was waiting with the coach to carry her away to safety.

Dolphie would then sprint back to her and pull on the dangling rope as a signal to her to follow him out. Two pulls for freedom. Two pulls, and she'd clamber out and abseil down the side of the house as fast as she could, trusting on Dolphie to break her fall if she slipped.

One pull? If that happened, she was to haul the rope up as fast as she could, close the window and sit tight.

Charlotte had been the one who'd stowed the ropes there, another of her fey inspirations that "it might be useful one day—like in a fire." Thank goodness her mother was a little fanciful.

Sarah's thighs cramped as she crouched at the window, sniffing at the dark perfume of the night, barely able to breathe for the hard lump in her throat. Late winter air, icy on her cheeks, and perfumed with astringent pine and puffs of fetid mastiff breath from Dancer and Blitzen and extra canines, brought in hours after Charlotte's disappearance.

"He doesn't know where you went," Dolphie mused to Charlotte, his demeanor as unruffled as always. "But he knows for certain he deposited you in that bed upstairs. So, he's making certain no one else gets in or out."

Their escape had become urgent once Jensen discovered Charlotte was gone. It was only a matter of time before Sam mounted a full search and discovered the hidden room. It amazed Sarah he hadn't done it already.

But maybe even more important than that, Sarah desperately needed to get out so she could monitor developments on her Freedom Project. Zach waited impatiently to give her his report on the latest from San Francisco.

She had to know what was happening to the share price, and whether he'd been successful in buying up the widow Whitecliffe's shares.

She wanted to analyze the latest numbers to calculate the optimum moment for announcing to the world what she'd done. How she'd pulled off the stock market coup of the decade and stolen Sam Hollows' most productive mine out from under his nose.

Despite the freezing air leaking in, Sarah's cheeks flushed with warmth. Money was the only power Sam and Clifford understood. She wondered how they would handle bankruptcy.

She heard a soft thud as Dolphie's legs hit the ground. The rope, which had stretched taut, slackened off.

Earlier in the evening, they'd heard the front door slam and then the sound of heavy footsteps tramping down the front steps.

They guessed Hollows and Jensen were going out on the town—something her stepfather and sidekick did most nights of the week. Dolphie and Sarah estimated they wouldn't return until around two a.m.

Any new security men were likely to slack off and find a warm corner to snooze in after midnight. Their perfect window of opportunity would be between midnight and two in the morning.

They had sat in disciplined silence waiting for the low whistle that had come a short time after the men left—Kaleo arriving with the sedative-laced meat for the dogs.

George sent someone to report to Kaleo and de Vile the moment the Hollows party left. There was the soft thump of the deer carcass landing, the eager rush of the dogs skidding across the snowy back garden, competing for meat.

Sarah tensed. She couldn't see anything in the low light, but she could picture it all in her mind.

The house at 146 D Street was the first and only family she'd ever had, theirs long before Sam became their step-father.

Thankfully, because George and Nessa had been with the family so long, they knew all about the secret hidey hole, a fun place for the girls to play with a more serious underpinning, and in the last twenty-four hours George had been a willing and discreet conduit.

If required, she could walk across the room in the dark and put her hand directly on her mother's treasures. As a child, she'd gazed at them as they snuggled into their haven while their mother read them stories. She knew by heart the photograph on the bookcase of Charlotte and Noah on their wedding day.

The young couple, so young, innocent and devoted. She loved the expression on her father's face as he gazed at her mother, one of unconcealed delight that this woman had consented to be his wife. A soft-eyed gaze she had never seen on a man's face when he watched her.

Beside the photo stood a small silver goblet, the cup from which they sipped wine at their modest wedding breakfast with close family. And next to that, a bunch of dried gray-green rosemary, tied by a silver cord and embossed silver-plated tag reading Noah Jonas Pike 1822–1852. The memento from his funeral.

And then it dawned.

This room is a memorial to my father.

She put her eye to the open chink at the blind's edge, resisting the urge to lift the blind even a half inch, because she was superstitious.

I don't want to jinx it.

She'd been sitting in the dark since nightfall, so her eyes were well-adjusted to the lack of light, but even so, it took half a minute to make out the vague shape moving to the back wall.

Dolphie, a faint wraith crossing the glittering snowy back garden, weaving his way to the back fence. Only one set of tracks, so he was still carrying her mother.

Charlotte would be annoyed and apologetic about requiring such help, but she didn't need to. The gunshot had not penetrated deeply, but her grazed rib cage was tender, and there was still a danger of her wound reopening.

She stared out until her eyes watered, trying to interpret the shadows. Dolphie lifted Charlotte over the fence. Kaleo received her on the other side. Dolphie was turning back to the house when he froze in his tracks.

Her eye followed his gaze, and she suppressed a sharp gasp. Bounding across the lawn, as if ready to play a game of tag, was one of the mastiffs.

Even in the dark, she could see its mouth was open, teeth gleaming. It wasn't an aggressive rush, this delighted prancing across the lawn. She recognized Dancer's joyous leaps, and she knew the dog was smiling. However, if she was running free, something had changed.

Dolphie threw a quick peek up to the window, and Sarah knew they were in trouble. Wordlessly, she began hauling in the rope, not waiting for any further signal.

In a few seconds, a dark shadow like that of a giant bat turned and vaulted the back fence. Dancer abruptly halted, went down on her front haunches and barked, as if to say, You spoilsport. Aren't you even going to stop and play?

And then the garden flooded with light, and Blitzen charged in behind his mate, barking wildly, indignant to be left in the rear.

Behind him thundered men. Huge men. Sam and Clifford and other muscle men she didn't recognize struggling in the snow, holding flaming torches at shoulder level, directing their beams here and there. The dogs bounded excitedly everywhere, covering over the traces of Dolphie's footprints.

She was smiling as she pulled the rope in. She hauled the last few inches and eased the window down from behind the blind, willing herself not to give away any telltale sign by bumping it and making it swing. The movement might catch their torch light.

The beam flew up to the ledge as she closed the last half inch. She slumped into herself, barely letting herself breathe out in case they heard from below.

Sam Hollows was not a stupid man. Nor was the domineering Clifford Jensen. It wouldn't take them long to work out what had happened. And then what would be her fate?

A shiver ran through her, which had nothing to do with the cold air from the window. Their discovery of her hiding place was inevitable. They would smash down the wall by first thing tomorrow unless something extraordinary interrupted them. She thought of her secret plan, of the imminent collapse they still didn't know was coming.

An image of a great clay dam, a towering wall of brick and plaster, flashed before her eyes. At the base of the dam, there was a small open plug hole, already leaking. She could picture the water leaking out, now a trickle, a portent of the catastrophe to come.

She needed to get word to San Francisco. She had to tell Zach what to do next. And she couldn't do it from this sealed room that was a mausoleum to lost love.

Chapter 41

By the time they got back inside, Sam had woken George Murphy and the library fire was blazing in the massive stone hearth. Will and Clifford changed their trousers and socks for dry, freshly laundered ones before returning to report to Sam.

"Someone definitely tranquilized the dogs. If we'd been much later, they'd have frozen to death." Clifford's voice shook with anger.

Dancer and Blitzen, together with a couple of imports whose names he didn't know, stretched out on a big Oriental rug to one side of the fire, further away than the men but close enough to get warm.

"Bet you they sedated them with poisoned meat. They were coming round when we arrived back. Their paw marks were all over the back garden, so we don't know what they covered up."

Clifford's dark eyes narrowed. "Sarah. Charlotte... Who knows...?" He took a big sip from the balloon glass in his left hand. "Right now, we've got more pressing issues. The Golden Bowl share price is plummeting. Our shareholders will revolt against any more assessments the way things are going."

Assessments levied on shares were one way mine owners got shareholders to pay exploration costs, hitting them up with extra fees on the promise of coming bonanzas. The Hollows crew had been adept at pumping investor's hopes up.

"And that story Sharon had tonight—about some widow owning a parcel of shares. That's a worry coming from Sharon. His intelligence is rarely wrong."

Sam snorted into his voluminous glass. "Unless he wants it to be. You know as well as I do, he's not averse to planting false rumors if it suits him."

Clifford shook his head. "Nah, I don't think he's doing that this time. He's giving us a warning. 'Sort it out or I'll call in your loans.' And you know damn well in the past he's pulled the trigger on bigger clients than us.

"He didn't get the nickname as the 'most hated man in town' for nothing. We can't afford to take the gamble." Clifford glared at Will, as if appealing for his agreement.

"What do you think, Will? Should we be worrying?"

Here I go… My chance to influence the course of history and get back at de Vile at the same time.

"If someone was trying to influence the Golden Bowl share price, who would you pick to be most likely?" Will asked, ever the new boy.

"Good question," said Clifford. "Someone who was well-versed in the local scene, with an insider's understanding of what influences share prices, and the network in San Francisco to place information with the right people."

"In other words, no one-bit-booster from Idaho?"

"That's right. Why do you ask?"

Will's heart beat faster. Whatever he said now might make things turn very nasty for Sarah if they ever caught up with her. But why should that be his problem?

Sure, she had been a great colleague. He admired her intellect, but she'd lied to them all for her own purposes. He owed her nothing.

"When Mr. Sharon was talking tonight, I suddenly remembered something I saw at Pike Consulting recently. Last week, in fact. It meant nothing to me at the time. I noticed it because it seemed a bit 'off' from our usual line of business."

"Oh, yes?"

Will could sense Clifford's pulse quicken. The little dip at his temples fluttered in and out.

"Yeah. I was searching for a purchase agreement on Sarah's desk and I came across a note there, on Hector's de Vile's letterhead. That's what caught my eye. It was very short.

"I suppose it was in the senator's handwriting. I don't know it well enough to tell." He flicked his eyes to Clifford, who was watching him like a hawk.

He gave a self-deprecating shrug. "It struck me as odd. Very short. A name, an address, and a few other details."

"Uh-huh. And what was it about? Get to your point." Clifford's voice was strained and impatient.

"The heading read 'Golden Bowl Takeover.' And underneath was a woman's name and address and a note. 'Buy Now.'" Will paused for effect, wrinkled up his brow as if genuinely confused.

"It came back to me tonight when Mr. Sharon was talking." He widened his gaze in a guileless question.

"Do you think it could have been the same widow he was referring to? The one with a load of Golden Bowl shares? And if it is, maybe it's the senator who's behind the whole thing?"

In his mind's eye, he saw again the note on Sarah's desk. One of her usual lined foolscap sheets filled with random jottings; reminders of things she needed to do, or snippets worth remembering. Paper covered in a mass of scribbles, and no sign of the senator's letterhead anywhere.

Boohoo. Too bad. He's a murderer who's done wrong to plenty of people. He deserves to pay, even if I have to lie to do it.

He blinked from the firelight to Clifford's eyes. Two onyx pools of malice.

He doesn't believe me.

"Now, why would the senator be bothering to give little Sarah such a valuable tip? If it was good information, he'd be off buying them up himself. He wouldn't be sharing the information with someone like her."

His mouth twisted into a mirthless sneer. "You've lost me there, Davenport. It makes no sense."

Will's middle region squeezed tight, as if caught in a vice. "I didn't say I knew why."

His voice, when it came out, sounded breathless and reedy.

"I know what I saw… I dunno. Maybe he didn't want to be associated in case his name came out. He's trying to be Mr. Good Guy now, isn't he? Courting public popularity."

Clifford shook his head again. "When was this?"

"A week ago. The day before you arrived, if I'm not mistaken?"

"De Vile would never let public opinion impede profit. It's not in his nature to do it."

Sam interrupted them. "I don't suppose you remember the name on the paper? Who this supposed widow was?"

Sam's red-rimmed eyes drooped. The flesh hung off his cheekbones, slack and sneering around his mouth, as if confident Will had hatched some shaggy dog story to impress them.

Will felt his insides relax again. He had a head for facts and figures, and that cryptic note had teased his curiosity.

Besides, the surname rang a vague bell with him. There was the faintest familiarity about it. He had meant to ask around, but with all the upheaval, it had slipped his mind.

"I do, as a matter of fact. It was Cassandra Whitecliffe. That was it. Cassandra Florence Whitecliffe. At 18 Vallejo Street, Russian Hill."

The room took on an astonished stillness. A grandfather clock tick-tocked in the corner, its mahogany case shining, the golden pendulum working ponderously back and forth. It was the only sound in the avid silence. The mechanics whirred, and Will realized it was about to strike.

Bong… It vibrated and rang through the cosy room. Bong… Two. Bong… Three. Then silence. Three a.m.

The last chime died away. The charcoal-haired sleeping dog whimpered and shivered, as if the temporal world disturbed his peace. His back legs twitched, unsettling the mushroom-and-sable bitch alongside him. She scrabbled her paws on the floor to resettle herself.

"Cassandra Whitecliffe?" Sam Hollows had been silent for so long Will had thought he'd dozed off with his dogs. Now his voice boomed in the space: "That would be Jonah Whitecliffe's widow, wouldn't it? Splendid fellow, Jonah. Pity he went as soon as he did."

"Never mind that," Clifford said. "We need to get hold of those shares. Now."

Sam nodded. "Absolutely. You'd better wire Butch as soon as the office opens in the morning."

He glared at Will. "If we miss out on this deal and discover de Vile is behind it, I'll have his guts for garters."

A comforting warmth flushed through Will's body, a sudden release that made him aware of how strung out he was.

At any cost, he told himself. At any cost at all, he'd get his revenge.

And the job's on the way to being done.

Chapter 42

"She told me what she's done." Charlotte Hollows lay back on her plumped-up fine cotton pillows and fixed the enthralled circle around her with glinting sapphire eyes. They held the same determination in her daughter's hazel ones, Kaleo thought.

Charlotte continued: "She's used Sam's strategies against him. He's going to know what it's like to find the scrip he holds is worthless. And he won't like it one bit."

She gave a soft laugh and sank further into her pillows. Kaleo guessed she'd used up most of her strength to make this defiant statement of solidarity with her daughter. Now she needed rest.

Elizabeth leaned over and pulled the covers up around Charlotte's shoulders. She cupped her hand and stroked down her cheek in gentle affection.

"Dearest Lottie. You and the girls have been through an ordeal, but it's ending. The good news is the doctor says all you need to get well is lots of good food and rest, and we're blessed to provide both."

Charlotte shook her head impatiently. "But what about Sarah? You've got to get Sarah. We can't leave her in that house with that man."

Elizabeth stroked Charlotte's arm, long soothing strokes down the pink brushed cotton nightgown sleeve. She flicked a glance over to Petra, hovering on the other side of her mother's bed, her face pinched and white.

"Hector, Dolphie, and Kaleo are working on a good plan right now, Lottie. We won't leave her there for a moment longer than we have to. Isn't that right, boys?"

Kaleo registered weary, deep lines around Elizabeth's eyes. Her mouth turned down at the corners, and her voice, despite her bravado, had a flat tone. Elizabeth Westerhoven wasn't admitting it, but she was exhausted.

"That's what we're turning our minds to right now, Charlotte," de Vile said in a tone that brooked no argument. "I want you to go to sleep, knowing we're onto it, and we won't let you or Sarah down."

They were leaving when Kaleo intercepted a quick glance between Elizabeth and de Vile. A glance that said what their words weren't willing to acknowledge.

How on earth are we going to pull this one off?

***

Back in Hector's suite, Petra and Elizabeth collapsed onto the velour sofa, despondency taking over from the fighting talk in the room next door.

Kaleo prowled the wall behind them like a caged tiger, while Dolphie lounged against the fireplace mantel, a battle-hardened veteran preparing for his next skirmish.

Despite the late hour—it was heading for three a.m.—Hector ordered hot chocolate and pastries. Failing to free Sarah was taking its toll on morale, and nothing worked better at boosting the mood than hot chocolate.

Kaleo's frustration boiled over the minute the door closed behind the waiter, the sweet smell of cocoa beans doing nothing to soothe his nerves.

"We can't leave her there. We've got to go back and get her now."

He glared around the dog-tired group. Kaleo was, thought Hector with inner satisfaction, magnificent in his intensity, a defeated general chomping to get back into the fray.

He gave him a quick, approving smile. "Top marks for persistence, Kaleo. But sometimes strategy comes before courage."

Kaleo snorted, but before he could speak again, de Vile raised his hand to arrest his next protest.

"We all share your anxiety, Kaleo, but we can't do anything more tonight. In a few hours, it will be a different story."

He pulled out the gold watch he carried on a chain inside his breast pocket and considered the time.

"First thing today, in fact. In three hours, we'll get the sheriff's department involved."

Kaleo leaned forward, his hands on the back of the sofa, shaking his head. "How do we know Clifford didn't see Dolphie and put two and two together? They could tear down that wall and get to her right now. We can't afford to leave it another minute."

His voice was ragged, and his breath uneven. He pushed back a long lock that had escaped his ponytail with a distracted air.

"I can't believe we had such bad timing," he moaned.

Dolphie's deep bass chipped in, bringing with it an immediate sense of calm.

"I would swear we didn't give ourselves away, Kaleo. The dogs were tearing all over the yard. They were so excited. And the torches they had weren't good enough in the dark."

Dolphie scanned the group, hands outstretched, palms up. "OK. They know someone interfered with the dogs. We can't hide that. But by the time Clifford got out the back, Sarah had the rope clear and the back window down."

He gazed back at Kaleo. "For all they know, it could have been that gang that's been robbing the mansions in that area. Remember, they hit the Gould and Curry vaults up there last month and ran into armed guards?"

His brown eyes flicked to Elizabeth, then to de Vile.

"Besides, from what I overheard, they've got other things on their minds. Sure, the night watchmen falling asleep on the job infuriated Clifford.

"But he's got a helluva lot more to be worried about with the steep drop in their share price. If we launch a counterattack first thing today, we've got a good chance of still catching them off guard."

De Vile drained the last of his chocolate and reached for a refill. "Funny you mention that. I saw Bill Sharon in the foyer earlier today. You know he lives here at the club?

"He's unhappy with the way the slump in Golden Bowl values is dragging the entire market down. You know Bill. Best poker player in all of California. His face gives nothing away.

"But I got the impression he was fishing for information. And it's pretty surprising he doesn't know who's behind the drop. He's usually the one playing dirty."

De Vile gazed around him. "He said something about a parcel of Golden Bowl shares that are up for grabs. And did I know anything about them? I played along, but I'm pretty certain he could see I knew nothing about it, so he shut up."

Dolphie abruptly turned away from the fireplace and dropped into the chair opposite. He steepled his fingers in front of his mouth.

"That's exactly what Mrs. Hollows was talking about earlier. Sarah's secret project. She told me a bit about it when we were waiting to go down the rope.

"Sarah apparently got her man in San Fran onto it shortly before we came up here, but being holed up, she hasn't found out yet what's going on."

De Vile rubbed his hands together, flushed with a new confidence. His chest flooded with a lightness that hadn't been there a minute ago. His lungs filled with new air. They were onto something good.

He didn't understand it, this sixth sense, a keen intuition that came upon him like a gift from heaven when he was least expecting it.

It guided him like the ship's barometers he'd relied on for storm warnings in the early days. He could read it with the same inevitability as a ship's barometer, the rise and fall of the mercury levels measuring the rise or fall of air pressure that predicted fair weather or coming storms.

Only with him, it alerted him to if a deal was sound. It had been with him ever since he'd left his father's house.

He straightened his shoulders, preparing for action. "I bet that's what Bill Sharon's talking about. And if he is, then you can assume Hollows will know about it as well. They've been in cahoots for years.

"That means we've one more reason to get Sarah out of there as soon as we can."

Kaleo licked his lips with cautious hope. "Will was gabbing on about Sarah's secret project when he was here earlier, though I've no idea how he knew about it if it was a secret. Maybe he spied on her.

"Whatever the story is, we're not sitting around waiting to read about it in the paper, I hope?"

Dolphie's eyes sparkled with wicked humor. "Calm down, old boy. She's precious to us, too, you know."

Elizabeth reached out and placed a consoling hand on Kaleo's arm.

"Don't let them get to you, Kaleo. And don't take tonight's disappointment to heart. You got Charlotte out. And we're going to complete the task later today."

She smiled around the circle, drawing in all of them.

"Right now, though, we all need to get some sleep, because first thing today, we're going back up the hill with the sheriff and his deputies in tow. We make a big song and dance about how we believe Sarah is there.

"And we demand they allow the sheriff to search the place."

Elizabeth rose from the sofa with a thin smile. "What could possibly go wrong?"

Kaleo rose to his feet, the jerkiness of his movement showing he was still unconvinced.

"What if they've found her and already moved her somewhere else? What if the sheriff Gerry O'Doole refuses to come? There are still so many things that could go wrong."

Dolphie turned from his post by the fire. "They won't find her tonight, Kaleo. I heard them. They've had a hard night of drinking. They're in their cups."

Elizabeth touched his shoulder, reassuring. "And we've got eyewitnesses, Kaleo. Dolphie and Charlotte. The sheriff will believe us."

De Vile rose slowly, ready to deliver the ultimate word.

"O'Doole will come," he said. "He owes me too many favors not to."

Chapter 43

"You realize Kaleo's going to hate you forever?" Elizabeth Westerhoven smiled mischievously at Hector and squeezed his arm affectionately. They were in the lead carriage heading for the Hollows' house, with Dolphie, Gerry O'Doole, the Virginia City sheriff and four deputies coming behind them.

De Vile smiled down at her and placed his hand protectively over the top of hers.

"It's the only way to do it, Elizabeth. Dolphie's been with Sarah in that house. He knows exactly where to go, and he's a better eyewitness. Besides, someone has to stay behind to make sure Charlotte and Petra are safe."

He recognized they were on the slight rise before the Hollows' house. "Besides, Dolphie's an experienced fighter, if it comes to it." He frowned. "As I've warned you already, Elizabeth. If things heat up, I want you to get out immediately. Out on the street. As far away as possible."

Elizabeth's smooth forehead wrinkled into worried grooves. "Oh, Hector, it won't come to that, will it? The sheriff's an experienced man. He knows how to run the show. And Sam's not stupid."

De Vile patted her hand. "You wouldn't be here if I thought there was any chance of that happening," Hector said. "I'm mentioning it in the unlikely case."

They drew up at 146 South D Street and waited quietly for the jingle of the approaching lawmen's horses. Outside the dimness of the coach, the light had the pearly iciness of dawn, untouched by the early sun. As they sat side by side in silence, their breath came out in little puffs of mist. De Vile pulled out his gold watch.

"Coming up to seven a.m. We're in good time."

They'd bailed up the sheriff at home, and pressed their request to him fresh out of bed. Because it was the senator asking, O'Doole had no hesitation in rallying a party.

The minutes ticked by. Faint, early birdcalls were the only sounds.

"We've certainly had our share of snow this winter," Elizabeth remarked mildly. She pulled back the curtain with a gloved hand.

"Goodness knows how Sarah's kept warm in that tiny room with no fireplace. I can't wait to get her home."

At that, O'Doole and his men arrived and de Vile opened the carriage door, letting in a draft of cold air.

"We'll bring her home," he said, as he made to step out. "Don't worry, we will." He handed her down.

George Murphy answered the door with an arched eyebrow. "Sheriff O'Doole! Senator! Countess!" His mild gray eyes bored into Elizabeth's dark brown ones, a knowing glint shooting between them.

"Whatever's wrong at this hour? Nothing serious, I hope?"

O'Doole, who fronted the group, took control.

"Nothing that can't be quickly resolved, my man," he said. "We need to talk to Mr. Hollows. Mr. Hollows and all the other men who might be present in the household. Please assemble them in the library. Immediately."

Dolphie had emphasized to de Vile the importance of not leaving Sarah open to attack by someone else, and O'Doole was taking no chances.

"The household is not long up, Sheriff, but certainly. Come this way. Mr. Hollows is already in the library."

Murphy led them into the library, where Hollows sat in his usual chair at his big leather desk by the fireplace.

"What in the name of Jove is going on here?" Hollows stared in disbelief at the sight of the sheriff. He pushed up to stand, his hands flat on the desktop to steady himself.

"By the powers of St. George, why the invasion, O'Doole? What's going on?"

His face flushed an angry beetroot red, his heavy dark brows glowered over glittering onyx eyes. Fat wet lips brought together.

"And you too, de Vile? What in goodness' name are you playing at?"

Hector waited for O'Doole to state the case, as they'd agreed.

"I believe you are detaining a person or persons here against their will, Sam. As you will understand, if true, kidnapping is a serious offense. I would have thought you'd already be aware of that."

"Kidnapping? What nonsense. Who am I supposed to have kidnapped?"

O'Doole shuffled his feet, momentarily discomforted.

Was it reasonable to charge a man with kidnapping his unmarried daughter when all he was doing was giving her a bed in the family home?

"A Miss Sarah Wyndham," said O'Doole.

He eyed the group clustered behind him, as if seeking corroboration. No one spoke, so he turned back to Hollows and continued.

"From what I am told, Miss Wyndham hasn't been seen for two

days, and the last place was here, at this house."

Hollows sat down again with a bump and issued a bellowing laugh.

"Sarah Wyndham? Otherwise known as my very own stepdaughter, Rebecca? Since when is it a crime for a stepfather to offer his daughter a roof over her head? If she was here. Which I am not saying she is."

O'Doole cleared his throat in obvious discomfort.

"That's why I've got my men with me here, Hollows. To ascertain whether or not she is here. And whether she wants to be here.

"With your permission, we'll take a look around. If you're not sure if she's here or not, I gather you won't mind."

Hollows again jerked to his feet, his face flushing an even deeper red. "A search? You dare to bring a search party here for my own daughter? The cheek of it."

There was a clatter at the library entry and George Murphy ushered in three more men. Clifford, Otis, and Will Davenport.

"The rest of the household," Murphy said to O'Doole with a nod, and slipped out again.

"Can you believe it, Cliff? They're demanding to make a search for Bekka. Can you imagine? I don't believe it."

Sam pointed a rigid arm at the doorway. "I am asking you to leave, Sheriff O'Doole. You and whoever else it is you've dragged here with you. And don't return until you've got a search warrant."

There was an ominous silence. Hector was counting the seconds in his head, like the moment between when lightning strikes and the thunder rolls.

Hollows stared at their faces, checking them out. O'Doole. De Vile. Elizabeth.

"That's right. A search warrant. Ever heard of those, Sheriff? The little piece of paper a judge issues before you charge into someone's house demanding to go over it."

He shook his head, and a sly smile spread across his fat lips.

"Really, Elizabeth?" he said in a mocking tone. "For your own niece? I thought you at least would've had more of a sense of decorum."

He glared toward the library door, where the visitors stood. "Show them out, Cliff. They've got no more business here. Not till they've got a warrant, anyway."

Two things happened then, in confusing succession.

Gerry O'Doole raised his arm, flashing a piece of paper. "A search warrant, Hollows. I'm one step ahead of you. We've got the darned warrant. So, stand your men down and let us get busy."

And in the stunned silence that followed, a feminine voice intruded.

"It's all right, Sheriff. You don't have to search any further. I'm already found."

Chapter 44

Clifford strode down to the telegraph office next door to the Virginia & Truckee Railway Depot in F Street and wired their man in San Francisco straight after the ridiculous scene with the sheriff. He still couldn't believe it.

Bekka appeared from nowhere as if she hadn't been missing for two days, and then wafted out the front door with de Vile and the sheriff as if it was the most normal thing in the world.

He was furious with everyone. But especially Sam Hollows.

He paused on the curb outside the office and waited for his racing pulse to subside. How could Hollows be such a beetle brain as not to know there was a secret hiding hole in his own house?

Like those priest holes in old English manors he heard about—except there weren't any priests that he knew of hiding in Nevada.

Why hadn't Will Davenport mentioned the business about the widow's share lot before now?

And while he was at it, damn the rest of them. Hector de Vile, the slippery snake, for launching the attack on the Bowl in the first place. That nosy fake Countess for interfering in her sister's life.

Countess my backside. She lies faster than my dog can trot.

And what about the Hawaiian gutter-blood who was always

popping up where he wasn't wanted? Bet he had something to do with it.

He nursed his sore hand, still bandaged from the hit he'd taken at the Hawaiian's house. Whenever that hog-in-togs came to mind, the pain worsened.

He would dearly like to know what was going on between him and Rebecca, because he certainly was a pretty boy.

He stomped back up the slope to South D Street. When he entered the morning room, Sam and Will were scoffing eggs and bacon.

"Everything all right?" Sam asked, his mouth full.

Clifford shrugged, and pain darted down his wounded side. "So far as I know. I sent Butch the wire. Told him to go for it with no delay. That's all I can do."

Sam must have picked up that he was shirty by the way he was talking.

Well, he can like it or lump it.

He was sick of being the one to always be pushing. It was time for someone else to share the load.

Davenport paused, fork loaded, an uneasy glower on his face. "You okay?"

Clifford plopped into an empty chair at the table and pulled a plate in front of him. "No, I'm not okay. How in Jehoshaphat's name could that woman have been in this house and you not know it?"

Sam chewed on and swallowed, seemingly unperturbed. "How should I know?"

"It's your house," Clifford retorted. "Who else would know about a tricky hiding place, if you don't?"

"It's not really my house. It was Lottie's. She lived here before we married."

"And you knew nothing about it? Like with the shares? They've been slipping down the drain for weeks and you didn't notice?"

"You're as capable of seeing that as I am, Cliff. You've been too preoccupied chasing that daughter of mine, that's a fact. Less tail, and more business. That's your problem."

Clifford's arm froze in mid-air, arrested in its journey to serve himself with the remnants of cold bacon and eggs. His blood surged with a furious heat.

He squeezed his eyes shut, blocking out a red mist that blinded him. For several seconds, he couldn't make out the food in front of him.

He wanted to punch Sam Hollows right between the eyes. He jammed his jaw down so hard a pain shot down his neck.

"You'd better pray Butch finds that widow and gets those shares, pal. Or I'll hardly trust myself not to come after you with a .44 Colt."

Sam merely shrugged. "Cool down, Cliff. We're not broke yet."

"If we lose control of the Bowl, you know damn well we will be. We're hanging on by the skin of our teeth as it is."

"Calm down, boy. We've still got options."

"Options?" Clifford was shouting. He didn't want cold bacon and eggs any more.

"What options? Your brilliant daughter's gone AWOL again. The senator's doing his best to ruin us. And sunshine here didn't think to tell us there was a parcel of shares rolling around seeking a buyer until yesterday."

"Hey, hey," said Will. "Leave me out of this. I didn't know the significance of that note until I heard Bill Sharon talking last night. That's not my fault. You guys are the big financiers."

Clifford's fury deflated.

"De Vile's the one you should be mad at," Will continued. "He's the one who's going after you.

"He's got a point," said Sam. "He's always had it in for me."

"Why is that?" asked Will.

Sam shrugged. "Nothing and everything. I got mines he wanted. I married Elizabeth's sister, and it hasn't worked out so well. He's always had a soft spot for Elizabeth. Who knows?"

"Someone should teach him a lesson," said Will. "He's got away with for far too many years."

"Oh yeah? Why do you say that?"

Will shrugged. "He just has. He's bad news." As if struck by a sudden thought, he set his fork down.

"You know, if someone taught him a lesson, it might make it easier to defend the share price. Think about that."

"Taught him a lesson? In what way?" Clifford felt a tug of curiosity. Hope, even.

Will leaned forward over his empty plate, hands clasped together, as if pondering.

"He's got this big meeting at Maguire's coming up. I don't know, maybe organize some hecklers? Throw it into confusion? Maybe rough him up a bit? To remind him he's not as smart as he thinks he is?"

Clifford hung back in his chair and laughed. "I like your thinking, boy. And while you're at it, arrange for Rebecca to get back here."

Sam tossed him a scowl that said he was off his nut.

"No joke. I'm not giving up."

"Giving up on what?" said Sam.

"On getting Rebecca back." He reached for the bacon and eggs one more time. "I think I know the deal to get her interested."

"What are you talking about?" Sam said. "Face it, Clifford. She hates your guts."

"That's of no consequence, Sam. I'm not contesting the popularity stakes. I'm interested in results, and I think I know the way to get them."

He loaded up his plate with bacon. "You accuse me of chasing tail, old man, but you know as well as I do, she's got more brains than the two of us put together.

"This slump in Golden Bowl shares would never have happened if she was here. She would've seen it coming a mile off."

Chapter 45

"A bath. My kingdom for a bath. And then my favorite hot java. But first, let me give you an enormous hug, Mother." Sarah's face was glowing, eyes sparkling, as she ran to Charlotte's bedside, leaning down and kissing her mother's pink cheeks. She stood back and took in Charlotte's face, flushed with pleasure.

"You've still got a way to go to get back to full strength, Mother, I can see that, but I'm so grateful that you're here, receiving the best care in the world!"

She beamed at her audience—the Countess, Dolphie, Kaleo and Petra—and circled the room, hugging each in appreciation. "I don't know where the senator is," she laughed. "But thanks to him, too."

"He's got that big meeting coming up, so it's all hands on deck," Elizabeth interjected. "You can thank him later."

"Honestly, dear ones, I can't believe I'm standing here with you. There've been times …" Sarah's excitement faltered, and her eyes were suspiciously bright.

She gulped for breath and continued. "Times when honestly I wondered if I'd make it." Her eyes lifted to Dolphie, and she snickered.

"Like when I saw Dolphie disappearing over the back fence last night."

Dolphie gave her a thumbs up with a grin. "You kept your cool, like I knew you would. Brought that rope inside before they saw it. You could join the Texas Rangers—if they took women, that is."

They laughed together and fell into a moment of grateful silence.

"I really have to clean up, my friends. I've spent too long in one dress. Then, let's get back to normal life—if I can remember what that's like."

"Hurrah for Sarah," said Petra with another laugh. "I've got you all to thank for my freedom, too. None of us—Mum, Bekka or me—will ever be able to repay you."

****

Much later that day, after Sarah had bathed, savored hot black coffee with a cheese and ham croissant, and taken a catnap, she sought Kaleo and suggested they go for a walk.

They headed along the Gold Hill track toward Mount Davidson. The ground was soggy from the recent snow, but many walkers ahead of them had beaten a pathway through, and the warm sun melted away memories of being shut up in one small room.

She'd worn her red jacket with a rabbit fur stole wound around her neck, and from the appreciative glance Kaleo shot her, she concluded he approved.

She strolled in silence, breathing in the pungent camphor smell of the gray-leaved sagebrush that covered the ranges backing the township. The landscape of her childhood, with Sun Mountain and Mount Davidson rising in a panorama above them.

Sarah felt a nervous tug in her stomach. As Kaleo measured his long strides to her shorter ones, the conviction struck again; she was in the company of a prince among men.

Tall, muscular, with a dancer's fluidity despite his size, he had an irrepressible grace, as if nothing would hold him down. The strong planes of his face kept a fresh glow, even after being shut up in a California winter.

She swallowed hard to clear a lump in her throat. She'd mistreated him. No other word for it. He'd dedicated himself to protecting and supporting her, and she'd lied, rejecting his determined chivalry.

She shook her head in self-warning. There was no way she could undo that damage, but maybe she could try to explain why she'd acted the way she did.

Pausing in her forward motion, she said, "You deserve an apology, Kaleo. An explanation. I've behaved badly, and I don't want to leave things like that."

His face was solemn, even wary, under his golden tan. His dark brown eyes bored into her, searching hers. Then he took another step forward, signaling something.

He didn't want to hear? He didn't care anyway, because he'd already moved on?

She suddenly couldn't stand the thought that this might be how it would remain between them forever. She had to repair broken bonds.

She reached out and gently grasped his arm to slow his pace. "No, really, Kaleo. Give me a chance to explain."

His cheeks flushed a deeper tan. "No need, Sarah. You've made your position perfectly clear."

He went to move on again. She clasped his arm more firmly.

"But no, I didn't. Kaleo. You don't understand. Please. I couldn't stand for things to remain like this between us."

"Like what?" He freed his arm with a purposeful assurance and stepped away, increasing the gap between them.

He considered her, his eyes reflecting a deep pool of calm, gazing into her messy well of doubt.

He isn't making this easy. The wounds go deeper than I realized.

"Please understand. I had no choice. I had to lie, because I didn't want you hurt, even killed. You don't know how ruthless they are."

He shook his head. "You made assumptions about who I am and how I'd act, without giving me the benefit of the doubt or attempting to explain. It'll take more than a few easy words to repair trust broken like that."

She remembered again how he'd told her the thing he hated most was dishonesty. Tears flooded the back of her eyes. She turned away sharply, gazing back over the township. They'd climbed a considerable distance, past several working mines.

High in the pale gray snowy sky, over the smoking chimneys of the houses below, a lark soared, a tumultuous song pouring forth from its tiny throat.

A glorious wave of sound that signals farewell.

She dashed her hand across her face to wipe away her leaking sadness.

She attempted to breathe in new strength as she feigned examining at the view, gazing skyward for the soaring bird, although she couldn't see for the tears that were forcing their way out.

She took a few minutes, breathing deeply, then turned back to face him.

His face was not angry, nor was it bitter. But it was implacable, the eyes like granite.

He seemed distanced, as if he'd already decided any friendship they might have had was over.

"You've won the battle, Sarah," he said in a low, soft purr. "You've defeated them all and come out on top. You shouldn't apologize to anyone."

She shook her head, unable to speak.

Oh, but I haven't, she cried out from inside. Not if it means we can't be friends.

Instead, she gave him a wobbly smile.

"I can't count my chickens yet, Kaleo. I won't rest till I drive the final pile into the shaft, so to speak."

She gave him another shaky grin.

"Whatever's happened in the past, I want us to be friends. I deeply regret how I've acted, even if at the time I felt I had no other choice."

The stony facade of his face softened, but his true feelings were still impossible to read.

"Friends, Sarah? Oh, I expect when this is all over, we can be friends."

Was it her imagination, or did he put an ironic emphasis on the word friend? She wanted to cry out. Wanted to pound her fists on his chest. Beat him into submission.

More than friends. I want it to be like it was before. Wasn't that more than friends?

She imagined him taking control of those hands pounding his chest and bending down and kissing her. She shook her head again.

Now you're being ridiculous. Does he give the impression of a man who's attracted to you? You've acted like a total bitch, and he's not returning for a second dose.

They stood in silence, staring at one another.

She sighed and turned away again. "Oh, Kaleo, I wish I could turn back the clock to how things used to be."

He laughed softly. "Don't be ridiculous, Sarah. Or should I be calling you Rebecca?"

She felt the jab like a knife in her heart. "I guess I deserved that. But Sarah will do, thank you."

"Sarah, then. It's all worked out pretty well for you, as far as I can tell. Aren't you on the home straight? You've regained your freedom, and you're about to collect a big reward. You've never been in a better place."

"I'd never have got here without the help of the rest of you," she said. She hardly dared meet his eye

"Despite my pleas for you to stay out of it, you didn't, and your help has been critical to our success."

She took courage and met his eye, hoping she wouldn't cry. "Thank you, Kaleo. Even when I tried to protect you, you insisted on fighting at my side."

She ran out of air and her tears did finally overflow.

He gave a light shrug of his big shoulders.

"It's nothing. Anyone would have done the same."

He pulled out a dazzling white handkerchief from his jacket pocket and passed it to her.

"It's going to be fine, Sarah. You've got everything you were hoping for." He gazed down the slope back toward Virginia City.

"They warned me about the thin mountain air up here, and I didn't believe them." He gave her an apologetic grin. He was signaling the conversation was over.

"This is about as high as I can go. My lungs aren't up for it. I'll make my way back down and catch up with you later."

He turned and strolled away.

And despite his pleasantries, she knew he was saying goodbye.

Chapter 46

She watched Kaleo's broad back disappear toward the town's smoking chimneys below with a heavy heart. Her attempt at reconciliation was a big fail, but she didn't blame Kaleo for his attitude. He'd always acted honorably toward her, while her whole life had been a lie, the thing he hated more than anything.

I can't do anything about that now, she told herself. I'm running out of time. It's been over a week since I gave Zach his instructions. There must be word today, surely.

All the time they'd had her trapped in her mother's secret room, the cloud of not knowing hung over her.

Had she succeeded in her takeover of the Golden Bowl? If she had, neither Clifford nor her father had any further power over her. She needed to know, and this was her first chance to check out if she had good news waiting.

A falcon gave a piercing call from high overhead. Her eyes searched the sky in time to see a large bird swoop with lightning speed on a flock of much smaller birds below.

She shivered. In the last few minutes, the weak sun had disappeared, and the air thickened. Snow was on the way again.

She wound her scarf more tightly around her neck and set off with fresh determination up the track over the Divide, and down to the Gold Hill Virginia and Truckee Depot.

By the time she reached the California Telegraph Company office in the railway station, she was weak-kneed and out of breath.

Kaleo's not the only one experiencing the effects of the altitude, she thought. *I've lost all my mountain conditioning from six months away.*

She stamped her feet a few times to shake snow off her boots and get her blood going again, and then headed for the familiar telegraph booth.

She'd made this trip often when she had worked for her father, and Johnny Skeates was a legendary tele operator. She enjoyed coming to see him. Besides, she was less conspicuous at this office, a mile out of town.

Johnny had the reputation of being the sharpest cipher clerk anywhere, as well as a young Canadian who was always ready to flirt with a pretty girl. He grinned brightly as he saw her approaching.

"Well, well. Miss Rebecca Hollows. I thought you'd be coming by one day soon."

His chair legs squealed as he pushed it back to stand and grin. "I've got something here for you. Been away in the big smoke, I hear?"

Sarah warmed inside. The day was suddenly improving.

"Something like that, Johnny. But I'm back now. Good to see you on the job."

He reached into the shelf behind him and shuffled through the filed sheets, hunting for her telegram.

"Ah, here it is." His eyebrows dipped slightly, and her heart stilled. From his fleeting, unconscious gesture, she could be pretty sure he already knew what the message said.

And she guessed it wasn't what she wanted to hear.

All the mining companies used ciphers for the daily reports they exchanged with their San Francisco partners. A constant stream of communication went over the wires, with mine managers reporting to the owners on the latest developments on new ore veins and what the test results were showing.

It was a flood of commercially sensitive information that would damage business if it ended up in the wrong hands—stockbrokers, investors, competitors or journalists who were always sniffing around for the latest in stock tips.

If word of a new strike—or of a failed probe—reached the market before the mine owners were ready, it could spell disaster for the entire enterprise.

Johnny, it was rumored, was too smart by half. He'd worked out the various company ciphers and was quietly stacking away a fortune from the insider tips he gleaned from the traffic that passed across his desk.

She stared at the telegram, lying under his hand on his desk. "Not what I'm hoping for?"

He hesitated, momentarily awkward, and then leaned in, shaking his head. "Probably not… but you know you're not the only one chasing this lot?

She stared at him in shock.

"I only mention it because Clifford Jensen is such a jerk."

She reacted by doing a quick survey of who was in line behind her.

The office would close in an hour, and there was always a last-minute rush to send end-of-the-day reports, but the closest person in line behind her was Arthur Galway, manager at the Bullion, who was hard of hearing from years of standing too close to the blasters. She leaned in.

"What are you talking about?"

"The Bowl. They're after the same lot you are. And they haven't found the lady yet either."

He waved the pale yellow slip between two fingers. "According to this, anyway. No luck so far. But I wouldn't leave it too long."

She reached over and grasped his hand.

"Thanks for the tip, Johnny. I won't forget your kindness."

"Always happy to help, Bekka," he said. "You deserve it."

Chapter 47

Clifford was in a foul mood all day. Thinking about it later, Will recalled the black cloud had descended after he'd made the trip to the telegraph office. He guessed his man in San Francisco hadn't tracked down the widow yet.

And that made Will nervous. If the tip he'd given Clifford didn't pay off, he'd need another ally in his campaign to get back at Hector de Vile. He couldn't afford for that to happen.

When Will finally coaxed the story out of him over a lunch of hot soup, he discovered Clifford's man Butch had gone to the address Will had given them, but there was no one at the house.

The nosy next-door neighbor told him Cassandra Whitecliffe was visiting relations and wouldn't be home for several months. She referred all inquiries to Cassandra's solicitor, and so far Butch had no success in tracking him down, either.

"There's no point in trying to break in there and steal them. They'll be in some bank vault or safe deposit box," Clifford moaned. "Butch says the neighbor made it clear she's an extremely organized lady, even if she is a grieving widow."

It was snowing heavily again, and Will had his own case of cabin fever. He hated spending all day cooped up in the over-heated library with the Hollows men and Jensen.

There wasn't enough air in the room for all of them. Sam Hollows' face turned a deeper shade of purple and his speech became more slurred as the day—and his drinking—progressed.

Today he'd started with whiskey in his mid-morning coffee and tippled regularly from then on.

Otis and Clifford played penny poker that turned nasty with their increasing boredom. Will withdrew to a corner and read a volume of Edgar Allan Poe stories he had dug off the shelves. He was pretty sure Sam Hollows had no time for macabre mysteries, so he presumed this was one of Charlotte's books.

At the back of his mind always came the niggling thought.

If Clifford misses out on these shares, where will that leave me?

It didn't take much analysis to know where.

Up the creek without a paddle.

Clifford threw down the latest hand of cards and stood in a frustrated rush. "I've had enough for today, Otis. I'm sick of your cheating."

"My cheating?" Otis squinted through his cigar haze in mock disgust. "What cheating?"

"You keep hiding cards in your sleeve. I've had it." He turned and plopped down in the armchair next to Will. "Found anything decent to read?"

Will laughed. "Decent? Not sure you'd like it. But certainly entertaining."

"What is it?" Jensen's eyebrows lifted, a smile puckered his lips.

Will shook his head. "Probably not your cup of tea."

"Tell me. What is it?"

"*The Masque of the Red Death* by Edgar Allan Poe. Heard of it?"

"No, I haven't."

"It's about a Prince who holds parties in lots of different rooms.

He hides away from a pestilence with all his rich friends."

"Sounds good," said Clifford with a laugh. "It reminds me we haven't had a proper hunt for the secret room. Let's do that. Find out where they've been hiding. Shouldn't be too hard…"

***

Half an hour later, curiosity satisfied, they returned to the library. "Fancy that being there and we didn't realize," Sam said.

"The women in this family are very tricky creatures, that's for sure," said Clifford with a grimace.

Will saw his opportunity. "Speaking of tricky, I saw Rebecca out with the Hawaiian yesterday."

He watched closely and saw the muscles in Clifford's jaw ripple under the skin.

"Whereabouts?" The words were harsh, clipped.

"On the track up to Gold Hill. They appeared to be having a nice little tête à tête."

Clifford scowled. "If it wasn't for that gutter-blood, everything would have worked out. She'd be back here now. My wife. And we'd be on the up and up with the shares again."

"Yeah. Apparently, de Vile's planning to give him a big parcel of shares in the Bonanza Mine as a wedding present. The old man wants a family and thinks he's left it too late, so he's sweetening the pill."

Sam Hollows' florid face noticeably paled. "He's what?" he spat.

"Yeah. That guy's really fallen on his feet. Apparently, De Vile is about to make him his official heir. From Rebecca's point of view, I guess he must appear a promising prospect."

"When did this happen?"

Will shrugged. "Oh, don't take it too seriously. It's probably all gossip. It hasn't happened yet."

He gave a sly sideways glance toward Sam Hollows, who was

staring at him with narrowed eyes.

"It's a pity you've fallen out with him," Will said. "I mean, think. An alliance with Hector de Vile. But it's not going to happen now they're all back with the Countess. Charlotte, Petra, and Rebecca I mean.

"Probably a bit of a lost cause now."

"No," Clifford yelled. He pinned Sam with his strange-colored eyes and roared louder. "It will not happen, Sam. You've got to stop this. She's your daughter. Do something."

Chapter 48

Sarah had been on a high when she'd broken out of her "captivity" at the Hollows house, but something had dampened her spirits overnight. Elizabeth could sense it. The buoyant, confident young woman of yesterday was subdued today. Maybe even despondent, as she stared into her coffee at the Silver Spoon Eatery on South C Street.

Around them, the room buzzed with conversation as the ladies of the Lode made their leisurely course through their day. For every woman forced to take in boarders or laundry or do needlework to make ends meet, there were others who were living the high life.

Women like Louise Mackay and Teresa Fair, both of them young widows who had married the wealthy Silver Kings James Fair and John Mackay.

As they sipped their coffee, Elizabeth spied Teresa and Louise at a nearby table, chattering with friends. The men of Virginia City might choose to wear rough miner garb whatever their status, but not so their womenfolk.

They liked to flaunt their wealth, and the ladies at Louise Mackay's table were competing to see who could make the best show. With the new fashion for bright colors, especially the decade's "new discovery" of synthetic magenta, an eye-watering mauvy crimson, they presented a rainbow of hues.

Teresa was in vivid pink cerise, while the friend beside her had chosen golden pheasant yellow. Another sported Vesuvius red and Louise Mackay was in a bright turquoise. Some of the beau monde set, Elizabeth noted, had adopted the coming fashion for face make-up, with tinted eyelids and painted lips.

They'd finished with a nod at the trend for wild jewelry. At their necks hung inch-wide velvet neck bands sewn with beads, or multiple chains of jet or gold.

From their ears dangled gold hoops, or drop earrings in the shapes of insects, or fish or birds. Elizabeth could see these women spent many hours studying the last fashion trends from London and New York.

Sarah didn't notice. She fiddled dejectedly with a half-eaten blueberry muffin, clearly finding no appetite to finish it.

"Sarah, what's wrong?" Elizabeth queried. "You don't seem yourself today."

She gaped up in quick surprise, as if she'd been miles away. "Oh, Elizabeth, sometimes it all gets a bit too much. I think I've got delayed fatigue or something, from everything that's been going on."

Delayed fatigue?" Elizabeth raised an eyebrow in wry humor. "That's a new one. Though I admit you have had a lot of recent excitement. But you're through all that now."

"Am I?" said Sarah. "I wish I was, truly. But we've still got some distance to go before everything's settled. What if it all goes wrong at the last hurdle? I couldn't stand to face the last couple of weeks over again. I couldn't stand it."

Elizabeth sensed a stricken tension behind the throwaway line. "What exactly are you frightened of?"

"Well, first, I haven't been able to complete the purchase of the

Golden Bowl shares. I need to seal the mine's fate. My guy in San Francisco—Zach—went to Cassandra Whitecliffe's address, and she's gone to visit relatives. The neighbors didn't know which relatives or where they live. So, we're no further ahead."

"Cassandra Whitecliffe? You mean Cassandra Hungerford?" Elizabeth's voice shivered with amazement, but Sarah wasn't picking up on it. She continued fiddling with the muffin.

Elizabeth nudged her hand. "Listen to me. I knew Cassandra Whitecliffe when she was Cassandra Hungerford. Before she married Jonah Whitecliffe. She's a pretty blue-eyed blonde—very like her sister over there."

Sarah's eyes shot up as if Elizabeth had prodded her with a hot poker. "What did you say?"

Elizabeth tilted her head ever so slightly over to the right-hand side of the room, where the women at Louise's table exchanged gossip interspersed with regular gales of laughter.

"Don't look now, but yes. I believe I can see her over there.

"She stands out because she's still in her black widow's weeds. Seated right next to her sister, Louise Mackay née Hungerford. The one in turquoise."

Elizabeth had to suppress a surging satisfaction at the shock on Sarah's face.

"If it's Cassandra you need to speak to, I'm more than confident I can arrange it."

She picked up her reticule from the floor at her feet.

"I'll write Louise a note right now and have Dolphie deliver it. Louise and John have been wonderfully supportive of my causes back in San Francisco.

"Louise hasn't forgotten what it was like to be widowed and left in debt with a young daughter who needed medical help. She had her days of pinching and scraping as a dressmaker before she married

John. They both know what it's like to be poor, and they've been very generous to my Tenderloin charity."

"Oh, Aunt, you're astonishing. Is there anyone of note in California you don't know?"

Elizabeth smiled across the table and put on her best deep, mocking voice. "I certainly hope not."

She took out her notepad and pen.

"Now you finish that muffin while I attend to the note."

Chapter 49

Sarah prided herself on being the most impervious of women—she'd had to be—but sitting in Alphie's at the same table as Clifford the next day, violent contradictory emotions buffeted her. One minute a secret exultation possessed her, knowing as she did that she'd secured Cassandra's shares and guaranteed her financial security, at least in the medium term.

The next minute, her hands trembled so badly at the memory of Clifford's attack she clasped them fiercely under the tablecloth to hide her distress.

She hadn't overcome her all-encompassing fear of him, buried it deep within.

She'd lived with the memories of his brutality every day for the last six months of her life. She recalled his iron rod arm hard across her throat, blocking off air so she'd feared she'd die at any moment.

Then the burning humiliation of his physical invasion, the blood, the slime and stink of him between her legs. What would he do when he discovered her treachery—and her success?

She scanned the room. The afternoon crowd at Alphie's was mainly older couples, out for a late lunch or an early supper.

The maître d' had led them to a round corner table tucked away at the back, where they could talk without having to raise their voices or be concerned about privacy.

In a few hours, the party-going crew and the single men out for some action would overrun the place—the miners, tradesmen, and professional gamblers who liked to stay up late, rabble-rousers who'd make normal conversation impossible.

Dolphie was his usual imperturbable self on her left, while Will sat on her right. She was glad Sam hadn't turned up, though his absence shot down her thought that the meeting might relate to her mother.

She would never have agreed to it without backup. Elizabeth wasn't available to join them at such short notice—she was out with Hector on a walk about town to prepare for his coming gala at Maguire's.

The man across the table from her, the man she'd fleetingly considered marrying, thrummed with a vital masculinity many women found bewitching.

She found it hard to believe that under the quick charm and engaging wit there lurked a monster who was happy to resort to brute force against anyone, even those he claimed to love, to get what he wanted.

Having to sit this close to him left her so anxious she'd become tongue tied. Already she'd twice halted mid-sentence, her usually fluid speech stopped short by haunting images of his rape.

She'd covered up these tense moments by fiddling with her food, but she knew what he was capable of. He would be forever a monster in her eyes.

"I thought today called for a little celebration," Clifford said, his smooth face glowing, his glass raised. He and Will were drinking wine. She and Dolphie had chosen iced water.

"I've every reason to believe I'm about to secure the last elusive parcel of shares in the Bowl. Can you believe it?

"There've been so many whispers about them—I'm sure you'll have heard—but I'm pretty confident I've done it. Not counting my chickens or anything. Let's say I'm pretty confident."

Her stomach lurched, and it took all of her willpower to keep her face a mask of mild surprise, even hinting at pleasure. Clifford was inclined to overestimate himself. Perhaps that was why he took losing so badly.

"Really? That would be something to celebrate," she said. "How long have you been chasing them?"

"Actively? Only for the last few days, to be honest. But you know me. When I want something, I don't waste my time before getting it."

He dipped his head in her direction. She read a fleeting defiance in his eyes as he lifted the crystal tumbler again. "Here's to many more years of high profits."

She straightened her shoulders. "That's certainly something we can all drink to," she said, shooting a colluding dart at Dolphie.

The waiter came then to take their orders—French onion soup with cheese croutons all round, and then veal cutlets with mushrooms for Sarah, and either beef hotpot or roast chicken with rice and string beans for the men. When the waiter left, there was a brief, awkward silence.

"So, tell us, Will." Sarah leaned forward, genuinely curious.

"You haven't said much so far. What's so urgent that you brought us here at short notice? I'm obviously surprised—even perturbed— to be invited. We're not exactly buddies anymore."

He was leaning with his elbows on the table, his hands clasped so tightly before him the knuckles were white. He wriggled uncomfortably in his seat at the question, but Sarah wasn't giving up.

"Let us in on the secret, why don't you, Will? What's so urgent it justifies a special meeting?"

Will gawked at Clifford as if uncertain whether he should take the lead. Clifford deferred with a magnanimous nod.

"Go ahead, Will. It's your thing as much as mine. Tell her."

"Well, Rebecca…" He paused. "You don't mind me calling you that, do you? It is, after all, your rightful name?"

She shrugged it off. "Call me what you like, Will."

"Sure. Back to your question. It's a little sensitive. I'm not sure if you know that Hector de Vile is my uncle? Our fathers were brothers."

Sarah inclined her head. "I heard something about that, yes. Rather remarkable, isn't it? That there were two of us incognito at Pike's at the same time!"

She darted a challenge Clifford's way. Two could play the game of masked messages.

Will unclasped his hands, seeming to relax a little. "Yes. Well, Hector and my father parted badly and never made it up, and that's upsetting. There aren't many of my family left now, and I treasure the ones that are here.

"I'd really like to make peace with the senator, but because of the history, he won't see me. He won't even recognize my existence."

He squinted nervously at Clifford, as if seeking approval. "I wondered if you could help bring us together? I'm sure he'd listen to you more than to either Clifford or me."

She stared at him, unsure of how to respond. "Oh, my goodness. That's a big one. I mean, I don't know the senator particularly well myself. What exactly are you expecting me to do?"

"Nothing really, Rebecca. Nothing major."

He sized up Clifford, and their eyes seemed to tangle.

"I haven't quite decided on the best strategy yet, but I'm thinking maybe you could have a quiet word. Encourage him to see me for a few minutes to make apologies on behalf of the family."

His pale gray eyes behind his gold-framed spectacles were pleading. "Maybe even at that gala at Maguire's in a few days. I could call on him at halftime to pay my respects, maybe."

She registered an uneasy niggle in her lower abdomen. Did this ring true? She wasn't sure it did. She wordlessly appealed to Dolphie for help.

"How long is it since you last saw the senator?" Dolphie inquired.

"Apart from brief glimpses when he's come to see Bully, do you mean? I was a kid when he visited us last."

Clifford intercepted. "We thought you'd understand, Rebecca. Seeing how important family is to you, I mean. You'll understand why Will wants everyone back together again."

She lobbed a dark stare at Clifford.

"And what interest do you have in this, Clifford? I've not known you to be sentimental about this sort of thing. And the senator has never been an ally of yours."

Clifford glowered with pure venom. At least the pretence was over.

"Will has proven himself a good friend. He was the one who alerted me about the Golden Bowl shares, if you want to know. If it keeps Will happy, I'm happy." He regarded her over steepled hands.

"Besides. I've still got plans for Pike. I'm thinking of buying out Bully's share and putting Will in to run it.

"It's in our interests to keep the senator on our side as a minority owner."

He sat back in his chair. "Who's for more wine? How about another toast? Life's too short to hold grudges."

He laughed in her face. And then he tilted up the glass and was about to drink when one of the restaurant staff interrupted.

A boy was at the front desk with a message for the gentleman. His cheeks flushed with rosy triumph.

He thinks he's won—he's acquired the missing shares.

An icy shiver ran down her backbone.

What will he do when he discovers he's missed out?

***

The staff cleared away their entrée plates and there was a lull as they waited for dessert—a selection of finger food items, shortbread and madeleines, and apple tarts.

Will was uncomfortably aware that under the polite exchange, a deeper message ran like an underground river. One with an edge so caustic he worried his flaming cheeks were giving him away.

He wished Clifford had not blabbed on about the Golden Bowl shares. He still nurtured hopes of everything going back to the way it was, with him managing Pike Consulting.

But as he had chewed through his beef hotpot, he sank into an Irish bog of despondency. He was never going back to Pike Consulting. Never working with Rebecca and Kaleo again. The most he could hope for was to avoid the hangman's noose.

For a fleeting moment, he asked himself if his version of winning was really losing. Then he remembered his father's raddled face, a man destroyed by his father's brutal murder.

He'd never recovered—the family had never recovered—from that travesty of kinship.

He was fulfilling the central truth of his life. His destiny was to be the avenger of past wrongs. And if he had to lie to Rebecca Hollows a million times to see it done, then lie he would.

Rebecca… He sounded the name in his head. *She'll always be Rebecca to me now. We'll never be friends again.*

***

Someone else—the Almighty knew who, because he didn't—had bought the widow's shares. Clifford stumbled back into Alphie's after he'd slipped into the men's room to read the telegraph Sam's boy had delivered, barely able to keep his eyes focused. He was experiencing an intense rush of blood in his head.

As he slipped back into his chair, Rebecca rose like a dreamy mirage on the other side of the table. Around him, voices faded into an undercurrent of meaningless sound.

He squeezed his eyes tight and in his head he went over the news he'd received.

Butch had written the message in their gobbledegook cipher, but the leap of his heart bore witness to its impact.

Someone else has beaten us to the widow's shares. We've missed out. We've lost the biggest gamble of the decade.

And soon all the telegraph wires would hum with news of their unthinkable rout. Uncle Sam Silver was about to be denuded of its primary asset, and he didn't have a clue how he could head off the disaster.

The years of selling yet more shares to raise funds for the fruitless search for another bonanza were over. They'd spent the last eighteen months falsely propping up the share price on the promise of a new strike, and now the chickens were coming home to roost.

Somehow, he maintained the semblance of good humor as he made his excuses. Sam had called him away on urgent business. They were finished anyway, weren't they?

He paid the account. Pointedly reminded Rebecca of her undertaking to assist Will. And then he set his desperate attention to defying his ruin.

***

By the time Clifford reached Sam in his fine mansion on South D Street, shock was giving way to fury. And the prime target of his red-hot venom was Hector de Vile.

How dare that jumped-up politician mount an attack against them? He was supposed to be protecting their interests in Washington, working on projects like Stopping Sutro's tunnel from getting federal funding and goodness knows what else. Not meddling in his business.

Will was panting along behind, half running to keep up with him. They pounded up Sam's front steps together.

"This must be de Vile's work," Clifford said, breathing hard.

"You said that memo on Rebecca's desk was from de Vile. They're obviously working together."

Will's eyes glowed with inner fire. "Sure. Stands to reason."

Clifford kicked at the shards of ice under his feet. "Why? Why does it stand to reason? They've never been close before."

Will shrugged, as if it was too obvious to explain.

"Kaleo. His newly discovered son." His voice was laced with poison. "I guess he's setting him up to run things."

He half turned away, hands in pockets, and stamped his feet to keep warm.

"That other son of his. Alex? He's a nice enough chap, but no businessman. All he's interested in is taking photographs. It's obvious, isn't it? De Vile is setting up Kaleo to run things, and marry Sar — Rebecca.

"There's something going on there. Haven't you noticed?"

Will purred with satisfaction. "It's what de Vile does. Sets up the world the way he wants it, no matter what."

Clifford whirled away, stepping to the front door of Hollows' house in a couple of big strides, possessed of a new energy. "Not when I'm the one he's dunning. He doesn't know who he's taking on."

Chapter 50

Elizabeth and Charlotte stared at Sarah in disbelief. "You're what?" Elizabeth asked, a staccato emphasis on each word.

It was a rhetorical question, because she answered it herself in the next breath.

"You're going to help Will Davenport 'make peace' with Hector because he's upset about the bad blood there for the last twenty years? Are you out of your mind?"

They were sitting in Hector's Old Washoe Club lounge room, the inevitable late-afternoon coffee spread out on a tray on the ottoman before them.

"Sarah, I don't think you've any idea what you're getting into. And I see no reason to trust anything Will Davenport says. He joined Pike Consulting under false pretences. Let's be straight up about this."

"Well, so did I, for that matter."

"Not at all the same situation, Sarah. Bully knew perfectly well who you were, and it was for your personal safety. That's completely different."

"And what's Clifford got to do with any of it?" asked her mother. "I don't want you going within a bullet's roar of that man. He's shown himself completely despicable."

There was a light tap at the door, and Dolphie poked his head around the doorjamb.

"Come in Dolphie," called Elizabeth. "I want your view on all this."

Dolphie cast a backward glance. "Kaleo's with me."

"Even better. He probably knows more than any of us what Hector's thinking."

The two men strolled in and perched, one on each side of a solid roll-armed chair.

"What's up?" said Dolphie.

"Sarah's been telling us about this strange meal you've had with Clifford Jensen and Will Davenport. What did you make of it all?"

Dolphie bobbed his head toward Sarah, as if denoting sympathy for being caught in the crossfire.

"I didn't hear Sarah make any promises to them, if that's what you mean. It was all left rather vague and up in the air. But they definitely were applying pressure with some cock and bull story about Will wanting to make peace with the senator." He dipped his head toward Sarah again.

"Sorry, Princess, but that's how I saw it. Total nonsense. He might have some other intentions he's not talking about, but he didn't ring true to me."

He hooked out a leg and tapped Kaleo on his calf. "What do you reckon, Kaleo? Would Will Davenport want to 'make peace' with the senator?"

Kaleo's face darkened, and his hawkish eyes flickered, first to Elizabeth and then coming to rest on Sarah.

"Will hates my father. He blames him for his grandfather's death. He claims Hector murdered his own father. That's what he's been told since he was a baby. And de Vile doesn't totally deny it."

He took a breath and regrouped. "Well, he 'kind of' does." Kaleo made speech marks in the air. "He says he's not guilty of what he's accused of, but he's sensitive about it. He doesn't like to discuss it."

He turned his attention to Elizabeth and Charlotte, who sat close together on a sofa with big plumped-up pink cushions. "If Will Davenport is making excuses to see Hector, I'd take a guess it's more likely to kill him than make up to him.

"That night I rescued him on the Embarcadero he called Hector a murderer and a cheat. He's not seeking reconciliation."

"How can you say that?" cried Sarah. "Everyone deserves a second chance."

Dolphie intercepted.

"Bunnykins, you're so soft-hearted, but Kaleo's right. And I think Clifford was running the show there, even though he presented it as Will's idea.

"He's positioning himself to crawl back into your good books. This was his first brief foray into exerting his influence on you again."

Sarah's face was pale and drawn. She rubbed her eyes and nodded her defeat.

"I guess you're right. Clifford mentioned something about 'having plans' for Pike's Consulting, didn't he, Dolphie?" She pitched a tired glance Elizabeth's way. "We don't know what's happening yet, about Bully's estate?"

The Countess straightened her back against the cushions. "Any day now, Sarah. The lawyer says probate will go through soon, and then we can talk about it."

Sarah nodded. "We can't have expectations, fair enough. But if I have anything to do with it, Clifford will go to Timbuktu before he gets through the door at Pike Consulting."

Elizabeth laughed. "That's more like it." She surveyed the circle. "So, we're agreed? No cooperation with anything to do with Will, Clifford, or Sam?"

Sarah thought back to Alphie's, and the familiar boy who had delivered Clifford the message late in the meal. When Jensen came back to the table, he was biting his lip, rattled and unhappy.

And what about that earlier remark about Will helpfully telling him about the Golden Bowl shares? As if she'd discussed the topic with Will? She never mentioned the subject, so what was all that about? It was all so confusing.

She drew herself back to the present and nodded around the family group. "Thanks for all your combined wisdom. I'll have nothing to do with any of them."

***

Sarah slipped out of the Old Washoe, wanting to stretch her legs briefly in the fresh air and get her mother some chocolate eclairs from the patisserie on the other side of the street. She'd barely exited Mrs. Emily Benson's premises when a freckled faced kid of about thirteen turned up.

She placed him instantly. He was Amos, the same boy who'd come to Alphie's Bistro with the message for Clifford earlier today. When Sarah thought about it, she was pretty sure that the earlier message was a telegram.

She'd glimpsed it in Clifford's hand when he'd returned to the table. The paper had the familiar opaque appearance of wire services stationery.

Amos had grown up a lot in the months she had been away, when he used to hang around on the street soliciting errands for small change.

He stepped in front of her, a note thrust out in his sweaty boy-man's hand, the fingernails bitten down to the quick.

The crowd jostled around them. A typical Saturday evening in Virginia City, with the gathering of the frenetic energy so typical of a party going populace gearing up for another night of telling tall tales and roistering.

"Amos. What do you want?"

"Message from Mr. Clifford, miss." The boy's eyes flashed with trouble. He'd heard the kitchen rumors, that was plain.

The Hollows girl. All banged up.

She cast her eyes down to the note to avoid meeting his.

"He says it's urgent." The boy's voice quavered.

She recognized his fear, flowing like a river. Amos was under threat as well. She flicked her gaze back at him and then unfolded the scrap of paper with gloved hands.

Enough of your games. Bitch. Do what he says, or Kaleo dies.

She stared up at Amos, her heart pounding, eyes wide in disbelief.

"What… what did he tell you he wanted me to do?"

"He's around the corner in a cab. He says you're to join him."

Her eyes flickered, searching for an alternative. Dolphie was nowhere to be seen. He would be furious, but what could he do, anyway? She had to see this one through herself. She braced her shoulders and told herself she was up to the task.

"Whereabouts?"

Amos puffed out a breath of relief. God knows what Clifford said would happen to him if he failed to bring her back.

"It's all fine, Amos. Don't worry."

He led her up C Street to where it met Sutton. Her stepfather's familiar black coach was drawn into the curb. A door opened simultaneously with her arrival, and her stepfather poked his head out.

"Ah, Rebecca. I knew you'd come." He nodded to Amos. "Vamoose."

He took her hand and backed in, drawing her in after him. Clifford Jensen sat on the opposite seat, his eyes glittering, a different man from the one she'd eaten with a few hours ago.

When he spoke, his voice had a dangerous hiss. "Ah … Rebecca." He shook his head in mock disapproval, like a parent disciplining a child. "Up to your old tricks, I see."

Her steady stare moved from him to her stepfather. "I don't know what you're talking about."

"How you must have been laughing up your sleeve this afternoon. Stupid Clifford, thinking he'd got the widow's lot. But you already knew that wasn't the case, didn't you?"

She knew he would've hated that more than anything. Imagining people were laughing at him.

"No. No." Her voice spiked with genuine alarm. She reined herself in. He also hated hysterics, unless they were his own. She shook her head vehemently. "I don't know about any widows."

Clifford's head waved like a snake rising to a charmer's flute. "Oh, Rebecca. What a pathetic liar you are. Will's already told me he saw the memo from de Vile on your desk. He's the one who told us about it."

Memo from de Vile? On my desk?

Now she truly was confused. She stayed silent, her heart racing, head dipped, eyes focused on the band of piping that ran around the edge of the red leather seat.

She recalled that brief occasion when he'd seen her jottings on her notepad. Somehow, he'd seen 1 + 1 and made it into 3.

So. Will is a spy as well as a liar. And now Clifford thinks de Vile is the one share raiding.

She took a deep breath and raised her chin from her chest.

Let him think that. It's probably better than him learning the truth. For now, anyway.

"Thing is, we can't have it, can we, Sam?"

Clifford prodded the older man's stomach with the end of his furled umbrella. "Because you're bright enough to understand. It would ruin us. We can't let that happen. Can we, Sam?" Another prod. Not gentle, either.

"I told you. I know nothing about de Vile. What he might or might not be doing. It's nothing to do with me."

Clifford appeared genuinely amused.

"So predictable. So you. Always playing nice."

His face darkened to thunder within the space of one breath.

"But it won't work this time, Rebecca. You're going to do exactly what I tell you to do, or I'm going to kill that lover boy of yours. He won't leave Virginia City alive. He'll disappear down a mine shaft, never to be heard from again."

She brought her hands to the front of her chest and clasped them tightly together.

My worst fears, all coming true. This can't be happening.

She eased her clutched hands apart, and they trembled violently. She quickly clasped them together again. "Clifford, what's that going to achieve? Kaleo has nothing to do with any of it."

His face screwed into a sneer, hatred etched in every wrinkled line.

"You'd know, wouldn't you, you little bitch? You'd know."

He scanned the street, where the crowds ebbed and flowed. Her stepfather's coach was parked outside Tom Cockerel's bar, famous for its boxing matches, cockfights, and the betting that accompanied both, which Tom regularly hosted in a sparring ring out the back in the summer.

Customers spilled out through the wide-open double doors onto the street and stood drinking under the red rooster painted sign that hung above them. Another typical party night on the Lode.

Clifford spoke in a pondering, deliberate tone, as if spelling out the obvious to a slow child.

"The Hawaiian is de Vile's heir."

A deep breath, almost a gasp. He was losing it.

"The old man's setting all this up for his son and heir to take over. What he's got isn't enough?" He snorted like a mad bull. "Well, he won't be taking my mine. I'll kill them both first."

My mine.

As if her stepfather, much as she loathed his weakness, had nothing to do with it. The mine had been Sam's until a year ago. Clifford was being ridiculous. She knew that.

But he was beyond the reach of reason. She thought of Kaleo. Of the risks he had already taken on her behalf. If she could do anything to even halfway repay him for his solicitude…

"What… What do you want me to do?"

Chapter 51

Deep inside Tom Cockerel's bar, the Irish band complete with fiddler and tin whistle worked hard to make themselves heard above the roar of men's voices. The air warmed with the lingering smell of malt—proof of the spills on the sawdust floor between bar and tables.

Kaleo and Dolphie stationed themselves near the doors, well clear of the polished oak bar top crowded with men elbowing their way forward to buy drinks, or negotiating their way back, triumphantly bearing pottles of beer.

It was the usual busy Saturday afternoon on the Comstock Lode and Kaleo and Dolphie wouldn't be in town for much longer. They were content to sip and people watch, neither of them being big talkers.

Kaleo slouched down in the hardback chair, shuffling his rump to make himself comfortable. They didn't build cheap barroom chairs for men of his size, even with his legs extended and crossed at the knees.

He registered a dull ache in his chest that had nothing to do with the bruising he'd sustained fighting off Otis Hollows over a week ago. He went over it all in his head once again, but no matter how many times he replayed it, he had to acknowledge he saw no prospect of a future for him and Sarah Wyndham.

Or whatever her name is, he thought sourly. Rebecca Hollows, I suppose that's it, even if she doesn't like it. That's what his head told him. His heart didn't seem to agree. Damned inconvenient, that.

He sipped his beer and savored the yeasty bite on his tongue. The middle of the room was hot—a combination of the warmth thrown out by a fire blazing in a big stone hearth at one end of the room and the packed bodies, some dancing, some standing shoulder to shoulder, yakking at the other end.

The place had few tables, so he and Dolphie had been fortunate to score one near the street, where the crisp air contrasted with the fuggy room, thick with smoke from a hundred cigarettes.

On the curb right by the entryway, a polished black coach stood, the pair of black horses at its head rugged up in handsome winter horse-covers with a coat of arms appliqued across their backs. A word was spelled out amongst the decoration. S-i-l-v-e-r. As he gazed idly out, Kaleo deciphered the letters. Something silver…

He raised an eyebrow in Dolphie's direction. "Is that Sam Hollows' rig?"

Dolphie flicked a glance to the curb. "I believe it is. He's always liked making a splash. Why do you ask?"

"Nothing in particular."

Dolphie grinned slowly, his skeptical eyes narrowed. "She's a good woman, Kaleo."

A crawling worm of irritation wriggled at the back of Kaleo's neck. What the heck? Did he need maiden aunt advice now?

He gave Dolphie an irritated grin. "I suppose I could play dumb and ask who you're talking about," he said. "So, let's get this over with. She's not for me, and I don't need Mother Mary's advice. Okay?"

Dolphie shrugged. "Just saying. She's been treated badly. And I've never seen a woman fight back the way she does. Doesn't mean she's perfect."

"I'm not expecting perfect," said Kaleo irritably. "But I do expect honest. Subject closed."

Dolphie's shoulders answered him with a twitch. "Sometimes life's complicated, Kaleo. You gotta do what you gotta do."

"Now you're a philosopher." Kaleo glared out into the street. His beer tasted flat in his mouth.

The coach blinds were down, but the door suddenly opened, and Sam Hollows alighted backwards. Stepping out behind him was… Kaleo stared, not wanting to believe the evidence of his eyes.

Sarah Wyndham. Their eyes met, and she flinched. They remained locked. He couldn't pull away. She whirled around, gave Hollows a perfunctory hug, and disappeared.

His eyes widened in disbelief. "Did you see that?"

They watched Hollows at the wide-open door. Beyond him, in the dimness of the cab interior, Kaleo could make out another man. A man who, even in the low light, personified arrogance. Clifford Jensen.

"Two hours ago, maybe not even that, she said she was having nothing to do with them. Did I hear that right?"

Dolphie shook his head slowly from side to side.

Hollows stepped back inside and parked his big backside on the leather seat, pulling the door after him with a sharp heft. Another few seconds and the carriage pulled out into the street.

Before he could draw breath, a hack pulled in to take its place, blocking his view. But Kaleo didn't need to look to know that the woman who'd caused him so much heartache wouldn't be in sight.

The slippery little cow would already be long gone.

***

"I told you. Sam simply wanted to talk. There's no law against that, is there? He is my stepfather. The only father I've ever known. And I don't know why it's any of Kaleo's business, anyway."

Sarah was restlessly pacing from one side of de Vile's sitting room to the other, her arms flying as she walked, while her mother and her aunt watched, faces stony. They'd been waiting, a reception committee of two, when she had got back to the hotel, the chocolate from her mother's eclair leaking into a cream-stained napkin.

She licked her fingers as she'd passed it over with a sinking sense of anti-climax. She'd wanted to make a loving gesture to her mother, and this was where it had landed her.

Word was already out. Not fifteen minutes, and they'd all heard about her silent encounter with Kaleo outside the Cockerel. Her mother interjected. "Darling, be fair. He's in a state of shock. We all are. It's only two hours ago you told us all…"

Sarah leapt in, so upset at being caught out, her tongue was on the offensive. "I know what I told you, Mother. Sometimes things change."

Elizabeth joined in. "We accept that. But can you explain what's changed in the last two hours to make this a good idea?"

Sarah paused mid-stride. She raised her hands in the air and then dropped them again in a gesture of hopelessness.

"Clifford… When he got back to Sam's place—just now—and told them they'd missed out on the widow's shares, they were furious. More than furious. Incandescent. Dangerously so. And Clifford's got the idea from Will that the senator is behind it."

She faltered. How much of the truth could she tell them? She didn't doubt Clifford would go after Kaleo if she told them everything. Kaleo would have a bounty on his head for the rest of his life—and she couldn't allow that to happen.

Elizabeth sat back, pressing her spine firmly against the sofa. Sarah recognized it as one of her telltale signs when she was girding herself for battle.

"But he doesn't know yet that you're the one who's got control?" Her voice was quiet and deadly.

Sarah shook her head. The thought of his likely reaction when he found out had her heart turning over in her chest. She licked her lips. She was as dry as the Nevada desert.

"He demanded a meeting in Sam's carriage up the street. Sam was there, too. When I got there, I discovered why. They wanted to find out how much I knew.

"When we'd met earlier, Clifford had been so confident he'd got the shares. He was all puffed up with it. I wanted to keep him talking, to stop him from doing something stupid…"

It sounded a pathetic excuse. She knew that, but she still silently cursed Kaleo for coming straight back here and blabbing about seeing her. The niggling truth was that his instincts were a lot sounder than hers. He knew this was trouble, but what choice did she have?

"Something stupid?" Elizabeth echoed her words. "What are you imagining? Do we need to get you and Kaleo out of here on the next train?"

Sarah's heart stuttered. Running would be a total disaster. Clifford had been emphatic about that… He was watching her, and he would still hunt Kaleo down. Escape wasn't the answer.

"No… no. Running won't work for a second time. It didn't pan out too well the first time, when you think of it. If it had, we wouldn't be in this predicament now. No. We have to manage the situation."

She gazed at her mother. "Don't you feel the tiniest bit sorry for Sam? He's an old man, and he's going to lose everything."

Her mother stared back, her eyes screwed up in disbelief. "Do I feel sorry for Sam Hollows, Bekka? No, I do not. Whatever fate awaits him, he brought it on himself."

Sarah's mouth dropped open as she stared at Lottie, who was standing before her with hands on hips. It was a long time, years maybe, since she'd seen her mother strong and staunch like this.

"I don't know what's got into you, my girl. I really don't. You know better than anyone that Sam and Clifford are capable of. They're not men to be trifled with. I don't want you having another thing to do with them."

Neither do I, Mother. Neither do I. Pity I don't have a choice.

Chapter 52

The crowd surged into the foyer of Maguire's Opera House, the noise of their excited chatter bouncing off the pine rafters and reflecting down on the crowd beneath, increasing the sense of tumult.

Senator Hector de Vile stood in the eye of the social storm with would-be candidate William Sharon. They were jointly presenting their platform on how best to foster the West's interests in Washington, and everyone who was anyone had turned out to hear what they had to say.

Sharon's usually sour face split in a broad beam as he basked in de Vile's popularity, lapping up the senator's endorsement simply by standing at his shoulder.

De Vile clapped his colleague on the back, as if to include him in his grandstanding.

"My friend here agrees. The Comstock doesn't need Sutro's Tunnel." A few of the men crowding around him cheered.

De Vile waved a hand in greeting. "But we'll tell you all about that inside."

Kaleo shadowed him, relentlessly scanning heads, his sides buffeted by elbows and shoulders as the good-natured burghers and mine owners thrust their way forward into the auditorium.

The tone was jovial, the movement the normal pushing and shoving of a sizeable crowd eager to get the best seats, but that was of small comfort to Kaleo.

Ever since he'd caught Sarah hobnobbing with Hollows and his creepy offsider, he'd been on edge. Something was off, and he couldn't relax.

His hawk eyes searched the crowd's outer edges, resisting distraction in the general melee. His height gave him an advantage. He'd warned his father of his fears of an attack, but de Vile was sanguine about the danger.

"I've always known there are risks associated with public life, Kaleo, especially somewhere like Virginia City, where there are more oddballs and gamblers per mile than practically anywhere else in the Republic.

"But I can't stay at home and hide. And I've got you and Dolphie to ride interference for me. I've got to get out there and do my job."

Kaleo had drawn himself up to his full six foot two, urgent in his need to communicate the dangers.

"This is more than a normal risk, Father. You've got idiots close by, intent on revenge. Will Davenport has a real chip on his shoulder. And I wouldn't trust Jensen either.

"Sam Hollows may be a wasted old man, but Clifford is dangerous. Between the pair of them… nothing good will come of it, that's for sure."

That had been yesterday, after he'd returned from Tom Cockerel's establishment. However, De Vile was adamant. He wasn't pulling out of the Opera House meeting, which he'd advertised far and wide.

The building of the Sutro Tunnel was a hot topic. Some owners were going cold on the tunnel idea, one they'd initially supported because of the scalding acidic water that rose in the mines the deeper they dug.

They'd agreed to pay a levy for the work, intended to dig a tunnel right through the rich ore ledge and provide an outlet for the water all the way along it.

It was a massive engineering undertaking, but as the search for the ore changed direction and the mines went even deeper, massive new pumps were being employed. The need for an expensive tunnel appeared outdated.

A growling undercurrent of opposition hadn't been quelled by the disastrous Yellow Jack Mine fire the year before, when over forty men died underground. Adolphus Sutro claimed his tunnel would have prevented the terrible loss of life, because the men could have escaped out of it.

Now, Senator Hector de Vile occupied center stage at the Opera House, holding a capacity audience in rapt attention as he thundered against the proposal, telling them that Sutro was nothing but a carpetbagger trying to get a slice of the Comstock.

The audience cheered.

Kaleo and Dolphie watched and waited backstage, each taking one side of the wings. From this vantage point, they could survey the audience.

Kaleo knew bigwigs like John Mackay and James Fair, owners of the Consolidated Virginia, were here, but he didn't know them well enough to recognize their faces.

He spotted the women of de Vile's household—Elizabeth, Charlotte, Petra and Sarah—prominently seated in the middle of the circle. The soft hair on his forearms prickled as he saw Hollows and Jensen, seated a few rows behind them. Far too close for comfort.

But there was no sign of Will Davenport.

He signaled to Dolphie across the distance of the stage. Pointed at the seats. Mimed their names. Made a gesture in their direction.

I'm going to get closer out there. You watch here.

Dolphie nodded and gave him a thumbs up.

Kaleo slipped away and hovered inside the doorway into the circle, keeping his eyes firmly on the seated audience. They leaned into De Vile's words, giving him the silence of their rapt attention.

It's the first time I'm seeing my father doing what he does best, thought Kaleo. He can hold an audience in the palm of his hand.

Then the senator introduced William Sharon, and a subtle change crept over the audience. Women's skirts rustled, as if suddenly the occupants found their seats uncomfortable.

Men pulled surreptitiously at their collars. Heads turned as folk celebrity spotted, pointing and whispering to their companions. One or two men near the row ends slipped out on tiptoe.

Kaleo focused his attention even more keenly on the trio behind Sarah, but they showed no signs of moving.

De Vile took over again before Sharon lost the audience entirely and offered a quick conclusion.

"We'll be available for questions for a short time after this presentation," he said. "See you in the foyer."

***

The crowd thinned. Soon, only a few hangers-on loitered, wanting to share de Vile's limelight for a few minutes more. The Hollows crew were not among them.

Still, Kaleo burned inside like a reef light, positioned to warn of peril close by.

The Old Washoe Club was within easy walking distance, and the congested wheel traffic on C Street made it easier for them to return to their rooms by foot rather than coach.

De Vile had insisted the women of the group remain behind to be escorted home by the men, so Elizabeth, Charlotte, and Sarah all hovered patiently to one side, waiting for the senator to complete his business.

"This is what it would be like to be married to a man in public life," Charlotte said in a soft voice to Elizabeth, who raised an eyebrow quizzically, as if to say, So what?

Kaleo was close enough to hear the exchange, and he slid a glance toward the two women, their heads tipped together, Sarah's mother's hand on the Countess's arm.

He hadn't missed his father's warm regard for the Countess. But he hadn't realized it might be a bit more serious than he'd imagined. Was Hector considering marriage again?

His mouth took on a grim smile. Wouldn't that be funny? His father marrying Sarah's aunt?

A sharp pain tweaked in his chest as his eyes darted to the woman he'd once imagined had captured his heart.

Tonight she wore a pale blue dress that enhanced the delicacy of her creamy complexion and fair hair. A white jacket piped with blue in snugly fitted panels overlapped her skirt, accentuating her slender waist. She stood disconsolate, eyes on the ground, lost in her own world.

I'll never be able to trust her, never again.

On the day she returned from Alphie's and swore to the family she wouldn't have anything to do with the Hollows mob, he'd wondered briefly if they could be friends. And then what?

Within two hours, he'd caught her in another lie. That finished them as far as he was concerned, even if she gave the impression butter wouldn't melt in her mouth.

The senator was shaking hands, moving toward the wide doors onto C Street, signaling his departure, and the women floated in a small knot behind him and Sharon as they exited. Kaleo was still on guard on one side, and Dolphie on the other.

They reached the street. Hector paused and took in the chilly air with an appreciative glance at the sky.

Kaleo felt for the pistol in his waistband and drew it out, pinning it unobtrusively at his side.

He shadowed the family group as they stood on the street, drawing their coat collars up, preparing for the brisk walk through the snow-cleared boardwalk back to their accommodation.

Hector turned and drew Elizabeth to his side. Charlotte and Sarah linked arms. Sarah's eyes flicked in his direction and darted away again.

He took up position at his father's shoulder as they stepped into the pedestrian flow. As they moved in a small knot, the senator attracted approving smiles and warm greetings from doorways where men gathered, some sipping ale, others playing dice on barrel tops.

As they closed in on the Old Washoe Club, the crowds seemed to thicken. This was the heart of the town's entertainment district, with a bar or gambling joint in every second doorway.

Pedestrians patiently circumvented a poker game in play on the boardwalk.

Near the curb, a pedlar had set up a table of three shells and a pea, moving three glasses with lightning hand movements, while an inebriated crowd around him offered ribald comments.

De Vile drew Elizabeth wide of the group with a fond glance, momentarily stepping off the pedestrian thoroughfare and into the street to make room.

The space between Hector and the following women opened up. Kaleo slipped into it. The high-strung tension he'd felt all night compressed into one concentrated moment.

He surveyed the street left and right of de Vile's back. And then he saw something. Or rather, someone. A gray shape, looming out of the shadow of a stationary cab, gun raised.

Then a yell: "Death to murderers."

Kaleo lunged shoulder first and slammed into a slight blond man, hitting hard on the arm that held the gun. The attacker veered off target and fell face forward. A gun blast roared skyward as the bullet discharged harmlessly above their heads.

De Vile reacted instantly, like he'd touched a hot plate with his bare hand, bending low and pulling Elizabeth with him back onto the pedestrian walkway.

The gunslinger righted himself and attempted to re-aim.

Kaleo thrust forward again and grabbed him around the throat, restraining him against his shoulder.

"Stop, Davenport. Stop right now."

De Vile's nephew was snarling, mucus spraying from his mouth onto Kaleo's throat. His position was hopeless, but he didn't give up. He reared back, wildly swinging the gun he still held. For a second time, it exploded with a roar.

Chapter 53

From the *Territorial Enterprise*, January 17, 1870.

Front Page

SENATOR'S TRIUMPHANT NIGHT ENDS IN DEADLY ATTACK

'Senator Hector de Vile was attacked on C Street in Virginia City last night after giving a well-received speech at Maguire's Opera House on the vexed question of the future of Comstock mining and the Sutro Tunnel.

The senator was returning to the Old Washoe Club after speaking to a capacity crowd when a lone man who witnesses say was yelling "Death to murderers" accosted him of the in C Street wielding a gun.

A member of the senator's party disarmed the man and thwarted the attack. In a letter deposited at the Territorial's office a short time before the rampage, the attacker claimed he was Senator de Vile's estranged nephew, Karl de Vile.

Territorial staff alerted the sheriff's office to the letter, but the sheriff's department could not locate Karl de Vile before he opened fire.

De Vile the younger died at the scene from an accidental self-inflicted wound.

More details of the incident, and the gunman's motivation, can be found in the letter deposited with this newspaper, printed in full in a separate story on Page 3.

Late yesterday afternoon, a man claiming to be Senator de Vile's nephew, Karl de Vile, delivered the following statement to the offices of the Territorial Enterprise.

The editor has no way of checking the accuracy of his identity or the claims made herein.

Suffice it to say, we place no credence on defamatory claims made about a respected community leader willing to stand up for the Comstock, as evidenced by the warm reception he received at the Opera House meeting last night.

We simply publish the man's statement in full as evidence of his state of mind in the hours leading up to his attack.

Sheriff Gerald O'Doole says eyewitnesses confirm the younger de Vile made an unprovoked attack on the senator as he walked home from the Opera House.

The man who saved Senator de Vile was a visitor from Hawaii. Sheriff O'Doole confirmed they will lay no charges, as numerous eyewitnesses reported he was defending the senator from an unprovoked attack.

The senator was too shocked to speak to the Territorial last night, but a spokesperson commented on his behalf that he did not know his attacker and was unaware of his claims of being related to him.

"The attacker at no time presented his credentials to me," the senator commented further. The statement left at the newspaper office is presented here in full, with no further comment.

The Gunman's Letter

To Whom It May Concern

My full name is Karl Bohesimus de Vile, and I am the son of Bernard de Vile, who is Senator Hector de Vile's younger brother.

For the last six months I have been living and working in California under the assumed name of William Davenport while I pursue justice against my Uncle Hector for grave wrongs done by him against my family, including the cold-blooded murder of his father (my grandfather) in order to gain access to a family legacy.

I have grown up all of my life knowing the details of this heinous crime, told to me by my mother Thirza de Vile, even though I was too young to be aware of the full story when it occurred.

According to my mother, who was an upstanding New York matron of virtue and character, Hector de Vile was thrown out of the house by his father when he was sixteen years old, but de Vile senior stopped short at disinheriting him.

Instead, he made a series of inheritance requirements Hector had to fulfill to claim the double portion that is usually given to the eldest son as part of our family tradition.

According to my mother, my grandfather banned Hector from the family because he'd proven himself to be unwilling to take instruction when assuming a position in the merchant house of de Vile and Sons.

The family did not hear from Hector again for fourteen years, when he arrived unannounced at our Fifth Avenue home shortly before his thirtieth birthday to claim on his inheritance.

In accordance with my grandfather's requirements, he presented documents he said met the conditions set. He was married; he had a male son, and he had accumulated a fortune amounting to one million dollars in assets and cash.

He demanded full payment of the double portion in line with family custom. When my grandfather objected and demanded further proof of marriage and paternity, Hector insisted he be taken to the family vaults and paid out in gold ingots that he knew my grandfather sequestered there.

An altercation ensued. Hector stabbed my grandfather, mortally wounding him, and left with the ingots. My grandfather never recovered, dying within the week, and my father's life was ruined. He never recovered from the shock and died a few years later.

As the result of Hector de Vile's despicable actions, our family lived in much reduced circumstances, and the merchant house of de Vile and Sons collapsed after the loss of its two principal partners. I was deprived of my rightful inheritance

It has proven impossible to pursue the senator for justice. In the way of powerful men throughout the land, he is untouchable. He has ignored my letters appealing for restitution, and he has ignored my mother's pleas.

I have no further avenue than this desperate act. Do not believe this man's outward appearance of propriety. He is a blackguard, a liar, a thief, and a murderer.

Let this letter stand as a declaration to all that I willingly trade my life to rid the world of his offensive presence.

Signed,
Karl B. de Vile, January 16, 1870 Virginia City.

Chapter 54

Kaleo dragged himself through the days after Will's rushed funeral, the taste of ashes never leaving his mouth. He'd barely slept, unable to dismiss the agonizing last few seconds of his cousin's life from playing over and over in his mind.

Recurring flashes came to him, of the warm pressure of Will's back against his shoulder, and the smell of cordite in icy air which seconds earlier had carried the aroma of roasted chestnuts from street-side charcoal burners.

The deathly silence that fell after the second blast. And then the babble of drunken voices as crowds spilled from bars to view Will's body. And as quickly return to carousing and chatting up barmaids who wanted to get home to their kids.

In a town where the secretive 601 masked vigilante group had hung men they considered murderers without fair trial, the only thing interesting about this death was that the killer had failed to take out a big name.

He'd felt like Atlas as he sprang to his father's defense, his muscles responding to the danger with instant power. But once he'd satisfied himself that his father was unharmed, Kaleo's strength drained away. His body felt so weak he could barely stand.

He was glad, of course, to have saved his father. But he took no triumph in Will's death.

He drained the last of his ale and thumped the pot down on the bar. Drawn back again to Tom Cockerel's by his black mood, he mused sardonically. All alone, his resolve floated like sea foam, homesick for Waikiki waves one minute, and determined to stick it out in California the next.

The only thing that didn't change was the flat feeling of defeat, not triumph at Will's death.

He supposed he should start calling the quiet clerk with questioning pale gray eyes Karl de Vile, but he couldn't find it in himself.

The clerk's death was ruled accidental, caused by a blast from his own gun as he had tried to wrench it out of Kaleo's grip. But to be hailed as a hero for saving the life of a man blackened by charges of patricide?

He wasn't due any honor for that. He stood and caught a passing waiter's eye. He'd have another.

If only Hector would talk about it and tell me what happened that night. Surely, he owes me that.

He sunk further into his chair and jumped at a light hand on his shoulder.

"I thought I might find you here."

His father's immaculately tailored figure loomed over him. In a fluid movement which belied his age, the senator slipped into the empty seat opposite him, his perfectly manicured fingers spread flat on the table before him.

"Mind if I join you?"

A ripple of annoyance ran down his backbone. He was in the mood for wallowing in self pity, a lone wolf licking his wounds, easily ignored by those around him.

"Only if you're willing to tell me the truth. I'm sick of being left in the dark."

Kaleo lifted his eyes in challenge and stared into his father's unfathomable, gold-flecked eyes. A flicker of light crossed them at his words.

De Vile rested his chin on his hands and considered his son in silence.

Kaleo stared back, unblinking.

"A fair request, considering everything," said the older man, his words muffled by his hands.

He placed them back on the table. Shifted in his chair. "Trouble is, I'm not sure I know the full story myself. But I'll tell you all I know. First, though, I'll order a drink."

Tom Cockerels expected their customers to approach the bar and order for themselves. All de Vile had to do was meaningfully catch the barman's eye. The manager was out from behind his post and standing beside them in a flash.

"Some of the local drop," de Vile said. "There's nothing like a Comstock brew. And another for my companion."

"I've already ordered," said Kaleo mulishly.

They sat in silence until the drinks arrived. The hum in the bar quietened when de Vile first arrived, but now wound back up to its normal level, loud enough to mask any private talk.

"That dreadful night—over twenty years ago, when I returned to my father's house? Don't think it hasn't haunted me. It's true that I faked some details to claim my share of the inheritance. And I arrived unannounced because I knew if I gave my father notice of my intentions, he'd block me.

"He'd get in extra security or something to make sure he didn't have to face me, because he avoided any sort of emotional scene."

He lifted his tankard and sipped appreciatively. "The Germans really know how to make a full-bodied ale." He sighed, as if reluctant to continue.

"Go on," said Kaleo. "I'm all ears."

"Okay… As I've told you already, I took Bertha and Alex with me to New York."

"Stop right there," said Kaleo. "Explain that part again. I know about Alex, of course. Your adopted son. So that, for starters, could make you a fraud. But who's Bertha?"

"I'll get around to that," said de Vile. "But first, I have to tell you, Kaleo. That stuff about me marching my father down to the family vaults and forcing him to give me gold ingots? It's pure fantasy, like the most of that madman's story."

***

New York 1851

When he'd left home at sixteen, his father ran the household like an army general. Stepping back through the chandelier-lit faux Classical Rome entry and being greeted by Big Alf, his father's go-to-man for all things to do with the running of the house, was like stepping back in time.

"Master…" Alf put his hand over his mouth. "I mean, Mr. Hector—Mr. Hector!" Alf greeted him with a broad grin. "Long time no see!"

"You too, Alf," Hector said, clapping the retainer on his broad shoulder. "Is Rolf home?" Calling his father by his first name… It was a habit he'd adopted to annoy his father and in the years away, he'd stopped thinking of him as his father altogether.

"Yes. He's here. He's got extras too." Alf turned pointedly to Bertha and the boy. "And these are…"

"Oh, yes. My apologies. I'd like you to meet my wife Bertha, and son Alex."

Alf's eyes widened momentarily, but he quenched his surprise as quickly as it registered. "Do you want me to announce you, or leave it for you to do?" The big Yorkshireman raised one bushy brow.

"Let me," said Hector. "It's probably better that way."

Alf led him through the spacious entry, past the classical statues posed on slim marble plinths, and into the formal dining room.

The closed red velvet curtains gave the room the atmosphere of a tomb, despite being lit with two hanging chandeliers and the silver candelabrum on a table set for formal dining. Their fluttering candles reflected off silver cutlery, white bone china, and crystal glasses, the cloying vanilla scent from the burning wax adding to the clammy closeness.

A quick glance told Hector they'd interrupted a normal de Vile family meal with the addition of a couple of guests he didn't recognize, a blond man about his own age with a handlebar mustache and a petite brunette who he presumed was this man's wife.

All conversation stopped dead as they entered.

His father had shriveled over his time away, but he was still a big-boned man, with ham-sized fists. Except now his tailored jacket hung loosely off his sunken shoulders. Blond hair that once glinted under the chandeliers like a golden helmet lay flat against his skull, lifeless straw no longer gleaming in the spotlight.

When he laid eyes on the son he'd banished fourteen years ago, Rolf de Vile's lips pursed in a familiar hard line, and his fists opened and closed in reflexive protest, like a showground clown.

The man who'd always assumed he was born to rule had crumbled around the edges, like a marble statue worn down by harsh weather. Ambiguous Athens had replaced militant Sparta.

***

Virginia City, 1870

"My father couldn't believe his eyes when he saw I walked in there. He was at a loss for words, at least at first. When he gathered his wits, he summoned the family lawyer—old Joseph Rietveld, to come immediately.

"They hastily arranged extra places at the table. All highly irregular, of course, for that regimented family. My mother was white with fury at the interruption. They'd finished their soup, so we were in time for the main meal."

He grinned at the memory. Old Joe had long, gray ear whiskers that had fascinated him as a young kid. Now he was exhausted, on old man on his last legs. He gazed at Kaleo, disbelieving.

"Joe was the de Vile family lawyer from Father's first days in America, and he lived a few houses down the street. He came immediately to inspect my documents. Of course, that didn't happen until after dinner, when we adjourned to Rolf's library."

He gave himself a moment to swallow, imagining the scene again.

"Bertha was a brilliant wife substitute. One of her gifts was turning on the charm for the old boys. Despite himself, my father liked her, and he was even more delighted with Alex.

"A grandson he hadn't known about? I sensed he was warming to the whole idea of having me back." He pushed his chair back a few inches and re-positioned himself to face Kaleo more squarely.

"But did I have any thoughts of re-joining the family business? None at all. It would have been completely impossible. I could never have done it. And the women of the family? My mother and Bernard's wife, Thirza?

"It appalled them when they sensed Father might thaw in his attitude towards me. My mother took an instant dislike to Bertha. She sniffed out immediately that she was a popsy wopsy. That my father enjoyed her flirtatiousness riled Mother to no end. She wasn't sorry when Bertha left early to take Alex back to the hotel to bed."

"And what about Thirza?" Kaleo asked. "She's Will's mother, isn't she? Is she still alive?"

Thirza.

He hadn't thought of her in years. Regal, ambitious and as cold as the Arctic Circle. Colder. Hector shivered at the thought of ever having to share a bed with her. She was two years older than him, and she'd set her eye on him as the de Vile heir from a ridiculously early age.

She'd written the script, and his mother was in the audience applauding. That was one thing he pitied about his brother Bernard. Having her as a wife. He recollected his thoughts, shaking his head. "She died a while ago, I believe."

"And Will's father, Bernard? Your brother?"

"Died years ago. Ten years at least."

Kaleo nodded, warmed up and engaged. "Go on."

"Thirza hardly said a thing through dinner. Probably because of the visitors. James Wollander and his wife Bea. James was another importer-exporter. A partner in Wollander and Mountfort, one of the biggest merchants in New York."

He fiddled with his beer and pitched Kaleo a weary smile.

"I'd heard rumors about the Wollanders. Particularly about James and Thirza. It was probably malicious gossip, but it made me wonder."

Chapter 55

New York, 1851

One minute Hector was warming himself at the library fireplace, enjoying an after-dinner brandy, listening to old Joe giving the family his report about how Hector had met all his father's legal requirements and was due the double portion payout. And the next Thirza was rushing at him, her face contorted in rage.

After that, for a period, he remembered nothing. When he came to, he smelled blood and a woman—he thought it was Thirza—was screaming. He lay on the carpet close to the fire. When he put his hand up to his shoulder, and it came away wet and sticky, he thought the blood he smelled was probably his own.

His mother was beside him, but it wasn't him she was concerned about. She was leaning over the body of another man near him. Bernard was there too, helping her roll the man onto his back, and he saw it was his father. And there was blood, a lot of it, like a red lake, pooling on his father's chest.

Everything slowed down then, but even in slow motion, his brain couldn't keep up. Gradually, it all came back to him. Thirza flying at him, holding something in her hand. A brass poker, he'd thought, snatched up from the hearth fire set.

She raised it above her head, and as he raised his arm to protect himself, the last thing he remembered was brandy spilling from his glass and showering his face.

***

Virginia City, 1870

The bar crowd had cycled through as Hector and Kaleo talked, the late-afternoon clerks and managers replaced by miners who'd come off day shift but weren't ready to go home yet, wouldn't be for hours. The noise in the place had risen another notch, but still no one was paying them any attention. And Kaleo was still drinking.

"How many of those have you had, boy?" Hector asked.

"Not enough." Kaleo softened the cheeky rejoinder with a smile. "You're not becoming an autocratic dad, are you, Hector?" he teased. "Like your own pater? Remember, you've only been my father for two months. And I am twenty-three years old."

"Wrong, son. I've been your father for the whole twenty-three years. Neither of us knew it, that's all."

Kaleo laughed. "Fair comment. I'm fine, Father. It's water for me from now on. But can I get you another?"

"No, thanks. Let's finish this story and get home."

"Sure. The water can wait. Tell me the rest of the story, although I think I've already guessed the ending."

"You probably have. Thirza grabbed a knife from the kitchen when we'd taken our break at the end of dinner. She concealed it under a voluminous duster coat she was wearing.

"I don't know who she intended to use it on. Me, Bernard, or Father? But when old Joe delivered his verdict, she rushed me. And my father intervened. He stepped between us. She caught my shoulder, and I went down. I knocked myself out cold on the hearth. She lashed out a second time as I went down, and my father copped the lot. Right in the chest."

He'd never spoken of that night to anyone before, and recounting it now left him nauseous. He folded over, pushing back the nausea inside.

Kaleo reached out, grasped his wrist.

"Are you all right, Father? Your face is ashen."

De Vile shook his head. "Not all right, no. Give me a minute, and then let's get out of here."

He cleared his throat, trying to dislodge the ache there, and took a few deep breaths to lighten the weight on his chest. He leaned in closer to Kaleo.

"My father didn't die that night. He lingered on. He developed an infection and succumbed a few days later." His lashes were wet with tears he'd never shed until now. "I was well on the road to California by then."

He shook his head. "I didn't wield that knife, Kaleo. Because they didn't want a scandal, they hushed it up. The doctor certified he'd died of a blood infection. But Thirza and my mother always blamed me."

He rubbed his side, where a knife-like pain lingered. "You can see how it was for Will—Karl," he said, correcting himself.

"Thirza poisoned him against me. I never wanted to talk or think about any of it again. I wanted to get as far away from them as I could. And until you came on the scene, that's how it would have stayed."

He gave Kaleo a watery smile. "One day I hope I'll decide it's all been worth it. But that's not today, I'm afraid." He gave a weak laugh and pushed himself upright. "Satisfied now?"

"I guess," said Kaleo. "I'm sorry for Will, but I'm no longer guilty about his death."

Chapter 56

Sam Hollows sat at the breakfast table, the oaty crumbs from his morning toast flecking his woolly beard. Typical, Clifford thought. The world was passing Sam by, and he didn't appear to notice or care.

Clifford sized up the view out the windows to the side garden. The snow had thawed in the last couple of days, and yellow daffodils were showing their heads under the cherry walk. By the time they were flowering this time next year, someone else would live in the house he'd once assumed would be his.

Any day now, the world will find out they'd lost ownership of the Golden Bowl, and he'd tramp the boardwalks in workman's boots, seeking for work.

Pretty well every adult male in Virginia City, from John Mackay to the newbie who arrived in town yesterday, wore the same rough workingman's trousers and calico shirts, but that didn't mean folk couldn't tell at a glance the Silver King from the four-dollar-a-day miner.

And he'd no intention of sliding down the social scale to the bit bars on the scummy end of C Street. He renewed his attempt to make Sam realize the consequences.

"You still don't get it, do you, Sam? Without the Golden Bowl, we're no better than losers scratching around in the dark at the bottom of a flooded shaft."

His voice sounded strained, even to his own ears. A mosquito whine. But he couldn't believe Sam's slow-witted reaction. What was wrong with the man? He was about to lose his fortune, and he didn't care.

"I'm too old to worry about it," Sam said. "I'm obviously past going down some mine again, Cliff. Thanks to me, you got the chance to take over, and you've blown it."

Not this again.

"If you'd treated Rebecca better, we wouldn't be in this spot."

Clifford's neck hairs rankled. "What are you on about? You getting all holy on me now? Some nonsense about being punished for our sins? Is that it?"

His jeering echoed in the high-ceilinged room.

There was a tap on the breakfast-room door, and Nessa Murphy tentatively edged through.

"Mr. Hollows, sir, a visitor to see you. It's Mr. Sharon. He says it's urgent."

"Show him into my study, Mrs. Murphy. We're finished here. We'll go straight through."

Sam and Clifford barely got themselves seated before Bill Sharon bowled in, peeling off his furry gloves and fleece-trimmed hat as he entered the room that was already warming up from George stoking the overnight embers.

Sharon settled himself in the chair before Sam's desk, self-important in an impeccably tailored, wide-lapelled charcoal shooting coat.

Underneath he wore a dazzling white shirt with a neat cravat tie edging the sharp points of the flat collar in black. William Sharon was the only man on the lode who always dressed like a metropolitan banker.

Sam was setting about lighting his first cigar of the day. "Can we get you coffee, or something stronger?"

The bank manager's presence sparked Sam out of his flat mood, Clifford noted.

"Too early for that, Sam, far too early for liquor. Coffee will be fine."

Nessa Murphy hovered at the door, and Sam gestured her in. "More coffee, Mrs. Murphy. And some of your oat cookies for our visitor."

Clifford knew the Hollows' house was familiar territory for the manager of the Nevada branch of the California Bank. From the early years, Uncle Sam's Silver was one of Sharon's biggest clients.

He wasted no time in getting to the point. "Disturbing news from Ralston overnight." He rubbed his hands in anticipation.

William Chapman Ralston was the King of San Francisco, founder of the Bank of California and the man who'd rescued Sharon from bankruptcy and sent him out to Virginia City to remake his fortune.

Sam frowned. "Oh yes? What's Billy's problem?"

"He's confirming what we suspected. You'll never guess who bought that last raft of Golden Bowl shares." Sharon's eyes narrowed with satisfaction at being "in the know."

Sam flicked a glance Clifford's way, and he responded: "We have our suspicions. Who is it?"

Sharon hesitated, happy to extend the suspense. He gave a wolfish grin. "Well, you know they were owned by Jim Mackay's sister-in-law?"

Sam's brow furrowed. "They haven't gone to Mackay, have they?" Everyone knew of the rivalry between the Irish mine owners and Hollows and Sharon.

"Funnily enough, no. There's a good reason the Bonanza King didn't snap them up." The corners of Sharon's eyes pulled down in shrewd wrinkles.

Another silence. Clifford snorted. "And that is…?"

"Probably because his sister-in-law felt sorry for the buyer and convinced Mackay to pass on them."

"Oh?" Sam's discomfort eased to a relaxed curiosity. "Why would he do that?"

Sharon twirled the umbrella that rested by his thigh. "Maybe out of a sense of chivalry for the fairer sex?"

The crease in Sam's brow deepened. "Chivalry? Now that's not a word I've heard applied to the buying and selling of silver scrip before."

Clifford couldn't stand the suspense any longer. "Oh, for goodness' sake. Cut the drama, Bill. What are you dying to tell us?"

Sharon took a gulp of his fresh coffee and grinned up from the steaming rim. "The new owner is a woman. A young and, it's agreed, rather attractive woman."

"Who?" asked Clifford with a scowl. "I've had enough of the playacting. And what does a woman know about running a mine?"

"This one knows a good deal. Enough to gazump you, at any rate."

Clifford's cheeks were flaming. He'd an uncomfortable premonition about what was coming next. "Quit the game, Bill. Who is this delectable rich creature?"

Sharon pulled a telegraph sheet from his jacket pocket and waved it in front of Clifford's nose.

He snatched at it and spread it out on his knee, smoothing the creases in the pale yellow paper as he read. When he finished, he locked eyes with Sam and gave a slow, disbelieving shake of his head.

He put his hand to his temple to ward off a rolling lightheadedness. For a few seconds, he couldn't see. Then he caught Sam's eye.

He opened his mouth to speak, but his vocal chords were on strike. Finally, he gasped enough air to get his mouth open. "No. I don't believe it."

Sharon shook his head gently from side to side. "I'm afraid it's correct. "

"Who is it?" said Sam. He sounded as if he were emerging from a long dream.

Clifford still couldn't get the words out. After a long silence, Sharon filled the gap.

"Your stepdaughter. She's opened a new company called Restoration Mines. And the owner's name on the stock trading certificate is Sarah Wyndham."

Sam Hollows let out a startled laugh. "See what I told you, Clifford? Smartest woman on the mountain." Sam seemed almost pleased to be proven correct.

Sharon hesitated, taking in his reaction. "Maybe so, Sam. But it leaves you with some questions to answer. Like how you're going to repay your loan to us when you've lost control of your biggest asset?" He swirled the dregs of his coffee in his cup and gulped them down.

"We're not a charity, boys. You know that." He gazed from Clifford to Sam and then back to Sam again. "So, tell me. How are you going to repay the fifty thousand dollars you took out as a personal loan, Sam?"

"Ease up, Bill. We're not broke yet. Let's see that telegram." Sam reached over his desk with a long arm and whisked the telegram out of Clifford's fingers. He read it in silence, an admiring grin lighting up his face as he came to the end.

"Slippery Sarah. Appropriate, don't you think? She was yours for the taking a year ago, my boy. All it required was delicacy and patience. Now you've let the biggest catch of the decade slip right through your fingers." He dipped his head toward Sharon.

"Can't make you too happy either, Bill. After all, isn't this the second time Jim Mackay has got the better of you? First, he took the Hale and Norcross out from under your nose and broke your milling monopoly. And now this.

"I bet part of the deal with Rebecca is that they change the mill they use for crushing to Mackay's one. That'll hurt, won't it?"

Sharon's complexion had turned a sickly pale gray. "They're kitchen-sink suffragists. They won't last."

"You said much the same when Jim Mackay got control of the Hale and Norcross, remember? Said you were going to send him packing back over the Geiger Grade," he said, naming the twistiest, steepest section of the railway track into Virginia City. "And we all know where he is now. Bigger than ever."

Sharon's face went from pale to ghostly. He shrugged, as if that was of no account. "It's not me who's going to have to sell his house," Sharon grunted.

"And what about you, Clifford? Are you planning to stay?"

Clifford scowled.

Touché, he thought.

Where the hell am I going to go?

Chapter 57

As Kaleo set off on his daily constitutional up Sun Mountain, he overtook a few small groups of Saturday picnickers headed in the same direction—to the bottom of Cedar Hill, where Mackay's Consolidated Virginia minehead sat, nestled at a junction point of the ranges.

Since Will's death nearly a week ago, it had been his daily ritual to climb to the top, and he was pleased to find his ability to maintain his pace at the higher altitude was increasing every time he walked it.

My lungs must be getting stronger. That'll be an advantage when— if ever—I get home again.

He paused mid-stride and lifted his head to take in the view up to the series of peaks. Miners had long ago stripped the hillsides of bigger trees, leaving stunted pines and sage bush as the only natural cover.

Any timber of any size was underground, holding up mine shafts down hundreds of feet. Kaleo admitted there was a barren beauty about the rising peaks and the track which wended its way over the ridge and down into the Gold Hill side of the ravine.

Once there were two separate settlements—Gold Hill and Virginia City. But the urban creep of a continually growing population had closed up the space between them until a continuous band of settlement joined the original hamlets.

Among the most famous mineheads, the Chollar and Yellow Jacket for example, affluent townsfolk were building fine, spreading homes away from the noise and dirt of the town center. He buried the lower half of his face in his scarf and strode on, pushing himself to do the trip in a shorter time today than he had yesterday.

It was all part of the game he played with himself, and he was getting faster every day. He was familiarizing himself with the different mines, too, identifying new shafts as he went higher and further north.

Mackay and Fair's famed Consolidated Virginia sat neatly above the so-called Bonanza Pocket; with the Yellow Jacket a little below it, and the Andes the highest of all, close to the peak of Mount Davidson.

In every direction working mineheads sat over a warren of tunnels, the chimneys bellowing smoke. For a man who took fresh ocean air for granted, he held no ambition to go underground, but was fascinated to see it all.

This was Sarah's world. She understood it perhaps better than most of the 25,000 others who lived here. But it would never be his world.

It differed greatly from his beloved Waikiki, with its golden sands, foamy swells, and salt-tinged breezes. The locals talked about the Washoe Zephyr—a destructive, howling wind that matched the wildness in the spirit of people and place. It was a summer phenomenon, so he was unlikely to experience it.

Despite his resolve, he felt a pinch in his chest at the thought. He couldn't deny that even in his disillusionment, a mutinous little voice echoed from deep within him.

She's a liar.

Yes, she lied, but did she have any other choice?

She misled you about her feelings.

Had she done that? Or did I misread the signals?

She was engaged to Clifford Jensen, and she never said a thing about it.

Was she engaged to him? I've only got his word for that.

What is with him, anyway? She tries to hide it, but she's terrified of him.

More secrets she's not telling.

Near the top, a few clumps of bushy shelter remained, a local park where enthusiastic picnickers settled with their wicker baskets of sandwiches and lemon squash—if not something stronger—on weekends.

He'd reached the bench marker where the road turned up toward the Bullion, the shaft north of Con Virginia, where someone had constructed a rough bench with a couple of planks.

Amazing no one's stolen them for mine shafts, he mused, as he squatted for a quick rest before turning back.

Overhead, an eagle soared, its harsh keening cry reaching him above the thunder of dynamite from deep underground. The mines went on a twenty-four-hour cycle, regardless of weekends. He pulled a canteen from his waistband and took a long draft of fresh water.

Sarah is one thing. My father is quite another.

Was Hector's version of the events surrounding his father's death true? He noted he made no mention of ever thanking his father. The man had died protecting him, and instead of showing gratitude, Hector had turned his back and fled?

Is that fair? Or is he hiding his feelings, a habit he can't break?

And how did he, Kaleo, fit into Hector's world, anyway? Did he fit at all? Kaleo took in a deep breath of icy mountain air and, head in his hands, stared at the ground.

Do I want to be in his life? And have him in mine? Or do I want to get on a ship straight back to Honolulu and see Malia and Titus?

At home, Malia, his sight-impaired little sister, was coming into her own, running the family sugar business with her lawyer-fiancé, and he was eager to see them again.

He heard the crunch of a boot on twigs. He dropped his hands from his face and ahead. No one was on the track in front of him.

Another soft footfall. And then hands closed tightly over his eyes from behind, and the cold barrel of a revolver pressed into his back.

***

"Keep still and you won't get hurt." Clifford kept his voice low, avoiding attention from the other walkers. "Make a move—any move at all, and I'll shoot. This is Virginia City, remember? Anyone who notices us will turn the other way. They know what's good for them."

Clifford stood close, the gun hard up against the Hawaiian's spine. "If this goes off, you'll never walk again, even if you survive. No more surfer boy."

He felt a tingle of pleasure at the involuntary stiffening in Kaleo's body at the impact of his words. He nodded to Otis. "Get the bandage out." He'd made it clear before they'd started out. Otis was here under sufferance.

"I'm not trusting you at the sharp end of the action any more. Not after you've stuffed up every time," Clifford had told him back at the house.

"Besides, your arm has only come out of the sling today, so you're not ready for heavy effort. The bandage will work nicely. We can get him down off the mountain without attracting attention."

Otis pulled the white square of cloth out of his trouser pocket and tied Kaleo's right arm up in a sling. "If anyone asks, you fell and broke it. We're helping get you to the doc."

Clifford maintained a steady pressure with the snub-nosed gun. With a jacket draped around the guy's shoulders, no one would be any the wiser.

The secret room at the Hollows' house had inspired his kidnap plan, and it worked like a charm. Within forty minutes they'd stumbled down the Mount Davidson track and had their quarry, gagged and bound at wrists and ankles, tied to the bedframe in the room where Rebecca—and he presumed Charlotte—had hidden out.

"Two can play that game," he said to Otis with satisfaction. "He's not going anywhere, and his friends won't have a clue where he is. Even Sam doesn't have to know."

Sam had been out when they'd returned. The only other person who knew of the guy's presence was George Murphy, and he would keep mum. Clifford was certain of that. His livelihood depended on it.

He savored the small victory. Small, yes. But a paving stone for bigger things.

First, the note to Rebecca, demanding she sign over all her Golden Bowl shares to him or lover boy would fall down an old mine shaft.

There were so many of them dotted around the hills, they were spoiled for choice. He would get the note written and on its way in Amos's reliable hands as soon as he'd had a celebratory drink.

Getting the shares transferred shouldn't take any longer than twenty-four hours. He would demand she telegraph the San Francisco share registry with the instructions.

Then he would get lover boy to write Rebecca a letter saying he was done with California and was leaving on the next train. He would write that damn letter or understand Bekka would end up at the bottom of a mine shaft.

A royal flush. Two birds with one stone! He would get the mine back—and it would be in his name this time, nothing to do with Sam, and he would have broken up the little love tryst. She would end up with no mine and no man. Like she deserved, the bitch.

And of course, with a signed letter in their possession saying Kaleo was leaving, no one was going to think twice when the beach boy was never seen or heard of again. Pity about that. Those shafts were damn deep, dark and cold.

Chapter 58

"You'll be touched to know Rebecca cares about you so much she's willing to sign over the mine shares to me to ensure your safe return." Clifford sneered at her stupidity.

Clifford was standing at the end of his bed they tied him to. They'd removed his blindfold, but he was still gagged and tightly tied at wrist and ankle. Already the skin at his wrists was rubbed raw and stinging.

From the direction of the slanting light from the blind-covered windows, Kaleo guessed it was Sarah and Dolphie's hiding place. A sneaked scanning of the space confirmed that suspicion when he spotted a photograph on a shelf. A wedding photo of a much younger Charlotte with a man he didn't recognize, Sarah's dad for sure.

He smiled beneath the gag as he detected tantalising wisps of Sarah's woodland mint perfume in the closed up air. If he was imagining it, he didn't care.

He stared at the ceiling and ignored the gloating man who stood over him.

"Soon I'll have the river of riches flowing back to where it belongs. Actually, I suppose I should thank Rebecca for finding the widow and negotiating the deal.

"Jim Mackay would never have agreed to me purchasing them anyway, if he'd had a say. And I'm sure he had a say." He settled his butt on the edge of the bed, like a brother leaning in to confide something important.

Gorge charged up Kaleo's throat at his closeness. Through the herby smell of his expensive cologne, Kaleo smelt something else: the stench of venality. The whalebone hook glowed softly warm in the hollow of his throat.

Yeah. The fathers who've gone before you know it, too. They're warning me.

He willed himself not to react, to keep staring blankly at the ceiling. Little jags of light played at the corners of the room, the last rays of the sun this day would see, dancing at the edges.

He wondered if he would still be alive to see them playing on the smooth white walls tomorrow. The light on the fringes. Like him. He'd gone too close to the edge, but he would do it all over again if he could.

Don't give him the mine, his mind willed Sarah. Don't believe him. Whatever he's telling you, you'll never see me again, alive or dead.

For a few seconds, he centered all his willpower on sending her the wordless message.

Don't do it.

Then he became aware again of Clifford crowding him on the bed. He's so impressed by his own shadow he doesn't understand. I'm truly not listening.

Clifford grabbed him by the right shoulder. A piercing nerve pain ran down his arm, and he gasped through the tight gag. "Do you hear what I'm saying?" Clifford hissed.

Kaleo rolled his head from side to side in dissent. The fingers dug in again, more deeply this time, right into the ridge of his collarbone.

"Do what I say and you can get out of here alive," he growled, his voice fierce.

Kaleo lowered his eyes finally, reluctantly, to stare into his captor's face. An intense glitter darted from the opaque orbs pierced by pinpoint black irises; his captor's cheeks blazed a hectic, unhealthy red.

He's mad for power, he thought. And he won't be relinquishing his desire for Sarah to anyone, especially not me. He softened his gaze, hopefully showing he was listening. Anything to buy time while he worked out a plan.

"You're going to write Rebecca a letter. A farewell letter, saying you're going back to Hawaii. The air doesn't suit you here or something. Whatever you like. Do that and I'll put you on the next train out."

He rose and sauntered toward the door. "Once I've got the mine back, of course. Not before that. I'm not stupid."

Neither am I, thought Kaleo. If you think I'd believe you'll put me anywhere other than down a mine shaft, I would have to be unforgivably stupid.

Halfway to the door, Clifford turned casually back toward him. So studied, Kaleo thought. As if this carefully rehearsed finale was a passing thought.

"Oh, that's right, I'll need something as proof I really hold you, of course. I promised Rebecca."

He was back at the bedside in two big strides, a pocketknife in hand. He leaned in and wrenched the binding holding the whale hook on his neck. In one slashing stroke, he severed the pandanus ties and cradled the hook in his hand.

"A barbaric thing, but beautiful," he said. "Not another one like it for miles, I'm sure, so Rebecca will know it's come from you." He pivoted to the door. "I'll be back with the pen."

It was as if Clifford had dragged the life force out of him. His neck stung from the point of the knife as it reached for the whale's tooth. Blood dribbled on his shoulder. But that wasn't the worst of it. He imagined the generations of warriors who'd worn this *waiwai*—his priceless jewel—before him and he called down their wrath.

Do your work.

Chapter 59

Amos delivered the first of Clifford's notes late on Saturday. Sarah didn't know if Amos could read or not, but saw from his darting slate-gray eyes and drawn mouth that he knew the delivery contained something bad.

He slipped up from behind her with a tentative "Miss" and thrust the paper into her hand. She whirled and grabbed his wrist just as he was about to disappear again.

"Amos," she cried out, her voice carrying a sharper edge than she had intended. "I haven't seen you for a day or two. How are you?"

He cast his eyes to the boardwalk, shuffled his feet, which were clad in boots at least one size too big, with scuffed toes and worn-down heels. Legions of feet had filled them before they found Amos, she thought.

"I'm all right, miss. I been here."

"I suppose you have. But a note? You rarely bring me notes, Amos."

He shrugged. "Jus' do what I'm tole, miss."

She still held his hand, convinced he would run away if she let him go. "I want you to wait while I read it. I might have a message for you to take back. Were you told that?"

He risked a quick glance up at her. His pale face, with peaked features that showed a lack of a good meal or two, was etched in misery.

Something serious then.

He shook his head. "Nah, ma'am. The usual."

"Well, I'm asking. Will you wait while I read it?"

He nodded doubtfully and backed away as soon as she let go of his hand to open the note.

She'd been loitering anxiously outside their hotel, surveying the street north and south, watching for Kaleo. He went for his usual solo walk ages ago—it seemed like hours. He'd been away for much longer than usual, and she had a niggle in her bones about it.

With the note's arrival, her fingers tingled with fear. As she opened it, her stomach dropped into her rubber boots. Just the right footwear if you were expecting to search the mountain for someone. She clutched her hand tight against her waist to hold in her fears as she read.

Worse. Much worse than I expected.

No wonder Amos was out of sorts.

Clifford had Kaleo and was threatening to kill him unless she transferred all of her mine shares to him. That would make him the majority owner of her father's mine.

What had been her father's mine, she corrected. She knew without a skerrick of doubt that even if she did it, Kaleo would die unless they found him first.

She allowed herself time to gather her strength. Take some deep breaths. Gird yourself for the next battle. And then she swung around, trying to appear like she'd barely a care in the world.

Amos stared longingly into the French patisserie where she'd bought Charlotte's treat more than a week ago. She wandered over to him. "Come on, boy, it's time we filled up those hollow legs."

He gazed at her, eyes like saucers. She could almost see the drool filling his mouth. While the girl behind the counter filled paper bags with chocolate eclairs and two ham-and-cheese croissants, she took a pen from her reticule, turned Clifford's note over and wrote on the back: Give me some time to arrange it.

She tucked it into the top pocket of Amos's heavy cotton shirt and gathered up the paper bags. They turned and exited the shop. On the pavement outside, she handed him the paper bags in one hand, and patted his pocket.

"Make sure your boss gets that. A man's life depends on it."

Then she went to find Dolphie.

***

"He won't keep his word. You know he won't. I'm blowed if I'm going to give him the shares. He's even fencing Sam out of it. But Kaleo's a dead man if we don't find him."

Sarah gazed despairingly around the family meeting. They were all there—Petra and Lottie, Hector and Elizabeth. And Dolphie. But she was pinning her hopes on Dolphie.

"You know how common it is for people to stumble on remains down mine shafts. Goats. Children. Unexplained deaths. No one gives a toss. Life goes on. That's the VC way."

Dolphie stepped close and placed a light hand on her shoulders. "Calm down, Princess. We all know the odds. They're not in Kaleo's favor."

She pierced de Vile with a 'tell me the truth' stare. "What do you think, Senator? Am I right?"

"Couldn't be more on the button, my dear. You'd be an idiot to transfer the shares with no guarantee except his word. I'd be the first to agree if I thought it would work.

"He's my son, my newly discovered son, for goodness' sake. I want him back as much as anyone. But giving in won't do it. Clifford's words are not worth anything, as you already know."

His gaze fell on Charlotte. "Lottie. I'm thinking aloud here. But what're the chances they'll be holding him in the secret room you and Sarah used? They know all about it now. It's not a secret anymore. But it is conveniently private."

Lottie nodded her head. "Quite likely."

Hector caught Sarah's eye. "First thing is, we get our own 'Amos.' A boy to follow Jensen's boy next time and see where he goes. That will be a good clue." He sought Dolphie out for confirmation. "What do you think, Dolphie? You're the security expert."

"Quite right, Hector. We need a plan, and we need it now."

"Petra, I'm wondering. When does Nessa Murphy do her shopping for the household? The butcher, the baker, that kind of thing?"

"Regular as clockwork. First thing in the morning after they've cleared away breakfast. Usually around ten a.m."

Dolphie inclined his head to Lottie. "And which merchants does she usually favor, Charlotte? I think it would be helpful to have someone bump into her in the shop or on the street outside. By chance, of course. You or Petra, maybe? Sarah's too obvious."

***

The second note arrived at dusk. Except it wasn't just a note. Amos carried a bulky envelope. Sarah's stomach heaved in shock, and she had to swallow the vomit that rose in her throat. They hadn't cut off one of Kaleo's ears, had they?

She didn't know where the unwelcome thought had come from, but once it lodged in her head, she couldn't shake it. She grabbed the package from Amos and turned away from him as she opened it, in case it was something disgusting.

Nestled in the paper was the whalebone hook, the emblem that had been so familiar around Bully's throat before his death. A lump hit the back of her throat, and she had to squeeze her eyes tight to prevent the tears from escaping.

How she missed the big man, the uncle who'd given her a chance when she'd escaped from Clifford by giving her a job at Pike Consulting. How pleased she'd been when she discovered he'd bequeathed his family heirloom to Kaleo.

He was the obvious one to inherit; of Hawaiian descent, part of Bully's extended family, his *ohana,* from childhood. With his father dying young, and de Vile not aware he was even still alive, Bully was the closest thing Kaleo had to a dad for most of his life.

And now Clifford had stolen the precious emblem of that bond and made a tool for extortion. Red-hot fury filled her as she stared at the curved object nestled in her palm, the surface gleaming softly from continuous contact with Kaleo's soft, unblemished skin.

How dare he?

She braced herself, unwrapping the note that came with the treasure, fortifying her spirit for what the message would contain.

Proof—if you needed it—that lover boy's life is in your hands. Make one wrong step and you won't see him again. I'm expecting the shares, signed and sealed, delivered within twenty-four hours.

Twenty-four hours. So that was the time frame.

She touched the boy's arm. "Thank you, Amos. You can tell him I understand. That's all."

As he turned to go, she caught sight of a lanky dark-headed lad—older than Amos, probably fifteen or sixteen—detach from the wall he had been leaning on and make off in the same direction.

De Vile's tail.

Game on.

Chapter 60

Nessa Murphy's brother Darragh O'Brien ran one of the most popular butcher's shops in C Street, with prime cuts freighted in several times a week and local hunters providing him with fresh trout and venison.

Customers always crowded the place, so when a shaggy chap wandered in wearing rough workman's gear, his hard-toed boots scuffing on the wooden floors, no one gave him a second glance.

They were all too preoccupied with finding beef or venison for Sunday lunch. It was a Virginia City tradition.

Eat out during the week at the bars and eating houses that thrived on C Street, but cook up pot roast and vegetables at home on Sundays, followed by steamed pudding if the cook was especially proficient.

The crowded counter at O'Brien Meats showed plenty of them were dab hands in the kitchen. Tall and short, fat and thin, in headscarves and woolly hats, Virginia City's womenfolk—and a goodly number of men as well—were out to ensure they didn't miss out on their Sunday cook up.

The last thing on their mind was a rogue four-dollar-a-day miner, spying out lamb chops. Or if they weren't available, ingredients for goat stew.

Nessa edged her way to the front, intent on planning her Sunday lunch, not noticing the shadow slipping unobtrusively to her side. She'd leaned in to give her order to Darragh when she heard a quiet voice.

"Nessa. A word out back, please."

She turned in the voice's direction and her hand flew to her mouth. She surveyed the people around her nervously, then leaned toward the man who'd accosted her. "Oh, my word, Adolphus," Nessa said." You gave me a fright."

***

Secreted out back, where they'd both quietly melted with no one noticing, Nessa's blue eyes grew wider as Dolphie quickly explained the situation. The conversation was mostly one-sided, with Dolphie doing the talking, punctuated by Nessa's softly spoken exclamations."

"Ness—you'd know if anyone would. Is Kaleo there? In the room Sarah and I used?"

She nodded wordlessly, then whispered, "It all came out in the kitchen this morning. Young Amos got talking. Seems Clifford has had him following Sarah's for days now.

"She's got a genuine fan in the lad, that's for sure. Don't they say the way to a man's heart is through his stomach?"

She bestowed a wide-beamed smile on Dolphie.

"She bought him treats from the pastry shop yesterday, and he was full of it. Told us how he's delivered stuff from Mr. Cliff to Miss Sarah. And how yesterday he saw that fancy thing that Mr. Manolo wears around his neck—the shiny bone. Mr. Jensen sent it to Miss Sarah, Amos said."

Her pale blue eyes narrowed in consternation. "Now, why would he do a thing like that?"

Dolphie ignored the question. "He's there? Kaleo? He's at Sam's place?"

She nodded. "George is the only one supposed to know. He's been there since yesterday. I don't think even Mr. Sam knows. That's what George thinks, anyway."

Dolphie nodded encouragingly. "Time's very important to us, Nessa. If we don't have him out by later this afternoon, I fear for his life."

Nessa's hand flew to her mouth. "Oh, my goodness, Adolphus. How can we help?"

"We have to move fast. Mr. Jensen will get antsy after noon. And we don't want that, do we?"

Nessa thought of the last upset when Miss Rebecca had run away. "No, we don't, Adolphus." She peered up at him in her short-sighted way. "So, what do we need to do?"

"I'll do most of it, Nessa. I don't want you getting into trouble. First, do you know if he's locked Charlotte's rooms? And if he has, where's the key?"

She nodded vigorously, the tight curls around her forehead bobbing with her eagerness. "I believe the room is locked, Adolphus. The key hangs on a hook in the kitchen. The master locked it up after Sarah was in there."

"Listen carefully, then Nessa. I'll need your help to get in. And to give me the key to that room."

"Smuggle you in, you mean," she said, her dimpled cheeks pink with excitement.

Dolphie shot her an amused grin. "That's right. Smuggle me in. Oh, and let Senator de Vile in by the side garden, too. And keep the dogs quiet if they're out."

He stepped back and adjusted the cloth cap on his head. "We'll do the rest. Shall we say a quarter past eleven?"

She nodded eagerly. "Then I'd better pick up some meat for the dogs, just in case."

Nessa Murphy bustled out ahead of him beaming, her expression showing she was as pleased as punch.

***

At 11:15 on the dot Dolphie and de Vile presented themselves quietly at the Hollows' back kitchen door, which whisked open before Dolphie had raised his hand to knock.

De Vile hung back on the porch. Nessa slipped Dolphie straight through to the kitchen and then returned with a parcel wrapped in white butcher's paper under one arm.

She led de Vile to the gate into the back garden. The only dogs there were Dancer and Blitzen, and they were delighted to see visitors and even more pleased with fresh meat.

"They won't bother you," said Nessa as she withdrew, bustling back along the veranda to the kitchen. "Good luck."

Back in the kitchen, she handed Charlotte's room key to Dolphie. "George has taken the morning tea into the library. Wait here."

She was back in what seemed like seconds. "They're all quiet. Coast's clear."

She opened the kitchen door and gestured for him to enter the hall. It was the work of a minute to disappear upstairs, unlock Charlotte's suite and lock it again from the inside, move aside the volume of Grimm's Fairy Tales and quietly turn the lever to swing the bookcase.

Kaleo lay tied to the bedframe, gagged but not blindfolded. He raised his head at an awkward angle at the sound of someone entering the room. When he caught sight of Dolphie, his eyes widened.

Dolphie flitted across the room like a big moth, pulling a pocketknife out of his boot as he moved. With a few deft flicks, he cut Kaleo free. He sat up and stretched.

"You might think it would be very pleasant to stay in bed for twenty-four hours, until you're forced to do it," he whispered.

He placed both feet flat on the floor and hesitantly raised his muscular frame upright.

"Ready for business. What's next?"

"We're going out the window like last time."

Dolphie was already drawing a long, heavy rope out from the canvas carryall he'd brought.

"Ease the window up as quietly as you can. Try not to draw attention while you do it."

Kaleo moved like a cat from bed to window and tentatively peeked under the closed blind. "Got it."

In lightning quick time, Dolphie eased the bookcase across the floor and dropped it onto the bed. He roped the whole thing as ballast to hold them steady.

"That was quick," said Kaleo.

"I've had practice," Dolphie replied with a quick grin. "We need as much weight as we can, 'cause we're going out together."

He moved to the window.

"Now for the hard part. We've got no time to waste. For starters, I'm not sure how much this bed will move with two of us on the rope. It might make a noise and attract attention."

"Will the rope stand the weight?"

"For sure. I'll go first. Count to five slowly and then come straight out after me. No seat like last time. Twist the rope around your hands and feet."

He coiled the flex from the loose end, counting quietly as he rolled it in neat coils, setting it at his feet like he was getting ready to launch a sail.

"You'll join me about here." He handed Kaleo the rope, marking the point with a fold. "Remember. Count to five. No longer. Then you're out after me."

With one leg over the sill, he added, "De Vile's at the bottom, giving us cover if we need it. And the sheriff should arrive with backup sometime soon."

And then he was over the sill and out of sight.

The moment Dolphie's weight hit the rope, Kaleo realized they were in trouble. The bed creaked, and he leapt to brace it in place, preventing a slide across the room on bare boards as he counted.

One… two… three… four…

He released his weight and the bed legs screeched.

Five …

He let go and ran for the window. As he sat astride the windowsill, someone began pounding on the locked door.

Thank goodness Dolphie had the sense to lock it from the inside.

He curled his hands and legs around the perpendicular line to freedom and let go of the sill.

With a final crunching shriek, the bed slid the rest of the way and slammed into the wall, shattering the window on impact.

Down below, Dolphie dropped the final eight or ten feet to the ground. Above him, Kaleo heard a relay of shots. Someone had shot out the lock.

He subconsciously ducked his head, refusing to check above him. If he was going to die on this rope, or fall off it, so be it.

Anything was better than being left for dead at the bottom of a mine shaft. Heavy feet thundered to the window. A bullet pinged off the vine that grew up the wall, and he flinched. They would get him next time.

And then a shot roared from the ground up. There was a scream, and a man's body plummeted past him, landing with a thud at the spot where Kaleo was about to put his feet.

He swung out from the wall and checked above him. Otis was leaning out, his mouth wide open. Kaleo pushed out again, landing softly on both feet, right next to Clifford Jensen's sprawled, contorted body.

Chapter 61

"So, would you have written the letter?" De Vile was glowing with a warm affection Kaleo had never seen on his father's face before. His dark eyes were shining with delight.

Kaleo laughed at him. "Why do you want to know? Does it titillate your dark sense of humor?"

De Vile snorted. "If they'd forced you to write something, I'm convinced you'd have given Sarah some hidden clue, so she knew you wrote it under duress. At least I hope you would have. You'd have been writing your own death sentence. You realize that? Giving him a ready-made explanation for your disappearance."

"Don't worry. I've picked up how they play the game out here." Kaleo swaggered deliberately to the fireplace.

They were back in de Vile's suite at the Old Washoe Club. It was the day after his narrow escape and the freedom to get up and move around had never felt so good. He rolled his shoulders forward and back, luxuriating in the ability to move.

His muscles and joints were still stiff and sore from nearly a day and a half of being tied to a bed, and he would need a few more daily constitutionals up Mount Davidson to iron those out, but he was in fighting form.

"I never realized how much I enjoyed exercise until I couldn't do it." He grinned at de Vile.

"I guess this means we're all even. I saved your life, and you saved mine. Can we call it square and promise never to get in that predicament again?"

De Vile hooted with delight. "Only if you promise to not hare back to Hawaii right away. At least not yet. Give yourself another few months to get to know the business and for us to get to know one another."

Kaleo smiled. "Seriously though, Father. I'm grateful beyond words. And warning the sheriff about it was so good, too. I sure appreciated the way he walked in as Clifford drew his last breath."

"It wasn't hard to explain what had gone on once he questioned Otis, Nessa, George and Amos." De Vile poured himself a whiskey. "Want one?"

"No, thanks, I'm fine."

De Vile raised his crystal tumbler in a toast.

"Here's to us. To many more years of happy cooperation."

He took a sip and put the glass down again. "I'm glad Sam Hollows knew nothing about that last stupid trick of Clifford's. And also, that he wasn't totally done out of that mine. It was originally his, and he brought Jensen in on it."

Kaleo nodded. "I agree. And with Jensen gone, maybe Sarah will forgive her stepfather and help him out a little. Do you think Charlotte and Petra will go back?"

De Vile scrunched up his mouth and stroked his chin. "Highly likely, I'd say. Clifford was always the problem. He was rotten to the core."

Kaleo fingered the whalebone safely back at his throat. Sarah had returned it to him immediately after his escape, and he was complete again with it around his neck. "You're right there. The whalebone hook knew that. So did the ancestors."

"What are you talking about?"

"The hook. It lets me know things. I reckon it's the ancestors talking."

"Spoken like a true *ali'i*. A chief. Just like your mother."

Chapter 62

Everyone gathered for breakfast the next morning in Mrs. Benson's pretty Old Washoe morning room. They were finishing up when a visitor arrived.

Hector sat at the table head like the patriarch he was, with Elizabeth at his right hand and Kaleo at his left. Sarah, Petra, Lottie, and Dolphie took up the other spaces around the table. The newcomer eyed the party and approached Hector's chair.

"Forgive me for interrupting your breakfast, Senator, but I'm James Wollander, and I'd appreciate an opportunity to talk."

At Kaleo's throat, the whale hook hummed with silent energy.

James Wollander. He'd heard that name before in the last few days. What was the connection? Before he could recall it, Hector was on his feet.

"Mr. Wollander. Well, well. It's been a good few years. Many years since we've been in the same room. What brings you West? As far as I understand it, you still head a merchant house in New York?"

That's where I've heard it, thought Kaleo. James Wollander and his wife were guests at Hector's parents' house the night Hector's father died. He listened intently.

"That I do, Senator. But the day has come when we can't ignore

California any longer. I'm here investigating the opportunities in this fair land. And while I'm here, I realize there's some personal business I need to sort out."

He surveyed the table. Empty plates and cups, the dregs of bacon and toast and fresh fruit, spoke of a meal that was well ended.

"I wonder if I could induce you to join me for a fresh coffee. I've got information that I believe may be of interest to you." He paused again. "Of a personal, rather than a business nature."

De Vile raised his eyebrows. "More than happy to oblige, Mr. Wollander. But if you don't mind, I'd like to have my son along with me and," he turned to Elizabeth, "Mrs. Westerhoven too, if she so desires."

Elizabeth rose in one graceful move. "Thanks, Hector, but I've got things I need to be doing. I'm happy to hear the details from you later."

She dipped her head at Wollander with a quick smile. "Nice to meet you, Mr. Wollander." She dropped her napkin on her plate. "I'll order fresh coffee on the way out."

The others followed Elizabeth's lead and Wollander took Elizabeth's chair. Hector cast a sideways glance at Kaleo. "Mr. Wollander was an associate of my father's back in New York. In the same business."

"I remember you mentioning him."

Hector gestured to Wollander. "My son, Kaleo. Now, how can I be of assistance?"

Wollander opened the briefcase on his lap and extracted a newspaper—the *San Francisco Chronicle,* from the masthead. He waved it in front of de Vile.

"Don't know if you've caught up with the way they reported that scandal down the line, but I thought this might be of interest."

Hector took the paper and his eyes settled on a report under the front-page banner headlines. The heading over two columns read SENATOR'S LIFE SAVED IN STREET ATTACK.

Kaleo was too far away to read any further. The senator studied it in silence for a couple of minutes. His eyes flicked to Wollander.

"I presume this is the story you wished to bring to my attention? I hadn't seen this version, but I've seen others like it. Why is it of any interest to you?"

Wollander's face colored.

"I had a long association with your family and the firm of de Vile and Son," Wollander said.

"My conscience doesn't allow me to stand aside and let damaging information circulate in the public domain without doing my best to correct it."

He put the briefcase down on the floor beside his chair and paused as an attendant poured them fresh coffee. Kaleo made a quick scan of the news report.

It repeated Will's unchallenged claims that the senator had killed his own father—Will's grandfather—and destroyed the family firm.

Wollander turned and pointed his index finger at the newsprint. "Someone's fabricated lies here, and I don't like letting it go unchallenged."

Kaleo saw his father's body tense in the chair beside him. His fingers pressed white on the coffee cup.

"It was an unfortunate episode," de Vile conceded with a courtly dip of his head. "And I can understand why the boy blamed me."

Wollander reached out with his left hand and clasped the back of de Vile's wrist. "No, Senator. I don't think you understand. You don't know the full story."

De Vile stiffened, and Wollander hurriedly withdrew his hand. Hector's spine was now ramrod straight, flattened against the back of the chair as if waiting for the executioner's blade to fall.

"Full story? You're right. I don't have a clue what you're talking about."

"That's what I thought. And my conscience obliges me to tell you."

***

De Vile's heartbeat elevated at such a rate, his hand went involuntarily to his chest.

"Father. Are you all right?" Kaleo leaned over into his line of sight. "You're pale and clammy." He peered at Wollander. "I don't think we should continue. Father's unwell."

At his side, de Vile protested weakly. "Let me get my breath," he panted. "I've spent nearly twenty years trying to forget that night."

He sat up straight, took a couple of deep breaths, and stared at Wollander. "You might understand. I'm reluctant to go back there."

Wollander nodded. "Believe me, Senator, you'll feel a lot better when I'm finished."

Whether he liked it or not, he was back there. His shoulder ached, reminding him of an ancient pain. No matter how many times he'd tried to forget, the memories rolled in. And yet even now, he was recalling details he had successfully suppressed for a long time.

Thirza's litany of accusations, for example.

How had I forgotten what she said that night?

"It's all his fault." Pointing at Hector with a bloodied hand. "He's always been nothing but trouble."

And his brother Bernard, his arms hanging at his sides, saying nothing, impotent to rein her in.

Then his mother Wilhemina had slapped Thirza hard across the face.

"Shut up, you little fool, and move out of the way so we can get him to bed."

Thirza's hand flew to her face, dragging blood down her cheek. "How dare you? You'll be sorry." Her eyes blazed with locked-up fury.

"And you!" She turned on Bernard. "You stand up to no one. Your father, your mother. Him." She flung a hand in Hector's direction. "Him especially. I deserve better."

His mother had called Alf then, and he and Bernard had carried his father to bed.

His mother's icy voice cut into his recall. "You can go. You've caused enough trouble here tonight. And never come back. He should never have let you in."

The clink of china brought him back to Wollander, who was staring at him, his face crinkled with concerned lines. "You're sure you are all right to continue?"

"There'll never be a better time., Wollander. Please, go on."

"I'm afraid I don't come out of this well, Senator. I hope I can make up for past actions by telling you all this." He drummed his fingers on the table edge. "As you know, I was a close associate of your family. Very close. We were in the same business, so we had interests in common.

"My firm, Wollander and Mountfort, was growing as de Vile and Sons was shrinking. An unfortunate business, but there was not much I could do about it. Your father... your brother..."

"I know," de Vile intervened. "You don't have to explain. It's why I left."

"Thing is," Wollander dragged on, "I was ... How can I say it ... Thirza compromised me. She ate me up. And I was too weak to resist."

De Vile felt a warm rush of blood in his veins, a restorative flood of sympathy for his long-alienated younger brother.

Poor Bernard. Deserted by everyone who should have loved him.

He expelled a long gasp. "Ah… so the gossip I heard years ago was true. She was unfaithful."

"She was voracious. Once she got her fangs in… But I don't want to make excuses for my behavior. Once she'd got me under her thumb, she threatened to expose us every time I tried to end things. Excuses, I know. All excuses. But the truth."

"A sad story, Wollander. But what's it got to do with me?"

"The last time I saw her—not long before she died nearly two years ago—she made a terrible scene."

"Go on."

"She had an inkling she was dying. She wanted me to know what she'd done for me. As she saw it, what she'd sacrificed for me. And wanted me to understand I hadn't appreciated it."

Hector nodded. His sense of rising anticipation faded, replaced by mild irritation.

Where is the fellow going with this?

"She took me right back to that night when she stabbed your father when she was trying to get at you, or Bernard. I was never sure which, to be honest.

"She was as self-justifying as ever." He licked his lips nervously.

"Thing is, the family has always said Rolf died from that attack. The abortive one the night he gave you your inheritance. It turns out that wasn't correct, but the only one who knew that was Thirza.

"The fact is, the stab wound didn't do him serious harm. He would have easily survived. The doctor told them so that night. But Thirza decided she'd done half the job, and she'd finish it."

De Vile heard an involuntary cry escape his lips. His chest was alive with pain. "No…" He cried out for the infuriating father he'd never properly farewelled. For the brother and family betrayed.

Wollander nodded silently, the deep vertical lines on either side of his mouth dark and drawn.

"That last night I saw her, she was justifying her actions, sharing out the blame. She wanted me to accept responsibility so I'd do the one thing she'd always wanted. Marry her."

He pushed his face into his hands, suddenly moved to tears.

"She confessed that night, in a spasm of self-interest, how she wanted Rolf gone. She thought she and Bernard would do better without him. In her opinion, she had the brains to run the company even if he didn't. The doctor had given your father heavy sedation to encourage rest and hasten his recovery. She knew that.

"A few nights after her attack, when everyone else was in bed, she stole into his room and smothered him with a pillow. And then she acted outraged when they found him the next morning."

Chapter 63

They were seated under gold-plated chandeliers in one of Virginia City's most sumptuous restaurants, the Crystal on C Street, with food said to rival New York's best. Theirs' was a large family group which included, unlikely though it was, Sam and Otis, as well as Lottie and Petra. The senator had invited James Wollander along too. And of course, Elizabeth and Dolphie were there. Kaleo and Sarah too. And the senator was paying.

The Crystal Bar had only been going a few years and already had a visitor's book which included the names of two Civil War generals, but the bar was strictly men only.

Not so the adjoining restaurant. The Crystal's owner, Grant Israel, hadn't imported the gold-tipped French chandeliers and matching Bohemian glasses for the benefit of the men. Ladies were welcome to dine and dance, and Hector had secured the best table in the house.

"It's almost certainly the last time we'll all be together like this," de Vile said. "And Virginia City's given us revelations that will change life for us all. We must mark the occasion."

Kaleo agreed. Wollander's announcement the previous day had brought an end to his speculation about what had happened to his grandfather. The New York merchant had settled his heart on that score.

He relished a new peace that was blossoming between him and de Vile, but he couldn't say the same about his feelings for Sarah. He didn't know if she intended to stay in Virginia City with her mother or return "down below," as the Comstock referred to San Francisco.

Tonight she sat between her mother and Elizabeth, more beautiful than he'd ever seen her in a celebratory pink organza gown.

It was a real party dress, with bows on the shoulders and a full ruffle around the top of the neckline. A satin ribbon in a deep pink circled her waist. Her perfect complexion glowed under the soft light refracted from the dangling crystal chandeliers.

She smiled as she caught his eye, and his insides quaked like jelly. He repressed the sensation with a grimace and fiddled with his glass.

Her ownership of the Golden Bowl made Sarah the richest woman on the Comstock. She'd been generous with it, assuring her stepfather she would not see him turned out of his house.

The green-flecked hazel eyes were shining and serene. She was queen of all she surveyed. No wonder Dolphie called her Princess.

She deserves it. You wouldn't begrudge her, after all she's suffered, would you?

He gave a reflective shake of the head. No. Of course not. But I can't help feeling left behind. Deceived. Banished. And now outclassed.

She had always done that, he reminded himself wryly. But it doesn't matter, because you don't want her, anyway.

Keep telling yourself that Kaleo. One day, you might even believe it.

He reached up and touched the smooth white bone at his throat for a few seconds, as if seeking reassurance.

Buck up, Kaleo. Self pity is pathetic.

De Vile stood and assumed the direction of the chattering table.

"I've arranged a set menu for us all, to make it easy for everyone," he said, smiling at Elizabeth and then Sarah. "But before our first course arrives, I'd like us to charge our glasses and make a salute with some much-needed toasts."

The waiters hurried to ensure every glass was overflowing and silence fell in the secluded corner where they could safely party without attracting unwanted attention.

"First, to my son Kaleo, for saving my life." De Vile reached out and squeezed Kaleo's shoulder. "I'm forever grateful."

Chairs rumbled as they pushed them back and stood, clinking glasses.

"And while you're standing, my warmest thanks to James Wollander here, for telling me what occurred in the de Vile family one fateful night twenty years ago."

Faces sobered, recalling Wollander's story.

"Grave but welcome news," de Vile added. "And now I think you can all be seated again. I believe Elizabeth has an announcement."

More chairs scraped as everyone except Elizabeth sat. Kaleo noticed she had a paper in front of her, which she picked up as she gazed around the group.

"Before I start, I'd like to thank Kaleo, Hector, and Dolphie for the stalwart support they've given us over this last week. I know I speak for all of us, but particularly Sarah, Lottie, and Petra, when I say we wouldn't be here tonight without your protection."

The table broke into spontaneous applause.

When it died down, Elizabeth opened the folded paper.

"I'm here as Bully's executor to let those closest to him know his wishes in terms of the distribution of his worldly goods. Let me first say I apologize for the time this has taken, but I think you all know lawyers move slowly."

She surveyed the table with a cheeky grin. "Unless it comes to presenting their bills."

Everyone laughed and relaxed.

"I won't go into the finer details. Those of you who are involved will get more information in due course.

"Basically, Pike Consulting is to be owned in equal shares by Senator de Vile and Sarah Wyndham. Effectively, Senator de Vile's minority share will increase to fifty percent, while Sarah inherits the other fifty percent."

Kaleo darted a quick sideways glance. Sarah sat with a hand raised in shock to her mouth. *She's going to be even richer than now.* And he guessed the arrangement put paid to any thoughts he might have of staying on in the business.

Elizabeth continued: "Kaleo?" She caught his eye and held it.

"You've already received Bully's totem, and I know it means a lot to you. In addition, Bully had a considerable holding of shares in several Comstock mines.

"He's bequeathed these to you, and also designated a certain annual dividend to be paid to you from the import-export business. We can explain the details of that later."

Elizabeth was still talking, but Kaleo didn't hear another word.

His head was swimming. *Mine shares.*

Maybe I won't waste this introduction to the Comstock after all.

His hand went spontaneously to the pendant. It was silky and warm under his touch.

See, the ancestors seemed to say, *that turned out better than you expected, didn't it?*

Chapter 64

Sarah was sitting in the Harquette Brothers Palace of Art Saloon on Post Street near Kearney, waiting for Dolphie to turn up. She hadn't seen him since they had got back to San Francisco from Virginia City a week ago, and she'd no idea why he'd asked to meet her here.

He was already five minutes late, unusual for him, but she had plenty to keep her entertained, observing the artistic display that surrounded her.

The "Palace" was at the top end of the San Francisco's Free Lunch circuit, one of the few houses that was open to women and a favorite with the fairer sex despite—or maybe because of—the walls being lined with male nudes.

Fine paintings, marble carvings, silver cups, cast-iron statuary and wooden objets d'art were all on display under crystal chandeliers because the Palace operated as both a museum and an eating house.

The "Free Lunch" on offer was superior fare, and any chaps who dined here knew a higher standard of behavior was expected than was normal in some of the other Free Lunch watering holes on the circuit.

Of course, the lunch wasn't entirely free. To qualify, customers had to buy at least one drink—wine, ale or cocktail, and the lunch was of a serve-yourself buffet variety. As she dallied, Sarah had already perused the menu and found a bewildering choice, from crab salad and Honolulu beans to terrapin stew and Saratoga chips.

The waiter showed her to a table, and she relaxed back in her chair. Dolphie would be here any minute. His timekeeping was usually as perfect as his fencing thrusts.

He'd shocked her by announcing his imminent departure to Europe, and her heart pinched at the thought of having to live in San Francisco without him.

He'd been back for such a short time, but he'd made himself invaluable. With Bully gone and her mother and Elizabeth in Virginia City at least in the short term, she drooped at the prospect of his desertion.

She'd lost Kaleo too, but she didn't dare let her thoughts stray in that direction. Every time she did, an overwhelming sense of her life being out of kilter ambushed her. She missed him bitterly, and she'd no clue how to mend the estrangement.

He'll never want me, anyway. Not once he knows what Clifford did to me. No man will.

Perhaps he'd already guessed. He'd made his feelings clear that day on Sun Mountain, and he hadn't wavered since.

When she was present, he acted as if she wasn't in the room. If he acknowledged her, it was with the most perfunctory attention, and it pierced her every time.

On the train back from the Lode, he'd ignored her and played euchre with Dolphie while she and de Vile hammered out strategies for the future of Pike Consulting together. Since she'd been back, she'd seen neither hide nor hair of him.

She kept in daily touch with de Vile, and he'd hinted that he and Alex were having dinner with Kaleo every evening. So, he was still in town. That was about all he knew.

She shifted in her chair, increasingly uncomfortable with sitting alone in a busy restaurant. She made another furtive scan of the room to see if she was attracting attention.

And then she saw him, striding across the crowded room toward her. The familiar figure who always made her heart double beat in her chest. Not Dolphie, but Kaleo, turning heads as he progressed to her table.

Was it her imagination, or did a ribbony trail of whispers follow him? Women hissing at their companions.

"De Vile son…"

"Shooting…"

"Rich …"

"Mines…"

She rose reluctantly to her feet. "Are you expecting to meet Dolphie?"

His jaw flexed. "How did you guess?"

Okay… Dolphie's set us up.

The breath whooshed out of her, and her mind went blank. She completely lost her composure. She stammered the first thing that came into her head.

"I don't know where he can be. He's never late. But if he's ordered a table for three, he should be along soon."

She slipped back into her chair.

Botheration, Dolphie. Why are you doing this to me?

A waiter came hurrying over to them, clasping an envelope. "Monsieur Dolphie asked for this to be delivered when you arrived, sir. And can I get you a drink?"

Kaleo fingered the envelope gingerly and ordered a beer.

Elegant handwriting covered the envelope. Kaleo considered the lettering. "It's addressed to both of us. Do you want to be the one to open it?"

Sarah's heart was a glowing coal in her chest. She could barely breathe. She took the envelope from him, sliding it delicately between two fingers, lifted the sealed edge, and drew out the sheet.

By the time you read this, I'll be on a train for New York. In a few days I'll be on a liner to London, then Paris. Life's too short, my dear friends. Ask yourselves—like I have—what's the most important thing for your future happiness right now?

Decide that over a sumptuous lunch at my expense and tell each other what that one thing is before you leave this table today.

That's all I'm asking. Easy, isn't?

Love to you both.

Dolphie.

She hunched forward, gripped with a sudden cramping in her stomach.

"What's wrong?" Kaleo sounded concerned. "Are you all right?"

She held the note out between two trembling fingers like a dirty rag.

Holy Moses, Dolphie. It's none of your business.

She shrugged. "Here. Read it."

How they got through the next few minutes of cringing embarrassment, she couldn't remember afterwards, but they did. The waiter brought Kaleo's beer and her wine.

Kaleo made a good show of treating Dolphie's intervention as a joke. "S'cuse my French, but it's none of his damn business."

"My thoughts exactly," she said with a wide grin. She hesitated. "Truly."

He gave her one of his incandescent Kaleo smiles and suddenly it didn't seem so terrible.

"I suppose we may as well enjoy the lunch. After all, he's paying. Even if it is…" She consulted the carved gilded clock on the wall nearby. "Four p.m. Rather late for lunch."

***

They filled their plates with delicacies. Shrimp and crab salad with Green Goddess dressing for her; French lamb chops and artichoke hearts with Hollandaise for him. They wended their way back to their table.

They sat down in unison, and she smiled at him again. "So… I have to ask. Do you know what the most important thing is right now, or do you need this delicious meal to help you decide?"

"Not that I'm a poker player, but I understand playing last brings the biggest advantage." He gave her a teasing grin. "But I guess you already know that."

"You want me to lead off?"

"Maybe. But let's eat first. Tell me how your first week as a business magnate has gone."

She settled into a familiar rhythm. One they'd enjoyed in the past days of their friendship, she realized. Question and answer, flowing back and forth, without equivocation. Her heart soared with surprised joy.

He was taking his responsibilities as a mine owner seriously, it seemed, doing the rounds of the papers' mining editors, getting introduced to the brokers who enjoyed the best reputations for accuracy, learning the business from every angle. He admitted that having de Vile as his father was proving useful for introductions.

"I've never eaten and drunk so much in one week," he said with a laugh. "I can't keep it up for much longer or I'll have to buy a larger pair of pants."

But deeper down in her belly, nervous tension blossomed like a thunderous cloud. How am I going to reply to Dolphie's question? And do I dare be honest?

They came to the final touch. Dessert. One that the Palace of Art Saloon was famed for. Spiced apricots. She dipped her spoon into the allspice and nutmeg-flavored jus.

Kaleo licked his lips, savoring the sweetness. "Have you decided yet?" he teased.

"Decided what? If I like the dessert?"

He laughed. "No. Not the dessert."

He gazed into her eyes. He was enjoying her discomfort.

"I think you'd agree I've always been a gentleman. Plus, I've saved your life twice."

He grinned. "I know Dolphie played the biggest part the second time round, but it still counts."

She dipped her head coyly. "Point taken."

"So, you owe me."

"Your point being?"

"I'm going to be truly chivalrous and allow the lady to go first."

She burst out laughing. Suddenly, it didn't seem so bad after all. "Coffee first. Then I promise."

"Promise what?"

"To tell the truth, the whole truth, and nothing but the truth. So help me God."

He gazed deep into her eyes, as if staring directly into her soul. "Now you're getting it, Sarah. I wanted nothing else from you but that." She blushed.

The waiter brought their coffee. They sipped the first few drops in silence.

She cleared her throat. "This confession will probably embarrass me forever more, Kaleo," she said.

Her voice quavered, and her brow folded into worried lines. "But here goes. The thing that would bring me the most happiness right now?

"It's not owning a majority in the Golden Bowl. Or half of Pike, marvellous as those things are. It's not that I'll probably never have to worry about money again in the same way I have the last six months. Not if I'm wise in how I steward it."

She hazarded a quick glance his way, and when she met his eyes, she could not pull them away again. A force she couldn't explain held her.

"The thing that would make me happiest is to turn the clock back to our early days. When we seemed to walk to the same drumbeat. When there was something magical between us."

She dragged her eyes away and examined her fingers, which she'd clasped in front of her. "I realize that's dreaming. And even if it wasn't, there's something else."

His dark eyes watched with an intensity that threatened to consume her.

"Something else? Like what?"

Her voice grew small and squeaky. "I'm soiled goods, Kaleo. I doubt any man would want me if they knew what Clifford…" Her voice trailed off.

She had to take another big breath to fuel the end of the sentence. "What Clifford did to me."

He reached out and clasped the back of the hand nearest him with a whispering touch.

"Never allow yourself to think that man could spoil you." His gaze was magnetic. "Never. He's gone now. He has no power to hurt you anymore."

Tears spilled out of her eyes and down her cheeks.

"Oh, if only that were true," she said. "The things he did to me? I don't know that I will ever be able to forget."

She drew her hand from his and rustled around in her reticule for a handkerchief. Dabbing at her eyes, she half laughed and hiccupped at the same time.

"Here I am supposed to be talking about what would make me happy, and I'm crying like a baby. What sort of crazy woman will you think I am?"

His face took on a serious tenderness. "No crazier than me," he said. He placed his hand back on top of hers. "It's my turn now. Right?"

She swallowed hard. She had a lump in her throat the size of a hard-boiled egg.

He gazed at her for a long minute, while her chest swelled with anxiety.

She steeled herself to hear something she didn't want to hear. The final death knell of her hopes.

"I've never met a woman like you, Sarah." He stroked her hand with gentle fingers. "And even if you decide to go back to being Rebecca, you'll always be Sarah to me."

She hiccupped a smile.

"I never expect to meet someone like you again. I knew from that first day, even in your disguise as an unassuming receptionist, that you were way out of my league.

"And now that you've transformed into this mining magnate and business mogul, you've proven it even further. So far out of my league, it's impossible for me to reach you, up in the clouds above my head."

He paused and gave her a sad smile. "You are truly extraordinary. Your strength and courage. Your ability to endure the unendurable."

She winced, and he shook his head.

"I mean it, Sarah. You've endured the unendurable. That's not something to be ashamed of. It's something to celebrate. Not the humiliation, but the rising above it."

She gave a soft laugh. "That's sweet of you to say, Kaleo. But put me out of my misery. What's the thing that would make you happiest?"

"Exactly the same thing as you, Sarah. To recapture that ease, the wonderful flowing sense of being of one mind we enjoyed when we first met. But I understand there's no way we can turn the clock back."

Her heart plummeted.

Here it is. Compliments and then the gentle let-down.

She felt unstoppable tears well up in the back of her eyes. She gasped and hiccupped again. "I suppose not."

He reached over and tenderly brushed away a tear that coursed down her cheek with one finger.

"Sarah," he breathed. "Why are you crying?"

"I'm waiting for you to get to the part where you explain why."

"Why what?"

"Why we can't go back?"

He spoke even more quietly. "Why would we want to go back when we've got our whole lives to go forward?"

He continued to stroke the tears away. His eyed were suffused with such tenderness and—love—yes, it was love, that her tears kept flowing.

She hiccupped again. "Are you saying…?" She couldn't get her breath. She tried again. "Are you saying that you want to go forward with me?"

Her voice grew in strength as she spoke. "That there might be a possibility we could be friends again?"

He withdrew his hand and shook his head. "Not friends, no."

Her chest filled with rocks again.

"We were friends before. That wasn't enough. For me, anyway. And I hope you agree."

She stared at him in wonder; the tears flowing freely now. "Oh I do, Kaleo. I do."

THE END

If you enjoyed Ancient Deception, you may also enjoy Dangerous Desires, Book 10 in Of Gold & Blood, a full-length mystery. Here's a preview:

One

Hector de Vile, California senator to Washington, sank his bare shoulders beneath the swirling rose-scented water and exhaled. The Imperial Spa on Montgomery Street was the most recent evidence that San Francisco matched London and Paris as one of the most metropolitan cities in the world, with its faux Greco-Roman baths open to any gentleman who was a paid-up member of the Imperial Club next door.

Hector closed his eyes and allowed himself to float off on a cloud of happy imaginings. His newly discovered son, Kaleo, installed at De Vile Holdings, married to de Vile's young business partner Sarah, producing a brood of brilliant grandchildren. His old friend, the Countess Elizabeth in an elegant yet simple wedding gown, eagerly awaiting his arrival at the altar.

He lay back, letting the hot water caress his neck and shoulders, and exalted in the moment. The only sound in the secluded, dim space was the mesmerizing bubbling of the moving water, pumped through jets into the mosaic-tiled private pool.

His eyes flickered open briefly, taking in the sense of luxurious enclosure the intimate bathing cubicle afforded. Like a Roman catacomb, lit by fluttering candles set in alcoves in rough brick walls.

He allowed himself a breathy chuckle. A catacomb, maybe, but one for the living. At fifty-one, he might be nearing the end of his earthly years, but he had much he still wanted to accomplish.

He sank deeper, and when the heat grew intolerable, he rose like a whale breaching; the water streamed off his shoulders, and he again laughed silently to himself. He'd been a whaler in Hawaii. And he'd moved on to know some of the most celebrated and the notorious identities of the young state of California.

John Sutter, the adventurer who started the whirlwind that became California when a worker found gold on his ranch. Jack Porter, the notorious bandit who'd hung out on Sundays at the Mission Dolores roadhouse, with his black beard, flowing hair, and glittering restless eyes, prompting fascinated terror as he drank with prominent Californios and soldiers before his crazed misdeeds caught up with him.

Hector had ridden the Pacific Coast north from the collection of huts that had been Yerba Buena to view the masses of seals on the rocks below Cliff House, before there even was a Cliff House.

And now he was a national figure, one of the richest men in the state, and about to propose to a woman for only the second time in his life.

Belatedly, he was hoping to enjoy a family life he'd not known in adulthood.

He'd accumulated children. Yes, by some miracle he didn't deserve, he'd raised a treasured adopted son, and he'd found the children who'd been withheld from him for over twenty years. Now he'd add a wife to the story and his life would be complete.

The candles audibly guttered. A subtle change in the surrounding airflow made him glance toward the arched doorway. His eyes widened. A woman, a barely mature blonde child draped in a towel which slipped to her waist, revealing pert breasts, approached him across the stone floor.

Before he had time to draw breath, she'd perched on the bath edge close to him.

She dangled slim white legs into the roiling hot water and paddled them, smiling from under long black lashes, as if it were the most natural act in the world for her to be keeping him company in the nude.

Alarm rose in his throat. What was this? Some plot? Entrapment? There were men, he knew, who fancied young girls, but he was not one of them.

He'd settled his haunch on one of the top steps leading down into the pool, but now he reflexively sank to a lower level, distancing himself from the mirage.

"There's some mistake," he said. His normally deep voice sounded breathy and cracked. "You've got the wrong place."

She smiled again and shook her head. Still, she remained silent.

Her hand went to her throat, and it was then he noticed something hung from a leather cord between her breasts, making a light rattle as she pulled the cord free.

"Oh nooo," she cooed like a dove. "No mistake."

She pulled the emblems out for him to see more closely.

He peered through the steamy bath vapor.

They resembled bone amulets—two of them, like the whalebone teething rings mothers gave their children in Hawaii—threaded through the leather string.

"Madame Moonlight says you'll be most interested in these…"

She leaned into him and rattled them under his nose.

"La Nera Notte is certain. You're to meet her in her private box at the opera on Thursday and she'll tell you more."

She stared into his eyes, seductive, offering the token.

"Moonlight? What the devil does Moonlight have to do with me? Or any of this?"

He pushed himself up the steps again, the water sloshing and slapping the bath's sides as he moved, releasing a cloud of rose-scented air.

"That's for her to know, and you to find out."

The outer corners of her lips turned up in a coquettish question mark. For a child—what was she—twelve, thirteen?—she had a precocious knowingness.

He stilled inside, his sixth sense overcoming the rush of anxiety. *Here be dragons.*

He'd seen it on the old maps when he'd sailed the China route.

The territory of ancient cartographers, marked as unknown and dangerous. By the time he'd been a captain, they'd included it more in jest than anything, but any mariner knew danger lurked in every storm on the high seas.

And this was a potential storm of cataclysmic proportions.

In one intuitive swipe, his right arm lashed out and caught hold of the leather cord.

The girl reared back out of his reach, but too late.

She clutched at her breasts, attempting to smother the fall of the antique rings, as the leather snapped.

In a flash, she swung her feet out of the water and rose, panting, hugging her cleavage in the towel.

Her eyes were intense and glittering, not in the least panicked, as she glared down, an angel lit in an avenging halo by the candlelight.

"Madame Moonlight insists. The opera on Thursday. Or you'll be sorry. She says if you don't come, the only person sorrier than you will be the Countess."

***

The only person sorrier than you…

De Vile groaned as the masseuse's nimble fingers worked into his foaming scalp, fingers and thumbs flexing the slippery shampoo with a pressure that was minimally short of painful. Was he groaning from pleasure or from dread? He didn't know.

In the seconds after the girl disappeared like a vapor, he'd stared into the empty doorway, asking himself if he'd imagined the entire encounter. Then his eyes dropped to the pulsing water, and he'd leaned into its depths, groping for something, anything, to prove to himself she'd really been there.

His foot nudged a small object. He'd leaned over and drawn out a dripping totem. A small bone ring, creamy with age, from which dangled a silver shield engraved with tiny letters.

He resisted the urge to race straight back to his house on Russian Hill and examine it with a magnifying glass. He'd paid for the full treatment at the Imperial Spa—shoulder massage, shampoo, shave, barber and a luxurious soak—and no courtesan, however dangerous and desirable, was going to panic him into going home.

Besides, the episode gave him time to think. Madame Moonlight, otherwise known as Sophia Morrigan, was a celebrated San Francisco hostess who owned this Imperial Spa premises beside the popular Imperial Club next door. She was famous; some would suggest notorious.

She'd appeared in San Francisco nearly twenty years ago and not yet twenty years old herself, a supposed European heiress with midnight-black hair and sapphire eyes that quickly earned her the sobriquet "Black Night," La Nera Notte. And not only because of her hair.

She'd gained early infamy when an engagement to James Willoughby, a rich English heir, turned sour and her outraged "guardian" sued for breach of promise. They'd settled out of court for an undisclosed sum, and that perhaps had encouraged her to try the same trick a few years later with another overconfident rich boy.

She's like Bertha used to be when she was younger, Hector thought, as the attendant briskly towelled his hair and sprayed his locks with a fresh-smelling eau de cologne.

But a lot younger than Bertha was.

She must have been a girl—fifteen or sixteen—when I was taking Bertha out on the town and she was luring wealthy men into public humiliation. She was reckless with her own reputation. Couldn't care less.

Like Bertha in so many ways. A beautiful woman, seemingly not interested in a conventional life of marriage and children. Hungry instead for riches and getting her own way.

And far too young to have had anything to do with Bertha, thank goodness.

Now in her thirties and still unmarried, Madame Moonlight operated in a twilight zone in the city's society. A brilliant hostess, she ran the Imperial Club and Spa with just enough audacity to keep her clientele enthralled without alienating their wives.

She engaged controversial, entertaining speakers like Mark Twain. Held soirees with risky guests like clairvoyant physician Ephraim S. Taylor, who enjoyed a brief season of popular notoriety as the doctor to the city's rising social "stars"—excitable but bored young women with more money than sense.

She staged dance parties where society women couldn't resist showing off the latest in fashion. Sophia never failed to earn some mention in the society gossip columns, either because of her own risqué ventures or the scandals of those who frequented her establishments.

Above all, she was a consummate publicist whom local editors knew they could rely on for a tantalizing yarn on slow news days.

He'd have to be careful, because she was exceedingly clever. A dangerous woman for a politician to get on the wrong side of.

But why bring Elizabeth into it? Was she threatening to sully her name by association?

He stepped out of the Imperial Spa into the dust and noise of Market Street, newly coiffed and immaculate, but not nearly as confident of his future as when he'd stepped through its perfumed archways two hours earlier.

Get Dangerous Desires at:

https://www.jennywheeler.biz/book/dangerous-desires/

Enjoy *Ancient Deception?*
You can make a big difference.

Reviews are the most powerful tools in my kit when it comes to getting my books noticed. Much as I'd love it, I don't have the budget of a big publisher to buy billboard ads and other national advertising.

But I have the promise of something more powerful—something publishers envy.

And that's a committed and loyal bunch of readers.

Honest reviews of my books help them gain the attention of others who might appreciate them too.

If you've enjoyed *Ancient Deception*, I would be grateful if you could spend a few minutes leaving a review (it can be as short as you like) on one of the listed book sites. You can jump right to the page by clicking below.

Post Your Reviews Here:
Goodreads: https://bit.ly/3GIxmwR
Bookbub: https://bit.ly/3qfWENl

Thank you very much
Jenny Wheeler

ACKNOWLEDGMENTS

Ancient Deception is the first in the Of Gold & Blood series largely set in Virginia City and it was such a pleasure to delve into the remarkable history of the Comstock Lode and learn how silver impacted on California's development.

Many of us know about the Gold Rush and the 49ers, but how man understands that the discovery of silver in Nevada was arguably even more influential than the initial rush for gold in the development of San Francisco and the West?

I consulted a whole range of research material but the key books—all of which I can recommend for those interested in the period - including *The Infamous King of the Comstock, William Sharon and the Gilded Age in the West,* by Michael J. Makley, *The Roar and the Silence,* by Ronald M James, *The Bonanza King, John Mackay And The Battle Over The Greatest Riches in the American West,* by Gregory Crouch, *Ralston's Ring* by George D Lyman (1937). and *More San Francisco Memoirs 1852—1899 The Ripening Years,* compiled and introduced by Malcolm E Barker.

I also found the Internet Archive invaluable for access to older material, including *Comstock Commotion, the story of the Territorial Enterprise and Virginia City News,* by Lucius Morris Beebe, (Stanford University Press, 1954) and *The Fantastic City, Memoirs of the Social and Romantic Life of Old San Francisco* by Amelia Ransome Neville, (The Riverside Press, Cambridge, 1932.)

As is accepted with popular fiction, I have taken a few liberties with the historical record, mainly in fudging the timing of some events, but the literature supports all the details and remarks I have attributed to known historical figures.

I am grateful for dedicated help from Stephanie Parent for editing and Nikki Crutchley for deep dive proof reading. Also, warmest appreciation to friend and journalist colleague Robyn Welsh for her work in a final read through to catch sneaky literals.

As is always the case in these matters, despite all of this very sterling assistance, any mistakes and errors are entirely my own. But with every book, there comes a time when my eyes cross over and I have to let it fly off into the universe.

I always feel a profound gratitude to the long dead people I read about when writing these books, and this was even more marked with Ancient Deception.

Oh, the ironies of history. Consider, for example, the two devoted brothers who could be said to have discovered silver in Nevada. Both died young within months of each other without seeing any benefit. Here's an excerpt from Legends of America:

> *"More ore deposits were discovered in the fall of 1857 by brothers Ethan Allen and Hosea Ballou Grosh, sons of a Pennsylvania minister and veterans of the California goldfields. However, before they could work or file the claim, both would die tragically. Hosea Grosh ran a pick through his foot, which eventually resulted in lockjaw (septicemia) and he died on September 2, 1857.*
>
> *His brother Allen, while traveling to Last Chance, California in November 1857, got caught in a snowstorm and suffered severely from exposure. Though he was found before his death, his legs were completely frostbitten, and refusing to have them amputated, he died on December 19, 1857."*
> https://www.legendsofamerica.com/nv-comstocklode/

I am always reminded how much we all have in common as human beings, despite the years that separate us. It's been a pleasure and privilege to peek into these lives and amazing times as I've created my own "series of unfortunate events."

Finally, thanks to the loyal readers and supporters who keep encouraging me, buying the books, and—in the case of my Advance Reader Team—take on reading the manuscript before publication and giving me feedback on it. It means a lot to know you have my back.

ABOUT THE AUTHOR

Jenny Wheeler is the author of the Of Gold & Blood Old California mystery series and host of the author podcast The Joys of Binge Reading, www.thejoysofbingereading.com

Poisoned Legacy #1
Brother Betrayed #2
Double Jeopardy #3
Tangled Destiny #4 (Christmas novella and prequel)
Unbridled Vengeance #5
Hope Redeemed #6
Tainted Fortune Book #7 Captive Heart–A Hawaiian Christmas Novella
Ancient Vendetta #9
Dangerous Desires #10
Boxed Set/Book Bundle Of Gold & Blood, Series 1 Books 1–3.
Boxed Set/ Book Bundle Of Gold & Blood Series 2 Books 1 & 4
Boxed Set/Book Bundle Of Gold & Blood, Three Holiday Novellas, Books #4, #6 and #8
Boxed Set/Book Bundle #3 Books 5 & 6
Boxed Set/Book Bundle #4 Books 7 & 8

WHERE TO CONNECT WITH JENNY

Jenny's online home is at jennywheeler.biz or email Jenny@jennywheeler.biz

You can connect with Jenny on:

Facebook: @JennyWheeler.Biz

Twitter: @Jenny_Biz

Instagram: @jennysbingereading

Pinterest https://www.pinterest.nz/Jennywheelerbooks

www.ingramcontent.com/pod-product-compliance
Lightning Source LLC
Chambersburg PA
CBHW021538110726
47902CB00004B/929